TOM E

Weep for the Dead

A CELESTINE COURBET MURDER MYSTERY

Copyright Page

This is a work of fiction. Names, characters, places, and incidents either are the product of the author's imagination or are used fictitiously. Any resemblance to actual persons, living or dead, events, or locales is entirely coincidental.

Copyright © 2023 by Tom Becket

The right of Tom Becket to be identified as the author of this work has been asserted by him in accordance with the Copyright, Designs and Patents Act 1988

All rights reserved. No part of this book may be reproduced or used in any manner without written permission of the copyright owner except for the use of quotations in a book review. For more information, address: tombecketauthor@gmail.com.

First paperback edition November 2023

Book design by GetCovers
Publisher: Colton Press

ISBN 978-1-7395117-3-9 (paperback)
ISBN 978-1-7395117-2-2 (ebook)
www.tombecketauthor.com

Translation of the inscription on the Grosse Cloche or Great Bell in Bordeaux

> I call to arms
> I announce the days
> I give the hours
> I chase away the storm
> I sound the festivals
> I scream at the fire
> I weep for the dead.

Chapter 1

It was already two o'clock in the morning, the work was going slowly, but Armand Verville was worried about more than that. He straightened up from the bench, laid down the grinder he had been using and pulled off his leather gloves. The tools were cheap, not really fit for purpose in his view, and that angered him too. He had his own tools, he had standards, even for a shit job like this one. His head was thick from the fumes in the building, from the stench of acid and scorched metal. The screech that came from hard metal scraping violently on steel was hurting him deep inside his ears. There were no ear defenders on this job. It was all so careless.

He stretched his back and turned away from the bench to look around. Half of the cavernous tin shed was in darkness, but he could make out the shapes of the big machines, like huge, quiescent creatures lurking in the gloom. There was a flash as someone welding struck an arc, and for a second, the wall behind them turned lilac. He blinked, and he saw that the other three were looking at him. There were the two small ones he called the ducks, expressionless faces half hidden by the goggles they wore, and Old Lionel Meslier, fish-eyed in his goggles, still managing to look anxious, always looking anxious, always there in Armand's life when he was standing in the wrong place. Was everything all right, he wanted to know. But it wasn't, it was not all right, not at all.

'I'm going for a cigarette. Keep working,' he said, making elaborate hand gestures. Only Meslier looked down and started grinding again.

Armand shook his head and moved away from the benches. A halogen lamp came on as he slid open the metal door at the back of the building and stepped out into the night air. He took a deep breath to clear his lungs of the fumes and the smell of burnt and tortured metal. He placed one finger on the side of his nostril and blew out snot and dust from the other one, then he repeated the process on the other side. Now he could smell the night scents of the long grass and the weeds in the wasteland in front of him. Now he could smell the wind and the river flowing smoothly past on the other side of the high fence. There was a half-lemon-slice moon lounging low in the sky, and he could see its reflection being rippled and buffeted by the currents. He couldn't make out the far side of the estuary, which was several kilometres wide at this point, but he could see the lights of a small settlement in the distance. But mostly it was dark all around. The river was dark and seemed sinister at night, to him; rivers and lakes and the sea, they were all sinister at night, he thought, maybe it's as though all the drownings they've committed could be sensed in the cold blackness. He shivered, although the night was mild, and he shook himself. Too much imagination for the two o'clock in the morning kind of bravery that had impressed Napoleon. I just don't have it, thought Armand.

He heard someone step over the metal runner and come out of the sliding door, pulling it closed behind him. Armand didn't look around. It wasn't one of the ducks; they wore slippers and moved so softly you never heard them until they were standing right next to you. He couldn't be bothered to turn around, he wasn't interested; he was interested in the way the moon rippled on the dark river's surface. He took out a cigarette and lit it, and holding it out at the end of his arm aimed it like a gun at the waxing moon. Yes, he was very anxious, not just about the work, but about the other, the side he hadn't known about for sure, until tonight. And now he knew, good money or not, this would be his last shift.

Predictably, at that point, a tune came to him, and *Rivers of Babylon* started up in that part of the mind that seemed able to run along on another level, for ages, no matter what else you were doing. He knew for certain that he'd be humming and singing the words in his head for the rest of the night. He knew a lot of songs, in French, in English and Spanish. That was ok. Music was the salve on the wounds of life. Who said that? He didn't know.

He heard someone moving behind him and he turned slightly, expecting to see Old Meslier standing there, with his slumped shoulders and vapid eyes. He started to say something and turned further, but it was another man, a younger one, big, not one of the metal workers. Armand took off the safety goggles he was wearing on the top of his head and nodded to the new man.

'Nice night,' he said. The other man raised the heavy wrench he was trailing in his right hand and swung it violently across Armand's face. Then he stepped quickly over to where Armand was reeling and brought the wrench down with all his strength on the top of his skull that cracked like an egg, and pieces of Armand's brains and masses of blood spurted out. He was dying quickly before his body collapsed and spread-eagled on the ash-covered ground.

The killer laid the wrench down carefully and called out. A second, much smaller man came up to him from the shadows. They took hold of the arms and feet and carried the body across the wasteland to a gate in the high mesh fence that surrounded the property. They laid the body down and prised open the gate. Then they picked it up again, face down so that the blood leaked less and instead soaked into the tight curly hair on either side of the crevasse in the skull. They stumbled down a low bank and onto an old concrete jetty that protruded for twenty metres into the river. They carried him clumsily, his belly scraping the surface when the smaller man loosened his grip. The killer growled at him. The waters surged under the pillars of the jetty, and it felt as though a great force was surrounding them, squirming and angry. At the end of the jetty, they stood sideways to the river, and on a word swung the body of Armand Verville into the Gironde. They stood watching for a few moments as the body floated and surfed on the current before sinking. The killer looked hard, puzzled, something didn't seem right. The water was moving in the wrong direction, not what he had expected.

'It all goes to the sea,' he said out loud. The other man understood nothing, silently waiting for instructions he continued to stare at the water.

'Come on clay face,' the killer said. 'It all goes to the fucking sea.'

Chapter 2

At seven o'clock in the evening, on the last day in April, Etienne Vaillancourt, Divisional Commissaire of the National Police Force in Bordeaux, left the Hotel de Police by the rear exit onto the Rue Camille de Roquefeuil. The sky was clear and it was still light. He crossed the road to walk along the pavement beside the wall that surrounded the huge Chartreuse Cemetery. He would have liked to have gone into the cemetery but it was closed at this time. He often wandered along those lanes of the dead where the city's traffic was muted by the high wall and the filter of stone crosses and mausoleums. As a younger officer, and now as a senior police official, he walked there to settle himself, to gain equilibrium and perspective. Perspective from the dead.

It was also a useful location to check if you were being followed; a random walk along the grids, a quick step behind a statue or a tomb and anyone following would almost certainly reveal themselves. There were also three exits - it was rare that anyone had the resources to cover all of them; and of course, there was also the unofficial fourth exit - a stepped mausoleum built too closely to the outside wall, where a nimble person could scale it easily and drop down beside a lamp post on the other side. He didn't think it was necessary tonight, but he was always nervous when he met these associates in public. He would have to be very careful, keep his cards close, listen and not drink too much.

He came to a main road and turned right, watching for a taxi with its *libre* sign lit. He walked for a few hundred metres until he spotted one coming towards him on the other side. He flagged it down and it circled at the lights and edged its way across the traffic to stop beside him. He gave directions to a street close but not adjacent to the one he was destined for. He paid cash and let the taxi drive out of sight before crossing the road and heading down a narrow lane. He emerged onto a quiet road, which he knew led deeper into a poorer neighbourhood. The pavements were quiet, there was little movement on the road. He stopped outside a restaurant where a faded canopy provided shelter for a few small tables and chairs. The paintwork surrounding the door and windows was a dull green, peeling in places where the wood showed through. Above the door was written in French and Vietnamese, Restaurant Pho Banh Cuon.

The windows were dark and it seemed to be closed. He tried the door and it was immediately pulled open from inside. The Commissaire stepped into the gloom and looked round sharply as the door was closed and locked behind him. His eyes needed to adjust to the dim light, but he could make out the slight figure of a young woman. She stepped forward and bowed slightly. She was very beautiful, with lustrous, jet-black hair and perfect features, and he noticed she was wearing the traditional Vietnamese costume of ao dai. He felt a tight frisson of excitement.

'Good evening, Commissaire Vaillancourt,' she said. 'Please come this way.'

She led him between the tables in the front part of the restaurant, which was unlit, into a room behind where there were lights and a table was set, and where the two associates he had come to meet were already seated. Both men rose to greet him, and the nearest, a short, broad man in an immaculate grey suit and open-necked white shirt, clasped his arms around Vaillancourt's shoulders and kissed him on both cheeks. Then he grasped his hand and shook it fervently.

'Etienne, my friend. Such a pleasure to see you. Looking so elegant and handsome as always,' he said.

'Didier,' replied Vaillancourt and raised his hand to both men. 'I am sorry if I am a little late. Work kept me longer than I anticipated.'

'Ah. It's nothing. I know, I know you servants of the public, you are worked to the bone.' He laughed loudly and clapped Vaillancourt on the shoulder. Vaillancourt turned to the other man and offered his hand. This man was different; taller, slighter, with very black hair, balding on top, and with a face and eyes that took in everything but gave very little back. He smiled at the new guest with his mouth, but his eyes seemed to be constantly appraising and sifting information. He was dressed formally in a black suit, white shirt and black tie.

'Welcome, Police Commissaire Vaillancourt,' he said and bowed slightly. 'Please sit on this side of the table, opposite Monsieur Zubizaretta.' He indicated with one hand where he wanted Vaillancourt to sit and where the hostess was already standing behind the chair.

'It is very considerate of you to invite me to this occasion, Monsieur Nguyen,' said Vaillancourt. 'But the restaurant appears to be closed. Is this not a day of celebration for the Vietnamese people?' Nguyen stood motionless and silent for a moment, and Vaillancourt shuffled a little uneasily, concerned that he might have pressed a nerve somehow. They could be so touchy, he thought.

'Please sit.' He gestured again to the chair to the left of him. 'I will tell you.' His voice was low and a little harsh, although the French was perfect. Vaillancourt sat down and felt the slight touch of the hostess' hand on his shoulder as she eased him into his chair. Nguyen remained standing.

'This day, the thirtieth of April, commemorates, that is the word, the fall of Saigon to the armies of the North and the Viet Cong. It is a day I might tell you, Commissaire Vaillancourt, that is contentious in the Vietnamese Community. Ha!

There is no community, communities. There is a schism I might say. And on one side of this schism,' he pronounced the word harshly, almost spat it out as though it was distasteful to him, yet apposite. 'On one side there is a celebration for this day. The Day of Liberation. Feasts in Hanoi and in Ho Chi Minh City. And in France too.' He was still standing and he held out his hands as though they were a balance, a scales. 'Others call this day, Black April, National Day of Shame. What a difference, what a people, still divided. For those people today is not one of celebration. No. It is a day of reflection, I would say.' He sat down. 'The restaurant is closed. I own this restaurant. I have many people on both sides of this schism. I do not want to alienate either side. So the restaurant is closed and I meet only with friends and associates who are not involved in this debate, let me say.'

'What about you? Do you celebrate the fall of Saigon?' asked Zubizaretta.

Again there was a pause before he spoke. 'I will tell you, but later, after we have eaten. I will tell you a story of the fall of Saigon and how it affected me and my life. And you can decide.' He clapped his hands and smiled broadly. 'Yes, you can decide if this is a day of celebration for Nguyen Ngoc Minh.'

He clapped his hands again and two more young women appeared, dressed alike in traditional costume. They laid a number of small bowls of food on the table in a circle, like a flower head. They brought glasses for traditional Vietnamese beer and rice wine.

Zubizaretta shook off his jacket and it was immediately whisked away by one of the servers, but he grabbed it back.

'No. Leave it here, on the back of this chair.' The girl glanced quickly at Nguyen, then draped the jacket carefully over the back of the empty chair beside him.

'You will not need your wallet tonight, Didier,' said Nguyen. 'Eat and drink as you please. I will try to explain to you what is in each dish and what it conveys.'

Vaillancourt had eaten Vietnamese food many times and he was only half listening to the explanations. He was thinking of his father, and what his reaction would have been to seeing his son dining with a gypsy industrialist and a Vietnamese boss. But the food was exquisite. The sauces were sharp, piquant, sweet and salty, each designed to contrast with the dish being eaten. He congratulated Nguyen a number of times on the quality of the food, but his host merely held up a hand in acknowledgement and smiled narrowly. He himself seemed to eat little, dipping into this and nibbling at that, without any obvious interest or relish. Zubizaretta, on the other hand, ate wolfishly, trying every dish, dipping into sauces and leaving brown stains on the table top. There were beads of sweat on his brow and the hair above his temples was damp. His shirt was unbuttoned and the black, wiry hairs on his chest were crawling out. Vaillancourt looked around at the simple decor of plants and coloured photographs of rice fields and fishermen on a wide river. The young women were more interesting; two looked like sisters, quite attractive, not so fine-featured yet pleasant and shapely as always. The other one, the one who had opened the door for him, she was stunning, unmanning. More beautiful even than Bahn, he thought, almost too exquisite to touch, like a precious ornament of fine glass; almost. They drank Vietnamese beer, which was fresh and light and helped counteract the saltiness of some of the food. Vaillancourt was careful what he drank, Zubizaretta was not and their host merely supped at his tea.

When the men sat back, clearly finished, Nguyen clapped his hands again and the servers removed the plates and bowls and returned with more beer and small glasses and a jug of rice wine.

'Ruou thuoc, medicine wine,' said Nguyen. 'Very good for many elements of a man.' He poured out three glasses and handed one to each man.

'Drink to this day,' he said. 'To this day of commemoration.'

'Fall of Saigon,' added Zubizaretta loudly and downed his glass in one.

'To this day, whatever it signifies for you Monsieur Nguyen,' said Vaillancourt, and sipped at the strongly-scented rice wine.

Nguyen looked at each man in turn and then placed his hands flat on the table.

'Before I tell you my tale of Saigon, indulge me, please. I want you to tell me, each of you, where you were born and who was your father, what did he do, how was he with you, and what impact he had on you as you are today. Humour me please.' Nguyen stared, unblinking, at the men on either side of the table. Both men shuffled in their chairs, a little surprised and aggrieved.

Finally, Zubizaretta spoke up. 'All right, I'll start.' He reached forward and refilled his glass from the jug on the table.

'That's easy. I was born in Bayonne. On the arse side of Biarritz. My father was a metal basher, a scrap dealer, and his father before him. How was he with me? He hit me many times. He lavished hugs and gifts on me and my brothers when things were going well. And when they weren't, he took it out on us and on my mother.'

Nguyen waved his hand as if to say, not about your mother, this is not about mothers, only about fathers.

'In 1981 when the French state began building the high-speed train lines, there were still narrow gauge lines running between small towns, although many of them were unused, defunct. My father bribed, threatened and won the concession to take up the tracks, the rails and the wooden sleepers, for long stretches of these lines in the south west region. Of course, these contracts were intended for large companies with extensive resources. My father had two men working for him, some old machinery and his three sons; two, including me, were still of school age. So we worked like devils for months, no rest days, no drop-off. And we cleared 150 kilometres of track and we started selling off all the wood, the oak sleepers, and the rails, so much metal. And the copper cable. Truly it was an Aladdin's cave, a gold mine.'

Zubizaretta paused and looked at Vaillancourt, searching for his reaction to this. Seeing nothing there, he continued.

'We went from being a small provincial scrap yard to a large regional metal factory in less than two years. Big bucks. You would think wouldn't you, that with that success my father would have mellowed and settled down a bit. But no. He drank now more than ever, he went whoring and fighting, and he beat us boys until we were big enough that he couldn't.' Zubizaretta looked up at the ceiling and Vaillancourt could see there was a dampness in the corner of his eyes. He is now very drunk, he thought.

'We put him in hospital, my brothers and me, so badly, he never walked again, and he died two years later.' There was a profound silence. Nguyen looked steadily at the man who had spoken. Vaillancourt looked down at the table.

'What did he do for me? What did you ask? What impact did he have on me? He gave me a business which I now own completely. He made me careless of other men who might get in the way. He made me an expert, a specialist in when to use violence when you want something. What else? He made me short and fat and ugly, just like him. Not like our elegant, handsome Commissaire, eh?' He laughed out loud and slapped the table.

'Eh, Etienne, do not tell me your father was fat and ugly.'

Vaillancourt smiled a little diffidently and took a sip of his drink. Zubizaretta held up his palms to say, I am finished, over to you. Nguyen had swung his gaze to Vaillancourt and nodded almost imperceptibly to encourage him to commence his own narrative.

'Nothing so colourful I'm afraid, gentlemen,' he began. 'I was born in Figeac, in the Causses of Quercy. Well to the east of here. My father was a schoolmaster and then headmaster of a lycée in the town. He taught me to study, to apply myself to mental tasks. He was never violent.' He paused, he could see his father now, hear his hectoring voice. 'No, that's not right, he was never physically violent. But he was extreme and very cold. I was an only child and he was sarcastic and belittling. Nothing I, or anyone else, could do was ever good enough for him. His students always failed him, he had few friends, he was…. But you are right Didier, he was tall and thin and I suppose handsome, although perhaps in features, not in expression. So I don't think he was an attractive man. And my mother left, and so did I when I was eighteen, and now I speak to him at Christmas. That's all. Nothing more to say.'

Vaillancourt looked suspiciously at Nguyen. He was unsure what magic had caused him to unburden himself so much in front of such unsympathetic strangers. He never spoke of his father to anyone. It was a kind of initiation, he decided. You must open a vein and let some blood flow out to mingle with the others. Your new blood brothers. He shivered and wished he could leave, but Nguyen was preparing to speak, his eyes were downcast and his hands were joined together on the table top in front of him.

'I was born in Saigon,' he said. 'I lived there for six years as a boy. I loved Saigon, I should say - the Saigon that was. I loved the tree-lined boulevards, French of course. I walked there with my mother. So many people, the men busy, talking, shouting at each other all the time it seemed to me. The women and schoolgirls in their ao dais, their traditional white and coloured costumes. Like these girls this evening. It was a rainbow of colours. And the smells; the river, the fumes from the motorbikes and the Honda cars. Noisy and smelly and alive. I was only six when I left but I remember the smells and the scent of jasmine when women, friends of my family bent over to kiss me on the head and their dark, perfumed hair fell over my face.'

Zubizaretta looked uncomfortable but Nguyen continued unabashed.

'It was a beautiful, ugly city, a glamorous city, quite exhilarating for a young boy. And we were quite well off. My father was a military attaché, quite high ranking.'

He paused and glanced up at his listeners. 'Now, everything is about him,' he said decisively. 'He was in the military in the South, although he rarely wore a uniform to go to work. Instead, he wore beautifully tailored silk suits and silk shirts and his hair was oiled. He was a god, you understand. We worshipped him, we all did, but he was a spy. His family came originally from the North of Vietnam, not far from Hanoi, and he was an "infiltrant". The spy and security services in the North were very sophisticated and professional. There were a number of supporters of the North who held advanced positions in the government and military in the South. My father was, I shall say, very effective. He passed so much critical information to the military commanders and the politicians in the North. He was undoubtedly responsible for the betrayal and execution of hundreds, perhaps thousands, of opponents of the North. We adored him, as I said, he was a god to us. Then one day, I do remember it like yesterday, I came home from school, I was six years old. The bougainvillaea was in full bloom on the veranda of our house, in a good area of Saigon. I came home happy, only to see my sister crying at the bottom of the stairs and everywhere chaos, cases, trunks, half-packed. I looked to find my mother, she was scolding the maids in the kitchen, organising the packing of the pots and pans, bowls and plates. I saw my mother's face and I didn't need to ask, I knew, even at that age, that life was going to change and that it would never be the same again.'

Nguyen paused and clapped his hands. One of the servers came in with more wine and tea, from which he drank thirstily. Vaillancourt glanced across at Zubizaretta. He was slumped down in his chair, his face sagging and his mouth partly open, but he was listening. There was no question of either of them switching off their attention. Nguyen started speaking once more in his quiet, harsh voice.

'My father came home shortly afterwards. We gathered in the large room where the birds usually sang in cages, but the cages were empty. I was looking at the empty cages when he spoke. He told us that we were going away to a far-off land, where we would be happy and safe. He made it sound like an adventure. I trusted him, he could do no wrong. It would be an adventure. He kissed my mother and held her, something he had never done in front of us children before. Then he kissed us both, my sister and I, on the top of the head and hugged us. Then he walked out of the door and I didn't see him again for another ten years. That's right, ten years. What happened?' Nguyen raised a finger in the air and looked at both his listeners. 'What happened? My father returned to the North, slid back along trails few were even aware of. He was in a rare position you see. He knew the disposition of the forces both North and South. And he knew the mental state, the convictions of the politicians, the leaders on both sides. He knew it was only a matter of time before Saigon and all of the South would fall into the hands of his comrades.

He also recognised that Saigon would become a treacherous and dangerous place for everyone and that we would be in especial danger once his actions came to light. We flew out early the next morning and three days later we landed in France. And they placed us, where do you think? Yes, in a former ammunition depot on the side of the River Lot, not so far from Bordeaux. A refugee camp, re-settlement camp, whatever you want to call it, for Vietnamese who had escaped.' He bent his finger like a hook and bounced his hand up and down on the table top. 'We slept on metal beds, all in the same room, in a wooden hut. We, who had dined off silver plates and bowls. Do you know Vietnamese silver? We who had slept in silk sheets, who had kept servants, who had dressed, my mother, who had dressed like a princess. This was our life in that place and I changed with it. I will not talk about the years growing up there. I grew, I got smart. I learned to take advantage of my smartness. I was sixteen and my father walked into that camp, back into my life. Although he clearly looked a little older, he was still a god. He had a swagger, not an exaggerated cowboy type of swagger, just a subtle movement of his hips, the way he held his head, the confidence in his walk.'

'Where had he been all this time? Ten years. That's a fucking long time,' demanded Zubizaretta, now raised from his stupor. Nguyen raised his hand, annoyed at the interruption.

'He had been preparing. Yes, preparing. With the unification of the country, he was granted a senior position in the new intelligence services. He watched, and he kept watching. He dispatched tens, hundreds of those who were unfaithful to the regime. Sometimes personally. He was a man of duty, I might say.'

'Did he stay in France?' asked Zubizaretta.

'No, not for long. He was here with a diplomatic mission to Paris, but also he had a mission of his own. There was in the camp, a group of people, growing in influence, who propagated stories against the Vietnamese Government. This at a time when the country was moving to a more liberal approach. These agitators had gained some credence with the French and other Western Governments. My father wanted them stopped. He spent the first day with us. He had brought presents and money for my mother. On the second evening, he took me aside, took me out of the camp to a bar on the edge of the town. It is still there. I look at it if I pass that way. In that bar, in a quiet dark corner, he gave me my task, my mission. He gave me a dao gam, a dagger, very, very sharp. He told me, his exact words; "I will open up the world to you, but first you have to open the throats of these three men." The agitators in the camp, you understand.'

'Jesus,' said Zubizaretta. Vaillancourt looked at the food stains on the table top and felt as though he was heading into a long, dark tunnel.

'He showed me how. Where to cut. How to do it silently. How to make it impossible to be traced. He talked about it as though it were as natural as, well, where to strike the football when taking a penalty. Father to son. He told me who the men were. I knew them, had spoken to them. We were not close but I knew them. I had seen them walking through the lanes between the buildings. I knew they had families. We talked more. He said he would return in five days. If the task, that's what he called it, had been achieved, I would enter into a new world; a world that would blind me with its possibilities. He left the dagger for me in a bag and walked out of that bar. I had to find my own way back to the camp.' Nguyen paused again and looked at his guests with an almost humorous look in his eyes. 'And now you are wondering,' he began.

'You are wondering whether I did that. Whether I completed the task. No?'

Zubizaretta was nodding vigorously, his eyes were shining. Vaillancourt tightened his lips, he saw that this was now the edge of no return. A part of him wanted to know, a big part wanted to be back out in the streets, in the air. Nguyen laughed, a sharp, harsh sound.

'Hah. Perhaps I should leave it there. A cliff-hanger, no? Like a TV serial. You must return next week for the answer. Hah, maybe. No gentlemen, of course I completed the task. I slit their throats, all three in one night. Silently, effectively, anonymously. It was quite easy I will say. Oh, the police came, but there was nothing to link them to me. Nothing. And I think they were not so very conscientious. The camp was known for its factions. Anyway, five days later I met my father again at the same bar. If he was proud of me, or surprised, he didn't show it. He just started talking, talking about the changes that were happening in his country, our country. The new embrace of a market economy, and he listed all the areas where he had influence, connections, leverage he called it. And I was to be his partner, here in the West. I had to learn quickly, very quickly, but I always had. Metals, armaments, drugs, people, whatever could flow at a profit from a, what should I say, bandit capitalism. No, that suggests something unsophisticated, unruly. Our approach was much more structured, more efficient than that. Legitimate businesses, others. And like you and your family, dear Zubizaretta, we grew very, very quickly. We moved out of the camp, but we stayed here in Bordeaux. Why? The port. The way in for so many of our commodities.'

Vaillancourt spoke up. 'Wouldn't Marseille have been a better choice? Better access. Most ships coming from Vietnam use the Suez Canal, I presume.'

'Too many gangsters, too much surveillance. No, I knew Bordeaux, and of course, for South America, it is more convenient. My father was as good as his word. Of course he was, he was a god and a very patient god. He had learned his tradecraft in one of the most treacherous, deadliest environments of the twentieth century. I did not. I learned mine here, from him and his experience.' Nguyen stopped again and looked each man directly in the eye. He seemed almost angry now. 'Trust. We do not do business with anyone unless there is trust. I had to complete my task, to kill those men, to gain my father's trust. And many times since I have required my associates, my workers, my business partners, to demonstrate they can be trusted.'

Oh God, thought Vaillancourt. He's going to task me to kill three policemen. His face must have shown his disquiet as Nguyen laid a hand on his arm.

'Do not worry, Police Commissaire. Nothing so dramatic is to be expected from you. Not unless it is absolutely necessary,' he smiled. 'Gentlemen, one more question and I will let you return to your normality. What does the Fall of Saigon mean to me? That was the question.'

Zubizaretta shook his head. He had nothing left to add to this night. He was drunk, but he had retained a hard kernel of attention and now he wanted to switch it off and relax.

'The Fall of Saigon meant one thing to you between the ages of six and sixteen,' said Vaillancourt. 'But after the meeting with your father, it changed, everything changed, and now you see the Fall of Saigon as a positive occurrence. Something that opened up that new world to you. Yes, a celebration I think.' Vaillancourt looked up eagerly at his host.

'Well done Etienne. You are absolutely correct. For me, it is a celebration. Without that, my country would never have united. Never have gone through the awful birth pangs, ten years of terror, never have emerged as this - what did you say,

Didier? This Aladdin's Cave.' He shook Vaillancourt by the hand and nodded. 'You understand don't you, Monsieur Commissaire? Now you truly understand.'

With that, he stood up. Vaillancourt was keen to leave. He felt like he had passed some kind of examination, but also that he had been drawn further in, deeper into a maze from which there was only one exit. The two sisters returned and handed the two guests a small package.

'A small gift. To remember this celebration,' said Nguyen. One of the girls helped Zubizaretta with his coat. He shook hands with the other two but said little, he seemed drained and empty. He left quickly. Vaillancourt shook hands with Nguyen.

'Thank you for a very special meal. The food was superb and I appreciate you sharing your celebration with us,' he said. Nguyen smiled slightly and waved his hand towards the exit where the beautiful young woman was waiting to guide him to the door.

'Until the next time, Monsieur Police Commissaire,' he said and sat back down at the table again.

Chapter 3

Vaillancourt stepped out into the street and drank in the air. The streets were dimly lit and quiet. He felt as though he was coming out of a theatre where he had been one of the supporting actors. It was as if he had been speaking and listening to dialogue that was strange and dramatic and unreal, for an audience that he couldn't see. He felt diminished when he came out into the living streets. He'd left the limelight and the grease paint behind him, and it felt a little tawdry and he was mortal again. He walked back the way he had come, along the narrow lane that led to the main road. He imagined that the buildings, the shutters and the doors were just props. He could open a door and there would just be an empty space behind. It was much darker now and it felt a little sinister, the way the rooms of a house can after you've been watching a horror film, he thought. He saw a figure walking along the pavement towards him and he deliberately crossed the lane to avoid them. But it was just an old workman in overalls, returning after his shift. He came to the brighter lights of the road and turned right. It wasn't far and he needed to walk, to clear his head of that vision of a young, sixteen-year-old boy slitting men's throats at the behest of his father. What people these were. Your people now, he thought. Then he wondered what task his own father might have set him, to gain his trust. But he was not a god to me, I would not have agreed to it, whatever it was.

He thought back over the evening, and then he recalled the light touch on his shoulder, inadvertent, but nevertheless real, by that exquisite creature in the scarlet ao dai. Now focus on the second engagement of the evening, the one you have been anticipating for days. He walked faster to stir up the blood, to get it moving faster around his body. After twenty minutes he came to a clean-looking, non-descript, three-story building in a quiet side street. He entered the lobby with a key and walked up the stairs to the third floor. There he stopped and rang the bell lightly. He had a key for this door also but he wanted it to be opened from within. It was the start of the formality, the ritual that he had created. It was just one symbol of the relationship, of the balance of importance of the parties. The door opened slowly and he walked in, not looking at the young woman standing there. He turned around when he reached the living room and the woman walked up to him and bowed slightly. He lowered his head and smiled.

'How are you, Bahn?' he asked.

'Very well, Etienne, and you, are you well?'

He nodded, and she stood silently as he appraised her. She was wearing a short, maroon, silk dress with slits in each side. The neckline was high and the fabric clung to her body outlining the shape of her firm young bust and slim waist and hips. Her hair was long and dark and framed a delicate face of near-perfect beauty; only her eyebrows were a little thin, but her eyes were deep, dark and soft and her lips were ripe and the colour of her dress. He nodded slightly again and she turned around so that he could look at her from behind. He let his eyes stroll slowly down the dark shiny slope of her hair, her back where the zip on her dress was straining a little from the tightness of the fit. He appraised the roundness of her buttocks and the firm legs, the delightful dip behind her knees and her feet angled into the red, high-heeled shoes.

'You look superb, come and kiss me,' he said.

She turned and came towards him, wrapping her arms around his neck and planting her lips on his. He could feel her young body pressed firmly against him, and it was so extravagantly thrilling, above anything else, so that the rest of it, the betrayals, were as nothing. It vindicated everything.

He did nothing, she did everything; except that he liked to unzip her dress from behind, watch it fall to the floor and cast his first gaze at her delicate silk lingerie. She undressed him. She led him to the bed. She brought him to his moments of ecstasy. This was about him, about his pleasure, not a sharing or a responsibility for the other. He liked to touch her, he liked the taste of her, but the focus here, the importance was that he be pleasured. And it was a relief to him, this lack of responsibility for another. When he lay there afterwards he felt quenched and generous. Then, when she curled her twenty-year-old body into his, he slept easily, it felt somehow deserved.

Chapter 4

It was nearly seven o'clock in the morning when Celestine Courbet stirred. In the dull, foggy borderland between sleep and waking, she could hear the jarring tones of a telephone somewhere in another room. She stretched out her hand to the other side of the bed but it was empty and cool. She felt a twinge in her stomach and it pushed her into wakefulness. She leaned up on one elbow, the pillow was plumped up, no-one had laid their head on it that night. She sought to remember; it was her husband of course, away on work business again, until tonight. The ringing stopped and she lay back and stretched her limbs luxuriously. But then it started again, and she forced herself out of bed and padded into the next room where her mobile phone was jangling and vibrating on the coffee table beside the wine glass from the previous night. She looked at the phone - official.

'Yes.'

'Capitaine Courbet.'

'Yes, but I'm off duty, it's Saturday. Find someone else.' There was silence on the other end for a moment.

'Sorry, Ma'am, I can't do that. Commandant Martel is on leave until Monday. There's a body, Capitaine. Found by the river. Foul play.'

'How do you know?' Courbet snapped.

'Well, suspected, you know.' Yes, I know, Courbet sighed. She had resisted, but she knew there was no alternative.

'What kind of body, man or woman?' she asked, although it made no difference.

'Man.'

'Ok. Ok. Call Lieutenant Dubois and Sorbot. No, not Sorbot, he has family this weekend. Brigadier Leger. Tell them to meet me there, and send me the exact location.' She ended the call and dropped the phone onto the leather sofa. 'Damn, damn, damn, damn, damn,' she said out loud. This was a day when I did not want to be dragged into another dark place. This was a day to run, to meet with a friend, to lunch, to gossip and drink too much white wine. It's a holiday weekend. She slipped off the short nightdress her husband had bought her and walked into the shower. She ran the water hot and then steely cold to stimulate her skin and draw deep breaths from her lungs. Let the other bits go, the disappointment, the resentment, she said to herself. Get yourself into shape and alert. The alertness you need for this job of yours.

Her apartment was in the fashionable Chartrons district, a little down the river from the centre of Bordeaux. On the southwest corner of the building she had a balcony that wrapped around and gave the rooms sunshine for most of the day and a view of the sunsets in the evening. It was a privileged location and she was pleased and grateful for it, but it was some distance from where the body had been found. The traffic out of the town and to the west was heavy already, as the Bordelais headed for the beaches on this long weekend. Courbet looked ruefully at the cars crammed with children, beach balls and parasols. How nice to be spending the day relaxing, splashing in the sea, laughing. She doubted there would be much laughter where she was headed. Oh, let it be an accident, she thought, someone careless, fallen off a boat, drunk and tumbling unconscious into the river. In the city, there were plenty of bars situated only a few metres from the River Garonne. She was tired of murders. There had been fourteen already in her city this year; most of them dumb, clumsy, angry bloodlettings by stupid, messy, fucked-up people. People whose lives had turned in an instant and left a legacy of pain and grief that would last for decades to come. Let it not be one of those, let it be a tragic accident that she could pass on, something she could unwind from swiftly, once the paperwork was done.

She turned off the main road and headed down one of the narrow lanes that led to the estuary. The land was flat but she caught an occasional glimpse of sun on water. She turned onto a minor road running parallel to the shore. She saw a police car and other vehicles already parked by the side of the road. It had taken her nearly fifty minutes to get there. Even then she had to leave her car and walk several hundred metres through rough grasses, shrubs and brambles to reach the stony and muddy shore. The scene was desolate; the land running down to the shore was scrubby, and the river beyond, running fast, looked brown and perilous. Seagulls keened in the air above, scavengers outraged that their meal had been disturbed by a bunch of humans. Courbet walked towards the spot where a small team of police officers and officials were gathered. Brigadier Leger was the first to look up and come towards her.

'Morning, Ma'am. Male, fifties, big crack on the back of his skull. Been in the water maybe a couple of days.' Leger said.

'Who's here?' demanded Courbet.

'Couple of local G's. Dr Delbreil, pathologist. Got here really quickly, very keen.'

'Keen! Who wouldn't be keen to size up a corpse on a sunny Saturday morning? Dubois?'

'On her way. She was out of town. Love tryst with a wine lord.'

'She's your superior, Stephane. You mind what you say. Techs?'

'Identity guys are on their way, too.'

'Jeez. I thought I was slow this morning,' said Courbet, shaking her head.

'It's Saturday, boss. Second of May. You don't expect to be working.'

'No. Damned inconvenient of a corpse to get itself washed up on a holiday. Who found it? No, don't tell me. Dog walker.'

'No. Two dog walkers. Three dogs.'

'God bless dog walkers. Would we ever find an outdoor corpse without them? They should be sponsored by the state. I see them?' She nodded in a direction some thirty metres from the scene.

'Yeah.'

'Statements?'

'No. I was waiting for you.'

'Don't. Get their statements now while it's fresh, before they turn to mush. May be something they saw.'

Leger walked over to where two middle-aged women were standing beside the shell of an old wooden boat. They were clinging on to the dogs, which were clearly over-excited and kept wrapping their leads around each other so that the women had to keep bending down to untangle them. They look disturbed, thought Celestine. I'll go and talk to them myself in a minute. I would like the forensic guys to check their shoes though, before I send them home.

She walked over to where the corpse was lying, the others nodding to her and taking a few steps back. She stood a metre away and looked at the scene before focusing on the body. She knew that once the body was in her mind it would be all-absorbing, and she wanted to be able to place it accurately in its setting. The river estuary was wide at this point and she stared at it as it swirled and rushed past on almost its last lap before the sea. The far bank was just a line of blue/grey shapes, smoky-looking and indistinct. On this side of the river, there was scrub, maquis, and she could see a thin path worming its way through the undergrowth parallel to the water's edge. Dog walkers, fishermen perhaps, she thought. There were no houses for half a kilometre or more. A light breeze was blowing across the water which smelled faintly of the sea, but also of the mud and the coarse vegetation. The tide was going out. There was a tidemark of detritus, of dead seaweed, small sticks, pieces of plastic rope which was at least a metre further from the river than the corpse. She stepped closer. The pathologist was kneeling down and picking delicately at the back of the head, which was hidden from Courbet. The corpse was splayed out on the mud and small stones, like human seaweed, she thought. Green strands were wrapped around his lower legs and feet. One leg was bare to the knee and it already looked bleached like a coral. His clothes, top and bottom, seemed to be the same colour, a blue, but badly stained now from the water. Overalls, that's what they were. So, a worker of some sort, or a do-it-yourselfer. The eye sockets were empty.

The pathologist stood up and pulled down his face mask. He was wearing thick, black-framed glasses in front of intelligent, wary eyes. His nose was ridiculously long and sharp and gave him a kind of bird-face look, and his lips were so thin that they disappeared completely when he smiled.

'Hi. Doctor Delbreil,' he said.

'Capitaine Courbet.' He looked surprised and coloured slightly.

'Capitaine, right,' he said. Celestine nodded towards the body.

'Oh. Dead male, fifties.'

'That I know. Cause of death?'

'Well, that's interesting.'

'Interesting?'

'Yes, I mean obvious, er, drastic, violent. Come and look.'

Courbet stepped carefully around to his side. He knelt down and with what looked like a spatula, she had one just like it for taking eggs out of the poacher, he pointed at the crack in the skull that ran from the cranium to the base. There was green slime on the head and in the crack.

'I've tried to clean it a little, but I don't want to remove what's there. Until I'm in the lab you understand. But, brutal huh,' he said.

'Could it have happened in the water? Boat propeller, something like that. Or a fall onto stone or concrete?'

The young pathologist looked at her with his keen eyes, magnified through the thick lenses of his spectacles.

'Possible.' But he sounded doubtful. 'I'll need to check what's in the lungs, blood etc. It's difficult when they've been in the water.'

'Dealt with many that have been in the water?' queried Courbet.

'Only a few. But, but this fracture was made with some force. Of course, it might have widened a little, with the buffeting in the water. Current's strong.'

'How long in the water? Could it have been left here?'

'No sign of that. Definitely not. Washed up. How long? Difficult to say. I would guess two days, max three.'

'How long out of the water?' Courbet asked. The young man paused and took hold of one of the hands that lay like a pale crab on the stones. He pinched the skin.

'Last tide, I would say. High tide last night must have cast him here. Any longer on these hot, dry days and he'd be less water-logged.'

Capitaine Courbet stood up and looked into the distance. She never could get over the sight of a life taken away before its time; whether by accident or crime. She was not squeamish; it was more a mood change that came over her, a cold anger, and it made her speak sharply, and sometimes thoughtlessly to her staff and other workers. She looked back at the river which was flowing strongly to the North West, and she could see that the feet of the corpse were already now two metres away from the water line.

'So, entered the water?' she asked, half to herself, half to the enthusiastic young pathologist.

'Upriver, washed down, caught in the tide, pushed back a little, swilled around, the current takes him, lies him down here on the beach for us to find.' Courbet looked at him, surprised.

'You think there's something working in our favour here?' she said harshly. 'This poor guy could just as easily have ended up in the Atlantic Ocean. And never turned up.'

'Statistically, because a bloated corpse will float for some time in the water, there is a fairly high possibility of such a corpse being deposited on dry land, at some stage,' said Dr Delbreil in a high and rather peeved voice. Celestine thought he looked as if he was going to start crying.

'You're right, you're right. But that still leaves a hell of a lot of possibilities of where this gentleman entered the River Garonne.'

'Monsieur Verville. Armand Verville.'

'You what. You know who this is?'

'Yes,' said Delbreil, pleased. And he reached down and passed her a small polythene bag containing a plastic card. 'Diabetic. Card they can carry. Tucked down in a pocket of his overalls.'

'So they are overalls?'

'Yes, and the boots, work boots, reinforced toe-caps.'

'Is there anything else? Wallet, phone.'

'Nothing. Probably in his jacket, hanging up on a nail somewhere.' Courbet looked at him again.

'You'll have to watch that,' she said.

'Watch what?' And confusion suffused his face again.

'You seem to have a rather vivid imagination. I'm not sure that's a real advantage in your line of work.'

He smiled then and relaxed, and the smile made him look even younger and slightly ludicrous, with the face mask hung under his chin and the top of his head covered by the hood of his protective suit.

'I will know a lot more, Capitaine, when I have him in the lab. I'll keep you up to date at all stages.'

'Good. I'm sure you will. One more thing. Do you think you'll find any evidence to give us a clue as to where he went in?'

'It's possible. But the river is such a blender, really. And a scrubber. Things attach and un-attach. It's hard to know where they were picked up.'

'Understood.' She paused to consider for a moment. 'I want to know what kind of work he did. He was a workman. His hands are the most obvious place; old cuts, scars, burns. And his lungs - what did he breathe in regularly?'

'And his stomach - what did he eat and drink? I do know these ropes, Capitaine.'

'I was thinking out loud. Of course you do, Dr Delbreil,' Courbet nodded.

'Julien, Julien Delbreil.'

'Capitaine Courbet. Good luck.'

Courbet stepped away from the body and looked around. Her lieutenant, Camille Dubois, was standing talking to one of the officers. She came over immediately.

'Boss, sorry I was …'

'Out of town. I know, and it's a pig getting dragged in on a day like this. But it looks 90% that we have a murder, and we have a name.' She showed the plastic bag to Dubois. 'Name's Armand Verville, that's a diabetic card. No other possessions, wallet etc. Wearing overalls and work boots. Got a savage crack on the back of his skull. Man in his fifties, balding. Find him for me, but if he has a wife, family, I'll visit. I want to know what kind of work Monsieur Verville did. Now go and have a look at the body and the scene, it'll be good for you. Make notes. I'm going to speak to the dog walkers.'

'It's always the dog walkers,' said Dubois. 'I had a dog once, never found a corpse.'

'Unlucky. Go on.'

Lieutenant Dubois was a hard little nut of a woman, compact, but with a substantial bust, thick auburn hair and a face that just looked lustful. She always had a man trailing after her, although she treated them with a level of disdain as well as generosity. Celestine liked her. She was a very clear-cut, no-nonsense cop that you could trust to have behind you.

Celestine walked over to where Leger was still talking and even laughing with the two women and their dogs.

'This is Madame Lus and Madame Rossignol,' he said. 'And this is. ...'

'Ok, Agent, thank you. Could you help Lieutenant Dubois, and go and have another look at the victim. I'll want to know what you think afterwards.'

Leger turned a little reluctantly and then waved a cheerful goodbye to the two women.

'He's nice,' one of them said.

'Yes. I'm Capitaine Celestine Courbet. I won't keep you. I know this has been a shock for you. But we really appreciate your service.'

'We come here nearly every day. Never seen anything like this, have we Val?'

'No, never.'

'And hopefully never again,' said Courbet. 'You must have been out very early this morning, is that usual?'

'In the spring and summer. Best time, quiet, birds,' said Madame Lus.

'And husbands,' added her friend.

'Husbands?'

'Yes. Before our husbands wake up and start all their blathering, you know.'

'It's a peaceful time. We like it.'

'Ok. What have you seen on your walks?' asked Courbet. The two women looked at each other and then back, blankly.

'What sort of thing?' asked Madame Lus.

'Well, other things washed up, things out on the water.' The two women looked thoughtful.

'Wood. A lot of wood, branches and things. Plastic, bottles, tubs. Child's bike once, little one, and plastic you know.'

'Ok.'

'A lot of birds. We watch the birds you see - waders, terns, all sorts.'

'Seagulls. We saw them hopping around the …'

'Corpse. Yes, I see. That boat.' Courbet pointed to the broken hull of a small wooden fishing boat. 'Do people fish from here?'

'No, I don't think so. Never seen them. There is a small harbour a few kilometres down, at Saint-Yzans.'

'So, this boat, how long has it been here?' she persisted. Again the women looked at each other.

'Oh, it hasn't always been here,' said Madame Rossignol. 'We noticed it, a bit surprised, wasn't we Dani? Maybe last spring, after the winter. Maybe a year or so.'

'Was it in that state?' asked Courbet.

'More or less. Maybe worse now. You don't really notice do you?'

Courbet looked inland. There was just a thick bank of scrub, at least a hundred metres wide, before it thinned out towards the road. There were no tracks except the narrow winding path she had taken to get here.

'How did it get here?'

'The... corpse?'

'No, the boat.'

'Oh, somebody left it. Been ruined beyond repair. Left it to rot away into the landscape.' The woman looked pleased with herself and nodded. Courbet was less convinced of this.

'Ladies. Thank you so much for your help. My officer has your details and we will be in touch if we need to speak to you again. Equally, if you think of anything that you think might be of relevance, call us. You have the number.'

'Yes. That nice officer gave us his card,' said Madame Lus. 'It's a tragedy.' The sudden change in the tone of her voice made Courbet look up.

'Tragedy?'

'Yes, to end there. A man, human like the rest of us. Washed up like so much driftwood.'

There were tears in her eyes now and Courbet knew that as the excitement waned, the full weight of their discovery was starting to sink in.

'Yes, it is a tragedy,' said Courbet. And I will get to the core of it, she said to herself. The women gathered their still excited dogs and were tugged off along the path that led through the scrub and the woodland.

Courbet looked again at the boat. It had been clinker-built, and although one side had been stowed in, the shape of the hull was still intact. It had been painted green, but most of that had peeled, dried and cracked in the relentless assault of sun, rain and wind. It was more or less on its side; the stern was completely splintered and parts of the hull were wedged in the mud and stones. There was no legible name on the parts that she could see, but it was possible that on the buried side there might be some mark of identification. She called over to Leger.

'Come over here and bring those two G's.'

The gendarmes looked surprised when Leger spoke to them, and they looked across at the female capitaine with some scepticism. But Leger knew better than to argue and he brought the officers over.

Capitaine Courbet pointed to the boat.

'I want you to try and turn that boat over. I want to see if there's a name on it.'

'What for,' demanded the older gendarme, a grumpy-looking brigadier with a swelling belly and a sneering mouth. 'It's got nothing to do with your dead man over there. He's not Robinson fucking Crusoe.'

The other gendarme laughed.

'Brigadier ..?' Courbet asked, staring him hard in the face.
'Gabel.'
'Well Brigadier Gabel and ..'
'Berger.'
'Turn the boat over, I want to see if there's a name on it. Help them, Leger.'

The three men hauled at the front of the boat but it wouldn't budge.

'It's stuck fast.'

'Got a spade in your car?' Courbet asked the younger of the gendarmes.

'No. Trowel maybe.'

'Leger. I want you to stay here. You go and get whatever you need to clear the earth away from that boat. I want to see what's on the other side. Leger, stay there until it's done and take a photograph. Any distinguishing marks, anything at all. Got it?'

'Do you want the techs to have a look at it?'

'No, Leger I don't. It's not evidence of a crime. But it might be useful in another way. Just do it.'

She walked back to where Camille Dubois was making notes from an interrogation of the young pathologist, who looked flushed again, as another strong, attractive female pressed him for answers.

'Anything more, Doctor?' she asked.

'No, no I don't think so. It's just that,' he paused.

'Just what?'

'The face. The nose is smashed, could have been in the water, it's a hostile environment you understand.'

'Yes, go on.'

'But it looks like his cheekbone is also broken. There's almost a line of broken tissue and bone, cartilage, across his face. As though maybe he'd been hit with something heavy. Something heavy that then cracked down on the back of his head. I hope I'm not being too imaginative,' he said and sneaked a look at Courbet's face.

'No, you're doing fine, Doc., whatever you find, whatever you think, no matter how imaginative, you keep it for me. Ok.'

She turned to Dubois.

'If you've finished, Camille, get back to base and find me an address for this man.'

'Done.' Lieutenant Camille Dubois walked over the rough pebbles towards the path through the undergrowth. Even on a lumpy, uneven surface, there was a slight sway to her walk that was just a little bit dirty, thought Courbet, in a nice, brash, sexy way. It was no wonder that the young gendarme joined her on the walk through the scrub to where the cars were parked.

Courbet moved away from the body to a slightly raised clump of earth and thin grass. She took another look around the scene. It was a bleak, lonely place. There was nothing attractive or picturesque about it. The estuary wasn't pretty at this point, it was strong, muddy and functional, and it had thrown this dead man onto its shore. But where did it accept him? Where was the first place he had met the water? That's what I need to find out if I'm going to discover who killed him, she reasoned with herself. The land upriver was wooded and protruded a little into the flow so that where she was standing was almost like a shallow bay. The two women had walked off on a path through these woods, and the wrecked boat was resting about twenty metres from the shoreline, almost in the lee of this wooded promontory. Courbet puzzled, she wondered how water behaved when it came down the river and around a point; did it surge into the bay, or swirl in, slowly, reluctantly, edged out of the main stream? What was it like here when the tide was coming in and the flow of the rivers met and mingled with the waters pushed back by the tide? It must be a real maelstrom, a seething mess of currents and eddies and whirlpools, she guessed, and she shivered. Nearly twelve years previously, she had experienced close up the dangers of a rising tide on this very coast. She had suppressed that nightmare successfully for a long time now. She mustn't let it interfere with what she had to do to work on this case. She needed to see this place when the tide was in. Was there such a thing as a map of the currents at different times of the day? That's fanciful, she thought. Who would do that? Who would make a map of the currents which vary every day, every hour? She had read of someone who was making models of all the great cathedrals of Europe out of matchsticks. He might have a brother or a cousin somewhere who was dedicating his time to mapping the currents of the Garonne and the Gironde Estuary and putting them online for their three followers. If there is, I'd like to meet them, decided Courbet. I'm pretty sure they wouldn't be the type to commit murder, just bore their visitors into an early demise. She stopped herself; something was agitating at the back of her mind, but she knew from experience that she would need to walk away from it for a while; these thoughts and inspirations were shy and liked to creep up to the front only when they knew you were looking elsewhere.

The forensic officers from the Identite Judiciaire had arrived and were pegging out a square around the corpse. She walked over to them and handed over the bag with the plastic card. The senior tech nodded to her; she knew him from far too many crime scenes.

'Nice day for the beach,' he said.

''Well, don't go paddling in that water, will you? I don't want to be looking at two washed–up corpses in a weekend,' she said.

'You suggesting I'm washed-up, Capitaine Courbet? Just overworked.'

Courbet smiled. 'Looking for pointers as to the work he did, where he fell in or was pushed. Well, you know, Jean-Luc. Enjoy the rest of your weekend.'

She had had enough now, enough time around the dead body of a man. They would probably discover that he worked in a factory somewhere, had fallen out with a mate over a woman, or a bet or something, and his mate had wrapped him one over the head with whatever he had to hand, then dumped him in the river and hadn't come into work for a few days. They'd find him hiding in a shed behind his uncle's house in Landes, and he'd be amazed that they'd found him so quickly. They had no idea, they always underestimate the resources we have, she thought. Amateurs do anyway.

She pushed her way back through the scrub and brambles and reached her car just as the young gendarme appeared with a spade that he had acquired from somewhere. He came up to her.

'Ma'am. I'd certainly like to work in your department,' he said and grinned.

'Just dig out that boat agent, and keep your mind on the job,' she replied.

Chapter 5

Courbet knew that she should head back to the commissariat, but instead, she started driving in the direction the car was pointed and followed the road that ran down the estuary. After about five kilometres, she came to a small village nestled behind a slight ridge and surrounded by vineyards. There was a church and a tree-lined square with a pétanque court. She parked on the edge of the square, got out of the car and looked around. There was no one in sight. She noticed there was a lane leading from the village towards the port, and she crossed the road and headed down to where it met the muddy creek, which was the harbour. With the tide retreating rapidly, there was just a basin of brown sludge where the few boats rested, stranded and looking oddly forlorn, she thought. She stood on the crumbling stone bank and looked around. There was a row of wooden, fisherman's huts, tile-roofed and squat, which she presumed was where they kept their fishing gear. It was at least fifty metres to the estuary and she walked along to a concrete platform that formed part of the harbour mouth. The waters had now receded so far that there was a thirty metre band of treacherous-looking mud stretching out towards the current. She walked back and looked at the boats. They were all very similar, about five metres long, some in better shape than others. Only one was of the traditional wooden planking, like the wreck on the beach. The others were of glass fibre or GRP, she guessed. A few had pots in them for catching lobsters or crabs, which she ate with relish but didn't know much about how they were caught. Another gap in my education, she thought.

She sat down on a concrete capstan on the bank and let her breathing settle and her mind calm down. It had been a shitty week and a shitty start to this one. She looked around. This was an unbelievably peaceful place, she thought; cut off from the hustle of the world, protected on three sides by vineyards and on the other by the great river running by. Did it feel claustrophobic at all? Maybe for the kids; she could imagine them feeling restricted and trapped here. But for the older ones or the ones who needed to retreat from life for a while, I guess this would be just fine. I think I could do with a short stretch of this right now, she thought. That's because you're going to be forty next year. You're on the slippery slope to your dotage. Push your meat, she said to herself quietly. She listened to the near silence. There was no one around. She couldn't remember the last time that she had been in a landscape so completely alone. Not in a building, or a room, or a car, but in an open space in the world. Careful, she thought, you'll let the real Celestine Courbet emerge if you stay here too long. Then there'll be some trouble, then all the cats will be in a frenzy amongst all the pigeons. Best get your arse back in the car and start doing your job again. She sighed, but her reverie was about to be broken in any case. She saw a man coming along the narrow lane, dragging a kind of a trolley behind him. He started when he saw her and the trolley banged into his legs. He cursed, and then with his head bent down he came onto the bank.

'Bonjour,' said Courbet, and stood up from her perch on the capstan.

'Bonjour, madame,' he replied and raised his eyes to somewhere near her shoulder line. He was very thin and wore jeans that were too large, and a faded blue shirt, buttoned at the cuffs and decorated with smears of white paint.

'It's a beautiful day, and it's so peaceful. Do you live hereabouts?' she asked.

'Yes. That's my boat, that one there.' He pointed to the wooden clinker-built boat, which was clean and looked freshly painted and varnished.

'Beautiful. Old-fashioned, no? With the wood.'

'Yes. Harder to look after, but I prefer it. Just the look of it, the feel of the wood you know. Foolish really. These other boats are a lot less work, and lighter too,' he paused.' But I don't mind the work, I like it see, it's a part of it.' He stopped himself, a little embarrassed at the length of his speech.

'Do you fish?' asked Courbet, then realised what a stupid question that was.

'Mm.' He merely nodded and had the courtesy not to show what he thought of the question. 'You interested in fishing?' he asked, and finally looked up at her face, which seemed to startle him again.

'No. Just eating them,' she replied. It was clear that he wanted to ask her what she was doing there but was too polite and slightly overawed to ask. I could have been a mermaid sitting on this rock and he would have just smiled shyly, she thought.

'I'm a police officer,' she said suddenly, and he stepped back involuntarily and his eyes opened wider.

'Police officer, you. You're a police officer. Ok,' he murmured.

Please don't give me the "well you've caught me red-handed, officer" quip, she thought. But he wasn't like that. He was a quiet, shy man, and telling him she was a police officer had merely shifted him into just a more official kind of politeness.

'I'm sorry, I should explain,' said Courbet. 'I was looking at a boat like that, but wrecked, washed up on the shore a few kilometres away.' She pointed up the river. 'It was completely wrecked.'

'Ah. That can happen. Don't do the maintenance.'

'Is that what happens? They're not maintained, so they sink in what, rough weather?'

'It can. Sometimes they're just left to rot. Fisherman dies, gets a new boat, can't be bothered with the painting and cleaning.' Courbet noticed that the trolley contained a small gas bottle and some brushes and scrapers.

'Any other reason?' she asked, smiling encouragingly at him.

'Reason?'

'Sorry. Reason why a boat might get wrecked and wash up on a beach.'

'Washed up on a beach. Storm maybe. Boats come loose. Not usually the rope that breaks. More the rings on the boat, where the rope is tied. Yes, boats get taken away in a storm.'

'That ever happen to you?' asked Courbet.

'Not me. I am a very careful man. You have a boat, like a dog, you look after it.'

'I'm sure you're right,' she said. 'Can you recall any boats being lost from here in that way?'

'From here?' He paused and looked into the distance and ran his fingers through his thick black hair.

'I wasn't here until last year, about this time. Moved down from Paulliac last June. Brought the *Belle Étoile* with me then. So not in my time. But it's possible. Tides and spates and storms tearing in off the Atlantic. You got to keep your boat and your house in good repair, and protected.'

'You're a very sensible man, I'm sure. I wish there were more like you,' said Capitaine Courbet; the patronising police pep talk to the populace, she groaned to herself. He simply nodded; he might have been pleased but he didn't show it.

'You know, it's the curse of the police that we just ask way too many questions, all the time. You'd think that was all we could do. I'm Celestine Courbet, Capitaine in the Police Judiciaire in Bordeaux.' She held out her hand and he took it and shook it firmly in a rough, strong hand.

'Alain Jarre.'

'Well, Alain. If for example, a boat broke away from here, in a storm one night, maybe late winter, where would you expect it to pitch up? Where would it land if you like?' The man looked again into the distance and pulled in his lower lip in concentration.

'That would depend on the tide, I would say. If there was a spate and an ebb tide, it would be washed out to sea in just hours, I would say. If there was a high spring tide, well it could wash about for a bit and end up almost anywhere, I would say.'

'Even upriver?'

'Upriver. Well, yes, possible, short way maybe, the right current. See it's difficult to say. The estuary's a right mess when the waters clash, and sometimes the tide comes in like a steam train, and sometimes the rivers run so full, well they're like a ... steam train going the other way.'

Courbet took out her notebook and pencil.

'Alain, you've been a great help, I mean that. Just one more thing. Can I take a note of a telephone number for you? Don't worry you won't be called except…well I'm hoping to have a name for this boat that's been washed up and I would like to know where it came from and when it was lost. If I got a name, do you think you could ask around, see if anyone from here, or nearby, knows of the boat? I'd like to speak to the owner. And they're not in any trouble, not in any way. It would just help in my investigation.' She looked him firmly in the face and held his gaze until he dropped his eyes.

'078356217.' He looked stunned but he rallied enough to ask her. 'This investigation, into what?'

'It's a murder investigation, Alain. We're investigating a murder. So any help you can give me would be very much appreciated. This is my card.' She shook hands with him and strode off up the lane to the road. She didn't turn round but she knew he would be staring at her back. Walking across the quiet square she felt a little guilty that she'd brought commotion into this peaceful place. But something was nagging at her, and she was never careless, always thorough, and she knew that at this stage of an investigation you just didn't know which of the strands, the tributaries that they followed, would turn out to be the main stream.

Chapter 6

It was just past eleven thirty when Capitaine Courbet pulled into the Hotel de Police on the Rue Francois de Sourdis. Camille Dubois was waiting for her as she came through the door.

'Got a match for you. There are a few in town. This one's got form.' She handed Courbet several sheets of paper, the one on the top had a photograph on it. They moved into Courbet's office and sat down on either side of her desk.

'Missing persons. Anyone report him, or any other Armand Verville missing?'

'No. No missing persons. Not that match the …. deceased. Kids mainly, a few kids, a wife.'

'So this guy is the only one we have details of?' demanded Courbet.

'Yes. About the right age, forty-nine, curly hair. I think the guy on the beach had curly hair, right? What you could tell,' added Dubois.

'So he did time, nearly eight years ago. Three years. Forgery. Forgery!'

'Part of a gang.'

'Minting notes. Does that mean printing money?' asked Courbet.

'I guess. But he could've been just a bit of muscle or a distributor or something.'

'It doesn't say much here. And nothing since?'

'Not even a speeding fine.' Courbet sat back and looked at the black and white picture of a man at least ten years younger than the corpse she had been looking at that morning. Could it be the same man?'

'If you were wondering if I was just a pretty face, well let me tell you, he is, was, a diabetic. Prison medical records.' Courbet looked up at her assistant.

'You are more than a pretty face. That's good work. So it kind of narrows it down a bit. Anything else on him?'

'Married, or was. Last address; 68 Rue des Vignes, Apartment 8.'

'In Saint-Michel. That's not the gentrified bit is it? Or maybe our man has been printing money again.'

Dubois shrugged, 'Don't know.'

'Ok, I'm going there now,' said Courbet.

'Take someone with you. It's better you know, with two. They don't turn on you as much, blame you for what's happened. In my experience.'

'Thank you, Camille. You are bursting with it today,' said Courbet with genuine approval.

'Just living the dream. Take Predeau, he needs a run-out and he looks like an altar boy.'

'An altar boy, preserve us from altar boys.'

'Anyway, he's hot. It's a distraction you know. They won't let themselves go completely if he's sitting there.' Courbet shook her head.

'Ok, fetch him, I'm going there now.' Just then her mobile phone rang. It was Leger.

'Boss. Got a name for you. Gemini.'

'Gemini, anything else?'

'No, it was a bitch to get to that. No name of a port or anything. Just Gemini.'

'Ok, good work. Where's it up to there?'

'Just bagging the body up now.'

'Right. Get some lunch and come back in here.'

She picked up the papers from her desk. Camille was right in one way. It was a bit easier to do this part of the job when there were two of you. But she needed his wife to talk as much as possible. She needed to get a handle on the man who had been Armand Verville.

Chapter 7

It was almost half past twelve, so Maxine took two bread flutes from the shelf and put them into her own bag. It would be just like the thing for someone to come into the boulangerie last minute and buy out the whole lot. She had seen it happen. She was going through the motions, the day-to-day, the mundane, it did her good to grumble. She shuffled things around, she brushed crumbs from the counter into a little pan. Then the customer who always comes in right on the button, twenty-nine minutes past, came in. Always one, not the same person, but really the same person. This one was all in mustard; blouse, trousers and hat. She smiled a thin smile at Maxine and let her eyes linger over the glass shelves as though she was looking for diamonds and pearls.

'Two flutes please,' she said. That only left one for Gabrielle.

'Patisseries, patisseries,' she was talking to herself. Oh, the dilemma thought Maxine. You can have my sodding dilemma, and I'll decide between the eclairs and the mille-feuilles. The customer finally waved mustard fingernails towards the cakes.

'Two and two,' she said. Maxine slid the cakes out with a spatula and shovelled them into a flexible cardboard box. Her hands were unsteady and she was struggling to slot the sides together. She was normally so dextrous. The customer proffered cash and Maxine had to point her to the machine sitting on the counter.

'You have to put the cash in there,' she said.

'But I only have a twenty euro note,' said the woman, flapping it from her mustard finger ends.

'It gives change. We can't handle money now. Not since Covid.'

The woman looked warily at the machine and angrily at Maxine. She finally put the note in the slot and gasped stupidly when the change tumbled back into the chute below. Maxine handed her the cakes and bread and followed her to the door.

'Bonne journée' she said automatically, locked the door and flipped over the sign to closed. Mireille, the manageress came out from the back.

'I have to leave now, straight away, is that ok?' Maxine said, slipping off her coverall.

'No, that's ok. I'll cash up. Gabi can clean. Do you want something else? They'll just be wasted.'

'I know, but no. I've got bread. I have to get away, I have to see somebody.' This was the first time she had said it out loud. That put a line under it. She did need to go and see somebody.

'Ok, have a nice weekend. Tuesday.'

'Yeah, you too.' Maxine slipped on her jacket, grabbed her bag and hurried out. Now it was in stone. Now she had a course to follow. Anything to cover over this big, yawning gap in her insides, anything to fill the hollow, desperate feeling that she had.

Outside the shop she looked up at the towering Flèche Saint Michel, pointing like a stone arrow to the sky. She saw it every day from the window of the bakery. Some days it seemed like an inspiration, but today she raised her head and let her eyes slide up the great spire and she was casting her fears and her anxieties to a god she didn't believe in. She walked quickly through the narrow ancient streets that the tourists loved, past the renovated apartments and the fancy restaurants. She turned into a sunless, uglier road where the old buildings were still mouldering in previous centuries.

The windows were nearly all shuttered and the shutters were unpainted. Not a pedestrianised way, so the cars came along here and the taxis filled the air with their fumes and noise. Maxine stopped by a dull brown door, half ajar, and pushed it open. By the side of the door, on the wall, were old worn plaques with barely legible names; a brief history of the inhabitants of the building for the last fifty years or more.

Her apartment, their apartment, was on the third floor. She wanted to leave her groceries there, brush her hair and change her blouse before she went out again. The apartment was small and gloomy with the shutters closed, but it was immaculately clean and tidy and smelled of patchouli and jasmine from the joss sticks that she burned. It was full of quirky things that belonged to them. Crazy things that he'd made, hanging from walls and the high ceiling, stuck on doors; a metal parrot that from another angle looked like a fish; comfortable things that she had sown from old material gathered at bric a brac shops or vide greniers, house clearance sales.

She went into the bathroom, took off her blouse and washed her neck and under her armpits. She combed her blonde hair out of the bun she wore to work. The dark roots were showing through even more now, and in the raw, fluorescent light she looked her age, maybe older, she thought. The creases in her cheeks and around her eyes were deeper. Smoking cigarettes all her life, that's a problem for women, he used to say, it creases them up, takes the juice out of their skin. She took a sharp gasp of breath. Perhaps that was why, why he didn't come home. He'd just gone, after twenty years. Perhaps she'd been missing the signs. Would that be a better outcome than some she had contemplated this week?

She added some lipstick and found a clean blouse in her bedroom. His clothes were neatly folded or hung carefully in the wardrobe, there was nothing lying on the floor. They were both very neat, very neat and very dexterous, she thought, surprising herself. Yes, we are similar in that way. She put on a light jacket and checked her handbag. There was a knock on the outside door. She jumped and for a moment stood rigid in the tiny hallway. There was a knock again, this time harder, a different hand. Her first thought was, it's him, stupidly, he's lost his key. She patted her hair and opened the door, a frown and a smile competing on her face. There was a woman standing there, a tall, slim woman with very dark hair and fierce, confident eyes. Behind her stood a young man, smiling at her, encouragingly. She didn't know them.

'Bonjour. Madame Verville?' asked the woman.

'Bonjour. Yes.'

'I am Capitaine Celestine Courbet of the Bordeaux Police Judiciaire. This is my colleague, Agent Predeau. May we come in and talk to you, please?'

Maxine stood holding the door, uncomprehending, but something was starting to smoulder at the back of her mind.

'Please,' said the tall woman and waved a hand towards the room. She held up a card.

'Police?' she said.

'Yes, Madame Verville. Police. We need to speak to you, now.'

'I was just going out.'

'Please madame, this is important, it cannot wait. Let us come in to talk to you.' The tall woman's voice was strong and impatient, the young man smiled at her again. Maxine turned and walked into the salon, the police following her, and the young one closed the door. They remained standing, Maxine looked at the floor.

'Madame Verville, is your husband Armand Verville?' asked Capitaine Courbet.

'Yes.' She didn't look up, she remained staring at a worn patch on the carpet where a table leg had once stood.

'Have you seen your husband? When did you see your husband last?'

There was a long pause as Maxine seemed to count the days, although she knew for certain.

'It was Wednesday evening,' she said finally.

'Wednesday evening, and you have had no contact with him since then?' asked Courbet.

'No.'

'Where was he going on Wednesday evening?'

'Work.'

'Work. He works a night shift?' Courbet asked.

Maxine just nodded.

'You didn't report him missing. Wasn't this an unusual situation?'

'Maybe. I expect he'll be back.'

Agent Predeau was fiddling nervously with his notebook. He had expected them to get to the point more quickly. He kept glancing at Capitaine Courbet.

'Where does your husband work, Madame Verville?'

Maxine shrugged.

'You don't know? … madame,' queried Courbet, incredulously.

'No.'

'You don't know where your husband works. Is that what you are saying?'

'Different places.'

'And this week?'

'Don't know. He never said. He never talked about it.'

There was silence for a minute, then Courbet took hold of Maxine's arm, gently, and suggested that she sit down. She guided her to a chair by a small dining table. Maxine sat as though she no longer had any volition of her own. She continued to stare at the floor.

'I'm sorry, this is very difficult,' began Courbet. 'But this morning we found a body, we believe it to be Armand Verville. We found a card, a diabetic card. Your husband was diabetic, no?'

Maxine nodded and then inhaled sharply and seemed to hold her breath.

'I'm terribly sorry, I really am. We don't know for certain yet.'

'Can I see him?' said Maxine suddenly. 'I'll know.'

'No, not yet. There are processes to be followed. We have to be very thorough. We'll let you know when it will be possible. And we'll arrange for someone to visit you, to help you through this, of course.'

Maxine simply nodded and continued staring at the floor. Then in a sudden change of tone, she said.

'Ok. Anything else?'

'Anything else. Yes, well we do need to know where he worked, so we can confirm the cause of death. You haven't asked where we found the body, Madame Verville.'

'Doesn't matter much now, does it? If he's a dead body he's a dead body. And that's that.'

Courbet was astonished.

'Perhaps I have not been clear and I am sorry if that is the case. We believe at this stage that your husband was murdered. We need all the information we can get to find those responsible. Do you understand, Madame Verville? We need to know about the kind of work he was doing, where, and who he was working with. Can you tell us anything at all?' pleaded Courbet.

'No. I've told you. No, I don't know any more.'

'Very well. We'll leave it there. Perhaps we can talk later. Here is my card. Call me at any time. And here are the numbers of the services who can help you.' She handed them to Maxine, who didn't move or look up, so she left them on the table.

'I'm very sorry again, madame. We'll see ourselves out. But I will come back, to make sure you're ok. And if you remember or think of anything. Call me.'

Maxine said nothing, and the two police officers left the apartment quietly and didn't speak a word until they were outside the building.

'Jesus. I didn't think it would be like that, boss,' said Predeau. His young face looked scared and his eyes were casting about for something to focus on.

'It's not usually,' said Courbet, coldly. 'I've never seen anyone take that kind of news in that way. They sometimes keep up a front, polite, that's because it hasn't really sunk in. You know when the door closes behind you they are going to crumble and the grief will come pouring out. Funny things humans, Predeau. God, you'll find that out in this job. Get in the car.'

They sat in the car, a short way down the street from the apartment.

'She knew, or half-knew, before we told her. There's something very wrong here. She's holding a hell of a lot back, not just emotional stuff. She must have had some idea of what kind of work he was doing and where.'

'Criminal work again, do you think?' asked Predeau.

'Wouldn't be surprised. But who murders people who work for them? If that's what this is.'

They sat in silence again, then Courbet said.

'She was about to go out, wasn't she? She said so. I thought it was just to get rid of us, but she had a jacket on, didn't she, a handbag. Predeau, I want you to follow her. See where she goes. It may be nowhere important, but we need some more information on that dead guy. Follow her and find out what you can.'

'Right, Capitaine,' Predeau nodded enthusiastically.

'And don't look so cheerful. You're a police officer, look a bit more...browbeaten.'

'Yes, Ma'am. I'll change my face, of course,' he grinned and opened the car door.

'Don't let her see you. She's sharp. I would say she's been round the houses a few times.'

'Yes, Ma'am.' He closed the door and moved over to the doorway of an empty shop, its windows plastered with old posters of circuses and closing down sales. Courbet drove off, her mind swirling, trying to see through the first fog of this investigation. A fog that Maxine Verville had failed to help clear in any way.

Chapter 8

Predeau didn't have long to wait. He sensed a movement by the outside door of the apartment building and edged further into the recess. He waited tensely in case she should come his way, but after half a minute he looked out and saw her crossing the road fifty metres away. He stepped out quickly to follow her. This area of Bordeaux was of old narrow streets with high buildings on both sides where sounds carried easily, heavy footfalls echoed and cars a hundred metres away seemed almost upon you. Predeau closed the gap between them; he knew she could turn to left or right quite easily and he would lose her. She crossed a small square and turned onto the Rue Porte de la Monnaie. She's heading for the river, he suddenly thought. What if she was intending to throw herself in? Would he be expected to jump in after her, into that muddy, coffee-coloured water? He quickened his stride and came even closer. There were more people around now, this was a more important thoroughfare, and it was easier to blend in. But she wasn't looking to left or right and to his relief she turned into another street just before she reached the stone arch of the Porte de la Monnaie.

Predeau stopped at the corner and looked round carefully. He could see her where she had crossed the narrow street and was hurrying along the pavement on the other side. There was no one else on the street, just a line of cars parked on the near side. He kept to where the cars were parked, ready to duck down quickly if she turned around. She walked nearly halfway along the street and then stopped and stood for a moment in front of a wide blue door. She seemed to be preparing herself for something; patting her hair, pulling at the collar of her jacket. He sensed she was taking a deep breath, and then she pushed open the door and went inside.

Predeau didn't really know this street. It looked shabby and down on its luck. The houses themselves could have been smart, they'd been well-built in fine dressed stone, with ornate balustrades around tiny first-floor balconies. Some of the balconies were supported by intricately shaped corbels, and there were carved stone panels above the windows. But they were unkempt, the doors were faded and unpainted, some windows were blocked up with concrete bricks and the whole street had an air of neglect. Predeau waited for ten minutes, then decided to risk walking past the door Maxine had entered. He kept on his side of the street and as he came level with it he glanced across and took two quick pictures with his mobile phone. The door was in the centre of a stone arch, where part of the sides and above the door were glazed, although the glass was dirty and opaque. There was another matching arched door further along in the same building, also painted a faded cobalt blue, and between them was a single blue door which, he thought, most likely led to the apartments above. It had clearly, at one time, been an attractive building, but the stone was water stained in places, and a pigeon, sitting on the ornate ledge that ran above the windows, was not the first to sit there and leave its white droppings to drip down the wall. Although the whole building looked deserted and unloved, Predeau could see, in the panel above the entrance door that a fluorescent light was burning. There was some faded writing on the glass panel next to the door which he couldn't make out, so he crossed the street quickly and walked past the building. He could just about read the writing which was etched in the glass. *S. Deprisse. Carpenter and Antique Furniture Restorer*. He hurried on and crossed back over the street to stand beside the last parked car. He took out his notebook and wrote down the name and the address, then checked the photographs on his phone. If he needed to show them to Capitaine Courbet he didn't want them to look blurred or careless. He put his phone away and turned back towards the building. Maxine was walking towards him and he had nowhere to go. She had her head bent down but when she stepped onto the pavement she raised her head and looked straight at him. She started, her face was blotchy with tears but suddenly there was anger and incredulity in her eyes. She stopped in front of him and said nothing. He tried to smile but he couldn't move. It seemed to last for an age, but she finally turned away, leant to the side and spat accurately by his feet.

'Madame,' he finally managed to say, but she had already started to walk off in the direction she had come from. There would be no point in trying to follow her now, he realised. He was starting to feel strangely guilty, but he looked across at the building; at least he could find out who she had come to see, he thought. Then he would have something to report to the capitaine.

Predeau took a deep breath himself and pushed open the blue door. At first, nothing connected. He seemed to have stepped into the Nineteenth Century, or perhaps even earlier. Apart from the fluorescent lights, everything else seemed to belong to a scene from one of the historical novels of his childhood. There were pieces of antique furniture everywhere; with intricate wooden stools on top of leather-topped desks, and armchairs with finely carved and gilded arms and legs and seats that looked to have exploded as tufts of horsehair spiked out through holes in the fabric. Even the smell seemed to be ancient; of old wood, centuries from its time as a tree, and some kind of glue, but not a plastic smell, of something more basic and earthy. Predeau looked around a little dazed and disconcerted, like a time traveller trying to establish in which era he had just landed.

As he grew accustomed to the light, he saw the unwavering eyes looking at him. A man was standing behind a very ornate table, and for a moment Predeau wasn't certain if he was even real or a part of this time hallucination he was suffering. The man was tall and broad-shouldered, solid looking, not fat; he was wearing a brown apron of a tough-looking material, and his sleeves were rolled up to display thick, sinuous arms. He was holding a small tool, perhaps a plane, in his right hand and his left hand was resting lightly on the table top. It was the head and eyes that were making Predeau nervous. It was quite a large head surrounded by a mane of grey-brown curls, he had a thick moustache and beard of the same blend of grey and brown which curled around his solid chin and thickish lips. There was something of the wild animal about him, and the eyes were large and seemed to be of some dark impenetrable blue, and they glared and hadn't blinked or stopped staring at Predeau from the moment he had come in. He cautiously approached the table.

'Monsieur Deprisse?' he asked. The man continued to stare at him in silence.

'He's not here,' he said finally.

'And you are?'

'Not he,' replied the man and then paused. 'I can give you his address though. He lives in Chartreuse, Allée Camille Goddard. You can't miss him. Stephane Deprisse, beloved husband. You should visit him, it's not far from where you work, I imagine.'

Now completely disorientated, Predeau took out his warrant card.

'I am sorry, monsieur, I do not understand. I am Agent Predeau of the Police National. I would like to ask you a few questions about the lady who just left here a few minutes ago.'

'No.'

'What do you mean, no, monsieur?'

The man put down the tool he was holding and came around to the front of the table to stand very close to Predeau.

'I mean, Agent Predeau of the Police National, that you should be ashamed of yourself. You have followed a poor woman who has just been told that her husband has been found dead, murdered. You follow her, and now you think you can interrogate me. You will leave my workshop now. Now,' he said loudly and Predeau stepped back despite himself.

'Monsieur. I, we are attempting to find out what we can, to discover who might have killed Monsieur Verville. We feel that Madame Verville has not been completely candid with us. We wanted…'

'Not candid with you. She has just heard that her husband has been murdered.' The man was shouting at him now and there was a fierceness and a strength that Predeau was shrinking from. 'Out, now. Harassment of the bereaved. Is that how you discover things? Get out now.'

Predeau turned and moved towards the door. He saw a small wooden box on a shelf which contained some business cards. He picked one up. At the door, he turned to the man and read off the name on the card.

'Jacques Lecoubarry. Is that you, monsieur? I will leave this for today, but you cannot obstruct the police or refuse to answer questions.'

But the man was already walking back behind the table and had picked up the little plane as Predeau closed the door

Chapter 9

It was early evening when Capitaine Courbet left the long corridors of the bland white chunk that was the National Police Station in the Rue Francois de Sordis. She was too tired and dispirited to be angry, but that was crouching there just below the surface. She had made one good phone call, to the fisherman she'd talked to earlier that day. It had been simple, amusing even, reaffirming. The phone had been answered almost immediately after two rings.

'Monsieur Jarre? Alain.'

'Oui.'

'This is Capitaine Celestine Courbet. We spoke earlier.'

'Yes. Police.'

'Alain, I have the name of the boat that was wrecked on the beach. I mentioned it this morning.'

'Yes, the wreck. Wooden boat.' The voice was slow and gentle, with just a hint of nervousness, or was it excitement?

'It was the Gemini. Nothing else, except it was green at one time.'

'Gemini. Ok, I don't know it.'

'No, but if you could ask around among the fishermen you know in that area, perhaps one of them will be able to say who owned it.'

'Yes, I will ask. I'll find out for you. Yes,' he sounded suddenly very confident and determined.

'You will. That's very helpful, Alain. I would really appreciate that. Call me if you find anything out.'

'Yes. I will telephone the number on the card. Yes. When I find out.' His voice was so slow and quiet and matter of fact, that for a moment she wished all the humans she dealt with had evolved in that way.

The second phone call was less helpful. The pathologist, Dr Delbreil, had telephoned to say that he had been called to another case, a suspected suicide, and the results for Monsieur Verville would be delayed. He was much more upbeat and sounded as though he had spent a thoroughly enjoyable day with his corpses. Courbet shuddered. So far the fisherman was leading hands down.

Then Agent Predeau had knocked tentatively on her door and advised her of the results of his actions of the afternoon.

'What, he just refused to talk to you? This Lecoubarry,' she asked angrily.

'Yes, Ma'am. Said we were harassing a bereaved woman and should be ashamed of ourselves, well myself.'

'And you just left it at that?'

'What else could I do? He was demanding I get out of his workshop. He was angry and bloody big.'

'He threatened you?'

'No, not as such. I mean he didn't say get out or I'll… But he knew I was a flic, soon as I walked in. Knew where I worked, here. Mentioned Chartreuse. Said I should visit this Monsieur Deprisse, who's dead, buried there, Allée Camille Goddard.' Predeau looked haplessly at the top of the desk as Courbet pondered this information.

'Do you think he was connected to Maxine Verville, a friend, more..?'

'A friend maybe, not more, if you mean… he was younger, quite a bit, she's kind of …'

'Old?'

'No. Haggard, you know, worn out.'

'But she had told him about the murder,' said Courbet, trying to imagine this conversation.

'Definitely. That's why he was so annoyed.'

'I wonder,' said Courbet and tapped her fingers on the desk top. 'Predeau, see if we've got anything on him. Criminal record. I'm going to talk to him myself. Fucking harassment. I'll harass him if he holds out on us; this is a murder inquiry. See if he's got a record, any links to the dead man. Ok, off you go.'

She had been looking at the business card and trying to break through the surface, the thin layer that was preventing her from going further into the depths of the conversation with Maxine Verville, and what Predeau had said about his meeting with this furniture restorer, when the phone rang again.

This time it was her husband, who sounded peevish and impatient. He wanted to know when she was coming home, why was she still working on a Saturday, what had she planned for their dinner that evening and more of the same. Biting her tongue, she had stuck to the facts, pointing out that, at this moment, eating was the last thing she was thinking about, but if would like to book a table or order a takeaway, she would go along with that. When he had started on about the state of the rooms, the dirty wine glasses in the sink and the clothes on the floor, she had put the phone down.

She had opened the blinds and stood looking out of the window at a corner of the Cemetery of Chartreuse. That was a strange remark this fellow had said to Predeau. "He lives in Chartreuse". Not just he's dead. Chartreuse was the largest cemetery in the city and had been welcoming guests since the seventeen hundreds. She had heard it described by some history wag as the oldest, living cemetery in Bordeaux - living because it was still interring people. There were older graveyards buried beneath the stones and the crypts of the churches, but they were no longer open for business. Too much death today, Celestine, she thought, you're getting flippant. It was a strange remark though that this Lecoubarry had made. Anyway, she would lay the law down tomorrow and he would most definitely come to heel and tell her what he knew about the activities of Monsieur Verville. And if he was involved, she would have him.

Just then the phone had rung again and reluctantly she'd left her place by the window and walked back to her desk. This time it was her Commandant, Martel, who as always was blunt and to the point.

'You are not to do any more work on this estuary case until I get back,' he said without even a greeting.

'Sir. It's important, you know. The first few days.'

'There's nothing you can do. You're supposed to be off duty. You won't get any forensics or pathology until Monday. It's a holiday weekend, so take a holiday.'

Courbet looked down at the strange drawing she had made on the pad on her desk - a design of river currents, eddies and waves. 'Excuse me, Sir, but how did you know about the case? I thought you were in Paris for the weekend.'

'I am. Dubois called me. As you should have done,' he replied testily.

'Dubois. No, Sir, you're on holiday. There was no need to call you. I'm dealing with it.'

'No, you're not. Nothing to be done. Wait till Monday. Understood.'

'Sir…' But he had ended the call. Damn, damn, damn, damn, damn, she had mouthed to herself for the second time that day. She certainly had not wanted a murder to arrive on the Saturday of a long weekend, but once it's there you've got to progress things as speedily as possible, while evidence is fresh, while hopefully suspects are still in the vicinity. It was the Dubois reference that had also really annoyed her.

What the hell was her lieutenant doing calling Martel? She had gone to see if Dubois was still in the office, but she'd already left, as had Brigadier Leger. Only Predeau remained at his desk, scanning his computer screen. 'Anything?' she'd asked him.

'Nothing. Can't find a thing. Seems clean, Ma'am. I had a look at the business. Stephane Deprisse died in 2009, Anne Deprisse in 2012. Some good write-ups on the business though, good reviews. "Good work; a magician with wood", one comment said; "Pleasure to deal with", etc. Nothing negative.'

'Ok, that'll do. Get away home now. We'll look at it again on Monday.'

'Monday, Ma'am?' queried Predeau.

'Yes, Monday. Commandant Martel's orders. Thinking about our well-being, I am sure.'

She had walked back to her office. Making disparaging remarks about a senior officer to a rookie, she shook her head. This is really getting to you, you need to let a few things go, she thought. But she knew that she wouldn't. There was a man lying in the morgue because someone had taken the decision that that person's life was worth less than their own interests. And while that person was out there she would not let anything go.

Chapter 10

Jacques Lecoubarry locked the door of his workshop and headed out into the early evening streets. The air was mild and a breeze was blowing up gently from the river. The sunlight was pale, casting the lower sections of the buildings into shade and bathing the spire of the Flèche Saint Michel in a pink and golden hue. He was striding purposively, but in reality, there were a hundred things running through his head that he was trying to place in some sort of order. He needed a drink; he needed to see Maxine again; he was hungry and he wanted some friendly company, even some passion. But inside he felt wretched, hollowed out and seared by the news of his friend's death, like a cold wind was blowing through his insides. He hadn't remembered how pieces break off when a friend's life ends; threads are pulled out, links are broken that can never be repaired. Armand Verville - he could see the man's face, the disjointed movements he made when music came on that he liked, the intensity of his concentration when he worked and the music he made with his hands when he was fashioning something in metal. How could a man who was so careful in his work be so careless in life? It was beyond comprehension, he thought. This was a man who did not make enemies easily. Why would anyone murder him? What nature of rough beast would not see that the world was shrunken by the loss of such a man? What could anyone gain from that? I need a drink before I head along too many dark streets, he thought, and quickened his pace.

He dipped into a small and gloomy café on the edge of the Place de Maucaillou. At a table by the door, there were four, middle-aged North African men talking quietly in Arabic and gesticulating gracefully with their hands. At the only other occupied table, three younger men were each staring at their cell phones, but they all glanced up at him as he walked in. The barman was short and stocky, with a shaved head so covered in scars and bumps that it could have been a contour map for his home village. He greeted Jacques with a slight raise of his head.

'Bonsoir, Fouad. How goes it with you?' said Jacques.

'Ça va. It goes, nothing more.'

'Pastis, if you please.' The barman poured a good measure of Rickard into a large glass for Jacques, filled a jug with water and placed it alongside on the counter. Jacques handed over some coins as he leaned towards him.

'Armand Verville is dead. He has been killed. Do you know where he was working, Fouad?'

The barman shrugged and shook his head. 'Armand Verville. I haven't seen him in months. He doesn't come in here. Killed. That's a pity.'

'You don't have any idea where he was working, or who with?' asked Jacques.

The man shook his head again. 'No. Like I say, I never see him. Seen his woman though. Works in a boulangerie near Saint Michel.'

'Yeah, I know. Maxine, his wife. We're old friends. Look, Fouad, if you hear anything, you tell me right.' The man just moved his head slightly from side to side.

Jacques picked up his drink and turned away from the bar.

'He used to like to smoke, you know,' said the barman, 'from boys here. But I don't see him for a long time.'

'Ok. Thanks, Fouad. I know he did, but not big time; he just liked to laugh and listen to music, and some bastard has killed him.' He said this with such force that the other men in the café suddenly went silent and glanced towards him. He took his pastis outside to sit on one of the plastic tables under the canopy. There wasn't much of a view, just the walls of a building, which, like his, had seen better days. He poured a little of the water into his pastis and watched as it turned to brown cream. He sipped it slowly, enjoying the bite as it caught his throat and sent aniseed fumes into the back of his nostrils. He sat deep in his own thoughts. He knew there was a disgruntlement there, a dissatisfaction with his daily existence. He was coasting, freewheeling, there were no great, bloody gobbets of passion in his life, just a repetition of the comfortable and the easy. And now this old friend had died and he could feel a spark and felt disgusted with himself, as if in some way he had welcomed this new interest. He shook his head, no, not that. That is unacceptable. You must do what you can for an old friend and his wife. They are not there to spice up your life. And he had a sudden memory of Armand, standing in the corner of a café in the Rue du Tertre in Nantes, making jerky, Joe Cocker-like arm movements as he sang along to *with a little help from my friends*. A man of music and metal. A sweet, funny man, a foolish one, one that he thought Maxine had kept in order. But he hadn't seen him for nearly a year, so who knew what things had changed or what had happened to him in that time? Something bad clearly, because you don't get murdered when you're in a good place, unless you're very, very unlucky.

Jacques stood outside the door of Maxine's apartment for ten minutes. She wasn't there. He was glad in some ways; there was something she needed to be away from. And he, coward that he was, didn't feel ready to deal with the images of his friend that the interior of the apartment would show. He leaned back against the door and smelt the mustiness and slightly rotten odours of the corridor - the smell of gentle poverty and gradual decay. He closed his eyes as if he could feel the answers by osmosis through the door. There must be answers there.

He left the building feeling depressed and unenlightened. He stood on the narrow pavement, searching for a direction to follow as a car drove by too quickly. If in doubt, turn away from pain, turn towards pleasure. Even the simplest, minute organisms knew that one; and he wasn't simple and he certainly wasn't minute. He skirted by the Marché des Capucins, where a van was unloading the carcases of pigs onto the bloodied shoulders of the labourers and the smell of old vegetables and seafood seeped out into the street. He walked along the Rue des Douves, which was still busy with cars at this time of the evening and where two girls were already leaning in one of the doorways. He crossed the small park to reach the theatre behind the church of Sainte-Croix.

The theatre was incongruous; it looked like a cottage at the corner of two streets, but it opened up into a small auditorium with a stage, seats for a hundred people and a bar running along one side. The door was open, although there was no performance due, so Jacques walked quietly inside and peered through the gloom. The stage was palely lit and he could see four characters standing stock still, bent in strange and ungainly positions. There was complete silence, it was almost as though they had been frozen in time. He stood behind the seats at the back and joined the silence. Then slowly, one figure, a girl, uncurled herself and floated, it seemed, to the back of the stage. This was followed by another, and now he could hear the low humming noise they were making. The third and fourth actors followed to the back of the stage. There were two girls and two boys. The humming had become louder and louder until it was like a swarm of angry bees. Then the pale light faded until there was complete darkness, but the humming continued, menacing now in the blackness. Finally, when the noise had reached a crescendo, it stopped and the lights came on. Jacques breathed again. On the stage, the actors relaxed and two of them burst into laughter from the release. A slim, elegant woman was standing at the front of the auditorium and she clapped her hands. Jacques clapped too, and the actors, startled, looked up, peering through the lights towards him. The woman turned round and Jacques walked up to her.

'Jacques,' she called. 'Jacques, so good, so good to see you.' She put her hands on his broad shoulders and kissed him robustly on both cheeks and then pecked him on the lips. She looked at his face carefully before turning away. She pointed to the stage.

'The sets, they are magnificent, superb, Jacques. They are, I should say, the exact counterpoint to what we are trying to say in the piece. I love them. They look good, no? They look untrustworthy.'

Jacques was looking at the backdrop now that the lights were on.

'Marc,' the woman called and waved her hands in the air. 'Turn the lights on full, onto the scenery.' A moment later a brighter light flooded over the stage. The actors shuffled as though the light was a heat that was touching them. The scenery, which Jacques had built, did look good. It was stark, three-dimensional, and it seemed to lean out towards the audience.

'It looks good,' said Jacques, 'but I think it's the painting that makes it.'

'Pah! The painting is simple. It is the structure, the way it seems to hang, and it leans out over the actors and draws the audience into the cauldron. You're a genius. The company love it. And they are a lovely group to work with, so loose and uninhibited,' she laughed.

'Is it ready, Candice?' he asked.

'Almost. Dress rehearsal tomorrow, and Wednesday the play opens.'

'Have you sold many tickets?'

'Oh, you know, Jacques, people come last minute. I am not worried.' She looked carefully at his face.

'But really, how are you, Jacques? You look discomfited.' She placed a hand on his cheek.

Jacques nodded. 'Perhaps a little, more than a little, yes,' he replied and put his hand on hers.

'Oh, my dear lion,' she said and kissed him briefly on the lips. 'You know, Philippe calls you Le Lion des Bois, the Lion of the Woods. He says you are a shape-shifter, you live with wood, in wood, but you shift and change sometimes into a man and come out into the clearing to ravish the maidens, to ravish his wife,' she looked at him gaily. 'He says you are mythological, a shape-shifter.'

'I didn't realise anyone knew my secret,' replied Jacques.

'Many have suspected, but it takes a poet to get to the truth of it.' She turned him around and pretended to look for his tail.

'Philippe?' asked Jacques.

'Is in Aix-en-Provence; workshops, readings, what poets do when they leave the garret,' she paused. 'He doesn't mind you know. I've told you that. He loves you. Says you are my lover from another world, so that's all right.'

'He is a very generous man, and I wish it was the law that everyone had to read his poetry each day.' Candice laughed and clapped her hands again. 'That I would vote for,' she said.

'You won't have eaten. Should we find somewhere to have dinner? When you are finished, of course,' said Jacques.

'Love to. Give me another fifteen minutes. One more scene I want to take them through. Sit down and enjoy it. It's quite difficult. You can be the critic of the Bordelais Bourgeois.'

The lights dimmed again and Candice gathered the actors into a group at the edge of the stage. Then she stepped away, clapped her hands and the actors moved to their positions. With a wave, the music started and the scene commenced. Jacques watched it and watched Candice as she moved from one side of the theatre to the other, her hands moving, encouraging, slowing down, her head tilted one way then the other. She was wearing a loose linen blouse and tight jeans, and around her neck and wrists were beads of all colours and different sizes. Her hair was blonde and thick and swung around her face when she became animated, which she did a lot. He couldn't see her face but he knew the expressions on it, knew it would be backlit by the verve and enthusiasm she showed for everything she did. She wasn't beautiful, but she was attractive, and like her actors, she was very uninhibited.

Chapter 11

At a few minutes after eight, Celestine Courbet and her husband walked into the pink and chrome décor of the QC restaurant on the Quai Chartron. They were shown to their table and took their seats in silence. It was instinctive for her to look around, to check out the other diners and confirm the exits and entrances. But this night she merely stared at the table until the menu arrived and then stared at it without really reading the words. She was hungry but she wasn't. Her body was empty, she had eaten little all day, but her mind was not interested in food or anything else. She chose the first item on the menu that she thought wouldn't stick in her throat, and drank deeply of the wine that they'd ordered as soon as they had sat down. Her husband looked at her critically.

'You know, Celestine, if you are going to bring your work home with you, perhaps it's too demanding, too serious for you,' he said.

'Too serious.' She looked up and pursed her lips. 'A man's been killed. Of course it's serious. Of course I take it seriously. I'm not fretting over a packet of biscuits that fell off a shelf I've been packing. I'm investigating a murder, the death of one human being caused by another.' She glared at him and drank down her glass of wine. He held up his hands with a gesture to keep her voice down.

'I'm just saying. Perhaps it's too demanding for you, I should move you to an easier position, one with less stress and responsibility. I'm thinking of you,' her husband said, and reached over to fill up her glass again, but she pulled it away.

'I do not believe that you said that, Etienne. I do this job, this job, because I'm good at it. I'm clever and determined. I don't do it because you gave it to me. And now you think you want to take it away,' she retorted. He topped up his own glass, took a sip and placed it carefully back on the table. He leaned towards her and said in a low voice.

'Well, if you want to keep doing this job, stop being so fucking female about it. Don't get emotional. Deal with the facts, follow that trail and then leave it at the door. Do you think I want this twenty-four seven?'

'Twenty-four seven! I haven't seen you for the last three days. Where were you? Yesterday, May Day, a Public Holiday. We weren't even in the same city, were we? In fact, I don't know where you were.'

'I told you, police business. And above your pay grade I'm afraid,' he replied cuttingly.

'I'm not asking as a police officer, you arse. I'm asking as a wife,' she replied, the anger barely restrained in her voice.

'Then I'm asking you as a husband, to leave work behind when you get in your car in the Rue Camille de Roquefeuil, and act like a wife when you get home. It's very easy,' and he put his hands out to each side like a balance. 'Wife, home. Work, police officer, senior officer. I really thought we had this sorted.' He shook his head as though disappointed. 'Now have some more wine. Relax a little. I'm sorry I was away for a couple of nights. It couldn't be helped. It's something big, organised crime, but I really can't say any more at this time. Relax, enjoy your meal. Tomorrow's Sunday. We could go to Arcachon, or have lunch at the sailing club.'

Celestine remained silent. She accepted some more wine and looked at the overblown décor of the place. The restaurant was full, this being Saturday night, and she recognised the people at a couple of the tables; but they were not friends, they were peers, she thought. Same look, same habits, same money just bouncing around. Was there one person who stood out? Perhaps a young, under-dressed couple. She watched them, they were intimidated by the waiter, but when they were left alone she kept giggling and he was clearly making funny comments which made her snort with repressed laughter. Celestine was envious. Her own husband was a handsome, confident man, domineering with waiters, successful and competent in so many things; but she couldn't remember the last time he had made her laugh. Perhaps she should take her plate over to the young couple's table and try to join in the laughter, but it would be such a singular thing to do that they would undoubtedly clam up and be embarrassed, and that would spoil the evening for them too. So she ate her perfectly cooked *Ris de Veau à la Chatelaine*, when it arrived, and drank another glass of wine so that a second bottle was needed.

Chapter 12

Jacques and Candice strolled along the narrow roads around the Church of Saint Pierre. The cafés and restaurants were filling up and the streets were bustling with mainly young people enjoying the gentle light and warmth of the late evening. He had been talking about the killing of his friend and every so often she would squeeze his arm to bring him closer to her side.

'And do you think he was involved in something criminal?' she asked quietly.

'It's possible, yes, possible. There are jobs that a man with those skills can do which are perfectly legitimate; we worked together on jobs like that. But those skills can also be valuable to people on the other side. And sometimes that pays better.' Jacques shook his head as though remembering something then pushing it away again. 'He was not good with money, I was going to say, but that's not right. With him, money flowed in and flowed out; and to me, that's what it's supposed to do. Armand was not a builder of dams, you know, he lived for today. He loved the flow. Earn and spend. But sometimes maybe the spend was greater than the earn, and possibly then he had to do things to improve the flow. Make more money. I don't know. I need to speak to his wife again. But whatever he was doing, he shouldn't have been at risk of losing his life.'

Candice put her hand on his head and ruffled his hair.

'Where are we going, Goxoki?' she asked.

'I thought so. Red pepper dishes, plenty of bite, red bite.'

'Food from the Pays Basque. Absolutely. We'll eat fiery Basque food and toast your friend in red wine. And we'll wing him up to where he should be. They must need metal workers up there. Those heavenly gates must be getting a bit rusty by now.'

In another fifty metres, they came to the restaurant behind an inauspicious exterior that you could easily pass by. But when you opened the door and stepped in you were met with a rich wave of hot food smells. The walls were red and the tablecloths red and white checks. It was already busy, with a mix of young and older, all casually dressed, and everyone seemed to be talking at once. The servers were young, kids really, fast and dextrous and cheerful. One of the girls, who knew Jacques, showed them to a table in a corner where the sounds were slightly muffled. Candice laughed, shrugged off her jacket and placed it on the back of her chair. Bread arrived immediately, and for a while they were silent, eating pieces of the tough rustic boule and looking at each other.

One of the waitresses had placed an outsized beret on the head of one of the diners and was dancing behind his chair singing *Joyeux Anniversaire,* happy birthday, with the other people at the table. People clapped when the song was done. Candice clapped.

'You know, I love this place. It feels like it's all one, everything is connected. I am part of the meal and part of the room and the other guests and the meal is part of me.'

'It will be soon,' said Jacques smiling.

'But you know what I mean. I know you do. It is a total experience. It's not singular. The waiters and waitresses are part of the whole, not a separate little functional unit. The people at the other tables are talking to each other, but their speech, their words are rising, are flowing around the restaurant. Somebody's epithet just dropped into your wine,' she laughed.

'And when somebody leaves, like those two guys leaving now?' asked Jacques.

'Then we are all slightly depleted by it,' Candice said solemnly. 'But we regroup, and perhaps another pair or a group will come in and soon their energy will be bouncing around the room, soaking into my food and wine.'

'Sounds unhygienic,' said Jacques.

'You don't feel that in many other restaurants,' she continued. 'They feel like… erm, a machine, a meal machine. Step in, sit down, make order, cold man goes to kitchen, cold man returns, plates on table, eat now, pay now, out now. That's just charging your stomach. This place charges your soul.' She laughed again and took the last piece of bread before Jacques could get it. He couldn't help smiling at her.

'Charging my stomach would be a great start right now,' he said.

They had both ordered *Axoa de Veau*, veal cooked with red peppers, onions, thyme and the *Espelette Pepper*, and when it came it was piping hot and spicy and they ate in silence with great relish. Then, when they had both finished, Candice raised her glass and said out loud: 'To Armand at the Gates of Heaven.' Several people turned around when she said that and smiled and raised their own glasses. The third time she said it she stood up and a few more tables joined in, until finally almost the whole restaurant was raising a glass and chanting 'Armand at the Gates of Heaven.' Jacques was fighting back the tears and he had to wipe his face with a napkin and cover his eyes until he regained his composure.

'You have to give the man the right recognition and send off,' said Candice, completely unabashed.

'Ok. But for Christ's sake, tell me about this play and don't mention Armand again tonight,' he said.

'Can't promise that,' she replied, 'but a little diversion to relieve the pressure might be a good idea.' She sat back and put her hands together. 'Betrayal,' she said, 'that's the central theme. But not betrayal on a simple level, not just the level of social mores or artificial standards.'

'Like husbands and wives,' interjected Jacques.

'Yes, and demographic groups, society, countries even. No, ultimately it's about betrayal of yourself, the originality, the uniqueness, the soul of you if you like. Four characters, all twisted by betrayal of the sorts I've mentioned. But the one, the most twisted one, is the one who is true to all the other elements, but not to themselves. You know which one that is.'

'The last one to unfold themselves. The most twisted one, literally,' said Jacques.

'Precisely.'

'And the humming? That was quite disturbing.'

'Disturbing, good. Well you'll just have to watch the whole play and then tell me what the humming was about.' She clapped her hands lightly and looked up at him in such a brazen way, with her dark eyebrows raised and her eyes flashing, that he waved to the waitress to bring him the bill. It was the same girl who had danced behind the table, and as she gave them their receipt she asked.

'Who's Armand?'

'A friend,' said Jacques.

'The finest damn metal worker since Vulcan the God of Fire,' said Candice and stood up.

'Great,' said the girl and smiled at them. 'Allez Armand.'

'Yes. Allez Armand.'

They walked briskly back to Candice's apartment on the Rue Margaux and made love almost as soon as they arrived. Later they lay close but not touching. Jacques was staring at the ceiling and she put her hand on his heart.

'You know, Jacques. Good friendships don't end when a friend dies,' she said.

'I wasn't a good friend, Candice. But I do want to see some bastard pay for this,' he replied.

Celestine Courbet was prickly drunk. Her husband drove them back and she sat playing with the clasp of her handbag. As soon as they had parked she got out of the car and stalked over to the outside door of the apartment block. She tapped in the code and let the door swing closed before her husband reached it so that he had to tap the number in again. She walked up the three flights of stairs, rather than wait for the lift, so her husband arrived at about the same time. Once in the apartment she went straight to the bathroom, drank some water and got into bed. Her husband came into the room a few minutes later, he was naked and lay down on top of the bed beside her. He reached over and began to stroke her head and the back of her neck, and she turned slowly. Then she felt the pressure on her head increase as he tried to pull her down towards his groin. She reared up and shook off his hands in a furious and clumsy movement. She couldn't speak. She stood up and walked into the guest bedroom, slamming the doors behind her.

Chapter 13

It was a little after midnight. All was quiet on the ship. He stood in the shadow of a container on the deck and peered through the railings. The lazy half-moon lay a pallid gauze of light across the land, which was good and bad for him; good, because he could make out the dark shapes of the containers standing in rows and of the cranes on the shore below; bad, because they could see him, if they were watching, and that he didn't know.

There was sound; the dull throbbing of another ship's engine as it lay at anchor half a kilometre away in the strand. Closer, there was a faint whistling sound as the wind squeezed through the metal pipes and railings of his own ship. He focused his hearing on the harbour yard below. There didn't seem to be any movement. Over by the buildings, which were well-lit, where the ground in front was stark in the white floodlights, there was no activity. Strain, stretch your senses, he told himself. Can you hear anything? Can you see anything? He leaned back against the container and took a deep breath, uncertainty, excitement and fear running through him. He lifted the small knapsack onto his shoulders and whispered a half-remembered sailor's incantation to the four winds. Then he slowly edged towards the steps leading from the deck of the ship to the quayside below. He stayed in the shadows as much as he could but there were lighted spaces that he had to cross; there he tried to think of his movements as like a dull beam of light or a pale flame, not a man, something nebulous that could be only slightly detected but not clearly seen. He believed in that; in the insubstantial landscape, even of metal bulwarks and steel frames. He had heard of animals that could move, blending light and dark, and never be completely seen, animals that could sift through a village and steal a child or a calf and only be detected by the slight distortion of the molecules as they passed and a faint vapour trail that lingered after they'd gone. He willed himself to be as one of those.

He reached the head of the steps where a low chain hung across as a barrier, but it was only there to represent the rules; if you were intent on breaking those rules the chain was easily disregarded. He crossed the barrier and stepped lightly, pausing after each step to listen. He reached the bottom of the stairs where another chain hung across like a reprimand. He crouched under it and stayed low to listen. He could hear his heart beating. He was on solid ground for the first time in weeks and he felt as though his heart beating was also the breathing of the earth. Now he could hear a low humming sound, the sound of a generator, off to the right where the buildings were. He sprinted across the space to reach the shadow of a crane and he soaked the darkness into him. There were no angry shouts, no lights flooding on, no dogs barking and straining at their chains desperate to chase and savage him. He was beginning to feel a little more confident, but then he heard the sound of a vehicle engine starting up. He edged around the great wheels of the crane and peered out from the shadow. He could see a small van pulling away from the front of the building and heading along the road between the containers that led to where he was hiding. He wondered for a moment if this was just a big trick, a game they were playing with him. He thought they had probably been watching him on their bank of screens, with their infrared lights, watching a stupid little man crawling like a bug, scurrying from crevice to shadow, like a bug. And now, tired of playing, they were going to catch him. He could feel his terror rising and he had to wrap his arms tightly around to hold himself together. The vehicle came closer, he was in the shadow, they couldn't see him, could they? Not unless they shone a light directly at the place where he was crouching. The van drove past without stopping. He could hear the tyres rolling roughly over the concrete; he could hear each wheel and for a second he glanced in the window and saw the head of the driver. I have seen my enemy, he thought.

He stayed in the same position, creased up, bent over so that his knees and ankles were stretched and aching. But he didn't move and he heard the change in sound as the vehicle was muffled and then it was coming back towards him on the lane he had crossed. The engine sounded different as it pushed the molecules before it. He couldn't crouch any lower, but he pulled himself in, in his mind, until he was just a wafer of shadow blending and diffusing into the darkness. The van came closer, then was level, then past, and after a few minutes the engine sound stopped and he heard car doors slam and faint, garbled, human voices travelling down towards him on the breeze. But there was nobody shouting - we know you're there, come out you human bug, its squash time.

He waited a little longer then started walking in the shadow of the containers, away from the lights of the building. He shuffled a few hundred metres like this until he came to the end of the line of containers and he could see the fence. He stopped in the shadow and studied the way. There were cameras, he could just make them out; they weren't moving, just staring, fixed at points along the fence and into the yard. How could he cross that space? How could he spend time at the fence without being seen? He looked from side to side and then he saw what looked like a giant capstan, but was in fact the wooden drum where some thick electrical cable had been coiled before being run out. It was like a large bobbin, with a flat round top, a narrow cylinder of a waist and a flat round base. It looked to be about two metres high, and more importantly, it had been discarded very near the fence itself. If I can get to that, he thought, I could hide under the hat where the cameras can't see me. He braced himself, he prepared to run as fast as he had ever run, so fast that even if the screen watchers glimpsed a movement, it would pass so quickly that they might think it was only a trick of the light, or a malfunction, or the passing of a dragon being, not of this reality. He honed into all the signals that the world could give him, waiting for the right moment to run. He felt a surge of energy and there was a click in his head like the sound when the two hands of a clock scrape together at twelve, and he sprinted like the four winds funnelled into one direction and dived beneath the overhang of the drum. He sat there letting his breath and his blood re-order themselves. Nothing. There was no sound, no alarms, no diabolical laughter from the screen men. Nothing.

He took a set of bolt cutters from his knapsack, fastened them around the first strand of the fence wire and squeezed hard. The metal snapped with a dull click, it was quieter than he had dared hope; you would have to be a dog, ears strained, to hear that. He cut another wire and then another until he had one side and the top of a square cut from the fence. He stopped to rest his hands and to listen again, but he started cutting again quickly; he needed to finish this, to move beyond this prison. When he had cut the last strand he pulled the square of wire mesh into the shelter of the drum. He pushed his head and shoulders through the gap to test it for size, then drew himself back again. He placed the bolt cutters back in the knapsack - he had no idea how many fences he would need to break through in this new world. He pushed the knapsack through the gap first, and then muttering another incantation, he plunged headfirst through the gap, snagging his leg on one side where the cut was rough, and tearing his trousers a little. But he was through, and he grabbed his sack and ran, stumbling on the rough ground, on the tussocks of grass and stunted wiry bushes he could barely see in the gloom. After a hundred metres he fell and banged his elbow on the concrete edge of a ditch he had fallen into. But it was dry, and he lay there on his back, breathing heavily, looking up at the stars blurred by the light of the pale hovering moon.

He could smell the margin of the sea; not the wind-scoured, salty sea of the ocean, but the rank, vegetative smell of creeping water sluicing the rocks, draping the weed and detritus on the shore, whispering as it made runnels in the sand and then sneaked back out again. He knew the smell well and it made him feel sad and homesick, and yet at home. He had always known that the ocean here touched the shoreline there, and visited the same sands where he was born. In his lifetime he believed every piece of the ocean visited every bit of the shore of every land. That gave him comfort, although he was alone. 'I have cracked the shell,' he thought, 'and now I will emerge new into this world'.

His arm was hurting but he knew it would pass. He lifted his head and looked back towards the fence and the harbour yard. There was no sign of activity, nothing; perhaps the screen men had been distracted after all. He walked along a path that ran close to the sea's edge and he could hear the slush and wheeze of the small waves on the shingle beach below him. To his right were the lights of a town, but he knew it would seem suspicious if he were spotted walking the streets at this time of night. He had no information on how many police there would be, waiting in their blue cars, straddling their fast motorcycles, watching for the likes of him. He decided to skirt around the town and then to head inland and to get as far away from the port as possible during the night, and then to lie low when the sun came up. Then he could make the call.

He walked for nearly three hours and saw no one. He heard one car on a road in the distance, it was as though the earth had gone silent and was suspended just for him. The countryside was much stranger than he had imagined; the smells were different, and the very air was different, drier, sweeter than he'd expected. He came by fields with rows of small trees strung on wires, which were pale and ethereal in the moonlight. He felt he was moving through a dream landscape until he heard the howling of a hound and that set his nerves on edge. He veered away from the origin of the sound only to be met with a different dog on the other side, yapping angrily at the strange scent and sound moving through its bailiwick. So he went from dream to wide awake and rigid, to dream again as he walked through the night. He saw the first tentative lightening of the sky directly ahead of him and he marvelled as the trees and the woods and low hills slowly absorbed the gold of the sunrise and started to form their shapes. Not long after the sun inched above the horizon he started to hear the sounds of the waking, rural people. He expected it. In Vietnam, the workers were already toiling in the fields when the full sun was on the landscape. He heard a tractor and then a car coming along the narrow road he was following. He ducked down by a hedge and watched the car go by. A little further on he saw a sign which he took to be the name of the village he had reached. He took a pen and notebook from his pack and painstakingly wrote down the letters, to tell her when he called. The village was only a few houses set to one side of the road. He was past it quickly and then he looked for a place to conceal himself. There was a field with a row of vines on one side and on the other a small wood. He walked into the wood for a few metres and found a tree with a bush growing in front that would shield him from the road. He sat down and leaned back against the tree, sniffing at the new smells. He took a small package from his knapsack and unpeeled the foil wrapping. He realised then how hungry he had become and he ate the mung bean cubes and deep fried dough sticks. He had nothing to dip them in so ate them dry and washed them down with water from the small bottle he carried.

He had done something, he had stepped out and he was in the new world now. Not so much an escape as a rebirth, he imagined. This new creature, that he was, did not belong to them and would have no part in their works and their darkness. He settled himself down to sleep for a few hours until he could make the call.

Chapter 14

Jacques Lecoubarry was back in his own rooms above the workshop when his mobile phone rang. He ignored it and it finally stopped ringing and clicked through to voice mail. One simple rule; if there's no message, it's either unimportant or spam. He heard the beep that said he had received a message. Reluctantly, he picked up the phone and tapped for the message to replay.

'This is Capitaine Celestine Courbet for Jacques Lecoubarry. It is ten oh five on Sunday morning. I need to speak to you with some urgency, Monsieur Lecoubarry. Please call me back on this number without delay.' Pause. 'I will in any case call you again shortly and on a regular basis until we speak.'

Jacques sighed; the voice was quite stern, fierce even, like an angry schoolmistress. He really didn't want to be angry this morning. He was still basking in the glow of Candice's warmth and generosity. But it was she who had pricked his conscience, who had orchestrated that requiem for his friend, and who had made it clear to him that his friendship could and must continue beyond death, that there were duties he had as a friend that had to be discharged. He picked up the phone and as he did so it rang again. This time he took a deep breath and answered it.

'Bonjour,' he said quietly.

'Bonjour. Monsieur Lecoubarry?' There was a pause. 'This is Capitaine Courbet, Bordeaux Police Judiciaire. I'd like to speak to you about Armand Verville. I am investigating his possible murder and I would like some background information on him. You knew him, yes?' The woman's voice was so cross.

'Yes.'

'Were you friends?'

'Yes.'

'Ok, look. I want you to come into the commissariat, I will need a statement from you,' she said.

'No.' There was a substantial pause and Jacques could imagine the anger level was tipping up to the red/danger point. But that wasn't his problem. Someone else's anger was for them to deal with, it was not going to influence him.

'No. No, you refuse,' the voice was harsh. 'I'll send a car now to pick you up and drag you here if necessary. I'm not pissing around, you understand. You're obstructing a police investigation. A murder investigation. Serious, Monsieur Lecoubarry, this is very serious.' Again there was a silence.

'Show me your warrant card,' said Jacques.

'My warrant card. Right, here it is, can you see it, on the telephone?'

'No, I can't,' said Jacques calmly. 'Therefore I have no idea if you are in fact a police capitaine or a pain-in-the-ass cold caller. It follows that I can't be obstructing anything. Secondly,' he continued not giving her an opportunity to speak, 'if you are a police capitaine, and if you were to send a car to drag me in, where would you send it? As a matter of interest.'

'We have your address, Monsieur Lecoubarry. One of my officers called on you yesterday afternoon.'

'It's Sunday. I don't go to work, I go to church,' said Jacques.

'Church?'

'Eighth Day Adventists. Yes. We believe that the world is quite clearly such a half-finished mess that an eighth day would have been useful to review the snagging list. That's what we do: try to correct the points on the celestial snagging list. It's hard work but spiritually rewarding,' said Jacques in a serious and deadpan voice. There was another long pause, but the voice when it came seemed to Jacques to have lost some of its harshness, some tension had seeped out.

'Monsieur Lecoubarry, are you trying to make me laugh? Are you really taking the piss with a capitaine of the National Police?'

'If that's what you are,' replied Jacques, calmly.

'If that's what I am.' Jacques could imagine the shaking of the head on the other end of the phone.

'Well, Capitaine Courbet, allegedly. I am not going to visit your establishment on the Rue Francis de Sordis. And if I were physically forced to attend there, which would be no easy matter, I can assure you, it would be a complete waste of time because I wouldn't say a word while I was there. Not a word you understand. And you could try and bully and threaten as much as you like but it would be in vain.' Jacques' voice was now raised and he was starting to sound angry. 'However,' he paused, and Courbet, who had been about to object, held her tongue. 'Armand Verville was a friend. I will talk to you, but I want something back in return.'

'Oh, what's that?' she asked.

'Reciprocation. Not a one-way street.'

'This is a police matter. I can't share details of an investigation with a member of the public; whereas you have a duty to share information with me.' There was another long period of silence. Exasperated, she finally said. 'Monsieur Lecoubarry, where can we meet this morning?'

'Do you agree?' replied Jacques.

'Agree with what?'

'Two-way street, a sharing of information.'

She was suddenly very tired and fed-up with this guy who was clearly being obstructive.

'I will keep you and Madame Verville up to date with progress on this investigation to the extent that I can. No more.'

'Sports Park, Saint Michel. Beyond the basketball courts. Eleven thirty.' Jacques said almost instantly.

'Eleven thirty. Ok, I can do that. I know the park. I run along there all the time.'

'I trust you are a hard-boiled, scarred, cynical flic, not like that altar boy you sent yesterday?' said Jacques.

'Scarred and cynical. Absolutely,' replied Courbet.

'The benches by the river. Just you. Two of you and I walk away.'

'There'll only be me, Monsieur Lecoubarry. I'll recognise you easily, I suppose.'

'I'll be wearing a look of casual disdain,' said Jacques. Courbet snorted and grinned despite herself.

'I'm not even sure what the hell that looks like,' she said, 'but I did get something of a description from my officer. He seemed to think you were unusual.'

'Eleven thirty.' Jacques ended the call. He sat quietly in the over-stuffed cabriolet armchair, running the conversation back through his mind. The woman's voice was strong - clarinet not oboe, he thought. That was quite unusual in a woman. Candice was an oboe, sliding up to a flute and descending to alto sax; a terrific range which matched the breadth of her passions, of her passion. This woman is just a police officer. What are you going to tell her? That's what's important. He sat there thinking of Armand, but also of what he had heard of the Bordeaux Police. Some of them. He was wary. Bordeaux was a small town really, words flew on the wind and down the narrow streets where he lived. He would need to be very, very careful.

He decided to get to the meeting point early so he could watch the approach of this police capitaine, and to see if she was really coming there alone.

Chapter 15

Celestine Courbet looked at the phone in her hand for a minute after the call, wondering how that had happened. Why was she going to meet this stranger in a park, instead of at the station or at his home, at her behest? She'd been worked and that didn't happen often. She felt her anger rising again but she decided she had to put it aside for now. She had already tabbed this guy as a vainglorious, tedious, asshole, who probably had a little bit of information, but wanted to big himself up to make it, and him, seem more important.

From where she was standing she could have run to Saint Michel in five minutes. She had left the apartment before her husband had got out of bed and had gone for a run to clear her head and shake off the hangover. She was dressed in running shorts and a thin T-shirt, which was not exactly appropriate attire for an interview in a murder case. She needed to look deadly serious and official. There was no question in her mind that she was going to put the son of a bitch in his place, once she had the information she required.

She jogged back through the streets of Chartrons to her apartment building hoping that her husband was still in bed or had gone out to find some breakfast. But when she walked into the flat he was standing by the coffee machine in the kitchen, wearing his silk dressing gown with the dragons on. She ignored him and went straight to the bathroom to shower. She dressed in the formal clothes she wore for work; dark trousers, white blouse and a fawn-coloured jacket. In a last-minute decision, she took off the jacket again and fitted her service pistol in its holster around her neck and under her armpit. When she looked up, her husband was standing in the doorway glaring at her.

'I have a lead,' she said. 'I'm going there now.'

'You were instructed to hold back until Monday. That's what you were told,' her husband said and filled the doorway.

'This can't wait. The guy could leave.' She pushed past him and collected her car keys and bag from the dresser in the hall.

'And you need your gun to meet this guy?' he asked, following her towards the door.

'It's official. It's for emphasis,' she said and walked out of the apartment.

Jacques watched the young boys playing basketball in the big wire cage. Their voices were shrill, full of urgency and youthful energy as they called to each other in the game. The park had been built since he was a youth growing up in Bordeaux. His playground had been the streets and occasionally the Public Gardens, but that was quite a distance and not many of his friends had wanted to go that far. They had to stay nearer home, waiting for a call from their mothers to run an errand, look after younger siblings, or sometimes to fetch their fathers from the café. Jacques had been lucky that way; he had no siblings, and his mother worked during the day, so he had had more freedom than the others. And he had used it. He would walk miles, through all the zones of the city, formulating a map in his mind's eye, memorising streets and unusual features in those streets; a barber's shop with a picture of a headless corpse in the window, or a church where the angels around the door looked like Disney characters. There wasn't much of the city that he didn't know well. It was all too, too familiar.

He walked past the courts and over to the benches that overlooked the river. There were two boys sitting on one of the benches and they glanced up at him as he approached. He smiled and they grinned sheepishly. One of them was rolling a joint and they both had earphones in.

'Guys,' he said. They each took out one earphone. 'You might want to go and sit somewhere less public. I've seen there are police about. Plain-clothes flics, you know. Maybe around that corner, where the bushes are.' He pointed to a place further along the riverside. For a minute they looked at him uncertainly. But then the one rolling the joint jumped up, gathering his stuff. He nodded to Jacques, nudged the other one and they scurried off without a word. They don't say much, sixteen or seventeen-year-olds, he thought. Perhaps if they'd had his number they would have sent him a text, 'Thanks, man. Cool for an old…'

He sat on one of the benches, there was no one else around. Then he stood up again and walked over to lean on the railings. The river below was full and a dingy coffee colour, a strong breeze was blowing from the west, skimming over the water, lifting up tiny waves and a white fuzz, which showed and was absorbed again so quickly it was almost imaginary. The current bumped rudely against the concrete bank and swirled around the broken piles that stood up in the shallows where the old pier had been. This was the edge of the city. There was development now on the other bank some three hundred metres away; but this was the edge of the real city, a city bound by this unending flow, a city that started and ended with this river - the source of its value and its restrictions. Jacques loved it, but it was perilous, and now it had puked out his dead friend, somewhere. He would need to find that out.

He turned away from the river and looked at the people coming through the park. There was a short plump man in running clothes whose face was as red as his legs were white. A mother was walking slowly with two little girls whose hair was frizzed up like springs sticking out of their heads, and they looked as though they had wet their fingers and stuck them in a light socket, Jacques thought. They were giggling and singing parts of songs that Jacques could hear but not understand. They stopped to look briefly at the boys playing, then turned back the way they had come. There was a tall, elegant-looking woman with shoulder-length black hair, smartly dressed, just lacking a poodle to walk on a Sunday morning. She was walking more purposively, looking around her, casually but methodically. There was something in the walk, almost a march if it hadn't been for the slight sway of the hips. It caught his attention and kept it there. She walked between the basketball and the volleyball courts, looking straight ahead now, looking at him. He looked back at her as the features of her face became clearer. He felt the movement of the hips, the firm sway, the directness. She held his gaze, her face unflinching and motionless. She didn't smile. She walked straight up to him. She was only a little shorter than he was, although much slimmer. She held out her right hand.

'Monsieur Lecoubarry.' It wasn't a question. He took her hand, it was dry and firm, with long fingers and he crushed it lightly in his own. For the first time, she looked away from his face as she reached into her pocket and pulled out a small clip.

'My warrant card. Capitaine Celestine Courbet.' Jacques looked at it carefully.

'I'm sorry, madame,' he said. 'I have a rendezvous here with someone scarred, hard-boiled and cynical.' He handed back the card.

'Believe me, Monsieur Lecoubarry, they are all there on the inside.'

Jacques smiled. 'Enchanté, Capitaine Courbet. If you're going to keep saying my name you'd better start using Jacques. Lecoubarry can be a bit clumsy.'

'It is unusual,' she replied and stood for a moment looking at him, weighing him up. There was the exuberant grey-brown hair, his size, but most noticeable were the eyes which were such a dark blue that they gave the impression that they could draw unwary matter into them, but not let it out again except at his volition. Yet, the eyes were young, not even middle-aged, and there were a bundle of laughter lines creasing out from both sides. She quickly re-appraised her opinion of him, this was no puffed-up lightweight. She would have to take this one seriously and tread very cautiously.

'Should we sit down,' he said and waved her towards the wooden bench as though inviting her to sit on a fine canape in the drawing room. They sat down a metre apart and she took out her notebook.

'Firstly, thank you for meeting me. I suppose this is more convenient for you,' she said.

'More comfortable,' replied Jacques, turning to face her. She was looking out across the river, seemingly gathering her thoughts, so he studied her face in profile. The long bevelled shape of her nose was definitely carvable; likewise the high cheekbones and the firm jawline. There was softness only in the lips which were full around a generous mouth. It was a face, or at least a profile, that he could carve in lime wood or perhaps cherry. It was a face of strong features, and the voice too was strong, but smoother and richer than it had seemed on the phone. She turned towards him.

'Let me give you some context, Monsieur Lecoubarry, Jacques. Context, because I want you to understand exactly what I expect from you when I start asking my questions.' She paused for a moment and turned further around to be able to look directly into Jacques' face. She continued; 'On Saturday morning the body of a man was found washed up on a beach between Pauillac and Valeyrac.'

'Pauillac?' asked Jacques, surprised.

'Yes, between Pauillac and Valeyrac. We believe the body to be that of Armand Verville; a piece of identification, a diabetic card, was found on his person. We believe he had been in the water for around two days. He was wearing overalls and working boots.' She held up her hand to stop him from interrupting. 'The back of his skull was cracked open to such an extent that part of his brain was visible. We believe he was also struck across the face with the same or a similar instrument, as the nose bone was shattered, along with both cheekbones. I don't have the final report from the pathologist, but that is our current understanding. It seems likely that he was murdered and his body thrown into the river to be disposed of. Monsieur Verville was last seen by his wife before he left for work on Wednesday evening at around seven p.m. The clothes he was wearing, the time in the water, and the fact that he did not return home on Thursday morning, having completed a night shift, would indicate that he was disposed of at some time on Wednesday night or Thursday morning. Disposed of. His head cracked violently open and then his carcass thrown into the river.' She stopped to let him react. Despite himself, Jacques had flinched and looked down. He knew why she was being so blunt and he disliked her for it. Such ugly information should not come from such a source, in such a way. There was in fact no source suitable for such horror. She started again.

'So, Jacques, what can you tell me about your friend Armand Verville that could have led to such a … situation?' She crossed her legs and rested the notebook on her knee, pen poised above the page. Jacques stood up and walked over to the railings to look out at the flow of the river. Something had settled in his mind like a stone, and it was going to take a lot to dissolve it. He walked back and sat down again. She offered no apology for her bluntness, she just sat there, expressionless, waiting for him to speak.

'He was a metal worker, a metal magician. Do anything, make anything in metal,' he began, not looking at her, staring over to the other side of the river.

'Criminal work?' she asked.

'I don't know,' replied Jacques. 'I haven't spoken to him in maybe nine months.'

'And yet his wife came straight to see you when she got the news of his death.' She raised her eyebrows and pointed her pen in his direction. 'Had you seen her in the last nine months?'

'Around. To say hello to. She works in a bakery by Saint Michel.'

'We know. Did she tell you where he was working?'

'No.'

'You didn't ask?'

'I did, when she came to see me yesterday. She didn't know.'

'You see, that's what surprises me. Nobody seems to know where he worked. Does that not surprise you, Jacques? You can see why I might find that hard to believe.'

'That's not my concern, what you believe or don't believe,' snapped Jacques. 'If I say I don't know, I don't know. If you question that again we don't move on. If Maxine says she doesn't know, she doesn't know. She would have told me. She came to me for advice. I was closest.'

'Then, what sort of work does a man do that he doesn't tell his wife or his friend about?' She left the question hanging there between them. 'Criminal work,' she said finally. 'We know he had a record. Served time for forgery. Is that what he was doing? I am asking what you think, not what you know.'

She could see that his hackles were up as he pushed his fingers repeatedly through the waves of hair on the side of his head.

'I think it's possible,' said Jacques reluctantly. 'But he wasn't a crook, he was an artist. He did work for money. He could do anything with metal, Armand; shape it, engrave it, he made locks for me and fingerplates. You gave him a template and he could produce the most perfect copy, ageing it so that you would swear it came from the eighteenth century, or earlier. He could repair so that you couldn't see the joins. Metal seemed to sing for him. Big pieces too; he could weld steel beams and solder the finest silver thread.' Courbet looked at his profile and her expression softened a little; she could see the emotion in his face and hear the memories catching in his voice.

'He was an artist,' Jacques continued, looking back at her now. 'But he wasn't good with money. It came in and went out, like the tide.'

'Did he drink a lot, could he have had an argument with someone?' she asked.

'No. He drank just the right amount. And he wasn't violent when he drank. He was just funny, funny and musical. He had a singing voice that was not quite as good as he thought it was. But he didn't care. This is not a man who could offend many people. You need to understand that.' He ran his hand around his chin. 'It is possible though that the work he was doing was not completely legitimate. If he was short of money, maybe.'

'What kind of work, Jacques? I need to know. If we can establish the kind of work and where he was working, we have a chance of nailing this down. What kind of work?'

'Could be a few things,' said Jacques.

'Forgery?' she demanded

'Maybe. Not money. He wouldn't do that again. It was a stupid move, stupid people.'

'What other kinds of forgery?'

'Vehicle marking, identification numbers…possibly.'

'Antiques?' she asked and looked at him with her dark, vivid eyes.

'Antiques. I don't think so. I think he would have talked to me about it,' replied Jacques.

'Because you are the big expert on antiques?'

'Partly yes. I know antique furniture well enough.'

'Yes, I've seen your card. What is that, historical irony? A woodworkers shop in the Rue Carpentyre. Cute, when the rest of the street is just about dead.'

Jacques sat stock still and looked at a face that suddenly seemed mocking and twisted.

'You really do have that hard-boiled cynicism inside you, don't you, Capitaine Celestine Courbet? I just saw it seep out into your face. You might know that that business has been there for tens, hundreds of years. It was my uncle's business, and his father's and grandfather's before them. From when it was the street of carpenters. Yes, really cute, ironic. Now is there anything else here?'

Courbet sat back and let out a deep breath. She turned with her palms towards him.

'Ok, I'm sorry. Let's get back,' she said. 'Please.' She could see that he was sitting rigidly, ready to stand up and walk off at any moment. She could almost feel the charge running through him, like static, or magnetism. 'I'm sorry. Is there anything else you can tell me about his associates, or people he might be connected with? Any link at all that we could follow up?'

Jacques sat silently, looking at her but not seeing, not interested now in the features of her face, not wanting to hear that harshness, that anger in her voice. Finally, he asked, 'Was the body washed down the river?' A little startled by the question, she fumbled with her notebook.

'We don't know,' she replied. 'The consensus was that the body came down the river. It seems more likely. But I'm not so sure.' She described to Jacques the location of the body and the wreck of the boat that suggested that it might have floated up the river on the tide. She told him about her meeting with the fisherman and her attempts to trace the origins of the boat. He listened carefully and nodded approvingly when she described what she had done. She started to realise that, for some reason, it was important to her to gain the approval of this man, she wanted him on her side - a much-depleted side it sometimes seemed.

'I'm going to narrow down the possibilities of where the body could have gone into the water. I'm going back up there this afternoon for another look,' she said. 'I also thought I would speak to Maxine again. See if she remembers anything else.'

'She's not there,' said Jacques. 'I called last night. She's gone. I thought she would. I probably even suggested it.'

'Why?'

'She's afraid. Wants some time.'

'Afraid of the killer?'

'Maybe. She doesn't know. We don't know. Perhaps he was killed to keep him quiet. Perhaps he might have talked to her. If in doubt, piss off,' said Jacques, echoing the words he had heard many times from various characters in his life. 'I might be able to find her. I'll try this afternoon. I'll also ask around a little more, see if I can pick up anything, but I'm not hopeful.' He smiled ruefully at her, but it lit up his face and she could see the humour in his eyes, behind the pain. 'I've lived in Saint Michel for nearly thirty years. It's a mixed bag, as I'm sure you're aware. Lots of good people, some very bad, quite a few on the margins trying to get by with their social hands tied behind their backs. I know a lot of people. But I'm not a criminal. I almost forgive you for that insinuation now,' and he waved his finger at her mockingly. 'But I know these people, they trust me. Someone may know something. Something you would never find out through them.'

Courbet studied him, puzzled. 'So you are going to help me?' she asked.

'To find out what happened to Armand. Yes.'

'Then why the hell was there all that fuss about coming to the commissariat or meeting up in the first place?'

'You don't know?'

'Know. Know what?' Jacques reached across and took the pen from her fingers. He held it up like the needle on a scales or the hand of a clock.

'I have had, fortunately, very little personal experience of the police in Bordeaux. But I have heard, from some of those very same marginals, that the lines there are not as straight as they might be,' he moved the pen to one side.

'Meaning?'

'Bent flics. A lot of graft, a lot of close connections to the wrong sorts, a lot of pressure put on witnesses and a lot of violence.' He moved the pen back and forward in a shaky motion as though measuring the actions of the police away from the straight line.

'There's always bent police. Always, everywhere in the world. But they are a small minority, especially in a force like that in Bordeaux. It's not huge, people can't hide,' said Courbet.

'Quite possibly, but they're mucky, and they've muddied up the waters for the rest. People won't talk easily. Nobody trusts them. I don't trust them.'

'That is so wrong. I know a lot of dedicated, honest police who just want to do a good job for the community we serve.' She realised that she was sounding like a PR release. 'We don't think most citizens are criminals, but the marginals in your little community think that all the police are corrupt. Maybe, it's just the perspective from where you're standing, in the margins. Fuck it, you trust me, you don't trust me. I don't care. Help me to find who killed your friend. That's all.' She stood up. Jacques remained sitting, looking now like a man enjoying a Sunday morning in the late spring sunshine.

'Can I ask you something, Celestine Courbet?' he said. She nodded, leaning back on her heels and pursing her lips. He looked up at her; she really was a very elegant and attractive woman, despite the sharpness and the hostility in her eyes.

'Why are you so angry?' he asked quickly. 'I swear, if I pricked your skin with a cocktail stick it would come back out charred. So much anger just below the surface.'

Courbet's eyes flashed and she tossed back her hair.

'What. Are you my shrink now? Are we finished here? Do you have anything else of value to add or ask?'

'Are you married?' Jacques asked.

'Fuck off. This is not a social thing,' she said and made as though to leave but just turned around on the spot. Jacques burst out laughing.

'What? What's so funny?' she demanded and stepped towards him. He pretended to search in his pockets.

'I think I have a cocktail stick somewhere here. I carry them around for anger testing and release,' he said. She sat back down and couldn't help smiling and shaking her head so that her thick dark hair flicked gently across each side of her face in turn. She leaned back, stretched her legs out in front of her and looked up at the sky.

'Are you really a carpenter?' she asked.

'Cabinet maker, furniture restorer. I am the wizard of wood.'

'You look like a wizard. Oh my God, you have no idea. Think flics are dirty, well it's a dirty world. I visit corpses on a beach, women beaten black and blue by the man who's supposed to protect them, girls as young as twelve, abused, raped to make them prostitutes. Dirty world. But, Monsieur Lecoubarry, I'm not a dirty cop. I don't take graft. I try, I try to solve crimes, to bring arseholes to justice. That's what I do. Maybe that's why I'm so angry.' She looked at her hands and then round at Jacques. 'And I would appreciate any help you can give me. Any help at all.' She handed him a card.

'It would be an honour,' said Jacques. 'Armand was a good friend. I wasn't such a good friend to him. I will help you. Can I call you on this number?'

'Sure. Anytime.'

'Ok. Let's do it.' Jacques said and sat up ready to leave. 'I'd invite you for lunch but this is not a social thing,' he said, his eyes creased with good humour.

'Lunch! I don't do lunch. I don't even eat some days.' She stood up and held out her hand. He took it and held it firmly.

'You didn't answer,' he said.

'Answer what? What's the question?'

'Are you married?'

She snorted. 'Yes. Yes, I am. He's a Police Divisional Commissaire,' she said and grinned at him.

'Shit,' said Jacques, forcefully. 'Oh well, I do love a challenge.'

They parted. He watched her go, walking along the esplanade by the river, with her confident, gently swaying march. He turned towards the town and the restaurant where his lunch was waiting to be consumed.

Chapter 16

He made the call at exactly nine o'clock. He spoke in whispers, rushing his sentences, desperate to impress on her the dangers of his situation. Already, three police vehicles had raced past on the narrow road and he had cleaved to the earth behind the bush. How many more had passed while he was sleeping he could only imagine. He could only imagine because he couldn't know; he was in a strange land where the rules and the numbers were different. He told her she must come soon. He invoked the spirit of his aunt, her mother. He promised news and aid. She must come soon, they would know he was missing by now. They have dogs.

He begged her, and Le Ho Linh could hear the distress in his voice, but still she vacillated. She was sitting upright on the edge of her bed. Another girl, who looked like her sister, was grumbling on the other side. The room was tiny, the walls a putrid green colour as the sun seeped through the lank, bottle-green curtains. The walls and the floor and the bed and even the air smelled of old cooking, stale fat and the smoke of burnt meat. She lived with her friend above the Pho Bahn Cuon Restaurant, and here she felt almost safe and protected. The call had not come out of the blue, but she had put the prospect of it out of her mind. This was a threat to that security and she was struggling to speak; it was as though he was speaking to her in another room, speaking to a different her.

'I have no car,' she said finally. 'I don't know where you are. I don't know.' There was silence on the other end of the phone as he tried to think clearly. He had become calmer as her agitation had grown.

'I will message you the name of the village. You must find it. You must find a car, a friend, anyone. I will wait here. I wait for you, I expect you. Soon.' He ended the call, and then taking the notebook from his knapsack, he texted her the name of the village, twice having to correct the text as he stumbled over the unusual letters. Then he sank back against the tree to wait. The birds were noisy in the trees now; some he recognised, others not, but there was no bird so very colourful he thought. One gave a cry of alarm, a high scratchy noise and he ducked down sharing the danger with the bird. 'Screech good birds,' he whispered out loud, 'screech if someone is coming, or some dog. Screech loud and early if the police are coming. Don't let them catch me unawares.'

There was only one thing to do. The day was starting to become warm and he took off his jacket, a little concerned that his bright yellow T-shirt with its grey globe pattern might stand out in the greenwoods. But he had worn it as a symbol, defiantly, it represented the world and his place in it. He would show Le Ho Linh and the others that he was a man who knew the world. He had only to wait.

The two girls sat talking in whispers on the bed.

'I don't know. He's a sailor. Left his ship, run away. Now he wants me to collect him. How I am going to do this?' said Linh, her eyes flitting around the room out of the dark shadows on her face.

'He's your cousin.'

'Yeah. I don't know him, Kim. Not for maybe five years, more. How'm I going to collect him? What can I do?'

'He's your cousin,' repeated the other girl. Then after a few moments, 'Pham Vinh has a car.'

'Pham Vinh, Pham Vinh has a car. So, Kylian Mbappe has a car. He's going to lend it to me? He's going to drive me? I can't drive.'

'He'll do it for me, Vinh, not Mbappe,' her friend sniggered. 'He'll do anything for me.'

'Just because you'll do anything for him.' The other girl slapped her lightly on the arm.

'Not like that. He's like family.'

'He's not family. He's not your family. He's a con do, a gangster,' said Linh.

'Con do. He makes his way. Hello, Linh. Everybody's a con do, everybody's a gangster. Nguyen Ngoc Khanh, you think he's not a gangster? He's the big con do. The biggest gangster,' she paused. 'Anyway, it's your problem. I say Pham Vinh has a car.'

'Shit, I don't know. What am I going to do with a cousin?'

'He's your cousin. You have to help him. It's blood, it's family,' said the girl Kim and lay back down to sleep some more. Linh sat staring at the phone and at the silver slippers that she wore in the restaurant and which cut into her feet so that each night the pain was more and more intense. Freedom for her was now epitomised by the liberty to never wear those slippers again. Perhaps this cousin was strong, perhaps he had money. Perhaps he could change her life. Then, she would burn those slippers and end the pain.

Chapter 17

Jacques' lunch sat heavily on him, along with a slight vagueness, like a mist, from the wine. Outside the restaurant he looked up at the unblemished blue sky and decided to walk; there was really no alternative, walking was his default setting. When he walked, he imagined that he shed the dead pelt and the scales and became clear again. He had always done it. It had always saved him, built his resolve, or scraped away the kerf that was clogging his view.

There were two subjects on his mind that needed to be given some air. He needed to loosen them like a knot so that he could see the individual strands. There was the murder of his friend Armand, which threw up a curtain of distractions, like guilt, anger, carelessness in friendships, but also a profound sense of fear that his own life was sinking inexorably into a slough of complacency and dullness. He had not visited Armand for nearly a year. He had stopped doing a lot of things. He could blame Covid, but you have to pass through that. You have to re-establish yourself. No excuses. No excuses for settling for a dull routine.

And then there was Capitaine Celestine Courbet; her of the eyes flashing with anger, mouth snapping out phrases, lips settling into firmness. His expectations after their initial phone conversation were so completely shattered that for a while it had felt as though he was talking to an impostor, a photo-shopped version of the picture he had formed in his mind. Yes, she was prickly, aggressive and condescending, but he could bundle all these aspects up in her anger and in something he was very drawn to, her honesty and her determination to find Armand's killer. He sensed that in a different context, these difficult aspects might fade, while the fire and the passion would remain to light up that remarkable face and the long, slim, direct body. And she is married to a Police Divisional Commissaire, so why don't you park all those aspects of Capitaine Courbet and focus only on her role in helping you, or you helping her, to track down Armand's killer? There, now there's only one point of focus, much easier, clearer. Now you are more likely to make progress. All the rest is peripheral, and if there is collateral damage there, it doesn't matter so long as the main object is achieved.

Walking was having the desired effect. He took the small road through the Parc Andre Meunier and crossed the wide Cours de la Marne. He walked the peaceful Sunday streets where cheap neighbourhoods gave way to the more genteel. He kept off the main thoroughfares, preferring small roads because of their greater intimacy with the lives of the people dwelling there. The day was warm and other people who walked were dressed lightly, legs were browning, hair was flowing, arms were bare and swinging or gesticulating in the sun. There was a sense of freedom. There were so many children, holding hands, skipping like horses, running along low walls with patient and impatient parents. Often the children would look twice at him, they always smiled when he smiled at them.

He skirted around the Bois de Thouars, went beneath the busy intersection and entered the leafy suburb of Rance. He had only been to the house once, two years previously, but he remembered the way. He didn't expect a welcome. The house was set back from a minor road, its rear garden backing onto patchy woodland. A high hedge of cypress trees hid the front garden, with its small swimming pool and porticoed entrance. The electric gates were open and Jacques walked up the drive and pressed a bell which buzzed nastily, like a sprayed wasp, inside the house. This was exactly the kind of house Simone had always wanted and which he could never have given her, nor had ever wanted to give her. He was pleased for her, they had not destroyed each other, just left one another with a few scars. They were both in a better place now, neither had been sunk by the other, which seemed like a thin recompense for eight years of marriage, but Jacques felt it was a victory of sorts.

Her new husband opened the door, and behind the surprise on his face tried to hide his displeasure with an extravagant smile and flabby handshake.

'Jacques. Mmm. Pleasure. Surprise,' he managed to say.

'Bonjour, Jean-Paul. Ça va? Excuse the intrusion, I would like to speak to Simone, if she is here,' said Jacques hurriedly.

'Of course, yes, yes. You look well. Pleasure. She is in the conservatory.'

He made as if to fetch her and leave Jacques at the door, before his well-trained manners pulled him up short and he stepped back to invite Jacques in. The hallway smelt of varnish and patchouli. He noticed the nineteenth-century Bordeaux majolica clock. Jean-Paul hurried ahead of him calling out, 'Simone, Sim, Jacques is here,' in order to give her time to fluff up her hair and set the rictus on her face. Jacques followed him through a kitchen into a small conservatory full of exuberant potted plants, where she sat like a pasha on a wide cane chair, looking shocked and anxious, her eyes blinking in alarm. She had told him, much later, that she had always been a little afraid of him, of his size and his presence, although he had never so much as raised a finger against her. It was noticeable that her current husband was a small, wiry man with significantly less hair than Jacques but significantly better prospects.

'Jacques,' she said, 'what…' She waved her hands to the side. She didn't stand up so Jacques bent down to kiss her on both cheeks. He nodded his head, as though in approval.

'Simone, you look very well,' he said. And in fact, she was still a good-looking woman, although her features had coarsened a little, and what had been a sensual reserve, almost coquettishness, had morphed into a complete lack of human interest or warmth. The lines that were appearing above her lips gave her a crabby petulant look, but her body remained full and generous. Her husband hovered as Jacques loomed over her.

'Please, take a seat, Jacques. Coffee? Something stronger?' he asked.

'Coffee would be nice, thank you,' Jacques replied and sat on the edge of the cane sofa next to Simone.

'Armand Verville is dead,' he said. 'He's been murdered.' She sat upright and stared uncomprehendingly at him.

'What. Armand. You came here to tell me that?' she demanded. Jacques nodded his head.

'Who? Who is this?' asked Jean-Paul.

'An old friend,' said Jacques. 'A friend of many years. Simone knew him well at one time.'

'Maxine?' asked Simone.

'Ok.'

'She wasn't?'

'No. It doesn't seem to have been like that.' Jacques turned to the husband. 'Maxine Verville was a close friend of Simone's, back in the day.'

'Although, she was quite a bit older than me,' said Simone. 'I haven't seen her in years.'

'Oh,' said Jean-Paul, and this seemed to give him some comfort as he disappeared into the kitchen to make the coffee.

'How?'

'We don't know yet. Dumped in the river,' said Jacques, brutally.

'Oh, my God. An accident perhaps?'

'No. Murder. His skull was smashed in.'

She closed her eyes and placed her hands on her head. Then she looked up with hurt, suspicious eyes.

'Are you involved in this, Jacques?'

'No. I'm trying to help.'

'Help what?' she demanded, her voice becoming shriller.

'I'm trying to find out some information. Where he was working. What kind of work.'

'Haven't you spoken to Maxine?'

'Briefly. She came to see me, but she didn't say much. She was in shock. Now she's disappeared.'

'Disappeared. You don't think?'

'No. I think she's afraid, and she wants some time. But I need to speak to her urgently. There may be some little piece of information that she can tell us, you know, about his work,' said Jacques.

'Did she not know where he worked?' she paused, and one of those looks came over her face which in the past had driven Jacques outdoors. 'He was forging again, was he?' she said.

'I don't know, Simone, honestly, I don't know. I haven't seen him for nearly a year. But look, I wondered, you knew Maxine better than I did. You spent time with her. You know her family, other friends. Is there anywhere you can think of that she might go to at a time like this?'

Simone sat back in the chair and turned to look out of the window. She would have liked to have shown off the house and the garden, the new summer kitchen and the pool, but she knew Jacques would have been unmoved, even unimpressed. She thought for a minute.

'She has a sister, Marie. A little younger than her. I went there with her on two occasions. It wasn't very nice, the area, the building. But she was nice, I think. She had children.'

'Where Simone? Where does she live? Do you have an address?' asked Jacques.

'No. No. It was Merignac, not so far as Merignac. It was a building near the lycées.'

'Could you recognise it on a map? If I pull it up on my phone.'

'Oh, I don't know Jacques. It's been a long time.'

'Try,' he said sharply, and she blinked and sat up in her chair. He opened a map on his phone and focused it on Merignac.

'Lycée Fernand Daguin?' he asked.

'Yes, I believe that's it.'

'That's a nice area. Look at the streets, was it in front, to the side, where?' He sat down on his haunches beside her chair and placed the phone in her lap, moving the map so that she could see it more clearly. She smelled of indoors and Sisley's Eau de Soir, and he had a sudden recollection of her which might have upset her new husband, who had just come in with the coffees, if he had known.

'That street there,' she said decisively. 'On the main road, a modern building, well reasonably modern, but a bit shabby, you know, already.'

'Which floor was she on?' he persisted.

'Second. On the corner. There was like a balcony.'

'Definitely that building, second floor.'

'Yes, yes. You could look over the bus stop and the tram stop where the children waited to catch their bus and trams. Yes, there.'

'That's fantastic, Simone. And the sister's name, her surname?'

'No idea. Just Marie. It was quite a long time ago,' said Simone, and then she did something that Jacques remembered she had also been capable of. She put her hand on top of his and said, 'I am so terribly sorry, Jacques. It's a dreadful world, and Armand, as I remember him, was a gentle, friendly, funny man.' She squeezed his hand. He looked up at her and her eyes were genuine and he felt the lump in his throat. He sat back on the sofa and gratefully sipped the coffee, which was black and strong. They sat in silence for some minutes, the gentle ticking of the Bordeaux clock in the hallway, slicing up the silence. A Jules Vieillard, thought Jacques, not the best, but not bad for a house in the suburbs of Bordeaux. 'You'll tell me when the funeral is set?' said Simone faintly.

'Sure. I have your number. It's not changed?'

'Not the mobile, no. You didn't call today.'

'No, I didn't. That wouldn't have been useful. And I needed to walk.'

'Will you try to speak to Maxine now?' asked Simone.

'Yes. Straightaway. We need information as quickly as possible,' he replied.

'We. You said we a few times. Who is we, Jacques?'

'Me,' he hesitated, 'me and the police. Trying to find out what happened.'

'You are working with the police?' she asked, not bothering to keep the scepticism out of her voice.

'Yes. Some people in the police.'

Simone looked at him quizzically. 'Well you be careful, won't you? That's not your natural environment,' she laughed sharply.

'No, it's not,' said Jacques. 'Not my natural environment at all.'

Chapter 18

The tide had turned. Celestine watched as the waters lapped a little higher, wriggling through the stones on the beach. It wasn't uniform; one small flow would open up new rivulets before seeping back, but the next few ripples would falter before reaching the new height. She hadn't thought about that for a long time. Tides come in and tides go out. She had forgotten how it was more insidious than that, almost creepy the way the water slowly repossessed the land. She remembered being aware of that, thinking that as a child, and having those nightmares. She shuddered as she recalled those moments of horror she had experienced twelve years before.

The spot where the body had been found was now partially under a thin skin of water. In another hour or less, it would be washed clean. What do you call the place where a body is washed up, she wondered? She couldn't think there was a specific term. It was a kind of delivery point where the water delivered up to the land. She was trying to visualise what happened to a corpse, buoyant on the water, then semi-buoyant, trailing limbs snagging on the stones, then the gradual easing away of the water and the body settling, its edges still tugged by the breathing of the tide, until it lay still, passed over to the earth while the water respectfully slid away.

Her phone rang and she snapped out of her reverie. It was Alain Jarre, the fisherman.

'The boat was lost by Vincent Pallet,' he said, without preamble.

'Vincent Pallet, that's good. Where is he?'

'Port-de-Goulée.'

'Port-de-Goulée. That's what, another five or ten kilometres down the river?' she asked, trying to picture the geography in her head.

'Seven.'

'Ok, Alain. Is that where he lost his boat? I would like to talk to him.'

'You want to talk to him?' he asked, in a voice that suggested that she was introducing a new element that he had not been expecting.

'Yes. I want to talk to him. Do you know where he lives?'

'No.' There was a pause. 'I know where he'll be,' he said.

'Ok, look. I'm just a few kilometres away. I can be in your village in ten minutes. Will you wait for me there?'

'On the Belle Étoile.'

'Ok, on your boat. I'll be ten minutes.' She rang off, and as she turned quickly to walk back to the road she thought she glimpsed something move in the periphery of her vision. She looked across to where the scrubland reached the group of trees that covered the small promontory. There was something again, just the faintest flicker of a movement. There was little wind and it was too high up to be an animal. She stared at the place and waited. There was nothing, but then she heard the definite sound of a branch breaking, of someone pushing past bushes. She started walking towards the spot but then thought better of it. It was probably just another dog walker or maybe some ghoulish local, come to see where a body had been found.

She returned to the car a little spooked, and was grateful when she was inside and the engine switched on. Never mind that young pathologist, she thought, you're getting too imaginative for this job. She pulled away and headed for the peaceful little village further along the shore. She didn't see the black SUV that crept out from behind an old barn and onto the road behind her.

She parked again under the plane trees by the square. Four old men were playing pétanque on the sand court and they looked up and stared when she got out of the car. She called out a greeting to them and, to a man, they nodded slightly and said, bonjour. She smiled; this was the courteous face of rural France.

She took the small road down to the harbour, expecting to see Alain Jarre sitting on a capstan, possibly smoking a pipe like Captain Haddock. Instead, she could only see his backside sticking up as he bent over something in the boat. She couldn't believe she was thinking that it wasn't the worst butt she'd ever seen. She called out and he stood up quickly causing the boat to rock a little from side to side. The tide was quite well in, and the boat had floated free from its muddy base and was hauled up closely to a wooden frame, which had a ladder leading down to it.

'Monsieur Jarre, Alain,' she called again, as he turned round making the boat wobble a little more.

'Bonjour, madame, pardon I was …' his face flushed.

'That's ok. Vincent Pallet?' she asked loudly and took out her notebook. He looked at her, puzzled. 'Alain?' she asked again. He shook his head as though to clear it.

'He'll be on the bank. I know he will,' he shouted. 'Tides coming in, moon's waxing, spring. He'll be on the bank. Where I was heading.' Celestine looked at him like a foreigner trying to piece together the words into a recognisable meaning. He saw the confusion on her face.

'Mullet,' he said at last, as though he'd been reluctant to divulge the final clue. And then it dropped into the slot. She walked onto the rickety wooden frame that served as a jetty.

'He's fishing?' asked Celestine.

'Yes, on the bank.'

'Which bank?'

'Haut Gautheys. It's only a few kilometres downstream, where the River Courbian comes in. There's a sandbank, underwater now. That's where they feed. This time of the year.'

'I see,' said Celestine, 'and what time will he get back to Goulée?'

'Not till later, I wouldn't wonder. When the tide gets muddled.'

Celestine was starting to feel incredibly stupid and she could feel her anger rising again. But she looked at his face, which was pleasant and open and earnest and she could see that he was trying to tell her something but somehow they lacked the common platform on which to communicate. And then it arrived, like a Rosetta stone. He picked up an orange life jacket and waved it towards her.

'That'll fit you,' he said, risking a glance at her body.

'You want me to come in the boat with you?' asked Celestine, holding onto the wooden rail.

'Course. You can't walk on water, can you?' and his face creased up and he started chuckling to himself. Celestine couldn't help smiling.

'No, not even police officers can walk on water,' she said. He continued chuckling and gently shaking his head.

'No, thought not. I don't know Monsieur Pallet to speak to, you understand. But there'll only be a dozen or so boats. We'll just ask.'

Celestine shook her head.

'Alain, that's very kind, but I'm not exactly dressed for a day's fishing.'

He dared another look at her. 'That's ok, I've got a spare waterproof jacket here, but you'll not need it. It is cooler out on the water, but not so much on a day like this. We won't stay out there. Just ask your questions. I'm not going to fish.'

'Just go there and come back?' asked Celestine.

He nodded and chuckled again. 'You're not dressed for fishing, are you?'

Celestine thought for a moment and then agreed. It was partly that she didn't want to go home just yet; not to a petulant husband and the questions he would ask, nor even to an empty apartment. But also she felt that it might help if she could find some additional information about the ways of the estuary. She wanted to understand this medium better and become acquainted with its moods and its vagaries. She was trying to plot the final journey of Armand Verville. She reached down and took hold of the life jacket; it smelled slightly of diesel and fish but she strapped it on over her fawn jacket. At least its bulk covered the fact that she was carrying a firearm. She didn't want to freak out her fisherman.

Feeling slightly ridiculous in her city clothes, she turned around and climbed down the steep, shaky ladder and stepped into the boat. She sat down quickly. Alain looped the ropes from the capstan and stepped past her to take the wheel. The boat rocked a little with the motion. He fired up the engine and glanced back at her.

'There's just enough water to get us out now. You ok, madame?' he asked, serious now and polite.

'I'm ok,' she smiled at him. In this parallel universe, at this time vector, I'm ok, she said to herself. But I did not expect to be sitting here on a boat on the estuary of the Gironde when I woke up this morning from an angry sleep.

Alain stood, legs apart, and steered the boat out of the narrow channel and into the mainstream of the estuary. The boat buffeted a little when it joined the denser, moving waters, but it soon settled into a rhythm that was steady and calming. Celestine watched him for a few minutes; he seemed less gauche, more in his natural element, and confident. She still couldn't believe that she'd caught herself looking at the man's butt in that way. But then she could believe it. Don't fool yourself, she thought.

She looked away at the nearside bank and saw how the land that crept up to the water was untidy, the branches and the trees were thin and straggly. The river was clearly an unruly neighbour to have. Out in the stream, there was a breeze and the sunlight on the water was bright and glaring. She wished she'd brought some sunglasses and some food. She had heard it said before that being out on the water makes you hungry, and she had hardly eaten a thing that day.

'How long will it take?' she called out to him, but he couldn't hear above the noise of the engine and the moving water. So she settled back, it would take as long as it did. It gave her time to think. She knew she'd gone a bit off-piste in this investigation already, or maybe literally off-shore. Her standard operational strategy was to relentlessly gather facts and impressions and then to extract the patterns and forge the links between the data, like a very complex joining up of the dots. She knew she could see wider and deeper than many of her colleagues, and she could detect any inconsistencies, they pulsed like a beacon in her brain and she couldn't leave them unopened. She had been accused of over-complicating issues, of seeing patterns that didn't exist. Police work was simple, she had been told; do the routine, the leg work, be consistent, thorough, don't try to be too smart, they aren't, the criminals, they are stupid and they make stupid mistakes. Use the science, do the leg work, be consistent. The hardest murders to solve are when there is no body. So, had it been a stupid mistake to put a body in the river, expecting it to disappear?

She looked out across the wide estuary, the largest estuary in Europe, as the tourist guides always said. If you wanted a body to disappear was this a good place or had there been a miscalculation and the corpse had resurfaced? Perhaps the one, or ones, who'd done the killing didn't care, perhaps they thought they were immune, untouchable. Well, they weren't. No one was untouchable, she thought.

Chapter 19

Jacques stood on the road by the lycée, looking across at the tram stop and bus shelter and at the building behind. It was an eighties apartment block of the type that had emerged from the brutal, functionalism of the sixties and seventies and had added a few additional features that gave it a friendlier, if still bland face. The apartments had a small balcony and there were black stains running down the concrete walls. Jacques watched the swifts swooping out from under the roofs and circling in ragged formations to the trees and back. He was focused on the apartments on the second floor. There was movement there; a woman with a child had stepped out onto the balcony briefly and gathered something from the washing line, she was wearing a bright green blouse. Jacques waited. After a few minutes, the same woman emerged onto the path in front of the building, she was holding the hand of a little boy. They crossed the street diagonally in front of the bus shelter, but she didn't look in Jacques' direction. The little boy did and his eyes widened slightly.

Jacques watched them walk along the road, the boy swinging and tugging at the woman's arms. He crossed the street and walked up to the second floor of the building. He knocked gently on the door. There was no response, but Jacques had heard a slight sound and he could sense there was someone in the apartment. He knocked again, put his lips to the diamond-shaped glass pane in the door and called out gently.

'Maxine, it's me, Jacques. It's Jacques. I have to talk to you.' He heard footsteps inside and a blurred face pressed against the opaque glass. The door opened and Maxine stood there, not looking at him, just staring at the ground. Jacques hardly recognised her, she seemed to have shrunk and thickened somehow, as though she'd melted a little in grief. He pushed the door closed behind him, stepped towards her and put his arms around her. She stood passively as he held her for several minutes, saying nothing. Then he felt the slight jerk of the head, the deep swallow and then she capsized on him and began crying in great heaves of breath. He held her a little longer and then led her to a sofa in a small but tidy living room. He sat next to her, his arm still around her shoulders and she leaned into his broad chest.

'What am I to do?' she said finally. 'What am I supposed to do?'

She turned her tear-stained face to him. It was a face that was lined and dull but which Jacques had always thought of as lively, even impertinent. He remembered her as feisty and gloriously sarcastic. He could picture her and Armand arguing, playfully; Armand making dry comments and Maxine cutting him to shreds with her sarcasm, and Armand loving it for the richness of the humour it brought, yet left him unscathed. He would become more and more fanciful just to spur Maxine on to greater heights of sharp abuse, relishing the words and collapsing finally with laughter, and Maxine smiling and trying to resist him as he tried to kiss her passionately, even in a crowded place.

She sat up and attempted to dry her eyes and re-arrange herself, although her hair was hanging in lank blonde fronds and she wore no make-up on her face. They talked briefly about simple matters; about her sister and the children and their kindness to her, and also of the brother-in-law who was less patient and worried. Jacques told her that he had met the police and that by helping them he could keep them away from her.

'But the most important thing is to find out where Armand was working. He didn't tell you anything?' Jacques asked. Maxine stiffened a little, then said.

'He wouldn't tell me. Said it was better. But he didn't like them. I can tell you that much.'

'Was it legit? No, it couldn't have been. Were you short of money?'

She nodded. 'Yes, yes, always, but yes. He'd discovered online gambling, with his phone. You know what he was like. He was always making fortunes. In his own mind anyway.'

'He lost?' said Jacques.

'Course he lost. So he had to take other work, you know, better paid, no questions.' She leaned her head back against the headrest.

'How long had he been working there?' asked Jacques.

'About three weeks.'

'And the money was good?'

'Very.' She looked out through the window into the distance and then back at Jacques.

'Would you like some coffee?' she asked.

'Sure, if you're having some.'

'It's all I have, coffee and fags. I have to go out on the balcony to have a cigarette.'

'Quite right,' said Jacques. 'Filthy habit, you should take better care of yourself, good-looking young woman like you.'

'Don't you start. There's no point now, is there? I'm an old …widow, Jesus that's what I am. Scrapheap, Jacques, nothing left. But you look lively,' she said, looking at him properly for the first time. 'You look proper lively. Not back with Simone are you?'

Jacques grinned. 'I thought you liked me, why would you say a thing like that? You know I only escaped by the skin of my teeth.'

'Yes. She was a bit taut, wasn't she? A bit out of place,' said Maxine.

'Not now. I've just seen her, she gave me this address. She's got a new husband who furnishes her house and her life, and she seems content. I'm pleased for her,' said Jacques.

'Good. Me too then.' She disappeared into the kitchen and Jacques followed her as she made the coffee.

'Did he only work night shifts with this crew?' he asked.

'Yeah. Ten-hour shifts, eight till six. He was always wrecked when he got back. But of course, I was just leaving then. Ships in the desert,' she said.

'Did he walk there, drive?'

'No car. But no, he got picked up.'

'Picked up by who, and where?'

Maxine turned to look at him. 'You sound very eager, Jacques. Is there something I should know?' she said, her eyes suddenly hard and her lips compressed.

'That's the look you need to work on,' replied Jacques. 'That's the old Maxine look. You're going to need that sharpness and aggression girl. You have to get through this and find a way forward.' She nodded and almost smiled.

'I want to know what happened, Maxine. I want to find out who did this,' he said forcefully.

'How are you going to do that? You're not the police.'

'No, I'm not, but I can help them. I can get information to help them.'

Maxine looked at him in some disbelief. She handed him his coffee.

'You, working with the police, those bastards. I don't see it, Jacques, I really don't see it.' So he told her about his conversation with the police capitaine that morning, and their agreement to assist each other and share information.

'Is that the hard-nosed piece that visited me, tall, black hair, sharp eyes?' she asked.

'Yes. Celestine Courbet.'

'That's her. Courbet.'

She looked at him and sneered. 'Attractive, if you like them like that. Is that it, Jacques? She's got you on the cock-a-doodle-doo. You scratching around the dung heap to fetch her some worms - bring her into your harem?'

Jacques burst out laughing. 'That's more like it, Maxine. That's the badness that'll get you through. But that is daft. Seriously, she seems to be straight and determined. I like that. We need to know where he was working. Come on woman, there must be more you can tell me.'

Maxine sat back down, her hands wrapped around the coffee cup. 'They picked him up at seven o'clock. Him and a few others. In a van. He couldn't see out and they took their mobile phones, so they wouldn't know where they were going.'

'Same place every night?'

'Yes. He wouldn't talk about the place.'

'Where were they picked up?' asked Jacques.

'Quinconces. Black van.'

'Every night at seven o'clock?'

'Not Saturday or Sunday.'

'Did he say anything about the driver?' Jacques asked. She shook her head.

'What about the people he was working with? Did he mention any of them?'

She looked around the room. 'An old guy he knew before. Ducks he said a few times. There were ducks. Do you know what that is?'

Jacques pondered for a moment. 'Maybe,' he said. 'I might have an idea about that. Anything more? The work he was doing, the place. How long did it take to get there?'

'I think an hour maybe, something like. He started at eight and finished at six, back in Bordeaux by seven. Yeah, so about an hour.'

Jacques could see that she was settling back into the state of lethargy she'd been in when he'd arrived.

'Is there anything else, Maxine? Anything else at all?'

She shook her head. 'He just didn't like it, I know that.'

Jacques nodded and smiled. 'That's really helpful, Maxine. I'll take this further. You just stay here for a while longer. Is that ok with your sister?'

'Yeah. It's family.'

'I won't let anyone know where you are,' he said.

'Not even your fancy police woman?' she retorted.

'Particularly not the police. It's better if no one knows where you are until there's some progress been made. I'll keep in touch. Answer your phone when you see it's me, ok.' He finished his coffee. 'I'll go now. Leave you in peace.' He stood up and leaned over to kiss her on the cheek but she turned away from him.

'Why didn't you come and see us, Jacques? It's been ages. Armand mentioned that. Said we didn't fit into your life anymore.'

Jacques took a deep breath. 'That's not true, I was always just a few streets away. It's been a strange time, Maxine. Covid and all that. I've been asking myself the same questions these last few days. And I am sorry, and I owe you and Armand something. I owe you answers and justice. That's all I'm trying to do. Just that.'

She turned towards him so he could kiss her on both cheeks.

'Get away you great hairy man,' she said. 'And it's retribution I want, Jacques. Retribution for a good soul like my Armand's.'

Chapter 20

As the river curved gently around to the left, Celestine could see the other boats. They were quite close to the shore, scattered like seagulls bobbing on the water. They were all facing in the same direction, breasting the tide, and they seemed to be an equal distance apart. She stood up and stepped unsteadily to the front to speak to the fisherman. She held on to the edge of the canopy and leaned towards him.

'That's them,' Alain said and took one hand off the wheel to point vaguely in the direction of the boats.

'How will you know which one is Vincent Pallet?' she asked loudly. He seemed to ponder this for a few moments.

'Well, we'll ask. Someone'll know him,' he replied.

Alain picked up a radio handset as they came closer to the boats and spoke. Celestine couldn't make out what he said or the replies. As they came within twenty metres of the first boat, Celestine saw a man there, gesticulating and pointing further into the pack. Alain turned the boat away and headed downstream. Celestine counted eight boats in total, and they really did look like seagulls bobbing up and down on the low waves. Each one had its rods and lines sticking out like spider's legs from different parts of the boat. As they neared the middle group, Alain spoke into the radio again, then he adjusted their course until they were heading towards a particular boat. They came level with it, about ten metres away, Alain constantly adjusting the throttle and the wheel to stay in the right position. He touched Celestine on the arm.

'Put those buffers out over the side,' he said, pointing to half a dozen rubber cylinders on ropes. Celestine edged gingerly along the side of the boat, lifting the buffers over the gunwale. She looked across at the other boat. There were two men in it; one was steering and looking anxiously at their approach, the other man, just a boy she realised, was winding in the fishing lines on that side and stowing the rods. Then he too pushed buffers over the side. Gradually, like two clumsy dancers, the boats came together, side by side. The swell was quite high now and the boats were frisky and uncooperative. Celestine appreciated the skill that brought them together. They touched each other's flanks, softly, and the boy threw a rope over to Celestine, pointing at the ring on the transom. She tied it securely and then Alain indicated that she should throw their bow rope to the other boat as well. At that moment, Celestine said to herself that this could have been a lot simpler sitting in a café, or in fact anywhere that wasn't lurching up and down and starting to make her stomach feel queasy.

The boy grinned at her. 'Vincent Pallet,' she said.

'My Dad,' he pointed to the man steering. The man said something to the boy, which was lost in the wind, but he took his father's place at the wheel, grinning still and looking over at Alain like two conspirators. The man came close to the side and leaned towards Celestine. There was a look of concern but also amazement on his face.

'Vincent Pallet. I am Capitaine Celestine Courbet of the Bordeaux Police Judiciaire.'

The man's face flicked from fear to excitement to bemusement. He had a long, lugubrious face and it seemed to stretch as he adjusted to the different emotions playing out. He glanced back at the boy to make sure he was controlling the boat. 'There's no problem,' said Celestine loudly. 'I just wanted to ask you some questions about your boat - the Gemini.'

'The Gemini?' he asked. She nodded. 'I don't have it no more. Not for a year back. I haven't done anything.'

'No, I know.' Celestine paused. She was having to shout over the noise of the engines and the moving water, and now the swell was rising between the boats and spraying her, every few seconds, with droplets of cold water. 'We found your boat, wrecked, washed up on the beach along the river. I want to know how it got there.'

'I know where it is. But I can't get it from there. She's wrecked. Can't get there, he said, glancing round at his son.

'When, and how did you lose it?' Celestine mouthed as loudly and clearly as she could. This was not the time for subtle discourse.

'Tore her moorings in a storm, oh, last spring. Round the equinox, when the tide's running high. Tore her moorings, never saw her go.'

'Can you be more precise about the date?' asked Celestine.

'Ten days before Easter, whenever that was,' he said firmly.

'Ok, that's good. And you keep it at Port-de-Goulée?' Celestine saw the uncertainty slide up his long face.

'Look,' he said. 'This isn't about insurance is it?'

'Insurance,' said Celestine. 'No, Monsieur Pallet, it's about murder. I don't care about your insurance.'

'Murder. Jesus. No, sorry.' He glanced up at the boy.

'Monsieur Pallet, where did you lose the boat from?'

'That's just it. Normally, ninety-nine times out of a hundred, she was kept at Goulée. Good mooring you know.' Celestine nodded at him to continue. 'But I've got a mate, keeps an ocean-going at the port at Grave. He invites me for a couple of days fishing on the sea. Well, he doesn't like to come all this way. So I takes the boat up towards Talais, near La

Plage, not a bad little haven. Ties the Gemini up to a buoy in the mouth of the little river there, and jumps into my mate's boat. We go out to sea, see.'

Celestine wanted to ask why he hadn't just driven up to the port and left his boat in its normal berth, but she feared being engulfed in a wave of fisherman's logic and logistics. And she didn't need to know and her stomach was nudging her to end the conversation sooner rather than later. She was leaning over the side, ear to the other man's mouth and the boats were bobbing and occasionally lurching beneath her.

'Where exactly did you leave the boat?' she asked.

'In the river mouth, Chenal Neuf. Storm blew up, we headed back to port. Stayed in Royan for a couple of days. Safer harbour, easier to get into in a strong westerly.' His mouth was almost touching her ear now, so she leaned back and reached inside her life jacket and struggled to pull out her notebook and pen.

'Give me a telephone number and an address please, Monsieur Pallet. Just in case I need to contact you further,' she said.

'I haven't done anything,' he said again.

'No, you haven't. But you may be in a position to help me in an investigation. Telephone number…'

She wrote down the number and address, sheltering her notebook from the spray. The writing was almost illegible but it didn't matter. She didn't expect to need to speak to him again, and they had other ways of finding addresses. 'Thank you, Monsieur Pallet,' she said and moved back. The man turned quickly and stepped up to take over the steering. Celestine untied the rope on the stern as the boy threw their rope back. Then the two boats peeled away from each other like lead dancers in a reel. Celestine sat back exhausted on the thwart at the back of the boat. Alain turned towards her.

'Got what you need?' he shouted. She put her thumbs up. Then he reached into the canopy and pulled out a large freezer box. He pushed it towards her with his foot. 'There's sandwiches, flask of coffee. Looks like you need it,' he said.

Celestine opened the box and took out a sandwich, she didn't really care what was in them. She took another one and handed it to Alain, who grunted.

'Alain,' she said.' How far along the shore is La Plage? Would it take long to get there?'

'Bout twenty minutes. Hard against this tide, but yeah, twenty minutes. You want to go there?' he asked. Did she? She really wanted to get back on dry land, sit in her car, turn on some music and close her eyes.

'Yes, if we can, if you don't mind. I'd like to get an impression of how far it is. If you don't mind.'

'Have some coffee. I'll have some after you,' he replied, and pushing the throttle a little higher, he grinned and gave the impression that he was having the time of his life.

The river mouth near La Plage wasn't much more than a slight indentation in the coastline. Alain brought the boat in close and Celestine could see where there were two small boats tied up to buoys, almost at the mouth of the river.

'Is that a very good place to moor a boat for a few days?' asked Celestine. 'Especially when there's a high tide and storms around.' It was easier to speak now in the calm of the little haven. Alain seemed to chew over the question, seemed to hesitate and then reached a decision.

'It's not a place I would tie up a boat overnight. Not a decent-sized boat,' he said slowly and carefully. 'It's got a little shelter, but when the tide rushes in it'll surge into a spot like this and there's not a lot of protection,' he stopped, although Celestine felt that he wanted to say more.

'Go on, what are you thinking?' she asked. He looked at her a little sheepishly turning his face only slightly towards her.

'Perhaps I shouldn't say. But, if I wanted to lose a boat, if a boat was maybe, beyond its useful life. Maybe it hadn't been well maintained.'

'Like yours,' interrupted Celestine.

'Ah. Maybe. He's a careless fellow that Pallet. I could see that looking at the boat he was on just now.' He paused again. 'If I wanted to lose a boat, get the insurance for a new boat, for example, I might think about tying it up here, not so securely, knowing what was coming in the tides and the winds. Yes, this wouldn't be a bad place to lose a boat.' He saw Celestine shaking her head and he quickly said, 'Not that I would do something like that. It's wrong. Boats should be respected, laws should be respected.'

'Yes, they should,' said Celestine, 'and I have no doubt you adhere to them as well as any citizen. But Monsieur Pallet's insurance scam is not of any interest to me. Tell me, what comes after this, along the shore?' Alain started to head the boat out into the main current again. 'No, I don't want to see them. I'd just like to know is all,' she said.

'More of the same, I guess. A few small havens, nothing important. Talais maybe. Some factories on the water's edge, vineyards of course, inland.'

'Factories?' asked Celestine.

'Looks like. I don't know. Maybe a substation or some such works. Sorry, never really looked hard.'

'No, that's great. You've been an amazing help. Can we go back now? I'm sorry I've spoiled your afternoon's fishing.' He shook his head.

'You ready to go back?' She nodded. 'Then hold on,' he was grinning. 'With this tide under us, we'll fly back, quicker than you can say capitaine of the police.' Celestine thought his face was just pleasant, open, honest and pleasant. She settled back to fly over the waters of the Gironde, her mind bursting with a hundred patterns, and she now needed the time to draw the lines between them. Her stomach had settled a little with the food and coffee, but she was so tired. She needed some sleep to help unravel the cares and the doubts and the even deeper questions.

She noticed very little of the trip back, it had certainly felt a lot smoother when they weren't butting into the tide. Alain guided the boat expertly into the little harbour and tied her up securely. He helped Celestine to climb up the ladder out of the boat and was quickly by her side as she walked along the bank, her legs uncertain, as though there was still water below her. They walked in silence until they came to the village square and then Alain turned half towards her.

'You need a stiff drink after that. A cognac'll settle you down.' He pointed to the small café on the corner of the street. Celestine stopped.

'That would be lovely, Alain, but I have to drive back, and I can't drink, I'm a police officer. But I'll take you up on that drink another time, when I don't have a murder investigation washing around in my head. I'd love to, you've been so helpful,' she paused. 'And I've never asked about you. Are you married? Do you have children?' he shook his head slowly.

'I was once, for a while, married.' He looked away towards the estuary. 'Got to where we couldn't see the point in each other, you know. After the frenzy wore off. No kids.' She placed her hand on his arm.

'Thank you again, Alain,' she said and started to walk towards her car.

'One thing,' he said suddenly and in a different tone completely. 'There's a man, over at Vayres he is. Pistouley is his name. Studies the currents and the tides. Written a book. I haven't read it. He knows all about the estuary, tides, and where the waters run. He's got a website. Puts warnings, information for fishermen, boat people, that sort of thing. I have looked at it. Very thorough. You might want to look at it.'

'Pistouley?'

'Yes, Hugo Pistouley it is. I think Vayres.' She made a quick note in her book, which was a little damp, with ink smudges in places.

'That was very interesting today Alain. It's a different world, isn't it? The estuary. Not the same from the outside.'

'Not a lot of things the same on the inside as the outside,' he said portentously.

No, but you are, thought Celestine. You are the same all the way through. She kissed him on both cheeks, much to his surprise, and opened the door of her car to climb in.

'That normal is it, for police capitaines?' he said, touching his cheek and grinning a little. Celestine smiled.

'No it isn't, not normal at all,' she said.

Chapter 21

Pham Vinh's car was not like a gangster's car, she thought; it was a short, black Audi with a leather steering wheel. He was dressed in black; black trousers, a black shirt buttoned at the cuffs and black shoes. He greeted the girls in a calm and friendly way, his eyes running up and down Kim's body in her short yellow dress. He kissed Linh on both cheeks and kissed and pulled Kim close to him.

'In the car,' he said. 'You know where we're going?' Linh nodded.

'West. I have the route on my phone.' She looked up at him, to see if he was serious, if he was really going to help her. His face was clear, his features were regular and evenly spaced, but he was not handsome. There was something missing, there was no animation in his face, it didn't draw you in, in fact, she felt a little repelled by its blankness. But he was helping her, helping her to find her cousin, who she now realised, she really wanted to see again.

She sat in the front next to Vinh. Kim lounged across the back seat in her yellow dress and Vinh kept looking back at her in the rear-view mirror. She smiled at him when he caught her eye, but most of the time she spent looking at her phone. He had agreed readily when Kim had called him, he had seemed excited about the idea of snatching a runaway from the arms of the flics.

They drove in silence apart from Linh's occasional directions. He tried to ask about the cousin; 'What was he like? Who was he?' but she had just shaken her bowed head and so he had left it. The road along the peninsula was dull, just woods, then rows and rows of vineyards, kilometres of them. He could not imagine being out here for any amount of time. People were alive and interesting, trees and green and vines were not. He drove too fast and aggressively, jerky on the winding roads, and Linh, after looking down at the screen and with the anxiety in her stomach, began to feel nauseous. She pressed the button to open the window and the air came in and blew back her hair and forced her to look up. Vinh grinned across at her.

'You gonna puke?' he demanded.

'No. Just a bit queasy,' she replied.

'Queasy's good. Just don't puke, not inside anyways. How far we gotta go?'

'Five kilometres. It says five kilometres.'

Just then they saw the blue lights of a police car rushing towards them. Vinh slowed right down and almost pulled onto the grass verge to let them go past. Linh looked across and saw the heads of two police officers, focused ahead. Sitting slumped in the back seat, staring blankly out of the window, was a little man in a bright yellow T-shirt. It was only for a split second that she saw him but she had a sinking feeling in her stomach.

'That's him. I think they've taken him,' she said, and unfastening her seat belt and sticking her head out of the window, she vomited along the side of the car.

'What d'you mean? It was like half a second, you couldn't see nothing,' Vinh said. 'You puked on my car.' She just shook her head, she couldn't speak. 'I'm gonna keep going. Could've been anyone in that car. It's your imagination girl. Can't believe you puked on my car. You're gonna clean it up.'

'She'll clean it up. Leave her be. Just drive. We'll go there. If he's not there we'll go back. Nice drive,' said Kim.

They drove on, Vinh just following the road as Linh wiped her mouth on a tissue and threw it out of the window. They drove around a bend and there were two police cars stopped by the side of the road, partially on the verge by a row of vines and opposite a small wood. There was just enough room to pass, but as Vinh slowed down and pulled out to overtake the cars an agent stepped out and held up his hand to halt him. Vinh swore viciously under his breath. He stopped alongside the second car, and another officer came around the front and rapped on his window. Vinh opened it and the officer looked hard at Vinh, then across at the girl with the washed out-face and the tissue by her mouth, then he looked at the legs, then the face of the girl lounging in the back.

'Where are you going?' he demanded, glancing back again at the girl's legs.

'Just driving. Afternoon off. Nowhere special,' answered Vinh in a neutral voice.

'Driving permit,' he demanded, and took down the details in his notebook. The other officer came around to the passenger side and looked at the discs on the windscreen: the insurance certificate and the contrôle technique. He also noted the vomit streaked along the side of the doors.

'Where are you going?' asked the first officer again.

'Just driving man. Having a day off. We work in a restaurant. Closed today.'

'Vietnamese?'

'Sure.' There was silence for a moment.

'You weren't coming to meet someone?'

Vinh shook his head. 'Don't know no one here. Just driving, driving around. Nice scenery, no?'

The officer looked over at Linh. 'You work in a restaurant? What's wrong with your face?'

'I was sick, winding roads. What happened? Was there an accident?' she asked.

The officer didn't respond. He walked over to his colleague and they talked together for a few minutes. He tore a slip from the back of his notebook and handed it to Linh.

'Write your names on the paper, and your addresses. You can write in French?' She nodded. She wrote down her and Kim's names and the address of the Pho Bahn Cuon Restaurant, then she passed it to Linh who scribbled his name quickly and added the restaurant as his address too. The officer took it, and after staring again at Kim's legs, waved them to go past.

They drove in silence for five minutes before Linh said,

'If you turn left here you can join the main road back to Bordeaux.' He turned without a word, and Linh tasted the bile in her throat and felt the thin shell of her safety and security begin to dissolve.

In the end, it wasn't the dogs who sniffed him out. He was discovered, and that was down to his own curiosity. He accepted that. He was in a new world and he was impatient to become acquainted with its strangeness and its different features. The bushes on the other side of the road were in straight lines, tied to a wire fence. He had studied the birds, looked at the trees, at the different leaf shapes and the bark. He had sniffed and smelled the dry, sweet air. He hadn't slept again. He had looked across the road at the strange bushes for a long time before, looking carefully from side to side, he had walked quickly across to them and stepped into the rows. He had knelt down to peer at the small tight flowers that were growing on the long thin branches. The short trunks of the bushes were like ugly old men, twisted and tortured by age, but the shoots, where the flowers grew, were lithe and supple and seemed to be thrusting with life - a life controlled by wires and posts and ties. He had sat looking at them for a long time. It was calm and nicely enclosed. He had felt he was saying his greetings to this new land, paying his respects to it. He'd fondled the leaves and the delicate flowers. Then he'd looked up. A man was staring at him. He was angry and he'd started shouting at him, but he'd also looked a little afraid. He was on a bicycle and as Quan came rushing out of the row towards the road, the man had cycled off, shouting and waving one hand in the air.

Quan had scurried back to his hiding place in the woods, breathing sharply. He'd tucked down behind the bush and tried once more to blend into the earth. That is where they'd discovered him. Two men in uniforms, staring at him, grabbing him by the arms, forcing him to stand up and shouting at him. They'd let him pick up his rucksack and coat and bundled him to the road and into the back of their car. They were still speaking to him, and although he knew words of French, he couldn't really understand what they were saying.

He sat back and watched the countryside go by. He was sad. But they were not taking him back to the ship - he could tell that by the position of the sun. If they were taking him to the authorities he could claim asylum. Then he would have time to work out his next move. He was not going back.

Chapter 22

Celestine's eyes opened slowly, hoping this was reality, hoping she was really awake and not just slipping into the next phase of her nightmare. In the murky depths of a river, she had been literally sleeping with the fishes. Grotesque, bug-eyed creatures had been nudging her and nibbling at her toes and fingers, but she couldn't move and she couldn't wake. Looking up, as she drifted through the waters, she could see light and the hull of a boat, but then a dark ray, like a huge water bat, swam over her, blocking out the light and covering her with its slippery, membranous wings. She gasped and shook her head to clear away the vestiges of the dream. As she sat up in bed she could feel the tension running through her limbs. She looked sideways, but she knew already that the other side of the bed was empty.

It was still very early when she pulled into the car park behind the building of the Police National, and she was surprised to see her husband's car was already there. She hadn't seen him since the Sunday morning and he hadn't called. I could be generous, she said to herself, I could suppose he has been working on major crime-busting since I last saw him in his dragon gown. Predeau was the only other member of the team in his place. At least he's keen, she thought, and he can't help looking like the really soft one in a boy band.

She had just sat down to collate her notes in preparation for the morning meeting when the call was put through to her. She grabbed her bag and called out. 'Come on, Agent Predeau. We've got another bloody corpse.'

Lying between the rubbish bins in an alley off the narrow Rue de la Sau, the body looked clumsy and frail. All four limbs were stuck at unnatural angles, as if they had stiffened instantly in the middle of a weird, robotic dance of death. Celestine's immediate impression was that it looked like the body of a man discarded, thrown in amongst the rubbish and the waste. As always, she stood back first, to take in the context. A very narrow, dark alley between high windowless buildings. The only door she could see was nearer the street - a side door to one of the houses. The street itself was a quiet thoroughfare which led to the rear of the medieval *Grosse Cloche*, the Great Bell, which the Bordelais were so rightly proud of. She sent Predeau to walk carefully along the alley to see where it led, but he came back almost immediately, it was a dead end.

She moved closer to the corpse. The eyes were open, the surface already dulled, but they still managed to look almost astonished at what had happened. She had seen that before. She looked at the wound, a dark red patch of blood had soaked into the pattern on the man's chest. She couldn't make it out, it looked like a globe, but the blood had rendered the writing illegible. The bright yellow T-shirt was stained and torn at the neck. There was a tear at the knee of the trousers. His hands were open, fingers spread as though he had been giving something out or releasing something. The birds of his spirit ran through Celestine's mind, but she cut herself short. Keep the imagination for later, she thought. This is about facts.

She called Predeau to stand beside her, he had been looking at the corpse sideways, as though he couldn't face the reality of a dead man.

'What do you see?' Celestine asked him. She could see him swallow and gather himself for the task.

'Male, East Asian. Not old, thirties perhaps. Blood on chest, stab wound?' He looked to Celestine, but she nodded for him to continue. He hesitated. 'Lying strangely, like he didn't just slowly die there. Like maybe he'd been thrown into this place.' He looked again for confirmation. 'No coat, just a T-shirt, stained, and trousers, torn at the knee. Nothing in the hands. Scratch on his right cheek, below the ear. Lying between two bins in an alley. Very quiet street.' He stopped.

'Good. Write all that down, let it sink in and see if anything else occurs to you,' said Celestine, not taking her eyes off the corpse. 'When we get the pathology report, and the forensics, link them back to the observations you've just made. We'll get the how and the when, and hopefully the who, from the science. Remember your question, the first thing we need to establish after that is the why.' She turned away and looked at Predeau's face, which no longer seemed quite so soft, but looked almost haunted. 'Why did somebody take this man's life and throw him down here between the bins like some human rubbish? Because he wasn't, he was one of us. Remember that, Predeau, he was one of us, a human being.' He nodded and started to turn away. She raised her hand and stopped him. 'This is very, very important, Predeau. Very soon this corpse will be a case number, an artefact in the mortuary, a series of photos and professional reports. Your job is to keep in mind always, that this was a man, not a case number.'

'Ok, boss. Got it. Can I … get some air?' She waved him away and looked again at the scene. Bordeaux, Bordeaux, she said to herself. Such a nice city, not a Paris or a Marseille. A city that has everything, but where nothing ever happens. Two murders in a few days, nothing ever happens. Very different these two murders, different kinds of people, different type of place, unlikely to be linked. Just an unfortunate weekend for some.

She walked back to the street. The Rue de la Sau was only wide enough for one vehicle to pass, and there were two police cars parked there already. She looked along the street and saw Commandant Martel, Dubois and Sorbot walking towards the scene, having left their cars in the wider road beyond. Commandant Martel didn't seem pleased to see her.

'You working nights now, Courbet?' he said.

She nodded towards the alley. 'Down there, between the bins. Asian. Stabbed in the chest.' Martel and Dubois entered the alley. Sorbot stood next to Celestine and took out a cigarette. 'You all right, Capitaine? Hear you had another one on Saturday as well. Holiday weekend, eh.' He lit his cigarette. 'Thanks for not calling me in.'

'Good weekend with the family?' asked Celestine.

'Yeah. Noisy, good.'

'Go and have a look. I'll appreciate your observations,' said Celestine.

She crossed the street to lean against the wall of the house opposite. The buildings were tall, three-storied, but only half of them were lived in now. These streets were dark and sunless and the houses were gloomy and unfashionable. She wondered if anyone ever looked out of these windows, there wouldn't normally be anything interesting to see, not even sunlight or birds or trees. She knew the crew was on its way, the same crew who had rummaged over the death place of the corpse on Saturday. It was becoming all too familiar.

The Commandant and the other two officers emerged from the alley and walked over to her.

'Lieutenant Dubois. I want you to organise the house to house, not just in this street but in the bigger one too. Once we know the time of death we can be more specific, but assume we're looking at any time between nightfall last night and early morning.'

'He was dumped there,' said Celestine. 'Must have been a vehicle. He wasn't killed there.'

Martel looked at her. 'We'll let the tech teams confirm all that stuff. Meanwhile, Sorbot, you liaise with the pathologist and the identite guys, when they arrive. Then everything comes back to me.' He turned to Celestine. 'We're going back to the station. I want an update on the body on Saturday.' He turned sharply and walked away. Celestine wanted to speak to Dubois, but she had avoided her eyes and was now discussing the setting up of a process for the house to house with one of the uniforms.

Sorbot shrugged. 'Cushy for some,' he said.

'Jean. Keep an eye on young Predeau there. I think he's keen to learn. From the best,' she added.

Her own car was parked a street away in the space under the arch of the Great Bell. These ancient areas of the city were not designed for motor cars and the room they needed. But she'd always liked this part of Bordeaux, steeped in its sometimes bloody history. She loved the history of the bell. She knew the text inscribed on the bell by heart ... *I chase away the storm, I sing for the festivals, I weep for the dead.* But it made her think of Armand Verville, and she thought of going to see that strange Lecoubarry - the Rue Carpentyre was only a few streets away. She wondered if he had made any progress or if he had any more information for her. But she was on thin ice already with Martel. She would call him later. In some ways, it would be easier to speak to him by telephone. Although she knew she was up to handling most people, he was a bit disturbing in the flesh, a little powerful and unpredictable. She got into her car to drive back to the commissariat. *I weep for the dead*, she repeated to herself. She knew she was getting very dark, and not for the first time she determined to maintain a distance between the work she was doing and the person she was. She would not be accused of acting too bloody female, by anyone.

Commandant Martel was waiting for her in his office. He waved her to close the door.

'Firstly, I hear you went to talk to a witness yesterday. Even after I had expressly told you to leave it until today,' he said. Celestine hadn't sat down.

'Christ, what is it in this department? Chinese whispers. I talked to someone that might know where the deceased worked. Might even be connected,' said Celestine, exasperated.

'And did he, she?' asked Martel.

'No. The dead guy, this Verville, was very secretive about it. Probably doing something illegal. He was a metalworker.'

'Ok. But when I say, when I give an order, a specific order, to take a day off, to wait until I am in position, that's what I expect to happen. It's not a request, it's an order. Is that understood?' Celestine said nothing. 'It's for your own good, Celestine. You take on too much. That's my job. That's why I have the extra stripes.'

Celestine smouldered, but let it go. Martel was not tall, but there was a belligerence in the way he stood, how he held his shoulders and the aggression in his eyes. He was at least ten years older than her, near the same age as her husband, but he looked much older. His hair was grey and cropped short and there were deep creases in his cheeks. His hands were massive - *Martel's shovels* they were called in the team. He could wrap his hands easily around someone's neck and hold two wrists together to clip on the handcuffs. His face wouldn't have been unpleasant, the features were clean, but there wasn't a gram of softness there to detract from the hardness of his demeanour. Celestine didn't feel like firing bullets at a steel target. He sat down and waved her to a seat opposite him.

'What have you got?' he asked. Celestine ran through the details of what was known so far, the identity, the attempt to find out where he worked. 'The wife's not speaking?' he asked sharply.

'Says she doesn't know. Now she's disappeared.'

'And this type you met. The carpenter?'

'Just an old friend. Doesn't know anything,' she replied, and wondered why she hadn't gone into detail. She also didn't mention her trip down the estuary, she only suggested that there was a line of enquiry she would like to follow. 'We haven't had the path report yet, so we don't know exactly how long he'd been in the water. But there's a definite possibility that he went into the estuary downriver from where the corpse was found.'

'Down. Towards the sea. That doesn't make much sense,' said Martel.

'It does if you take the tides into account. A strong tide could have carried the body back upriver,' Celestine insisted.

'Nah. I don't think that's likely. Leave that one alone. We'll see what the boffins say, but I bet we'll find he went for a swim somewhere in Bordeaux, after a bust-up or a deal gone bad.' He stood up.

'He was wearing overalls and work boots. His wife said he worked night shifts,' said Celestine.

'That's what I want you to do. Find the wife. She'll know more than she's saying, for sure. Tell me straight away, as soon as you find her. I'll speak to her. She won't keep secrets from me.' He dismissed her with a wave of his hand.

Celestine walked out of his office and along the corridor to where the Divisional Commissaire had the large corner office on the same floor. His assistant called out to her.

'He's not in, Capitaine,' she said. She was a new junior officer that Celestine hadn't really noticed before.

'His car's there,' said Celestine. The girl looked surprised.

'Is it? I haven't seen him today. But he must have been in yesterday, perhaps he left it then.'

'Yesterday?'

The girl nodded. 'Logged in mid-afternoon. Think he left a few hours later. I could check, but, well…'

'No, that's all right. Don't bother.' She walked back to her own office and closed the door. She tried to call him but it went straight to his messaging service. She started to leave a message. 'Etienne. I just…' But then she stopped. I just what? I just wanted to know what the fuck was going on. I just don't care. I just… She ended quickly with, 'Just call me.' She pulled out her notebook and started transcribing onto another pad that had more room for thoughts and comments. The first notes covered that unusual, helpful, but uneasy conversation with the Lecoubarry guy. She could still see the humour in his eyes as he was talking about cocktail sticks. What a character. Then she looked at the water-stained scribble she'd done during her trip down the estuary with another character, another man, very different, but who also had a vein of humour ready to burst out through his eyes and his grin. Yesterday was definitely a day of out-of-normal body experiences. She found the name of the expert the fisherman had told her about and looked him up and instantly found his website and contact details. She called him and he answered almost immediately. He didn't sound at all dull, as she'd expected. In fact, he sounded enthusiastic, almost gushing. She made an appointment to visit him that afternoon. Funny, she thought, she hadn't thought of informing her superior officer of her plan. But then she didn't intend to argue, she was just going to do.

Chapter 23

Jacques' enquiries took him into the shifty sands of the Bordeaux underclass. In Fouad's café, he sat down with a young guy who knew Armand as a customer, remembered him from a few months back, said he was a nice guy, talked a lot, thought he worked for a jeweller in the Rue Thiac. The jeweller admitted he'd been there for a while, but it hadn't worked out. Left suddenly, left him in the lurch.

'You tell him from me,' he started saying until Jacques glared at him.

'He's dead,' snarled Jacques. 'If you'd paid him a decent wage.' The jeweller was silent, then frightened. He shook his head and waved for Jacques to leave. There were other friends, not many, they had only a few friends in common. No one could help, no one knew anything. Did they ever?

He wasted a morning pounding the streets of the old quartiers, racking his brains for a name, any contact he could approach. Finally, he sat down at a small table outside a café in the Place de la Victoire and ordered a coffee. Above the tall, disjointed, rose-coloured column, the sky was a strange pallor, there was a sickly green tinge to the clouds - a storm was brewing. The air seemed suddenly tangible as though something, an energy, was filtering through it. The clouds were thickening and bustling across the sky and darkening. A cold wind suddenly blew across the square, lifting the papers from the table tops. Jacques put his hand over the ashtray where the bill was lying. He had been thinking of what Maxine had said, more specifically about who Armand had been working with. An old man he had worked with before and some ducks. But duck was an English word, canard in French. Jacques had sometimes heard Vietnamese people described as ducks for the way they talked - a duc sound that seemed to recur frequently when they spoke their language. It was disparaging, Jacques thought, but Armand had never been politically correct. He pulled himself up. Hey, don't start thinking ill of your friend - faults are too easy to find. He tapped his fingers on the table. But where could he be working with Vietnamese? I guess they have factories and workshops. Why not? He hadn't really thought about it before.

Just then the first fat raindrops landed on the table top. He grabbed the bill and ducked into the café to pay. By the time he turned round to leave, the heavens had opened and the rain was bouncing off the pavements. He hesitated at the door. He was only wearing a thin shirt and trousers. The boy behind the counter called out to him.

'Monsieur wait. Wait here, it's too heavy.' Jacques turned around and looked at him. He had a soft, almost pretty face, and he look concerned. Jacques grinned at him and raised his hand. Then he plunged out into the street.

He was drenched in no time. A few people with umbrellas were cowering as the rain pounded down on them, but most had scurried into doorways, or into shops or stood below café awnings. Jacques walked like a ship breasting the waves of a storm. The water ran down his head and face, his hair stuck to him and he had to keep shaking the rain from his eyes. His shirt clung to his chest and rain soaked his trousers from the top and splashed up from the pavement at the bottom. He walked through the streets like that, feeling as though he was fighting something, braving something. He felt that he wanted to be lashed, to be pelted with these cold torrents of water. He noticed a woman in a doorway looking at him strangely, then he realised that his mouth was open and his face was set in a mirthless grin.

By the time he reached his workshop in the Rue Carpentyre, he was as much water as man, he thought. He stumbled up the stairs, tore off his wet clothes and sank into a large armchair, with two towels around him, to let the madness abate. Sometimes, he thought, you just have to let the wild things in, just to shake out the feeble bits and check that you're still alive. He felt so much better now.

The telephone rang as he was pulling on his working boots. He ignored it. He had settled on a course of action for the day and the evening. He had some delicate, challenging repairs to make to the surface of a lovely, nineteenth-century, kingwood bureau plat. It would take all his skills to match pieces to the broken surface and to bring the fine leather inlay back to life. He was looking forward to the work, to being totally engaged and absorbed in something that wasn't related to the darker side of life. He went downstairs into his workshop and picked up his apron. The phone rang again. This time he was only a few feet away so he stretched for it, ready to be rude if necessary.

'Jacques. It's Louise,' the voice said. There was a quietness and a tremor there which he picked up immediately.

'Bonjour, Louise. How are you?' he asked, but she didn't answer immediately. There was a short silence.

'Jacques, are you in Bordeaux?' she asked finally.

'In Bordeaux. No, I'm in Kuala Lumpur. Of course I'm in Bordeaux, my dove. I am always in Bordeaux. And come to think of it, this telephone only rings in Bordeaux, it's attached to the house. What's the problem?'

'Could you come here? Come to see me. I think I have seen something,' she said.

'Seen something. A vision, a ghost. You know they don't exist, no?'

'No, Jacques. Something in the street. It's been a long time,' she said. There was a plaintive note that Jacques knew he wouldn't resist.

'Ok. It's only been a few weeks, but of course I'll come and see you. I have to get some work done today, so say about five. Coffee and cakes.'

'Coffee and cakes. Five o'clock. Thank you, Jacques.' She rang off. I'm not going to disappoint another old friend, thought Jacques

Chapter 24

Celestine was caught in the storm when she was halfway to her meeting in Vayres. The rain flowed down the road in shallow rivers and squirted up in sheets from the tyres of the vehicles. Her wipers were working at full speed but she still had to peer ahead, driving more in hope than certainty. At least she had to focus on something else, something that wasn't work or home, or both. The route wasn't particularly attractive, taking her through some of the industrial suburbs of the city, but it didn't matter, as she couldn't see a thing, couldn't take her eyes off the road ahead. What is it with water at the moment, she wondered?

She was late for her appointment, and she was never happy with that. As she approached the outskirts of Vayres, the rain stopped suddenly, the clouds scudded away and blue sky poured through from the west.

She pulled off the autoroute, she could see the wide river below, curving up to the town and away again in an oxbow. The house she was looking for was a kilometre out of the town, downstream, past the grand chateau. She had a brief glimpse of the gates as she drove past.

Dr Hugo Pistouley's bungalow appeared to have grown out of the cliff. The wall of random, white stone matched the chalky rock face to the side and above. The undergrowth that curled around the windows and the door were overshoots of the plants clinging to the cliff and squirming through the crevices between the great slabs of white rock. The house was like a growth, linear and regular, but somehow organic, as though it could be easily drawn back into the base rock at any time. She wondered if she was about to meet a troglodyte.

He was certainly tall; at least one ninety, thin and articulated, she was reminded of an anglepoise lamp. As he greeted her at the door, smiling and shaking her hand, all parts of his limbs seemed to be moving like a mechanical toy. He had a face that was odd, yet still friendly and interesting, with long, thick, dark eyebrows like caterpillars, jointed, as though they'd been pinned there as they'd wandered slowly across his face. Above, his brow stretched high and back into a tonsure surrounded by thick dark hair. He wore half-lensed glasses, which couldn't hide the liveliness of the eyes that were almost staring at Celestine. She wasn't uncomfortable, it just felt as though she were being classified. She waited until he spoke first.

'Captain Courbet,' he said finally. 'It's been a long time.'

'Dr Pistouley. A long time. Have we met?' said Celestine, confused.

'Come in, come in. Yes, quite a few years. Oh, seven perhaps.' Celestine was racking her brain to remember where she'd been seven years before. 'The ritual killing,' he continued. 'Drowning of a young man, below there, half a kilometre downstream. The timing was everything. The height of the tide, at the exact hour. Earlier or later and he would have survived, and they had to have known that. I was questioned. Of course, I was.' He was talking without pause as he conducted Celestine along a passageway into what was clearly his control room. 'But when I was discounted, off the hook. I am a man of science, I'm not interested in barbaric cults of nature. I was able to demonstrate the time when the youth would have to have been pinioned there. And by this, they were able to confirm the whereabouts of certain parties, and well, case solved. Sorry, did you want coffee?'

'That would be very nice, thank you,' said Celestine, drowning a little bit herself.

'Well, sit in that chair, no, that one, while I make Pistouley's brew. Columbian.'

Celestine sat down where she had been directed and looked around. It seemed she was in a conservatory, but when she looked to the side, she realised she was actually on a platform, protruding from the rock. With glass on three sides, it seemed to teeter right out over the river some thirty metres below. The view was stunning, but not comfortable for anyone suffering from vertigo. The rear wall was stone, but was almost completely covered with maps of the rivers and the estuary of the Gironde, along with charts of the phases of the moon and even of the stars. In one corner was a large desk on which sat three computers, including a large Apple Mac. Celestine imagined it was almost like being on the bridge of a ship, or a spacecraft that had docked onto the cliff face, but could be released at the touch of a switch to go drifting over the river and down the estuary to the sea.

Dr Pistouley returned with the coffee on a tray. He placed it on a small table and looked at Celestine from an angle and a great height. 'I am terribly sorry,' he said. 'I realised when I was making the coffee that you probably didn't have the faintest idea what I was talking about just then. I meant, of course, the last time the police consulted with me. Not you, a very thickset man, whose name I have long since shredded from my mind.'

Celestine couldn't help smiling. 'It's quite all right, Dr Pistouley. I was a little confused, but it was very entertaining. I'm afraid my request for your assistance is rather more prosaic.'

'Well, well. Nevertheless. I am absolutely delighted that you have come here. Delighted. Courbet. The dark bird. I shall remember.'

'Celestine. Celestine Courbet,' she said. 'This is a most remarkable ... home you have here. Have you lived here for many years?'

'Many, many years. Really, since the madness took me,' he chuckled. 'Oh no, not that kind of madness. I refer to my overarching passion, my total absorption - hydrography; but in my case the very focused study of the waters of the Dordogne, the Garonne and the Estuary of the Gironde.'

'The largest estuary in Europe,' said Celestine

'Quite so,' he suddenly looked disappointed. 'It's not the size, you see, that matters, or not so much, it's the density and variety of its vagaries. It is the very devil to monitor. Keeps me on my toes, each day,' he laughed. 'It's an uneven contest of course. One man with all his gimcrackery, still can't predict or comprehend its every way. But one tries, you know. And the fight is a good one.' He drank deeply of the coffee in his cup, sat down and seemed to fold himself into a resting position. 'What is your query, Capitaine Courbet?' he asked.

Celestine put down her own coffee cup and placed a notebook on her knees. She described the finding of the body on the shores of the estuary, the timings of when the pathology report had now indicated the body had entered the water. She mentioned the wrecked boat washed up on the same beach, and the information that she had gathered from her trip down the estuary. Throughout, Dr Pistouley looked sternly at her face, listening carefully, making no comment, almost motionless in his tucked-up, angular pose. There is something of the praying mantis about him, thought Celestine. Perhaps that's how they look when they are about to be devoured by their mates. When Celestine had finished, Dr Pistouley sat back and unfolded himself. He sat quietly for a minute or so. Finally, he said.

'This will take a little time. You will have to show me exactly where the man's body was found. Dreadful, unlucky fellow. You have a dark occupation sometimes, Celestine. Really dark. Dealing with the tragic. But let us see if we can shed a little light on it.' He stood up.

'It does seem dark at the beginning,' said Celestine. 'But if I can discover where this man was killed, then I am closer to knowing why, and then who.'

'And that is important to you.' It was a statement.

'Very, very important. It's justice. It's the reason for my occupation,' said Celestine strongly. He nodded and smiled at her.

'Show me on this map exactly where you found the body, and I will endeavour to calculate where his final journey began.' Celestine studied the large-scale map on the wall and eventually pointed to the place where the body of Armand Verville had been discovered. Dr Pistouley noted the coordinates. 'Now we shall do it again on the chart on this computer. It is easier to recognise once you have located a point on the paper map. Celestine pointed to the spot again on the screen of his large computer. 'Very well. And the dates and times are as I have written down there?' He pointed to a note he had made on a pad on his desk.

'Yes, that's right.'

'Very well. I suggest you sit down over there and wait. Real magic is not an instant thing. If I were to mention terms such as co-efficient, undular, and lunar draw; you see there are so many parameters. The River Garonne begins its life in the Pyrenees. The gorgeous River Dordogne wakes up in the Massif Central. These watercourses are affected by all the precipitation, or lack of it, in the lands in between. But their effect, except in times of spate, is less than that of the white goddess - the moon; oh, and the stars, and the shifting topography of the lands below the waters in the estuary itself, and the strength and direction of the wind. Would you like me to explain it to you? I am not being patronising in any way, I can see that you are a bright and intelligent woman, but perhaps I should just find you an answer, eh?'

Celestine nodded her head. 'If I had more time. But please... I will sit here and enjoy this wonderful view.'

'The kingfishers are active. You will see them swoop and return if you look attentively. Second clutch already,' he said. Then he opened his other two computers and started inputting data.

Celestine decided that these moments were outside of the normal haste of the day, and vowed to think of nothing, to just be and to watch. The river was wide at this point but she could see downriver where it swelled and then curved around and out of sight. If I could shed some of the angsty bits that keep me so agitated, I could sit here and look at this all day. Then she thought again of the man with the cocktail sticks, and how he was absolutely right, she was so angry under the surface. She gave herself time to picture him; he looked and sounded so strong, as though he was standing on firm ground. She shook her head gently. Just look for the kingfishers, she told herself, stop the rest of your brain from worthlessly spinning around.

After fifteen minutes, Dr Pistouley called to her.

'Where, my Capitaine, do you imagine the journey began?'

'Er... that is the question,' replied Celestine. 'The consensus is that he fell in, or rather was thrown in, somewhere upriver, possibly even in Bordeaux itself.' Dr Pistouley gave a loud 'humph'.

'But I had my doubts as I explained,' Celestine added quickly. 'So, although it was not very scientific, following the course of a wrecked boat, I will plumb for down the river.' She stood up and walked over to him.

'And you would be right. Top marks. Observation, intuition, science. Is that what a good detective uses, Celestine?' He looked genuinely interested.

'That and shoe leather,' she replied. That delighted him.

'Yes, shoe leather. We still need shoe leather. Me too. I walk kilometres every month along the banks of these rivers. I suppose that is the equivalent. Anyway, look here.' He pointed to the large chart on the screen of his computer.

'Of course, we don't know the exact time, so I have worked on thirty-minute intervals. It does make a difference, but in essence, I would suggest that your poor victim was entered into the tide somewhere along this line of coast. A stretch of perhaps five kilometres. I can't be any more exact than that.'

Celestine felt a tingle of excitement in her stomach. She looked more closely at the screen. She picked out the names she had recently learned to recognise. She was right, Dr Pistouley had highlighted in yellow a stretch from North West of Valeyrac to just beyond Talais. Downriver. Armand Verville had been killed down the estuary. He had been working at some location there. This was massive progress, and she suddenly felt emotional and vindicated. She smiled at Dr Pistouley who was trying to look modest.

'That is fantastic, Dr Pistouley. You have no idea how important this could be. You are a magician,' she paused. 'A scientific one of course.'

Dr Pistouley smiled broadly, and his eyebrows seemed to tremble as though ready to walk off his face.

'There,' he said. 'I'll print it out for you.' They talked a little longer as he explained various aspects of his work. Celestine was interested, but he caught her glancing at her watch. 'Very well. I am sorry, here I am wittering on and you have dangerous villains to catch,' he said. 'I had hoped you would meet my wife, she should be home shortly.' Again his relentless stare saw the flicker of surprise in Celestine's face. 'What? You don't expect an oddball like me can have a wife? Remarkable woman, teaches at the lycée.' He became conspiratorial. 'She tells people I have a hobby. A hobby!' he grinned. 'It's she who has a hobby. Me. I think perhaps that if polyandry were an acceptable practice in France, she would retain a whole collection of oddballs, in various outlandish locations like this, according to their *hobbies.'* He laughed delightedly, and his limbs moved in a gentle mechanical motion. 'As it is, she only has me.' He handed the printout to Celestine.

'Anything else, any time, dear Capitaine. Oh, and you can pay me.' Celestine looked a little uneasy. She hadn't expected there to be a cost, but there again, there was no reason why not. She was about to suggest that he send her a bill for services rendered, when he said. 'The Festival of the River, here in Vayres, in September. To celebrate the Mascaret. The great bore that surges its way up our river. Surfers, canoeists, those paddle boards, grand sight. This year I will be exhibiting a scale model, a moving exhibit, you understand, for the children largely, but of course the adults will be intrigued.' He paused. 'And you must come, you must promise me, here and now, that you will come. There is food you know and games. It's a marvellous festival. You must come. That is the payment.'

Celestine was speechless for a moment. 'I've heard of it of course, but I've never been. I will come to the Festival. It would be a great pleasure. And thank you again, Dr Pistouley, for your invaluable assistance this afternoon.' He shook her hand and led her to the outside door. She noticed that the walls of the hallway, and the small sitting room she could see to the side, were covered with pictures and large photographs of the moon - in its different shapes and phases.

'My wife,' said Dr Pistouley, 'she loves the moon, she is a little fanatical about it.' He shook his head. 'I worry that it has really become an obsession.'

Celestine drove away, smiling to herself. At last, she felt she was on the upward slope of the investigation. But of course, she said to herself, things can go back downhill again very quickly.

Chapter 25

Louise Brabant's apartment was on the second floor of an attractive building in the Rue Buhan. She had lived there for nearly thirty years, and for half of that time she hadn't crossed the threshold to go outside. She was a rare case; an unfortunate victim of the uncontrollability of the mind, a mind that had seized up on her. For fifteen years she had been a prisoner, unable to leave the house, held captive by her agoraphobia - a purely psychological condition, for there were no physical reasons why she couldn't go out. Her husband had been a tall, strapping, retired sergent-chef, a sergeant major, who had collapsed and died of a massive heart attack in the streets nearby. Louise had been with him, and she had been unable even to lift up his head. She had sat by him, dumb-struck, rigid, for fifteen minutes until someone had come along. Since that day, Louise had been unable to leave her gloomy apartment in the Rue Buhan.

When Jacques walked in, she was laying small plates and napkins on a very fine Charles X, rosewood drum table.

'You mind what you're doing with that table top,' Jacques said. 'I'm not going to repair it again. I'm too busy and you don't pay well enough.' He kissed her on both cheeks. She had been a tall woman but was now stooped, and her clothes hung off her, which gave the impression that she didn't have a fixed shape at all.

'Well, if you don't want me to use the table, then you can do without any cakes. Cos, that's where they're going,' she said, and placed a cut-glass cake stand nearer to where she was going to sit. She brought cakes and a steaming pot of coffee and they talked quietly. 'It's Columbian, Bourbon Rouge, from Café Pina in Rue des Ayres. They send it up, you know. It never changes.'

'I know, you said. They're good in there. I hope they survive,' said Jacques.

'They'll survive me, that's all I care about. And the cakes are from Guillaumes in the Cours Pasteur. I used to leave it to the manageress there, Olivia, but she left, and then they started sending me all kinds of things - doughnuts, whatever was left on their shelves. So now I order exactly what I want. Now they understand. Doughnuts, when you want canelés!'

She told the same story every time he came, but he just nodded. 'These are good,' he said. 'So tell me about this vision. What did you see that's got you so worked up?'

She looked around the room as though searching for something she had mislaid. Then she settled on a large mahogany cabinet at the other end of the room.

'You know that dresser you like. That one,' she pointed. 'I think I might sell it after all. But you'll have to tidy it up a bit. It looks a little shop-soiled.' Jacques laughed.

'Louise, you talk about selling that piece every visit I make. If it's not that, it's the credenza or the comtoise clock.' He shook his head and raised a finger towards her. 'But what I want to know is, how are you going to find two elephants to haul it downstairs? It must weigh a ton and a half.'

'Pah! Two men carried it in and two good men could carry it out.' She pouted her lips in defiance.

'Who? Who carried it in? Jock?'

'Yeah. Jock and old Vinni Antonietti. You remember Big Vin, Italian guy, had a stall in the Marché Capucins.'

'Jesus, I remember. It's a long time ago. He was a monstrous guy,' said Jacques.

'I know. Him and Jock. And they cursed so much carrying it up the stairs, I said we'd need to call in the priest to exorcise the whole building,' she chuckled.

'Vincent Antonietti. You know, when he died, he was so big, they couldn't get his casket into a hearse. They had to take him home to Chartreuse on a flatbed truck,' said Jacques.

'I heard that, I heard that,' she cackled.

Jacques laughed. 'Yeah. It was on a float, left over from the carnival. Still had the bunting and the paper flags and tinsel on it. Big white casket. And when it got there, the boys at Chartreuse thought they were burying Elvis.' Louise collapsed in a paroxysm of laughter, spluttering and wheezing with delight. Jacques smiled. 'Well, I'll ask around, see if he left any giant offspring in the neighbourhood. I haven't seen any walking around.' They both shook their heads sadly, because Louise hadn't walked around the neighbourhood for nearly fifteen years, and from the windows, she could only see a small part of the transit of the population of Bordeaux. 'So, what did you see, Louise? Come on or I'll arm wrestle you for the last cake.'

Louise grinned. 'Ok, listen.' She leant towards him, fine crumbs, like a tide mark, stuck on the light hairs above her lips. 'They found a body, didn't they?'

Jacques looked surprised. 'Who did?' he asked.

'The police, or at least someone, found a body in that street there, in an alley off the Rue de la Sau.'

'I didn't know. When was this?' asked Jacques.

'Today. Just this morning. The street was filled up with police cars, and an ambulance, must have been six or eight. Taking up half the road.'

'Do they know who it was?'

'Murdered, you know. They were murdered.' Jacques sat up now and studied the look in Louise's eyes. She was deadly serious.

'How do you know all this L? That they were murdered,' he asked.

'Because they came here. The police. Young, under-schooled guy. Asked me if I had seen or heard anything. Was I out in the street last night? Me, out on the street.' She paused. 'I said, "I don't answer questions unless I know what it's about". So he told me. Someone found a body in the alley off Rue de la Sau. Been murdered. "Oh," I said. "Well I don't ever go into Rue de la Sau. Fact is, I don't go anywhere and I don't see anything". And he went away. Just like that.'

'Ok. So what's the problem? You've got an alibi of sorts.'

'No, no. I mean. I asked him, "When did all this happen, this murder?" He says, "Sometime last night, after dark. Maybe through the night".'

'Yes.'

'Thing is, Jacques. I did see something. I don't sleep, you know that. I read, I watch some shit on TV. I listen to music. I was listening to the Chorus of the Hebrew Slaves, you know it.'

'Sure. Sing again the songs of our homeland.' Jacques bawled out two lines.

'That's it. But you know, when music like that stops, it's like the silence after it has a tone of its own. That's when I heard a car. It was after midnight. We don't have a lot of cars, but you do hear some down the street at night. I looked out. I saw it. I saw a police car.'

'A police car?'

'Yes. Definitely a police car. It was parked. Just on the corner, that corner there.' She took Jacques by the arm and led him to the window.

'Where?' he asked.

'There. Just on that corner. You see how I can see one side of the Rue de la Sau. But it's a narrow street. The police car was parked there.'

'Could they have seen down the Rue de la Sau?'

'Yes, yes. Parked so as their front end was sticking out. The guys in the front could see right down the street.'

'Did you see who was in the car?' asked Jacques.

'Just a head, or rather an arm, on this side. They didn't get out. Just parked there. Must have been fifteen minutes. I watched them for fifteen minutes. I have clocks.'

'Yes, you do,' said Jacques ruefully.

'Police, Jacques, there at that time. And there was a murder. I don't know what to do. What should I do?'

'You didn't say anything to the flic who came to the door?'

'No, I didn't think of it at the time. I was a bit…offhand. He was so plebeian.'

'Snob.'

'No, but, I didn't think. I was insulted in some way. And I wanted to know his news, that's what I wanted to hear. Like I want to hear your news when you come here. I can talk to myself all day long.'

'Ok, ok, calm down.' Jacques thought for a minute. 'Maybe nothing,' he said.

'Maybe something,' she said, and Jacques could see that she was really shaken. He looked at her carefully; it was clear she was fading a little more each time he visited her, as though, through the long years, the juice had gradually drained away.

'Look,' he said. 'Don't worry about it anymore. I'm going to talk to someone. Someone discreet. You don't need to worry. It's probably nothing. But she'll make inquiries, you know, quietly.'

'She?' Louise looked at him.

'She's a police officer. A capitaine. I happen to know her on another matter. I can't talk about that.'

'I see, I see. So you don't think I should worry, or phone the police, someone?' Louise asked, sounding less substantial than he had ever known her.

'No, I don't. Leave it with me. I'll have a word, tomorrow. And I'll call back the next day when I have something. I'm sure it's nothing for you to worry about,' said Jacques.

Chapter 26

The first thing Celestine noticed as she pulled into the car park was that her husband's car was no longer in its place. It was pointless to speculate, she thought, but she was conscious of another pang of sadness and loss in her stomach. She sat for a few minutes enjoying the anonymity, sitting on the stool in the blue corner, waiting for the next round to start. In the foyer of the Hotel de Police, a female officer called her over to the desk. She pointed to a young woman sitting hunched up on the benches by the wall.

'Sorry, Capitaine, but that girl came in a couple of hours ago. Asked to speak to Commissaire Vaillancourt. Nobody else.' She shrugged apologetically. 'I know it's not your…I mean, Commissaire Vaillancourt isn't here. We don't know if he's coming back today. I tried calling but there's no answer.'

Celestine sighed. 'Did she not say what it's about?'

'No. I said she had to give us her name.' She looked down at a pad in front of her. 'Le Ho Linh. Vietnamese I think.'

'Vietnamese?' asked Celestine quickly.

'Yeah. "I want speak Commissaire Vaillancourt, alone". I think she meant only. Said she'd wait. Seems really nervous.'

'Yes. This is the place for nervousness,' said Celestine. 'But Vietnamese. She speaks French?' The officer nodded. 'Ok, I'll speak to her, is there a room?'

'Yes. Take any one.' Celestine approached the young woman, almost still a girl, who looked frail and drawn in on herself. Celestine sat next to her on the bench.

'Hi, Linh. I'm Capitaine Celestine Courbet, you wanted to speak to Commissaire Vaillancourt. You know he's not here at this time, don't you?' The girl nodded. 'So what you want to say, is it urgent?' The girl nodded again. Celestine could see that she'd been crying. God I hate to do this, she thought. 'Linh. Commissaire Vaillancourt is my husband. Can you talk to me and I will make sure he gets the message as soon as I see him. Only him.'

The girl looked up sharply. 'Husband?' Celestine nodded. The girl seemed to wrestle with this.

'Look, we can speak in a private room. You tell me why you are here. I will tell Commissaire Vaillancourt,' said Celestine, placing a hand on the girl's arm and nodding encouragingly. The girl seemed to come to a sudden decision.

'Ok. Commissaire Vaillancourt, alone,' she said.

'Alone, only, yes. Only for Commissaire Vaillancourt,' Celestine assured her. The girl stood up as Celestine took her arm and guided her into the interview room. 'Sit down Linh, there. Would you like a coffee or water or something? You've been here a long time,' asked Celestine. The girl shook her head. Celestine had a sudden dread of what she was going to hear, but just be professional, she told herself. She opened a notepad in front of her. 'So, Linh. Tell me how you know Commissaire Vaillancourt?' she asked. The girl kept her eyes on the table.

'He comes to the restaurant. I work in a restaurant - Pho Bahn Cuon.'

'Ok. So he comes to the restaurant there. Often?'

'Sometimes.'

'And do you speak to him?' Celestine asked.

The girl shook her head. 'Good evening, you finished, sir, Good night. Waitress.'

'I see, but why do you want to speak only to him about this urgent matter?' asked Celestine. The girl hesitated.

'He is friend of my boss. I think he will know what to do,' she said finally.

'Your boss. Who is that?'

'Nguyen Ngoc Khanh.' Celestine determined to remain calm, although she felt like there was a tight muscle twitching inside her guts.

'So, Commissaire Vaillancourt is a friend of your boss, and you think he can help you,' said Celestine. The girl nodded again. 'What can he help you with? Why are you here?' Slowly, and in uncertain French so that Celestine had to keep interrupting to make sure her understanding was accurate, Linh told her about the phone call from her cousin, how he wasn't there when they went to meet him, and how she was sure she had seen him in the back of a police car. 'And this was yesterday afternoon,' said Celestine, 'and he hasn't been in contact, no phone calls since?'

'No. No calls. I try calling, send messages. No,' she looked up for the first time and Celestine could see just how young and afraid she was. 'I think he is here, in the big police station. I want to explain. He is my cousin. He is a good man. He is not here to do bad things. I explain to Commissaire Vaillancourt. He is big boss, he can help my cousin. I take care of him. Help my cousin.' There were tears in her eyes.

Celestine wondered again why so many people have to suffer and how there is so much collateral when someone is killed. It could of course be a coincidence, there are a lot of Vietnamese men in Bordeaux. But she had a horrible, dark feeling that she had discovered the identity of the corpse in the Rue de la Sau. She told the girl to wait as she made some enquiries.

'There was a Vietnamese guy brought in yesterday afternoon. Who brought him in?' The desk officer referred to her computer.

'Lieutenant Frezouls and Agent Pinet. Three fifteen.'

'Are they here?' demanded Celestine.

'Off duty.'

'So where is the Vietnamese guy? He was brought in, so he must be here or he must have been signed out.' The officer looked again.

'Not signed out.' She twisted her lips. 'Can't see where he is though.' She looked at Celestine apologetically.

'Who was on desk duty?' demanded Celestine. 'You?'

'No. I think, yeah Froissart and Lagarde. Sunday, only two.'

'Get them on the phone now.' There was no answer to the first call. The second picked up quickly, it was a woman's voice at first, then a man came on the phone. Celestine leaned over the desk, 'The Vietnamese guy brought in yesterday afternoon. Where is he?' demanded Celestine. There was silence for a moment.

'I don't know, Capitaine. I thought he was downstairs, you know, holding cell.'

'You thought?'

'Yeah. I mean that's where he was taken.'

'You didn't see him?'

'I saw him being taken down. Frezouls and Pinet took him. But look, he was interviewed, you know. You must know.'

'Who by?' demanded Celestine.

'Who by. Commissaire Vaillancourt, your …. He interviewed him. Then he left.'

'You saw him leave?'

'Sure. He spoke. Said something like, "Just leave him there, we'll make some enquiries". Yeah. Then he left.'

'Did anyone else interview him, or go down to the cells?' asked Celestine.

'Didn't see it.'

'But there were others in the building?'

'Sure, in and out all the time.'

'When are you back in, Lagarde?' Celestine demanded.

'Wednesday. I worked the weekend.'

'Well don't go far. You might be called in early.' She nodded for the officer to end the call. She looked puzzled. 'There's no way he could still be down there?' she asked. The officer shook her head.

'They do a sweep. All recorded. He can't be there. They must have let him out. Happens. A few questions. Nothing going on here.' She was starting to regret involving Captaine Courbet in this.

'Has there been anyone from Immigration in touch? This is a guy who jumped ship. An illegal. It's a job for Immigration,' said Celestine.

'I can check, but there's nothing on the records.'

'What was the name he gave?'

'Er...Ho Thi Quan.' Celestine wrote it down.

'Check with Immigration,' she said fiercely, and walked back to the interview room. The girl had barely moved. 'Ho Thi Quan. That's the name you gave me,' she said, reading from her notes. The girl nodded. 'Ok. He did come here yesterday,' said Celestine. The girl looked up, a flicker of hope on her face.

'He is here?' she asked.

'No, he's not. Do you have a photograph of Quan?' Celestine asked.

'I don't see him for five years. No photo.'

'Ok. Can you describe him? Any distinguishing features? Anything at all?'

'Normal, I think. Just a guy.'

Celestine was at a loss. She didn't want to upset this girl more by mentioning the body they had found. Not until they had some clearer facts. She came to a decision. 'Linh. I will have to make some enquiries and speak to Commissaire Vaillancourt. Leave this with me now. I want you to go home. I will be in contact when I have something to tell you. Don't go far from the restaurant. Ok?' She paused. 'Linh, when did you last see Commissaire Vaillancourt at the restaurant?'

The girl smiled briefly. '30 April, Fall of Saigon. Important dinner,' she said.

'Important?'

'Yes. Celebration. Monsieur Nguyen, Monsieur Zubizaretta and Commissaire Vaillancourt. Very happy. Very good food. Special.'

'Special. Ok, thank you, Linh.' Celestine escorted her out of the building and stood with her on the top of the steps. She gave her a card. 'Linh, call me if you need to. It's no problem,' she said.

Celestine watched the girl as she walked away along the street. Her feet seemed to be stepping on hot coals and her shoulders were hunched. She looked like a piece of human flotsam that had somehow made it further inland. Like a human being that had no control over their lives at all. Celestine returned to the desk.

'Nothing from Immigration. They don't know anything about it.' The desk officer told her.

'Stay on it, Lieutenant. I want to know when Monsieur Ho left the Precinct, when and under whose instructions. I want every detail. Speak to every officer who was in the building yesterday. Every one.'

'That's not my job, Capitaine.' Celestine had turned away but came back and leaned towards her.

'It's your section. You are responsible for who comes in and out. Get me that information or get your section chief to give me a call.' Celestine stared at the officer until she looked down, then strode away and took the lift up to her floor. There was no one working there, not even Predeau. It was nearly seven o'clock. She slumped down in her chair to begin unravelling the strands of everything that had occurred that day. But she was tired and dispirited, and very, very anxious. She decided to go home, although she knew there was every chance that further confusion and unpleasantness would be waiting for her there.

Chapter 27

It was nearly seven o'clock in the evening. Jacques was sitting astride his motorbike on the edge of the huge square at Quinconces. He was sweating profusely in full black leathers and a black helmet which covered his face and mane. The square was busy with the Bordelais, strolling in the evening warmth. Jacques was envious, but he was watching a small group of four men who were leaning against a wall in the shade of the plane trees. They were not talking, just standing there, clearly waiting for something. There were two Asian men, a little shorter than the others, a tall broad character and an older man whose head was bowed and turned away, looking down the avenue towards the river. Jacques was forty metres away and as he watched them the older man turned and looked in his direction. Jacques pretended to be adjusting something on the bike, but in that quick moment he had recognised the man - it was Lionel Meslier. Jacques knew him because he had seen him standing next to Armand Verville at their trial for forgery, some years before. He had had nothing to do with him, but he had seen him on occasion in the street, on a tram, smoking outside a bar. Bordeaux was a small city, and if you lived in a certain quartier you were bound to bump into people now and again. So that was the old fellow Maxine had mentioned.

Just then a black van circled the square and stopped in front of the men. Jacques couldn't see them boarding or if there was anyone else in the van, but the broad man came around the front and climbed into the passenger seat. Jacques started his motorbike and prepared to follow them.

In the city it was easy, there were other vehicles around and he could slip into the flow and weave in and out to keep the van in sight. In his mind, he'd been expecting to head north along the river road towards Pauillac, but instead, they drove through Le Bouscat, under the ring road and joined the main road, the Route de Bordeaux. This road was straighter and faster, and here too it was easy to keep the black van in view from a distance. There were long stretches where he could see half a kilometre or more ahead. The sky was clear, and the sun was still quite high in the sky, but it was getting lower, and at times it was directly ahead of him and more often to his left where it flashed and dazzled on his mirrors. The land on either side of the road was gently steaming with the heat after the rain, and the gutters and edges were treacherous with pools of water. He rode through kilometres of vineyards, their rows of famous grapes marching over every hill and dale. He passed the opulent gates of some of the famous wine producers of the Medoc, and there was a great urge in him to turn into one of these gates, although he knew they'd be closed. But, in his fantasy, he could pull up on his motorbike, step into a barrelled cellar where the tables were old hogsheads and the walls were lined with great vintages. He would take a comfortable chair, and the pretty waitress would bring him glass after glass of glorious red wines to drink until he was as merry as a robin in a worm farm. There would be music and singing, and Armand Verville would be leading in the chorus, slightly off-key, and taking the others with him because he was so animated. And Jacques acknowledged that some of the best drunks he'd had in the last twenty years had been in the company of that man. Not the heavy, maudlin, drown-your-sorrows drunks that everyone has at intervals. No, the glorious, let it all go, what-the-fuck drunks, filled with daftness and laughter. This was not a man who could easily offend. He remembered saying so to that physical police capitaine. Getting drunk would have to wait. He returned to reality and drew a little closer to the van in front as the road curved around the village of St. Laurent-Medoc, and Jacques could see the fine steeple of the church glowing on its west side in the lowering sunlight. But the van didn't turn off towards Pauillac - so they were going even further down the estuary. He'd been following them for a long time, and now the traffic on the road was light. He wondered if the driver would start to notice the dark motorbike that was keeping its distance behind them. Jacques eased back a little further. The road was as straight as an arrow, so on a stretch of dual-carriageway he speeded up and rode past the van, keeping his head to the front, conspicuously not paying it any attention. He rode on quickly until he reached the small town of Lesparre-Medoc, and as the road curved he braked and turned into a side street, did a U-turn and tucked himself behind a tree at the side of the road. As the van came slowly past he took a quick photograph on his mobile phone. I am really making this up as I go along, he said to himself. I have no idea why I did that last manoeuvre. He rode back onto the main road and was just in time to see the van turning right onto a minor road, heading towards the estuary. Now we're getting to the nitty gritty, thought Jacques. Now you really need to focus. He hesitated before turning, to give the van sufficient time to be out of sight. He knew these roads curved around fields and steadings, but he imagined there were few enough places where they could turn off. He rode slowly up to each bend, stopping and peering around them, before accelerating quickly along stretches that were clear. He nearly caught up to them at a crossroads, but they set off again and he was able to tuck himself up on the grass verge, out of their view. That's the advantage of a motorbike, he thought. It would be much harder to remain unnoticed in a car, which he didn't have, or worse, a battered white van, which he did own.

Soon, he could catch glimpses of the sun gleaming on the wide estuary before him, and he could smell the freshness of the sea air, brought in with the tide. He was just in time to see the van turn left at the T-junction in Valeyrac, and then onto a narrow road that ran not far from the waterside. The road was quite straight, and there was barely room for two vehicles to pass. They travelled for another five kilometres, past marshes where the water seeped from the flat, saturated land on both sides, leaving dark wet streaks across the road. It was quite desolate here on these uninhabited margins, and Jacques was starting to feel a little uneasy.

He rounded a curve, just in time to see the van turn off the road onto a minor track. He pulled into the side, out of sight, and waited a few minutes. Then he rode slowly up to the junction and looked down the track. There was a thin copse of pine trees and behind it, he saw the long metal roof of a building. He switched off the engine and rolled the motor-bike a little way along the track. He saw an old gateway and pushed the bike through and hid it behind some scrawny shrubs and undergrowth. The whole area had a feeling of desolation and waste. It really is the backend of beyond, thought Jacques. What the hell am I doing here? Just get back on your bike and ride home. You've found something out. Go tell that capitaine that you've got a worm for her. See how she looks at you then. But he ignored himself and walked slowly along the track, ready at any moment to fling himself into the trees or behind the scrub which grew on both sides.

When he came to the copse he moved into the trees and felt less exposed. He stepped forward cautiously until he could see the building through the last line of trees. He leaned against the bole of one of the bigger ones and peered out. The building was large, at least a hundred metres long. At the front and to the sides ran a chain link fence with razor wire along the top. Behind the fence he could see the van, parked with a few other vehicles; he could see a black SUV and the canopied trailer of an HGV. There was a name on the plastic curtains on the trailer in faded red letters - the name began with a Z, but it was difficult to make out the rest of the letters. Suddenly, the wide cargo doors slid open and a man stepped out. Jacques could see it was the broad character he'd seen at Quinconces. The man was speaking on a mobile phone, but Jacques couldn't make out what he was saying. At one stage the man looked up and Jacques leant hurriedly back behind the tree. But he had to stare again; he wondered if this man knew what had happened to his friend, Armand, and he wanted to call out to him, to grab him, to throw him to the ground and put his size forty-nines on his neck until he squealed. But he just watched as the man finished his call, spat on the ground and went back inside. Before the doors closed, Jacques could hear the clamour of metal hitting on metal, and he wondered what the hell kind of work Armand had been doing in there.

There was nothing more to be done, so he walked quickly back to his motorcycle, eased it out of the gateway and back onto the road. He didn't think of anything on his way back to Bordeaux. He rode fast and focused, the setting sun no longer a problem for him, and he turned into the Rue Carpentyre forty-five minutes after leaving the building. There was nothing he needed more at this juncture than a large glass of red Bordeaux wine.

Chapter 28

Celestine knew, as soon as she pushed open the door, that Etienne was in the apartment. She found him sprawled on the sofa, an empty glass on the coffee table beside him. She stood over him, having so much to say, having nothing to say. She looked at his eyes, which were bloodshot, at the designer stubble now a scruffy three-day beard. His face looked drawn, there were bags under his eyes and he seemed almost traumatised. Just for a second she even felt sorry for him. He smiled at her, but it was just his perfect teeth sliding out quickly from straight lips.

I used to have a wife like you,' he said. 'I wonder where she went.'

Celestine knew she wasn't ready yet. She walked into the bedroom, undressed and stepped into the shower. The day felt like it had started at the crack of dawn and was ending at the crevasse of sunset. But it wouldn't really end until she had answers to a lot of questions. She dressed comfortably and went into the kitchen to prepare some food, or rather to slide a packet into the microwave. She poured herself a glass of wine and sat at the island, scribbling down a list of questions. When the microwave pinged, she set out two places and called for Etienne to join her. There was no answer. She walked into the living room, where he was lying asleep, his mouth open and one arm dangling off the sofa, his hand bunched up on the floor.

She finished her own meal, poured herself another glass of wine, and armed with her notebook, she returned to the living room and sat down opposite her husband. She watched him for a minute or two, so many conflicting emotions running through her. Then she leaned forward and slammed her notebook down on the coffee table as hard and as loud as she could. She saw his head jerk and his eyes flick open.

'Wake the fuck up,' she said. 'I want some answers to some very important questions.' He struggled to an upright position, she saw annoyance and petulance on his face, but very little resistance. It really did seem that his internal structure had melted away, or that the strength had been drawn from him. She had never seen him look lost before. He picked up his empty glass and looked around for a bottle. 'After. After you've answered my questions,' she said. He slumped back and shook his head a few times. 'There was a Vietnamese man, Ho Thi Quan. You interviewed him yesterday. Why? What did he tell you? What did you do with him?' Vaillancourt managed a quick smile, as though relieved.

'Yeah, I interviewed him. Said he came off a ship at Le Grave. He's an illegal, wants to live in France, get good pension. So what?'

'Why you?' demanded Celestine.

'Because, because I was the only senior officer in the building.'

'And that's the job, is it? The great responsible job of Divisional Commissaire, to interview an illegal immigrant.' Celestine was scathing.

'What can I tell you? I was there. They wanted someone to talk to him. I said, "ok". It was just five minutes.'

'You went down to the holding cell.'

'Yes. That's where they took him.' He stopped. 'Anyway, what has this to do with you? I'm sorry, is that the job of a crack detective?'

'He's disappeared,' said Celestine, and watched his face closely. For a second, the briefest of hesitations, she saw the sign that he was not reacting but thinking about his reaction.

'What do you mean disappeared?'

'Yes. After you interviewed him. He disappeared. He's not in the cells, not in the building, no one signed him out. But let me tell you, Etienne; first thing this morning, I was looking at the body of a dead Vietnamese man, in a sleazy alley in the old town, stabbed to death, and I'm betting you it's your interviewee.' She watched him as he closed his eyes and saw the chewing of the lower lip, the nervous tapping of his fingers on his knee. Then he shook his head as though to banish the thoughts that were there. He opened his eyes and looked directly at her.

'If that is so, then someone must have let him out. But it has nothing to do with me. He was in a cell, behind a locked door when I left him.'

'What was he wearing?'

Vaillancourt shrugged. 'I don't know, jacket, trousers.'

'T-shirt? Come on, you're a police officer, you're trained to remember these details.'

'Yes, then. A T-shirt. I didn't take a lot of notice.'

'Colour?' Vaillancourt closed his eyes again, as though trying to recall. 'Was it yellow?' demanded Celestine.

'Yes, I think so.'

'Yellow, with some sort of globe pattern?' She glared at him, daring him to not give this the attention it warranted.

'Yes, ok, yellow, some sort of globe, some writing.'

Celestine sat back a little. 'That's where the blood came out, Etienne. Hard to read the writing when it's drenched in congealing blood.' She left him with that image for a minute, then said, 'Did he say anything to you? Anything that could lead to this?'

'No. He just spoke in broken French. Said he came off a ship, wants to live in France. Nothing more.'

'Nguyen Ngoc Khanh. He's Vietnamese,' said Celestine sharply. Again he looked up and she saw the uncertainty flick into his eyes, before he gathered himself.

'What? I guess so.'

'You have meals in restaurants with Nguyen, who we both know is a Vietnamese crime boss. In fact, you had dinner with him on Thursday night, the night you told me you were out of town,' said Celestine.

'I didn't say I was out of town. You just assumed I…'

'I assumed, because if you had been in Bordeaux, I might rightly have expected you to spend the night here, in this apartment, with your wife.' Celestine paused, to let her breath catch up with her anger. 'But let's leave that one to a little further down the page. Nguyen?' Vaillancourt waved his arms around feebly, as though he was pinned on a wire but still just about able to move.

'It's work. I told you. I can't tell you anymore. I'm investigating, you know, police work.'

'Work?'

'Yes, work. I told you. Organised crime,' he said.

'And you slept where that night? And last night and Friday night?' demanded Celestine, who was gulping down large drafts of wine and working herself up to a pitch.

'I can't tell you. I just can't,' said Vaillancourt and opened his body up to appeal to her. 'I can't, it's just work. When it's over, I'll explain it to you. Really, but not now.'

'And that's why you keep appearing and disappearing from the Commissariat. Why you don't answer your phone. Why you don't answer your phone to me.' He leaned over and stretched out to take hold of her hands. 'Who are you working with in this investigation? Who in the force? You can't be doing these things alone. So who else? So I can confirm your alibi,' she said mockingly.

'No. A few people at the very top. But they'll deny it. Have to, it's too sensitive.'

Celestine had interviewed a lot of suspects in her nearly twenty years in the police force. She leaned towards him and he opened his arms as if to hold her.

'You're a lying bastard, Etienne. And I am very, very tired of this version of you. Go back to sleep on the couch. I don't want to be anywhere close to you.' She stood up and walked into the guest room, closed and locked the door. A little later, she thought she heard the outside door open and close. For a minute she panicked, she had never really considered that it would end, even though she knew they had been hanging on by a thread for months. One part of her had always hoped that it could be mended, that the problem was situational, external factors. But she took a deep breath. You need to be honest, you always need to be honest, that is what she believed, what she'd been taught. And honesty told her that they had passed the terminal phase and were now just looking at the burial arrangements. Then her phone rang.

'Capitaine Celestine Courbet?' a deep, lightly accented voice spoke.

'Monsieur Lecoubarry, Jacques. How are you?'

'Very well. Have you exercised today, or have you been sitting in your car or at your melamine desk in the white biscuit box?'

Celestine was slightly disconcerted by the questions. 'Sitting, driving, viewing corpses. Just another day. Why do you ask? In fact, what do you want Jacques? It's late.'

'I feared as much. You like to run, don't you?' he asked.

'Yes, I do.'

'Then the best time to run is before the clatter of the day begins. For example; I am going to suggest that you go for an early run tomorrow morning along the promenade by the river, where all the joggers go to mingle with their herd.'

'Yes,' she said impatiently.

'At 7.30, I will be sitting on a bench you know. I have worms for you. I know where Armand Verville was working,' said Jacques triumphantly. Celestine was suddenly alert.

'Where? Along the estuary, no? Beyond Valeyrac.'

'Yes. But I have been right up to the door. Meet me there, Capitaine,' he said.

'Ok. … I have something for you too. In the spirit of reciprocation, you know.'

'That's good. I'll see you there, Celestine,' he said.

'Yes. Bonne soirée.' He rang off, and she sat looking at the phone. Her mind seemed to clear just a little; a little light, the faintest shaft of sunlight, not even a dawn, just the rumour of a sunrise. She lay back down to think, but she was fast asleep in minutes.

Chapter 29

She studied the profile of the man for the first time. His body was hidden by a low bush but his head protruded above it, and he was leaning on the metal railings and looking out over the river. There was something classical, old-fashioned even, she had seen a picture like that of some historical leader staring over the stern rails of a ship that was pulling away from the shore, taking him into exile. She had been walking the last fifty metres and now she stopped and observed him closely; he seemed absorbed, and there was something unassailable and enigmatic about him. And then he turned, and there was no mock surprise, just a big grin that lighted all his face and made his eyes seem to glimmer with life.

'Capitaine, my Capitaine,' he said loudly, as he looked her up and down. 'Like a gazelle.' She took a thin jacket from her small backpack and slipped it over her T-shirt.

'Hardly,' she said. 'Just a sweaty police officer halfway through her run. How's it going, Jacques?' He was still looking at her with undisguised admiration, then he took a step towards her and looked very directly into her face. He noticed the dark shadows and the tightness of the lines at the side of her eyes.

'Ok. How are you, Celestine Courbet? You seem to be suffering a little.' She brushed past him and sat down on the bench. She took out her notebook.

'What do you know?' she demanded. Jacques sat down alongside her and stretched out his legs. Next to her lean, muscular ones, his looked like hinged gateposts. He turned and smiled at her.

'Right. Armand Verville.' He told her about the information that Maxine had given him and his trip following the black van.

'So that was where your friend was working. But we don't know what kind of work. Was the building next to the estuary?' she asked.

'Must have been. I didn't go around the side of it, but it must be close,' said Jacques.

'So, that's probably where they put his body in the water. Unless he was killed somewhere else.' She explained about her trip to Vayres which had confirmed the approximate location. Jacques looked at her in approval.

'You are very thorough, Capitaine Courbet.'

She ignored this. 'What about this old guy, Meslier?' she asked.

'I'm going to try to find him this morning. He's been on night shift, so he'll welcome a loud wake-up call from a big hairy bastard who's going to kick the shit out of him. I mean, of course, interrogate him under the rules of the Geneva Convention.'

'Take it easy. Once you do that you're going to tip our hand. They'll know we're interested in them. I don't want them to clear out before we've had time to search the place,' she said.

'Understood. Can you locate people? With a name. Do you have a system that will turn up an address? A kind of big brother system?' asked Jacques.

'If he has things registered at an address, probably. But it's not fool proof. And it's not big brother,' she said firmly.

'I know. It's to keep the citizens safe,' replied Jacques.

'And there were two Asian men?' said Celestine. 'Vietnamese.'

'Yes, ducks. That's what they call them sometimes. It's derogatory but...' Celestine looked up and out over the river. She was silent for a few minutes and then she turned to Jacques.

'I'm going to tell you something, but it mustn't go any further. It's not public knowledge. You mustn't talk about it except to me.' Jacques nodded. She told him about the body that had been found, and how it was a Vietnamese illegal immigrant.

'Came off a boat. You mean like a runaway?' asked Jacques.

'Exactly that,' replied Celestine. It was Jacques' turn to look into the distance.

'I know about that murder,' he said, and told her what Louise had seen.

'A police car?'

'A police car at the end of the street. Parked there for fifteen minutes. But look, like you asked me, this mustn't go any further. She's a frail old lady. She's had a tough time these last, well, fifteen years,' said Jacques.

'Agoraphobic. She can't leave the building for anything?'

'The apartment. She's a prisoner. Gets her food delivered. Looks out of the window and sees the rest of the world moving along, and she can't join it,' said Jacques. Celestine shook her head.

'Jesus. And she's reliable? About the police car, she wouldn't make that up?' asked Celestine.'

'Not a chance. She's an intelligent woman. It's a bloody shame.'

'I won't say a word,' said Celestine. They were both silent again, digging deep into their own thoughts.

Finally, Jacques broke the silence. 'So we've got a dead Vietnamese. At least two Vietnamese at the place where Armand was working. What's the link, Capitaine? What is the

Vietnamese connection?' Celestine started to speak and then stopped herself. She nearly mentioned the link between her husband and the Vietnamese mob boss. But she wasn't ready to sweep that into the same pile yet. She wanted to follow that uneasy thread herself. Jacques noticed the hesitation.

'There are Vietnamese gangs in Bordeaux, as in all the cities in France,' she said.

'I guess I knew that, but I've never really come across them. What is their main area of interest?' asked Jacques.

'Drugs, people trafficking, guns, protection, prostitution,' said Celestine.

'No kindergartens then?' said Jacques.

Celestine snorted, 'No, no kindergartens,' she said. 'They're very violent, often with their own people. They're quite discreet in their dealings.'

'Decent of them,' said Jacques. Then suddenly he remembered something. 'Yeah, I nearly forgot. The trailer at the building. The name started with a big Z. Name of a company?'

'Zubizaretta,' said Celestine.

'Footballer?'

'I think not. I'll look into it. I want to look inside that building,' she said.

'Can't you? Can't you raid it or something, blue lights flashing?'

'It's not as simple as that,' admitted Celestine. 'I'm just a capitaine. Things like that have to be authorised higher up, and right now I don't have a lot of goodwill towards me.'

'I thought your husband was a big chief,' said Jacques, and saw the sudden glint and pain in her eyes.

'I don't do that,' she said simply. Jacques raised his hands in apology.

'Ok, but do you have any idea what is going on here? Dead Vietnamese. Is this a gang warfare thing do you think?

I want to find out what happened to Armand, but I don't really want to land in the middle of two groups of karate-kicking, knife-wielding, oriental gangs. Forgive the stereotyping,' said Jacques.

'I honestly don't know, Jacques. I didn't tell you; the Vietnamese guy, he disappeared from police custody. I'm going to try to get to the bottom of that this morning.'

'And then he's dead.' Jacques looked grim. 'And there's a police car parked by the end of the street where his body's found. This feels mucky.' He glowered at her. 'I don't want to say, I told you so.'

'Just leave it off with your mucky police. If there are any bent flics, it'll be only one or two.'

'Two at least,' said Jacques.

'Ok. But I'm not going overboard with this.' She glared at him angrily, her face taut and flushed.

'That's it,' said Jacques. 'Why did he go overboard? Why leave his ship? Just for a new life in France, or to get away from something. Why was he killed if he was just an illegal immigrant?'

'I've thought of that. He must have seen or known something.'

'Perhaps that was the same for Armand,' said Jacques, and the light went out of his face.

'We need to know what is in that building, and maybe what the ship was carrying,' Celestine said and started making notes on the pad. Jacques watched the long quick fingers as they wrote, and then spread themselves out like a fan as she paused to think.

'Do you have any leather gear, Celestine?' Jacques asked. Celestine finished what she was writing and then turned to him with raised eyebrows.

'What exactly are you asking me, Monsieur Lecoubarry?' she said, half smiling.

'Just if you have any motorcycle leathers, you know, a jacket, trousers?' He smiled. 'What did you think I meant?'

'No, I don't. Can we get back to this?'

Jacques nodded. 'I just thought. We could visit that building ourselves. Maybe quieter during the day. If we went on the motorbike it's easier to park, it's more discreet, you can go across fields even, if necessary. Not as obvious as a car.'

'Go together, on your motorbike?' she asked.

'Exactly.'

Celestine appeared to think about this for a second. 'Or I could go myself, in a police car. I have a badge. I can ask them to open the door.'

'Without a warrant, they wouldn't open it, would they? And then you'd get shot. And that would be a nuisance for me,' said Jacques.

'A nuisance. Well, I wouldn't want that,'

Celestine said. 'Look, I have to go. I'll see what happens when I get in to work. See if I can get some leverage.'

'We could go to the port, too. See what that ship was carrying,' suggested Jacques. 'I have a spare leather jacket.' Celestine looked at him sceptically. 'Not mine,' he said hurriedly. 'It belonged to my ex-wife, Simone.' He appeared to measure her up. 'She's shorter than you and the terrain is more mountainous, but I think it would fit. It gets cold on the bike, even in the sunshine.'

Celestine stood up and looked at him, frankly. 'You know, maybe it's me, but I swear I only understand fifty per cent of what you're saying.'

'Fifty per cent. That's good in the early stages,' replied Jacques. 'Just wait until you've known me for a few weeks, your average will rise considerably. Ninety per cent has been recorded.'

Celestine laughed and shook her head. 'You take care, Jacques Lecoubarry,' she said. 'I'll be in touch. I'll see if I can find Meslier for you.' She turned to go.

'You take care, my Capitaine. There seems to be a lot of muck around. You keep your boots on.'

Chapter 30

In the conference room in the commissariat, Commandant Martel glared at Celestine as she walked in, but said nothing. Camille Dubois glanced quickly towards her then turned away again. Jean Sorbot was standing by the board.

'Stabbed. Fifteen-centimetre blade. Bled out quickly, the path said. Dead when he was dumped. Probably around midnight. Techs have got a couple of things. Take time to get the results. No signs of a struggle.' Sorbot sat down.

Dubois moved to the board. 'Nobody saw or heard anything, except one old guy who thought he heard, quote; "bin lids being violated", he assumed by a fox. Complained we should be taking foxes more seriously. Personally, I do.' There was a light ripple of laughter.

'What time?' asked Martel.

'About midnight. Lives down the Rue de la Sau a little way.'

Commandant Martel walked over to the board. 'Anyone got anything else?' he demanded.

'Ho Thi Quan. That's most likely his name. But I have some checking to do,' Celestine said loudly. Martel stopped moving and stared at her. He started to speak but she continued. 'If this is our guy, he was in police custody yesterday afternoon. And then he disappeared. Nobody let him out and nobody saw him go. Although, we know that can't happen.'

Martel strode over and stood in front of her. 'You want to talk to me about this in my office? I don't know what you're ranting about.'

'No,' said Celestine calmly. 'I'm happy to talk about it here, because there's some action needed.' She walked over to the board. 'I'd like someone to go through all the CCTV in the cells and other parts of the station for yesterday afternoon; from about three in the afternoon onwards. We're looking for a short guy in a yellow T-shirt and anybody who was with him.' She glared at Martel defiantly.

The Commandant walked right up to her. 'My office, now,' he said.

She leaned around him and looked at the other team members. Dubois looked shocked, Jean Sorbot concerned, Leger looked amused and Predeau, embarrassed, was making notes.

'He was an illegal immigrant, he escaped from a ship at Le Grave. Not a druggy or a gangster. Brought here by two police officers of this force – Frezouls and Pinet. They need to be interviewed. Disappeared and was brutally killed. Questions?'

Martel pushed her physically away from the board. 'That's enough, Courbet, I said. My office. I won't have you spreading that stuff around. Your duty is to inform me of any information that you think is relevant to these cases.'

'I just did,' said Celestine, and strode out of the room. Martel came out immediately behind her. They went into his office and he slammed the door behind him.

'Don't you ever show that level of insubordination to me, Courbet. I don't care who your fucking husband is,' he shouted at her.

'This has nothing to do with my fucking husband, as you call him. This has to do with how a man held in custody, in a police cell, here in this building, suddenly ends up dead in an alley in the old town?' She looked at Martel, her mouth set firmly. Martel appeared as though he could detonate at any moment, but she could see that he was calculating, running the possibilities through his head. 'Armand Verville was killed downriver. I think I know where he was working. We should go there now,' she said, defiantly. Martel now looked shocked, as though she had gone so far she was now well out of reach.

'Verville was killed by a drug dealer in Aubier. He was brought in this morning. If you'd been here on time you would have known that,' said Martel, his voice hard as flint.

'That's bollocks,' retorted Celestine, all caution now cast to the wind. 'He wasn't a druggy, he was a metal worker. He was working illegally, somewhere down the estuary. His body was thrown into the tide. I have expert testimony. That's why he was washed up where he was. So that's bollocks.' They were now standing only a metre apart, both glaring at each other like fighting cocks.

'You're off the case. Both murder cases. You're finished with them. There's been a violent robbery up in Chartron. That's your poncy neck of the woods, isn't it? That's your case. Step out of line anymore and I'll suspend you. Get out.' Celestine opened the door and stepped out into the corridor and then leaned back into the room.

'If you don't investigate these two murders properly, Commandant Martel, I will torment you.' She stormed away and walked along the corridor to her own office. Within a few minutes, Camille Dubois walked warily into the room. She was carrying a thin brown file, which she laid on the desk.

'Robbery in Chartron,' she said. Celestine sat down. She didn't say anything for a few moments as she tried to control her breathing. When she did look up at Dubois she couldn't trust herself to speak. They stayed like that for half a minute; Dubois caught between justifying herself and walking out. Finally, Celestine picked up the file and handed it towards Dubois.

'Put that on Leger's desk. He's too flippant to get involved in murder. And I've got two of them to solve,' she said.

Dubois shrugged. 'I was told to give it to you.'

'And I'm telling you what to do with it. Now, unless you have something to add, perhaps to show some concern that we have two murder victims now and the whole posse is being sent in the wrong direction. No? Then piss off and close the door. And you can call that through to Martel if you wish.' Dubois walked out without the file and closed the door. Celestine realised that she was trembling. She felt as though she was standing on the top of a volcanic plug and she could sense the ground grumbling under her, feel the heat building up and see the tell-tale wisps of steam. Yes, she thought, the earth beneath her feet was definitely heating up and moving, and she couldn't see that there was anywhere safe to stand.

Chapter 31

Divisional Commissaire Vaillancourt enjoyed the nights more than the mornings at the home of his mistress. When he saw Bahn in the mornings she seemed even younger, just out of childhood, and that's when the guilt nagged him most. And she was slovenly away from the programme of lovemaking. Parts of the apartment were squalid, as though she hadn't yet grown into the responsibilities or the habits of adulthood. The kitchen was dirty and the food for breakfast was cheap and junky. Even the coffee was bitter and coarse. She rarely rose when he did, sometimes, he knew, she slept through until midday. This morning though she came into the kitchen as he was making coffee. She perched on one of the high stools, her short silk gown so loosely tied that when she moved he could see a strip of her body from her throat to the top of her legs. He stared at it for a few moments.

'She knows now, my wife. She knows I sleep somewhere else,' he said. 'She suspects, no, she knows I'm with another woman. She doesn't know it's you. A woman.'

'Now you are not so careful,' she said. He sat next to her, his knee touching her thigh.

'No, you're probably right. But she is not responsive.' He stopped himself. Even at this low ebb he wasn't prepared to blame Celestine. He shook his head. 'No, it is me. I want to spend every night with you,' he said, and ran his finger down the side of her face.

'Every night, then you get tired of me. Then you get tired,' she laughed coarsely.

'She knows about Monsieur Nguyen. Knows I have meetings with him. Knows about the sailor, even knows I interviewed him. She's a good detective, my wife. She is a very good detective. She won't drop it. She'll keep worrying it like a dog with a rat,' he sneered and his eyes became harsh and petulant. 'She won't let it go.'

Bahn stood up, deliberately letting her gown open completely, and she climbed up to straddle Vaillancourt on his stool. She wrapped her arms around his neck and placed her head on his shoulder so that he couldn't see her face. He put his hands around her back under her gown and pulled her body tightly to him.

'You are a witch, Bahn. I would do anything for you,' he said.

Later, sitting in his car, away from the enchantment, he wondered if there was a route through all of this, a route that would bring him out into a sunlit valley below. But he couldn't see it at this juncture. He was committed, his very existence was indentured to this dark bargain. The woman, the exquisite woman, and the money, more and more money. It was life-changing money; money to take him light years away from the claustrophobic, small-town pettiness, drabness and self-conceit of the place where he had grown up. A million kilometres also from the dull existence of a pensioned civil servant with another ten years to go in an office, followed by retirement to a neat bungalow in Arcachon, with a wife who was drooping and crabby. But now it was getting really desperate and dangerous and evil, and somehow he had been able to disavow these things in his magical thinking. He had thought he was prepared for the ruthlessness, the callousness and the violence, but he wasn't. He knew at heart he was still that middle-class, parochial son of a school teacher. He had boundaries and limits but they had none. And that was how they could control him, always, because they would gladly go way beyond any limit that he thought existed. They didn't care. He heard the words of Nguyen again. "I will open up the world for you, but first you must open up the throats of three men." Well, his world had certainly opened up, but there were cracks appearing and he was getting scared, very, very scared.

When Vaillancourt reached his office, Commandant Martel was almost immediately at his door. They spoke together in private for fifteen minutes. Martel left and Vaillancourt leaned back in his chair, pondering. Now is the time to think very clearly, he said to himself. He placed a notebook on the desk in front of him and picked up the phone.

Celestine had forced herself to calm down and to focus. Firstly, she started researching the Z and the business of Monsieur Zubizaretta: metal bashing, steel stockholders, and heavy machinery agents. She ran through the details on their website and read a couple of articles that showed up in her search. Their activities seemed fairly widespread in France, and in other countries in Europe. She knew enough to know that a website can look like anything you want it to, it can be part of, or the whole story, or a complete camouflage. Although Linh had told her that Zubizaretta had been present at the "special" dinner the previous Thursday night, what she couldn't see was the link to Nguyen and the activities of the Vietnamese gangs. There was a picture of Zubizaretta grinning out from the web page, below him was an anodyne advertisement describing the care and concern the company displayed for their customers, their workers and the environment. He looks like a little thug, thought Celestine. She tried to imagine the dinner with Nguyen, her husband and this tough-looking, heavy metal industrialist. What could they be discussing? What were the links? She could see the patterns, she just couldn't link it all up yet. Then her phone rang and one of the guests at the feast was on the line.

'Capitaine Courbet. Would you come to my office, please? Now,' Vaillancourt said formally. Before Celestine had time to answer, the phone was dead. She collected her notebook but turned over the top page. Now, they were on official ground and she would behave as a responsible, respectful member of the force. At least initially. He had showered and looked smart in his Saint Laurent shirt with the Van Cleef and Arpels cufflinks. Although his eyes still looked a little red and puffy, he had restored himself from the mess he had been the last time she'd seen him. He didn't smile but nodded towards the chair.

'There are a number of items on the agenda this morning, Capitaine, but the most serious, and the one we must deal with first, is the insubordination you have shown to your superior officer and the reckless and unfounded accusations you have been hurling about. Things that should have been discussed with the Commandant before you exposed yourself in front of the whole team of detectives.' Celestine kept silent but continued to look straight at him. As she didn't speak he went on. 'Commandant Martel is well within his rights, it would be standard procedure, to institute some form of disciplinary proceedings at this juncture.' He held up his hand. 'I have persuaded him not to do so, not to suspend you. I explained that you are under a lot of stress.' Celestine flicked her tongue between her teeth and raised her eyebrows a little. 'That you have been working very hard. And he has agreed to lessen your workload at this time. I understand he has allocated you a burglary case to deal with; violent, but thankfully not resulting in death. And just around the corner from our apartment, as it happens.' Again Celestine remained silent. 'So please, just keep out of Martel's way for a few days. Do a good job on this robbery and let the rest of the team handle these murders.' He looked for her acquiescence, but there was something about the stubbornness of her silence and the hardness of her look that he knew she was taking none of it on board. 'For Christ's sake, Celestine. Do you want to be suspended? Do you know what that will do to your career? Just step away for a few days, a week or so. Even take some time off. Please, for your sake.'

'You said there were other items on the agenda,' Celestine said coldly. He turned over a page of his notebook and his eyes darkened.

'All right. They are related to the above, but to be more specific, the murder of the man found in the estuary on Saturday - Armand Verville. A man was arrested this morning. A known and major drug dealer operating out of Les Aubiers. A witness saw Verville with this man. A weapon has been found at this man's flat, which has traces of blood, hair and, I am told, brain matter. They are waiting for a match to the victim, but that shouldn't take long.'

Celestine couldn't help laughing scornfully. 'That is one careless murderer,' she said. 'Presumably, he lives near the river and yet he didn't think to throw this "weapon" in after the body.'

'They are careless, Celestine. You know that. A drug addict. What do you expect?'

'What do I expect?' she paused. 'Well, I expect professionalism, honesty, and care for a start. Armand Verville's body was dumped in the estuary between Valeyrac and Talais. That's where he was working. I know where he worked. We should be searching there now. That is what I expect.'

Vaillancourt rapped his pen on the desk top. 'That's exactly what I'm talking about. Random, unfounded ideas. Where are you getting this information from?' She caught the sudden tightness in his eyes.

'And the second murder,' she asked calmly.

'Yes, this Vietnamese. We'll make enquiries of course. See what happened to him when he left here. We'll make some enquiries, not you. You're too…'

'Female, about it,' she snapped.

'Too unhinged, too passionate, too unruly,' he said.

'Etienne. There was a police car seen at the entrance to the Rue de la Sau, at around midnight, when the report suggested the body was dumped there. A police car, two officers from this building. Is that a coincidence? Is that unhinged?'

'That is unhinged. How could you possibly know that?' Vaillancourt demanded, his voice getting higher and thinner.

'Because they were seen, by an old lady looking out of her window.' The moment she said it, she bit her tongue. She saw the change come over her husband. For a split second, he glanced out of the window, over the stone orchard of the Chartreuse Cemetery.

'Well then. I heard there were no useful sightings. Who is this old lady? Where does she live? We'll send someone to interview her properly. How did you know by the way?' Celestine shook her head. He waited, pen poised over the pad on his desk. 'Name, address. You can see why there is now a credibility question hanging over you, Celestine.'

'I don't know the name or address. It came from a source. A reliable source,' Celestine said evenly.
Vaillancourt sneered.

'A reliable source. The same reliable source that told you that things, bodies, flow up the river, not down as we've thought all along.' He waved his pen at her. 'You won't have another chance, Celestine. Take it. Take it with both hands. I'm sorry things have been tough with us in the last few weeks.'

'Months.'

'Months then. But you have to see, most of this is down to the way this job has got to you. It's twisting you inside out. You're never calm. Never balanced.'

Celestine's face hardened and her eyes blazed. 'Are we finished, Sir?' she said. 'I believe there has been a robbery in Chartron. There's a lot of criminal behaviour now in Chartron, I've noticed. Yes, it's very close to home.' She stood up and walked out. Vaillancourt's head sagged on his shoulders. He picked up the telephone.

Chapter 32

The old town of Bordeaux has had such a rich and varied past, from the Romans to medieval times to the great surges in the eighteenth century, that everywhere there are hints, some obvious, some coy, of its great history. Jacques Lecoubarry had learned to read this urban landscape over the years. His freelance wandering still saw him placing his hands on the stones of a decapitated portion of the town's fourteenth century walls or found him staring upwards, shielding his eyes from the sun, and marvelling at a fine piece of stonework on the high façade of a building. Still, after thirty years, he refused to become complacent and he could still take pleasure and find interest in the city. So many of the places held memories and associations for him. He was standing by the Monument aux Girondins and trying to follow the line of all the limbs of the mythological beasts, the careering horses with their fishtails and all the extravagant creatures in the undergrowth below the statues. It came to him that it was here that he had finally accepted the end of his marriage to Simone. There had been something in the unruly twisting of the figures, embracing and contorting, that helped him recognise the contortions they were both going through to try to hold on to something that had broken loose. This was where he had become reconciled to it. So, it was a symbolic place for him; the symbol of something ending, but perhaps also of a beginning? He could feel something surging in his spirit, like a new drug that was not only relieving symptoms but was also spiking new cells into growth. And now he knew where Lionel Meslier lived. The man was a wraith. Jacques had asked in all the bars and cafés where he thought he had seen him in the past. No one could even put a face to a name. He seemed to have slid in and out of places without registering a note. But one name came up twice in his brief conversations - that of Albert Mandel.

That was a name that Jacques did know, and he had a fair idea of where to find him - that was if he hadn't changed his rat run in recent times. If you could string a net across a number of the narrower thoroughfares around the edge of the old town, Jacques thought, you'd definitely find him wriggling in the mesh when you came to draw in your catch. Failing that option, he decided to position himself at the neck end of the area and hope to spot him as he entered or left the zone. He sat outside a small, traditional café, with his sketch pad, and settled to wait; although he had an uneasy feeling that he was wasting his time and should really be working his way through the backlog of jobs building up in his workshop. A quick phone call from the ungrateful Celestine Courbet, saying; "Here's the address, found instantly on our citizen-watch system. He's at home now, watching daytime television, blue door, Yale lock, in arrears for his rent, problem with his kidneys". But nothing, and perhaps Meslier was a ghost in their system too, or perhaps she had bigger problems to face down.

He sat for over an hour, and the early lunch crowd were starting to fill up the tables and the waiters would soon become restless. Then he saw him, or at least recognised the shape of his walk. The man made short uneven steps, where his left foot seemed to extend less far forward than his right one so that every four or five steps he had to extend his left leg substantially to get back on the line he wanted to follow. It gave him a strange, crab-like gait. He was quite short and thin, and his shoulders were tucked up as though he was expecting something to fall on him from a height at any moment. Jacques spotted him walking towards him, his eyes on the ground and his hands clenched. Jacques took the twenty euro note from his pocket and stepped quickly from his seat into the man's path. The reaction was instant, the man tensed and glanced away, as if looking for an escape route, before he looked up at Jacques. There was a slight relaxation in his eyes but he remained wary. Jacques held the note up in front of him and the man's hand shot out like a lizard's tongue at a fly.

'Bonjour, Albert. A simple request, nothing to delay you long. Join me for a coffee,' Jacques said, while taking hold of one arm and gently forcing him towards his table. The man sat on the edge of the chair and looked down. 'You know me,' said Jacques. The man looked up and nodded.

'Antique furniture, Rue Carpentyre.' The words squeezed out of the thin slit of his mouth had no tone at all.

'That's right. I restore antique furniture, and I need a metal worker to repair a frame on one of the pieces. My usual guy is not available, but I was given the name of Lionel Meslier. Problem is, I don't know where to find him, where he works or lives.' Mandel's expression didn't change and he continued to look at the floor. Jacques had the impression that somewhere, behind the thin, drawn face, there was a mind, and it was like an old-fashioned filing system. Something in the man's head was leafing through ledgers, tracing files and flicking through an index until he could draw out the relevant card with the details on it. Albert Mandel was a runner and a stooge. He took information and other items from one place to another, and he gathered up snippets of gossip and facts like a sheep gathers burrs. Facts and information which he sold, sometimes weeks or months down the line. His memory, and the extent of his knowledge of just a few quartiers in Bordeaux, was legendary.

'Lives with his daughter. Want me to tell him you got work? Give me your card,' he said finally.

'No. I don't want anyone to speak to him first. I don't want him putting his rates up. I want to see for myself how he's fixed. Just want the address. I'll go there myself,' said Jacques.

Mandel thought for a moment.

'Fifty,' he said.

'Jesus, that's steep. I already gave you twenty,' said Jacques.

'I don't give change,' he replied. 'I know the building, need to check on the number. Meet me at the Girondins in an hour.' He stood up. For the first time, he looked Jacques in the eye. 'We good?' he asked.

'Good,' replied Jacques, and Mandel was gone.

And now, just over an hour later, Jacques had the information he needed, handed to him on a strip of brown paper in exchange for fifty euros. It was in his hand and the money removed in seconds. Albert Mandel was a model of efficiency in his particular line of work.

Chapter 33

Linh slipped quietly out of the front door of the restaurant. Her hand trembled with the lock and she glanced nervously around. Outside, she walked away quickly, down the narrow street that led to the main road. "On the corner, by the boulangerie, in the place where the buses stop". She looked quickly up and down the road. There didn't seem to be anyone looking at her, or interested in what she was doing. Ever since she had received that call from her cousin she had felt prickly, as though her nerve endings were being scraped by some watching force that knew she was stepping out of line. She hadn't really thought about her cousin or even thought that she cared about him until he had called her. Now it seemed the most important thing, he seemed the most important thing, a link back to her past and her family. But it wasn't simple. She had heard snatches of conversations. Vinh had appeared at the restaurant, and she had seen him talking intensely to Kim and seen them glaring in her direction. Monsieur Nguyen had arrived. He was always polite but he carried with him a coldness that sometimes chilled Linh to her roots, and she could see that he was angry. Nobody talked about the cousin and nor did she. But she thought about him all the time.

She walked as quickly as she could along the street, keeping close to the buildings, as though it was safer there. She hesitated when she saw the car parked by the boulangerie. It felt like a point of no return. But really she had passed that point when she had gone to the police station in the first place.

She walked past the car and turned the corner into the side street. She stopped, moved closer to the edge and peered across at the car. There was only the woman there, the one with the dark hair and the fierce eyes and the kind way. Linh took a deep breath and walked over to the car, opened the door and climbed inside. The woman looked unsurprised. She had the air of knowing and controlling everything around her. She smiled at Linh and laid a hand on her arm.

'This is better,' she said. 'I didn't want to call on you at your work.'

'Yes, much better,' said Linh, and sat back, leaving Celestine to control everything.

'I'm going to drive a little way and then I need to talk to you seriously. Ok?' said Celestine. The girl nodded. She could smell the woman's perfume in the car, it smelled subtle and expensive and somehow it gave her confidence.

'You have found Quan?' she asked.

Celestine just held up her hand. 'I'll tell you when we stop,' she said.

They drove for ten minutes through the stop-go Bordeaux traffic, until Celestine pulled into a car park by a large concrete building. She switched off the engine. Linh knew now that what she was going to hear was not good. She had sensed that in the silence, in the lack of the normal pleasantries. French people were very polite when you met them; always bonjour, always au revoir, bonne journée. Polite. Celestine unclipped her seat belt and turned to face her.

'Linh, I may have some very bad news for you,' said Celestine slowly. Linh gasped despite herself. 'We have found a body, you understand, a dead man. I'm afraid it might be your cousin Quan.'

'Dead man,' Linh repeated. 'Quan?' Celestine nodded.

'I think so. But Linh, I need you to identify him for me. That will be difficult. I will be with you. You will have to look at the face of the dead man and tell me if it is your cousin Quan. Can you do that for me?'

Linh didn't know. Didn't know what she could do or not do, but it didn't seem to matter now. There was always a hollowness inside her, and it was swelling, and she thought it might consume her completely. So it didn't matter what she did. You tell me what I can do. I can do what you tell me. She nodded at Celestine. 'Yes, I can,' she said.

They walked into the building, along white, sterile corridors that smelt of the disinfectant they put down the drains in the kitchen in the restaurant. It smelled coarse and pungent and it caught at the back of her throat. Celestine led her into one of the small rooms and they stood behind a glass screen. A young orderly stood by a steel table, a metre from the window, waiting for Celestine's instructions. She looked across at the girl. Linh was standing stock still, rigid but calm, intent, staring at the covered body on the table. Celestine nodded to the orderly, who pulled the covers down, leaving the head and shoulders in view. Celestine looked again at the girl who was still staring intently, but there was a look of puzzlement on her face.

'Linh,' said Celestine gently. 'Can you identify your cousin?' It wasn't her cousin of course. It was the dead shell of something that had been her cousin. He wasn't there now. He was memories and childhood laughter and big talk. He wasn't this lifeless carapace. 'Linh,' asked Celestine again. The girl turned to her and nodded once. 'You are sure?' pressed Celestine.

'Sure,' said Linh calmly. 'This was my cousin, now he is dead.'

Celestine took her by the arm and led her up some stairs to another floor in the hospital, where there was a small café for the staff and visitors. She ordered two coffees and brought them over to a quiet table by the window. Linh hadn't spoken since they'd left the morgue.

'I am so very, very, sorry, Linh,' said Celestine, and placed her hand on top of the girl's. 'This is a terrible thing and you have been very brave and strong. Strong for your cousin.' The girl withdrew her hand and placed it around her cup of coffee.

'Why?' she asked. 'He was a good man.'

'I'm sure he was,' said Celestine, 'and that is why I am going to find out what happened to him. I think you can help me. Tell me about him, Linh. Help me to see who he was.' Linh talked, slowly at first, and then more fluently, about the cousin she had known in Vietnam; older, but always funny and kind to her.

'How long was he a sailor?' Celestine asked.

'Maybe ten years. Always he wants to be a sailor. See the whole wide world. See the whole goddam world, he said.'

'And did he? See a lot of the world?'

'Oh yes. America, Chile, China.'

'But not Europe?' asked Celestine.

'Only this time I think. This is the first time. He wanted to see Europe, Paris. So he changed company. I didn't hear for maybe two years, more. Then, suddenly, he called. It was night, during the night. He spoke quietly, not usual, not joking, not saying funny things. Quiet. "Linh I'm coming to France. I'm coming to see you. Live there in France". I thought he was joking, but he was not, that night. He was very serious. I said, "Why, why now"? He didn't say. But he sounded sad, anxious, not usual for him. "Ok", I said. "Call me when you are here". "I will Linh. I will, I go now". And I didn't hear more for weeks. Then he called. "I am here. I have escaped", he said. "I am in Leluc". I don't know where it is. "You must come and get me. You must help me now". I told you, I went there, but he was gone, in a police car. Now he is dead.' She stopped talking then. She looked drawn from speaking so much, and now there were tears. She drank down her coffee, and when she looked up at Celestine her eyes were wet and angry. 'Police don't keep him safe. I don't trust police.'

Celestine nodded. 'I understand, I understand. I don't trust some of them myself at this time. But look, Linh, I will find out what happened, and those responsible will be brought to justice. I know that isn't much consolation for you right now, but…'

'I can trust you?' Linh demanded and looked up.

'Yes, you can. I promise.'

'You will find who killed him?' Celestine nodded. They sat in silence for several minutes. Celestine was surprised that the girl hadn't broken down. She seemed to be holding herself well, she appeared to be more angry than sad.

'Linh. At the special dinner last Thursday, you said Monsieur Zubizarreta was there. Did you hear what he was saying?' Linh thought for a minute.

'No. He is difficult to understand. He has an accent. He is a nong dan, a peasant, no, a pig. I don't like.'

'And Commissaire Vaillancourt?' Celestine couldn't help herself. 'Did you like him?' The girl glanced up quickly at Celestine.

'He was very polite, very quiet,' she said. Celestine smiled.

'And Monsieur Nguyen?' She saw the girl stiffen.

'Very important man, very rich man, powerful.'

'Dangerous?'

'Yes. Very dangerous. Very dangerous man.' The girl actually looked around the room, as though he could be standing there, or one of his henchmen.

'Linh,' Celestine persisted, 'I need to know what Monsieur Nguyen and Monsieur Zubizarreta do together. What their business is together, you understand.' The girl looked doubtful. 'It may have nothing to do with your cousin, but there has been another murder; a man was killed who may have been working for Zubizarreta. There are other people feeling very sad and angry in Bordeaux today, because of this.' And a picture of a tall, angry, complicated man, with the head of an ancient hero, came to her mind with a warmth she hadn't expected. 'Yes, there are other people who need answers. You may be able to help me get them. But,' she added hurriedly. 'You must not take any risks. If you hear anything, and you can let me know safely, that's good. But only if you can keep safe. Now, let me take you back to the restaurant. I'll drop you at the end of the street.'

Linh stood up, she seemed only partly there and partly in another place. Celestine suddenly felt guilty. Perhaps she shouldn't get her involved, shouldn't put her in danger. But there were fine margins and sometimes small things could tip it over to your side of the net.

Chapter 34

'I've never stepped into the past, before,' said Celestine, as the door closed behind her and she took in the jumble of dusty furniture jammed together and cowering from the twenty-first century in Jacques' workshop. Jacques grinned.

'You must have done. We slip in and out of it all the time. You walk through a few streets in Bordeaux and you're inches from it. It's like a wind-borne lens - we see things through it, it colours our views...' He stopped. She was looking at him strangely.

'You've thought about this a lot, haven't you?' she said.

'Mm. I have. Perhaps I have become attuned to the past.' He lifted his hand to his ear, then burst out laughing and shook Celestine's hand. 'My emporium is blessed by your presence,' he said, grinning all the while.

'I don't know about that,' replied Celestine, but couldn't help herself from smiling. 'And you live here also?' she asked.

'Upstairs, first and second floor.'

'And is it furnished in eighteenth, nineteenth century style?'

'Pretty much. Some of the best pieces saved over a lot of years. I do have a Wurlitzer jukebox from the 1950s and a 60s wall lamp by Florian Schulz.'

'Wow. Almost within living memory,' said Celestine.

They stood looking at each other for several moments, uncertain whether the banter had gone too far. Jacques was strangely embarrassed, which was something he rarely experienced. Celestine put her hands on the surface of a small table, its surface covered in an intricate pattern of flowers and scrolls. She looked more closely.

'This is beautiful,' she said. 'What do you call it? Is it very old?'

'Marquetry. It's a card table from the early nineteenth century, Louis XV style. The marquetry is about two weeks old.'

'Two weeks?' She looked at him, expecting to see him laughing.

'Yes. It's not finished. There's still the final polishing. It was a devil to match. Only a small section of the original was intact.'

'Just a minute. You made this. This marquetry.'

Jacques nodded. 'That's why I have to slip back into earlier centuries sometimes, to ensure the authenticity.' Celestine ran her fingers over the work.

'I didn't realise. I didn't think it was… artistry that you did. It's so delicate.' She looked up at Jacques, frowning. 'Just when I think I have a handle on you, Jacques Lecoubarry, you surprise me and turn into somebody else.'

'A shape-shifter. That's what a friend calls me.'

'Mm. Tricky though, you're definitely tricky,' said Celestine.

'Not to a brilliant detective like you. You must be a good reader of people,' said Jacques.

'I used to think so, Jacques. I can usually tell when someone is lying, or embellishing or avoiding. But I seem to have misjudged quite a lot of people in the last few weeks or maybe it's months.'

Jacques studied the tension lines on her face and for a second there was pain and uncertainty there. And then it faded and the fierce strength came back.

'Your motorbike's not from the nineteenth century is it?' she asked. Jacques faced her and frowned.

'Let me tell you. My motorcycle is a Peugeot 515. It won the Grand Prix, Motorbike of the Year in 1933. Best in class.'

'You are kidding me,' retorted Celestine, looking appalled.

Jacques laughed. 'Yes, oh yes. It runs on two stroke leaded petrol and old cognac, and it is recommended to keep a chicken strapped to the pannier at all times.' He stepped closer, placed a hand on her arm and bent down to look up at her. 'Actually, it's a BMW, S1000. Four years old.' Jacques clapped his hands. 'Come on, let's get you kitted out.'

Celestine shook her head, wondering why, in a matter of days, her life had turned unrecognisable from what she was used to before. She was determined to see for herself the place where Armand Verville worked, and had called Jacques after she had left Linh at the end of her street. She had made a quick visit to the scene of the robbery at Chartron, made some notes and spoken to the forensic guys. The victims were still in hospital so she had decided to leave those interviews for later. Then she'd called at the apartment to change before driving to Rue Carpentyre. And now she was wearing a black leather jacket that was a little short and decidedly roomy in front.

'Girl on a motorcycle,' Jacques said approvingly.

'I want to go to the port first. I want to know what the ship was carrying, to see if there is any link to what is in the building.'

'Understood,' said Jacques. 'One thing, Celestine. Just so I know. You are armed, aren't you? That is a real gun.'

'Yes, and a badge. This is official, even if the transporter isn't.'

'Joking aside. People like this, they don't mess around.'

'Nor do I,' said Celestine fiercely.

It took longer than Celestine expected to reach the Autonomous Port, a hundred kilometres away, almost at the very point of the Medoc peninsular. But once she got used to it, it was quite calming sitting behind the broad back of the man in front, arms wrapped loosely around him. He certainly sheltered her from the wind, and she could even lean her helmeted head against his shoulders. There wasn't much point in trying to talk, as the engine roared back against the wind, so she had time to think. In her own mind, she was gathering enough evidence to swing peoples' opinions her way. If she could take something concrete back to the incident room, something they couldn't possibly ignore or dispute, then she would be vindicated, the threat of suspension would be lifted and the whole team could follow the right direction and catch those responsible for the two murders.

But there was still the uncertainty; the police car at the murder scene, the removal of the sailor from the Hotel de Police. And what of the link between her husband and a Vietnamese mobster? It was horribly murky, mucky the man in front had called it. Could you ever get clean after this? Could you ever untangle yourself from such complexities or would there always be traces left, like sand found in a bag six months after you'd visited the beach?

She sat up straight. She could see the estuary and could smell the ozone in the wind. Jacques pulled the bike over to the side and stopped. He turned his head towards her, they were so close, but the heavy clothes and the helmets made it seem as though they were on either side of a thick screen.

'Go straight up to the gate. They'll have to let me in, with the badge. You stay outside if you want, or they may wave you through.' Jacques nodded.

They rode alongside a high chain link fence for several hundred metres. However did that poor sailor get out of there, she wondered? At the gate, she dismounted, took off her helmet and shook out her hair. There was a barrier across the entrance and a box where two security guards were watching her with interest. Jacques smiled as their attention changed from casual to intense, to where they almost saluted her. An arm came out of the glass box and pointed towards a building inside the complex. Celestine waved back towards Jacques and he saw a head nodding rapidly. She walked back to the bike. Jacques was sure the badge helped, but the lady has some power, he thought. Inside the building, Celestine was taken to the office of the Senior Controller. She explained what information she required.

'Is the ship still here?' she asked.

'Departed yesterday, five a.m.'

'For where?' The controller referred back to his computer.

'Rotterdam.'

'So a cargo was unloaded here. Do you have a record of what that cargo was?' She saw he was chewing his lips nervously.

'There is a record, yes,' he replied. 'It's really a matter for customs, you know. But we need to keep records. Statistics.'

'Yes, I understand. So, what was unloaded and in what quantity?'

The man looked anxious. 'I shouldn't really say. Records are confidential.' Celestine stood up and leaned over the desk towards him.

'Monsieur. Nothing is confidential in a murder investigation. A man left that ship, walked through your security and ended up dead in Bordeaux. I am investigating that murder and I expect and demand full cooperation from you. Previous protocols go out of the window and obstructing an investigation is very, very serious.' She watched the slight stubbornness tightening in his eyes. 'This morning I viewed the body of the poor man. I went there with his cousin, a young woman who is mourning his death. Now I will ask you once more, before I pull the handle, what was unloaded from that ship?'

The controller looked back at his computer. 'Twelve containers,' he said quietly.

'I want a printout of what was in them and who collected them. Can you print that out for me?'

The man nodded. Within minutes Celestine could hear the clatter of a printer in the room next door. The man walked out and came back with two sheets and handed them to Celestine. She scanned them quickly.

'Thank you, Monsieur De Plessis. I appreciate your cooperation. Is there anything else you can tell me about the ship and about how the sailor escaped from this compound? I presume it's fenced all the way round.' The man nodded.

'Yes. Cut through the wire, late Saturday night. We didn't know anything about it until the ship told us someone was missing. Then we found the hole in the fence.'

'Who did you call?' asked Celestine.

'The local police initially. We assumed he'd be found nearby and brought back quickly. Dash for freedom you know.'

'Does it happen often?'

He hesitated. 'Not often. But it does happen. Normally we catch them in the grounds. Some of the ships can be quite brutal, you know. Some of the sailors see Europe as the Promised Land. That's why we have such security.'

'Such security,' said Celestine dismissively. 'Last thing. That ship, it came from Vietnam, right? So do a lot of boats from Vietnam call here?' The controller consulted his computer again.

'Been a three-fold increase since 2010.'

'And do you have a record of all of them and their cargoes?' demanded Celestine.

The controller closed his eyes and sighed. 'Probably. Yes. On the system. But I couldn't possibly find that information out now, this minute.'

'No, of course not. Just get one of your staff to dig them out in the next twenty-four hours and email them to me. The address is on my card. Thanks again for your cooperation.' Outside Celestine looked around. It didn't seem very busy, but she assumed the work came in bursts, when a ship docked, and went quiet between those times. The motorbike was there, but Jacques wasn't. She looked over to where a truck was parked, a container resting on its flatbed. The driver was leaning against the cab and laughing. Jacques was standing with his back to Celestine and seemed to be gesticulating towards the container. The driver laughed again and nodded. Celestine saw them shake hands and Jacques walked over to her. 'Old friend?' she asked. Jacques shook his head and climbed onto the motorbike.

'Got what you wanted?'

'I think so.'

'Good. Are you ready for stage two?' he asked.

'Yes.'

'I'm going to get as close as I can, but we'll have to walk some of the way. I looked at the map. There is a lane leading down to the estuary about half a kilometre from the building. I'll take us down there.'

Chapter 35

It took twenty minutes to reach the place. Jacques parked the motorcycle in a small patch of trees, and they hung their helmets and leather jackets on the handlebars. A light breeze was blowing, but it still felt hot and airless on the fetid bank of the estuary. They followed a narrow path that was no more than a shallow indentation in the earth, flattened gently by wild animals or rare feral humans. In places, the path skirted right up to the water's edge and it felt perilous. The tide ran bloated and urgent beside them as they walked in uneasy silence, like trespassers in an unwelcome place. Jacques walked in front and brushed down the scrawny branches of the shrubs that grew along the way. The land curved gently to the right and they caught their first sight of the metal roof of the building. Jacques stopped and let Celestine come alongside him. He pointed.

'We should come to the fence soon. I don't know if it comes right down to the water.'

'Let's find out,' said Celestine, and moved past him to lead the way. They came to a narrow creek, still lively with the previous day's rain, which blocked their way. Celestine pushed upstream past low branches, her feet sinking slightly into the soft clay on the edges, until she came to a place where it narrowed and she could jump across. Jacques looked doubtful.

'It's all right for you winged gazelles,' he whispered.

'Jump it or walk through it,' said Celestine without sympathy, and taking a few strides back, ran and cleared the water with half a metre to spare. She didn't wait to see how Jacques was tackling it but pushed her way back along the other bank towards the estuary. Jacques took half a dozen steps back, ran and threw himself over the water, landing just on the edge, his boots slipping slightly in the soft margin, but his momentum carried him forward and he landed on his hands and belly. More of a floundering wildebeest, he decided to himself, and hurried after Celestine.

The trees thickened as they came closer to the building and they couldn't see the fence until they were almost next to it. It was set back at least five metres from the water's edge, and the path continued along the estuary. Celestine peered through the branches into the piece of weed-filled wasteland between the building and the fence. Jacques crouched down beside her and they studied the back of the building in silence. There was one large sliding door, almost in the centre and another door at the top of a metal stairway.

'There must be a second floor or a mezzanine,' said Jacques.

'Yes. I'd like to get in that door, but it'll be locked for sure,' said Celestine. 'If we could get in there quietly, we might be able to see what work they're doing, without being seen.' Jacques looked at his feet where the mud had splashed up his leather boots.

'Locks are not always a problem,' he said and glanced tentatively at her face. She looked at him, sucking in her lower lip and raising her eyebrows.

'No?' she said.

'No. Antique furniture, always old locks to …manoeuvre.

'Manoeuvre,' she replied. 'And you think you might be able to manoeuvre the lock on that door?'

'Possibly.'

'Possibly. Ok. First, we have to get through the fence.' They continued along the path by the fence until they came to a high gate where a concrete pier jutted out into the estuary. Jacques pushed gently at the gate and it moved in his hand.

'This wasn't locked,' he said.

'No, it's been opened recently; look at where it's scraped along the earth and flattened the undergrowth,' said Celestine. Jacques looked at the building and then turned to look at the concrete jetty. He suddenly felt cold. He walked to the end of the concrete and stopped at the edge, looking down at the swirling brown water.

'This is the place,' he said, but Celestine was twenty metres away studying the lie of the land leading up to the building. There was a narrow but well-used path from the gate to the sliding doors. She heard Jacques mutter something and turned to see him crouched down on his haunches, his hands on the concrete, staring into the water. She walked towards him and heard him say again, 'This is the place.' She looked at his thick, unkempt hair as it curled around the back of his neck, almost touching his shoulders. For a moment she had the urge to run her fingers through it, to comfort this big man who was hurting. Somehow, it seemed more poignant when a large animal is in pain, she thought, like an elephant that walks slowly away from its dead mate. She put her hand on his shoulder.

'We shouldn't stay here, Jacques,' she said. 'We could easily be seen from the building if someone comes out.'

'It was here,' he said, in a voice that was deep and desolate. 'This is where they put Armand in the water. Just here.'

'We can't know that for sure yet,' suggested Celestine. 'The heavy rain will have washed away any traces outside,' she paused. 'Jacques, we have to get inside, to really find out what's going on in that building. Come and help me.' He stood up and for a moment looked out across the water. He turned to Celestine.

'I'm sorry. But some bastard is going to get his,' he said.

The wasteland was full of old debris: metal frames, rubble and old containers, and through them the weeds had grown and softened their angles and almost blended them into nature. They walked along the cinder path at first, ready to hurl themselves into the undergrowth if there was any movement from the building. Then they left the path and cut across towards the metal stairway. Jacques crouched down behind an old oil drum and gestured for Celestine to tuck in beside him.

'I'll go up to that door. There's no point in two of us being exposed,' he whispered. 'If I can open it, I'll glance inside. If it's clear I'll signal and you can join me.'

Celestine nodded. 'Go quietly and be careful, Jacques. No heroics.'

'No. That's not my mould,' he replied.

For a large man, he walked very lightly on his feet. Celestine could barely hear his tread on the metal stairs. At the top, on the small landing, he knelt down by the door and studied the lock. She saw him reach for something in his rear pocket, but she couldn't see what it was or what he was doing. Perhaps that's just as well as she thought, honest deniability, if required. She heard a faint metallic click and then he stood up and glanced back towards her. He turned the handle slowly and eased the door open, just wide enough to be able to see inside. It was dark, but he could make out the dull shapes of boxes in stacks along the wall. There was no sign of movement so he eased the door open wider and stepped through, pulling it to behind him. People notice a quick change of air, a new draught, predators do in particular, he thought. He realised he was on a wide gantry with a handrail along the edge, where there was light shining from the floor below. He stood listening intently; there were scuffling sounds and the occasional sharp clang as of metal being struck. He sniffed, the air was acrid with the smell of scorched metal and fumes. He edged further onto the gantry, which was in darkness and ran the whole length of the building. There was no one there, whatever action was going on was happening down below on the ground floor.

He opened the door again gently and looked down to where Celestine was waiting anxiously. He waved for her to join him, and she sprang up and seemed to float across the ground and up the stairs without touching them. She brushed past him and he closed the door quietly again.

Jacques could feel his heart beating and his mouth was dry, yet Celestine appeared calm, glancing around in every direction, getting her bearings and tiptoeing up to the handrail at the edge of the gantry. Maybe it's knowing you have a badge and a gun, he reasoned, or maybe she's just a tiger. She moves with the stealth of an animal, he thought. She crouched down on the floor and crawled to the edge to look down into the main building. Jacques stood back, his bulk was easier to spot, but she waved to him to crawl alongside her. He looked through the rails; below them were the dark shapes of large pieces of industrial machinery; some pieces were partially dismantled, their integuments lying in heaps, their interiors exposed as through a mechanical post-mortem. Jacques glanced across at Celestine who looked stern and puzzled.

'There are people working at the far end, where the bright lights are,' Jacques whispered in her ear. She didn't respond; he could sense that she was running patterns through her head, trying to find a match or a link that would explain the scene below. Finally, she gave an almost imperceptible shake of her head and pointed towards the far end of the building.

'I'm going there,' she mouthed. 'You should stay here, keep a lookout, and make no noise.'

But Jacques shook his head and gestured that he was going there too. So they edged gently away from the rail and stood up. They walked slowly, heel to toe, as quietly as they could. The light became brighter as they approached the far end of the building. There were a few small stacks of cartons on the gantry against the wall, and at the farthest point there was a boxed-in office and a metal stairway leading to the ground floor. The noise was getting louder and the smell was more pungent and caught in their throats. Celestine dropped onto her knees again and crawled to the edge to look down. Almost directly below, she could see three men standing around a large steel component, about a metre round with curved sides. Next to it was a forklift truck, and it seemed to Celestine that the object had probably been brought there after being removed from one of the large machines at the other end of the building. It looked approximately heart-shaped, like the extracted organ of some large metal being. The top was sealed, and the workmen were alternatively heating the bolt heads with a gas burner and then turning the bolts with large wrenches. Smoke and fumes rose from their work, and Celestine gagged as it caught in her throat. She looked around. Jacques had moved silently to the office and was peering in through the glass walls. The door to the office was at the top of the stairs and she thought it could be seen by the workmen below. The three men were wearing blue overalls and large eye protectors, so she couldn't make out their faces, but they seemed short and their hair was black. One of them suddenly looked up and seemed to be staring straight at her. She froze, although she knew only the top of her head would be visible. But the man simply shook his head, as though to clear it of fumes, and set back to work again.

There didn't appear to be anyone else in the building, but there were workbenches, lathes and other pieces of machinery and steel spread over the floor. She glanced carefully across at Jacques who was standing stock-still in a deep shadow by the wall of the office and seemed to be staring into space. He must have sensed her looking as he turned towards her and she gestured for him to join her by the gantry rail. He nodded and edged cautiously along the rear wall and then crawled to a place alongside her. She brought her lips to his ear.

'Careful, but take a look. What do you think they are doing and what are those metal components from?'

Jacques inched closer to the edge and peered down. The workmen seemed to be making some progress. The two with wrenches were chattering to each other, he could hear the high-pitched, excited tone in their voices. The man with the gas torch turned it off and stood back, lifting the visor over the back of his head. It was apparent to them both that he had an Asian face. One of the others made a few turns on one of the bolts, and then the turns became easier, and pulling on a gauntlet, he loosened and extracted the bolt. He also stepped back and straightened up, stretching himself. The third man had put down his wrench, and with a bladed tool, was moving around the bolted top, easing it from its housing. The second man started from the other side and they gradually loosened the flange, and then with gloved hands, they lifted it up and dropped it heavily on the floor. The sound echoed around the building, and Celestine felt her ears were being assailed but she didn't move, she was excited, she had a sense that they were on the cusp of learning something crucial.

One of the men disappeared from sight below the gantry and for a second Celestine was worried in case he was going to come up the stairs. But he soon appeared again dragging a large wire basket across the floor and he pushed it up to the metal component. Then the three of them stood back and Celestine heard a new voice, harsh and authoritative. A fourth man came into view, taller than the others and younger in his movements. He adjusted the position of the basket and then thrust his hand inside the component. He drew out a foil bag, larger and flatter than a flour bag. He leant down and dropped it into the basket. He put his hand in perhaps fifty times, and each time drew out a foil bag. His head almost disappeared inside the component as he scratched around to ensure that all the bags had been removed. Then he stood up and waved at the three workmen, snarling at them in a language that was not French. They took hold of the corners of the basket and dragged it over the floor. They came under the gantry and Jacques and Celestine could hear them grunting and the basket scraping on the concrete ground. They seemed to move it some way and Jacques estimated that it must be somewhere near the sliding doors. When they stopped, the silence in the cavernous building was absolute and eerie. Jacques imagined that even his breathing could be heard, and he could sense the tension and rigidity in the woman lying alongside him. They heard the footsteps of the men coming back. The taller man said something and there was some nervous laughter. He clapped his hands against the shoulder of one of the workers and jerked his head towards the door at the front of the building. They walked together, one of them grabbing a water bottle from the bench, and Jacques and Celestine watched them go through the door, which clanged shut behind them.

Jacques started to move, but Celestine held up her hand. She was listening intently for the sound of anyone else in the building. All was silent. Jacques breathed deeply and eased himself into a sitting position. He looked at her questioningly.

'Interesting,' he mouthed.

Celestine moved away from the edge, stood up, and gestured for Jacques to join her in the shadows by the back wall. She leaned against his arm and brought her mouth across his face and close to his ear. He realised he was intensely aroused. She whispered to him.

'I have to see inside one of those bags.' He started to speak but she put her fingers over his mouth. 'Do you have a knife?' He nodded, and reaching into his pocket, pulled out a battered old Swiss army knife. 'I'll just open one of those bags, not on the top. I'll make it look like a tear.'

Jacques mouthed 'How?'

'You go back to the door. I'm going down the stairs. I have to do it quietly before they come back. I'll try to get out through those sliding doors. If I do, lock that top door and join me outside.' Jacques looked at her as though she was unstable. She put her fingers over his lips again and then she was gone. He watched her glide along the gantry and disappear down the stairs. His stomach was lurching and for a moment he was struck with admiration and fear for her. He listened carefully, but couldn't even hear her footsteps in the great echo hall of a building. Then he took a deep breath himself and tried to emulate her stealth as he moved along the gantry, staying in the shadows where he could. He reached the door and eased it open, taking one last look and listening for any sound. Then he stepped out into the fresh breeze from the estuary and blinked in the bright sunlight as it flared from the surface of the water. The air tasted of honey and ice after the harsh atmosphere in the building. He crouched down by the door and inserted a short, shaped rod into the lock until it clicked. Now it could be opened from the inside, but only from the outside by a key. He tiptoed down the steps and hurried across to the oil drum they had hidden by before, and waited.

Celestine could see there were four similar baskets resting on the floor by the large sliding doors. She assumed the basket she had seen being filled was the one furthest from the doors, but it didn't really matter. She plunged her hand about a third of the way into the basket and drew out one of the foil bags. Taking Jacques' knife she made a small cut near the edge about halfway down the bag. Then she noticed that a few of the metal strands of the basket were broken, leaving jagged ends sticking out. She pushed the bag onto one of those strands and tore the hole a little more, to look untidy and natural. She pushed a finger into the hole. There was another plastic bag inside, which was also torn. She could feel the contents; the bag was full of pills. She hooked her finger around one of them and managed to manoeuvre it out through the hole. She looked at it quickly - it was white and unmarked. She slipped it into her trouser pocket and placed the bag back, part of the way down, with the torn side resting against the basket. She took a deep breath, and just as she was preparing to move, she heard the door to the building open and heard the sound of voices and footsteps on the floor.

She ducked down quickly and shuffled around the baskets to crouch behind them. Then she heard the forklift truck whine as it started up and began to move in her direction. She glanced around, rapidly assessing her options; the double sliding doors were five metres away; the hulk of a machine stood close against the back wall, offering dark spaces in which to hide; or she could stand up with badge and gun. The forklift wheezed past and she watched as it lifted up another piece of equipment from the pile before swinging around and taking it over to where the men were waiting. She didn't hesitate. Hoping the electric whine of the engine would cover any noise she made, she moved quickly, and half-running, half-crawling she headed for the doors. Desperately hoping they weren't locked, she grabbed a handle and tugged. The doors slid noisily to the side. She stepped straight through and pulled them closed behind her. She saw Jacques' head appear from behind the oil drum and gestured wildly for him to head to the fence, but she didn't wait, she ran as quickly as possible along the cinder track to the gate and passed through onto the path outside.

Jacques was up like a startled bird from the undergrowth and picked his way quickly through the wasteland, cursing as he caught his shin on a piece of rusted metal frame. He reached the gate and glanced back, but the doors were still closed. He scurried through the gate and plunged along the path towards where Celestine was waiting by the trees. As he reached her she turned immediately and started running again. There was no need to speak.

Jacques paused for breath when he reached the creek and looked back. Apart from the light rustling of the wind in the trees, and the low murmur of the water, there was silence. It didn't look as though they were being pursued. He felt his breath go deeper and realised that he had been holding himself as tight as a spring for what seemed like hours. He joined Celestine by the place upstream where she was preparing to jump. She was looking at him and her eyes were almost glazed with excitement. He touched her arm.

'Are you ok? Do you think you were seen in there?' he asked.

She shook her head. 'I don't think so, but I don't know. The door was a bit noisy. We'll have to be careful.' And then with an almost hysterical laugh, she clapped Jacques on the arm. 'You did well Jacques. You did well. But that made me shiver, really.' And she shook her head and looked up at Jacques and he had no idea what she would do next. She seemed a little crazed and as taut as a violin string.

'Are you all right?' he asked again.

'Sure. We should go,' she smiled, and then she was back down to earth. She took two steps and leapt over the stream.

Jacques made no attempt at that, he ploughed into the fast-flowing water, resisting the tug of the current, and emerged out onto the other side. He shook himself like a long-haired hound. Celestine was laughing again, laughing at him now, but there was a high, hysterical note in her voice. Jacques frowned at her.

'Come on, you need to get to the bike. I think you've gone a little haywire,' he said gruffly.

'Fuck you. I was right. Right about the murder scene, right that there's something serious, very serious going on there. Now they're going to have to believe me.'

'Yes, but we need to get away from here. Just run. Ok.'

Celestine turned away and began pushing her way back to the path, and when she got there she started running as fast as she could along by the estuary. Jacques trotted more slowly and at intervals he stopped and listened. But there were no sounds coming from the building. When he reached the motorbike, Celestine was already wearing the leather jacket and helmet.

'Sorry,' she said. 'I'm not usually so excitable.'

'No, I wouldn't think so. It's ok. You were bold in there. Maybe having a badge and a gun, but you were…' he hesitated.

'What? I was what?' she demanded. He shook his head.

'No. I'm not going to say it. Maybe if I knew you better. Nobody wants a police officer with an ego.' He pulled on his leather jacket. His legs were soaked and his boots were full of water. 'We need to be careful now. If someone did see us, they could be waiting for us when we get to the road. So, there's a farm track about halfway. I'm going to cut across that and then go west before joining the main road again. We don't want to go past those gates.'

Chapter 36

Jacques started the bike, and as they headed up the track he could feel the hard presence of the woman clinging to his back, and for a moment he imagined what that would be like without the thick jackets between them, with nothing between them. Then he snapped into focus, and when he reached a small farm path he turned the bike carefully onto it. The ground was rough and the bike bumped and bounced its way along a line of stunted trees. He could feel Celestine gripping more tightly, but he didn't slow down. They rode along the edge of a field of barley where the green, whiskered-heads were already showing and rippling in the breeze. At the end of the field, he turned towards the road again, and the path became a grassy track, where tyre marks showed and there were pieces of farm detritus, plastic tubs and bits of pipe stuffed into the field headland. At the road, he turned away from Bordeaux and continued for a few kilometres before he could turn left onto another minor road. All this time Celestine said nothing. She now felt like a dead weight on his back, as though she was sleeping, or cowering, he thought. He stopped at a junction on the main road. He nudged her and turned a little in his seat.

'I'm going to head back to Bordeaux now, on the main road. Hold on tight. I thought you were getting a bit limp back there.'

'Ok. No, I'm hanging on. It's not that comfortable, but you are a hell of a windbreak.'

He turned onto the main road and accelerated. The sun and the wind were drying out his clothes, and the sight of the vineyards and the vibrant new growth on the vines lifted his mood. They travelled like that for thirty kilometres or so, before Jacques suddenly slowed down in a small village and turned into a car park set beneath the shade of some ancient chestnut trees. He switched off the engine and nudged Celestine to climb off the bike. He pulled off his helmet and shook his head. Celestine looked at him quizzically.

'I need a coffee. There's a small café on the edge of the square,' he said.

'Coffee?'

'Yes. But…we need to talk. You know, there's something very wrong here.' He rubbed his hand around his chin. 'That didn't feel like a very police thing this afternoon. It felt a bit, a bit …freelance.' Celestine stared at him, her eyes hardening.

'Coffee then,' she shrugged, and walked off towards the square, leaving Jacques to prop up the bike and follow after her, his boots still squelching a little as he walked. The café was dark inside but there were chairs outside under an awning, and although there was no one else there, Celestine sat down at the table furthest from the door. Jacques ordered a strong espresso for himself but Celestine wanted only water. They sat in silence for some minutes, Celestine looking down the road, and Jacques' gaze moving between his coffee and her profile. Finally, he said.

'I am willing to be corrected on anything I now say, believe me, this is conjecture. But I would like you to be straight with me on this. Ok?' Celestine merely nodded almost imperceptibly, and continued looking down the road. 'Ok. I guess those were drugs you found in those packets. What was it, cocaine, heroin?'

'Pills.'

'Pills right. Not slimming pills, not hidden away inside some machine parts. So we are talking illegal drugs. A big quantity. We have murders. A murder scene, most like. Now, I would have thought that a police officer, finding that, seeing that, would immediately be on their phone, calling in the drug squad, armed units, murder squad, I don't know who you've got. And I would expect to see blue lights, red lights flashing through the window in the rain. You know. Police arresting bad guys, in force, big bust, evidence of crimes.' He paused and touched Celestine on the arm until she turned to face him. 'Am I right, or is there some other play going on here? Celestine, what you did this afternoon was scary, reckless, but where is your backup? Level with me.' Celestine shuffled around in her seat to face him directly, and he saw that there were streaks below her eyes where she had been crying or perhaps it was the wind on the motorbike. She took a sip of water.

'Level with you. Ok, here's the whole thing. And I shouldn't be sharing even half of this with a civilian, but I seem to be so far out of line now, I don't even know where the line is anymore. My position is so precarious.'

So she told him about the situation in the Commissariat, the threatened suspension and being taken off the murder cases. 'I didn't say anything because I didn't want you to stop helping me find Armand's killer.' He listened quietly, watching the play of emotions on her face. She mentioned the Vietnamese girl and the fear she had for her. And then, despite herself, she talked about her husband and her suspicions, about the time he was spending with a mob boss and Zubizaretta, whose building that probably was. Jacques watched as anger, frustration, fear and uncertainty played with her eyes and the features of her face. He was listening but also watching and feeling, and he had the terrible impression that he was looking at the face of someone who was sinking slowly into quicksand.

'That is really hard, Celestine. I am sorry. I had no idea you were having to handle so much. You can't even trust your husband. Do you really think he's involved with these mobsters? Could he maybe be investigating them?'

'I don't know. I don't know, Jacques. I really don't. When I spoke to him last night, what he said didn't ring true.' Her voice was strained with emotion. 'And if I call this in, it has to be my boss. I don't trust him a centimetre. He would speak to my husband. Would they tip them off? They could be gone. We'd have nothing. And frankly, at this moment we have nothing.'

'Nothing!' Jacques raised his voice.

'Yes, nothing. We have no evidence that the murder was committed there or by those people. And the pills; until I get them tested and can prove that they are illegal drugs, they're just pills.'

'It's a bloody unusual way of transporting - just pills,' said Jacques,

'I know. But... you don't understand. I have to be one hundred per cent on this. Wrong, and I'd be suspended for disobeying orders again. Maybe worse.'

'Worse?

'Yes. Fired maybe. Or... we have two murders so far. Why do you think they were murdered, Jacques?'

'Because they knew too much, or saw too much and weren't willing to keep quiet.'

'Yes, exactly. I know too much, you know too much,' she said earnestly.

'They might kill a hairy carpenter, but they wouldn't kill a serving police officer, would they?' Jacques was suddenly conscious that his feet were cold and he felt that the sky had darkened and he was sitting in a more sombre shade. He looked across, Celestine was clearly thinking hard. She raised her face and her lips were moving. It was remarkable how quickly her mood seemed to change. It was her quick mind, he knew. It could pick a strand and suddenly it was following it and building a whole new set of possibilities. She raised a finger and waved it gently at him.

'Assuming nobody saw us this afternoon. They don't know what we know, yet. They're worried, but they think they can direct me, that the threat of suspension will keep me from taking this further.' Jacques sat back, it was his turn to look into the distance. 'And they don't know anything about you,' she continued. 'They don't know you're my source or…'

'Co-conspirator.'

'Something like that.'

'But how will you take it forward? Isn't there someone else you can go to, in another station, higher up again, or in the drug squad?' She shook her head.

'That's not how it works. No one assumes anyone is, what did you call it, mucky. There is a line of command.'

'Ok, and shoot me down. But isn't there an examining magistrate or judge or something?' Jacques asked.

'There is. A juge d'instruction. If I could put together a detailed report, a file of evidence.'

'You could do that.'

'I could. I just could. I'd have to be very careful. I would have to keep any evidence safe until it was all gathered. And neither my office nor my home is…secure from prying eyes.'

'You could keep it at my place. The Rue Carpentyre has bolts and locks going back to the middle-ages. I could repel the Black prince if I had to.'

Celestine smiled weakly. 'You're serious. Why? Is this just about Armand Verville? Wanting to find his killer? You must have really cared about him.' Jacques nodded slowly.

'Yes, about Armand. I have to go the whole distance to pay my debt to him. But now you've introduced a poor Vietnamese sailor who wanted a better life and maybe wouldn't go along with something bad. I'm assuming that's what got him killed.' He hesitated, strangely embarrassed. 'And now there's Capitaine Celestine Courbet. In trouble. I can't leave her to the dragons. But…' he added quickly, 'I wish my feet weren't so bloody wet and cold. You've ruined these boots.'

'I have? You should have jumped the stream. And I don't need an amateur knight in armour, Jacques. I just need somewhere sound to stand. I can beat the dragons myself.'

'As you say.' They sat looking at each other's faces until they both gradually smiled, Jacques' eyes lit up and he wet his lips and fought back the urge to lean over and kiss her. She saw it and sat back.

'Come on, we need to get to Bordeaux. I have to interview a couple in a hospital who were attacked in their home yesterday. I have to be seen to be working on other things.'

'So what's next? You need more evidence?' asked Jacques.

'I'll get this tablet tested. I need to find out who took the sailor out of the station. I need to know exactly where the dirt lies and how deep. It's you and your mucky flics. I'm beginning to suspect everyone and that's not fair.'

'It's a good start. I'll pay a visit to Monsieur Meslier tomorrow. Would that be ok?'

'Yes, I think so. Don't say too much. Just ask him about Armand. Say you heard he was working with him.'

'Ok. And you should stand beside the Girondins,' said Jacques.

'The Girondins? The monument? What the hell for?'

'Spend some time looking at the weird nature of some of the creatures.'

'And then what?'

'And then you'll know if your marriage is over,' stated Jacques firmly. 'You'll let me know.' Celestine looked at him in amazement. She shook her head and her thick dark hair swung gently around her cheeks.

'Come on,' he said. 'You still have many kilometres more pleasure this afternoon on the Winged Goddess, before you return to your humdrum life.'

'Humdrum. I wish.'

'No, you don't, Celestine Courbet. I saw you when you came out of that building. No, you don't.'

Chapter 37

Vaillancourt was looking into the dark, pitiless, unblinking eyes of a snake. It was unusual, almost unheard of, for him to be invited to one of Monsieur Nguyen's homes. Their relationship was of necessity, discreet. They ordinarily met in a restaurant, or the rear of a club, in a car, even on a boat on the Garonne once. But this afternoon he had received a call telling him that a car would pick him up on the southwest corner of Place Gambetta at three o'clock. He had rushed to prepare for the meeting. He had called in Martel for an update on the two murders and had sat quietly, his elbows on the desk, hands over his mouth, listening to the gruff commandant as he cursed his way in monosyllables through his report.

'Will it stick?' he'd asked finally. Martel had snorted, but there was no humour there.

'Will it stick? It's a plaster over a wound. There's the weapon and a vague witness.'

'You'll have to sharpen up the witness,' said Vaillancourt, through his fingers. Martel had looked at him with distaste and even a little contempt. He had leaned forward and rested his hands on Vaillancourt's desk.

'Will it stick? Will the witness be sharp enough? It will, it might, if there is no other narrative here. But if somebody comes up with a plausible alternative, and maybe produces evidence that cannot be ignored. Then it won't stick. Then it will peel off like old paper. Then it's a bitch's pie.' He had sat back and waited for his superior officer to comment or to display some element of leadership, but Vaillancourt had remained silent, his eyes turned away, looking through the window at the picturesque, tranquil permanence of the Chartreuse cemetery below.

'How much does your wife know, Sir?' Martel had asked finally. Vaillancourt had looked back.

'Where is she?'

'Her car is parked in the old town, near St. Michel. She visited the scene of the robbery in Chartron a couple of hours ago. Went home, then drove to St. Michel. They didn't follow her out of the car.'

'So, not near Rue de la Sau, and not out of town.'

'No. But you should have let me suspend her, Sir.'

'It may come to that, I thought…'

'You're too close to it. She needs to be silenced.' And now Nguyen was saying exactly the same thing but with much greater menace and in a way that brooked no argument.

'Commissaire Vaillancourt.' He had greeted his guest with his customary stiff politeness. The beautiful girl from the restaurant had shown Vaillancourt into a kind of study, but it was a room of darkness. The wood of the doors and the bookshelves and the furniture was jet black and lacquered so that it reflected the red glow of the lamps. There were thin golden sculptures of mythological creatures, dragons and coiled snakes fixed to the walls between the shelves. Vaillancourt was unnerved, there was no comfort to be found here. It could be the Devil's waiting room. Nguyen had entered through one of the black doors and taken Vaillancourt's hand coldly, but firmly, holding on to it a little too long and looking hard at him, unsmiling.

'Commissaire Vaillancourt. I am disappointed that we are meeting like this.' He gestured for Vaillancourt to sit down on a low, black, leather chair, and settled himself on the other side. He was wearing his customary dark suit and white shirt. Vaillancourt started to speak but Nguyen held up his hand to forestall him. They sat quietly for a moment as Nguyen gathered his thoughts, his hands clasped together loosely on the table top. He looked up. 'A man was killed. That is on Zubizaretta. Another man was killed. That is on my associates in the shipping. There will be corrections there. But these parties add many pieces to the game. Zubizaretta with his factory and his machines. The shipping associates, transport, discreet, an essential element in this enterprise. They are paid well, but they will lose a little because of these disruptions.' Vaillancourt sat silently, uncomfortably, the voice was harsh but somehow mesmerising. Nguyen continued; he hadn't moved a centimetre, his position, his posture and his gaze seemed cast in stone. 'Your role, Police Commissaire, in this enterprise, your piece is to ensure that if there are any disruptions, they do not put the whole in jeopardy. They are contained. There are no unwanted interruptions to our project. Your work is to slice off the rotting flesh to leave the rest of the body whole. And for which, you are also well paid and rewarded.' There was a pause, and in the near silence, Vaillancourt could hear a thin slushing sound as Nguyen sucked air and spittle over his lower lip and teeth. 'I must say, other than these two interruptions, those two parties are delivering in their roles. We have a very substantial quantity of product. Thirty-five million euros at wholesale value. We have the machinery, another twenty million. One shipment, one shipment, Commissaire.' Nguyen was raising his voice now. 'Fifty-five million euros and at the moment it is a sitting duck because it is all in one place. We need two more days at least, preferably more. But if someone should discover that place, a police person for example, that is when you have a role to play, Police Commissaire,' he almost hissed when he said the word. 'That is when you have a role.

That is when you earn your corn. I thought I had made my expectations very clear the other evening. Did I not?'

Vaillancourt almost stammered as he found his voice. 'Of course, Monsieur Nguyen. But you are wrong to think that these matters are not under my control. We have a suspect for the first murder, and the second is being treated as just a gang-related matter. We have, I have, cauterised the wound. You should have no concerns for the enterprise. None.' He attempted to smile but knew even to himself that it sounded hollow and Nguyen waved his hand impatiently.

'No, Commissaire. It seems you are not in control. Do you think I do not know what goes on in your precinct? Do you think you are the only eyes and ears I retain?' Nguyen's voice had settled down again, and now there was no change in the tone, no emotion, which to Vaillancourt was almost more disturbing. He remembered the man discussing the slitting of three throats in the same even voice. 'I have been told that Capitaine Celestine Courbet knows the location of the factory.' Vaillancourt started to ask how he knew that, but Nguyen cut him off. 'This police officer knows that the sailor was not a casualty of gang warfare. Knows he came from our ship. What else does she know, Commissaire? And she is your wife, and she knows that you are connected to me. And she is your wife and you cannot control her.' Nguyen sat back, placed his hands together and looked down for a moment. Then he looked up and fixed Vaillancourt with his dark, pitiless, snake-like eyes. 'I see now that you are a dreamer, Etienne. You dream that you can have a beautiful young mistress to attend to your desires. And you can have money, foolish money for a man who is no more than a state functionary. And you think you can have this and not have to dirty your well-manicured hands sometimes.' He paused again, and if a forked tongue had slipped out between those thin lips, Vaillancourt would not have been surprised. 'Your wife is a threat. A threat to this enterprise, to me, to you, and she will never trust you again. She will always be watching you, waiting for you to make a mistake, waiting for a connection, waiting to ensnare you.' Nguyen almost smiled, grimly. 'I admire her. I really do. It seems she is true to what she does. Truly admirable, but not helpful or tolerable. She must be eliminated from the equation. Now, by you, swiftly. It will be hard. I know it is hard. But you will. There is no alternative action you can take.'

Vaillancourt felt as though the venom had entered his body without him even seeing the strike. He was rigid, locked and cold, unable to tear his gaze away from those terrible eyes. Unable to think except in a tiny screaming portion of his mind. He heard himself say the word,

'How?' But he couldn't be saying: how do I kill my wife? Nguyen released him from his gaze. He stood up and walked over to a small ornate cabinet on the wall behind his desk. He opened the cabinet and took out a small plastic packet containing a dirty white powder. He stood over Vaillancourt and handed him the packet.

'All of it. It is tasteless and relatively quick. In food or drink. When it is done, phone the number. We will arrange the disposal. There will be no trace this time. A disturbed mind, a suspension, an element of obsession, clear for all to see.'

Vaillancourt held the packet in his hand, but it was not real, it couldn't be. But then he knew that this was just normality in the world he had chosen to enter. He had known for a long time that he was permanently exiled from that world he had known before. He stared at the packet for several minutes until there was a tap on his shoulder. The girl was encouraging him to stand up and leave, and he saw that Nguyen had already departed through one of the shiny, black doors, and he was now alone on the edge of his existence.

Chapter 38

Jacques watched Celestine walk away until she reached the corner of the street and was lost from his sight. In his rooms above the workshop, he showered and poured himself a beer. Then he sat down in his over-stuffed armchair to rest and gather his thoughts. He had to admit that he was drained, physically and certainly emotionally, and that his nerves were raw, the skin scraped off in strips by the fear and exhilaration of the activities of the afternoon. He noticed that there were messages on his answerphone, but he didn't listen to them. He didn't want to introduce anything new into his thoughts until they were calmer and more settled.

Much later, after he had made himself a quick meal and was drinking his third beer, he picked up a writing pad and pressed the replay button. There were six messages. The first one was in the warm, husky tones of Candice; reminding him that the play opened on Wednesday evening at eight, and asking how many tickets he wanted. The next two messages related to work and he jotted them down to speak to the next day. The fourth message was from Louise; it sounded panicky and vague as usual, pleading for him to call her back; "something has happened". The fifth message was no message at all, just a silence, but not quite a silence, there was a low ticking of a clock and the sound of a gentle aspiration of air. Someone had stayed silent for the whole of the recording time, saying nothing, but being there. And Jacques took that as a message too, and a thin cold current ran up his spine. He felt a reluctance to listen to the sixth message, uneasy that it might be more of the same; but it was Maxine, in a voice scoured by a thousand cigarettes. He called her back first.

'Bastards know I'm here. Did you tell them?' she said without any greeting.

'Who?'

'Police. Did your tart send them? Pull it out of you?'

'No, no. I haven't told anyone. Calm down. What actually happened?'

'Came to the door. Two of them. Asking for Marie, then asking if she knows where I am. I'm in the back room. She didn't say. Said she didn't know. Been her man, he would have said. How did that happen, Jacques?' Jacques thought for a moment.

'They didn't actually know you were there, did they? They were making enquiries.'

'They went away,' said Maxine. 'I have to stay away from the windows, can't smoke on the balcony. Fuck Jacques. I don't want to talk to them. I've got nothing to say to them.'

'Ok. Ok. Firstly, it's got nothing to do with me or the police capitaine. Nothing at all, all right. They obviously do want to speak to you and they're trying to find you. They'll always approach family. They have systems. That's how they trace people.'

'So, what am I supposed to do? I don't want to get in a car with them. Don't know who's who in this masquerade.'

'Masquerade. You're absolutely right. That's what it is. You have a way with words Maxi. You could have been a poet in another life.'

'Don't you fucking soft-soap me. What am I going to do? And what have you found out?' Jacques told her that they had discovered where Armand had been working.

'I'm going to speak to the old guy he was working with. When I say speak, it might be more physical than that. But look, if you want to go and see the body, Maxine, I'll take you there. The police will want to interview you but I would be with you. You wouldn't be on your own. It could be safer, more comfortable for you.' There was a long silence while Maxine thought this through. She coughed and then when she spoke it was in a sad, flat monotone.

'Thing is, Jacques. I don't want to see him. I don't really. Not like that. I want to see him next to me, laughing, being stupid. He's still with me like that, he's working away. When I see him flat in a box, I'll know I've lost him. So not yet. You understand?'

'Sure. Then wait a few more days. I'll let you know if things…. If there's any progress. But if you have a problem, call me. Ok.' He rang off and sat back. Another litre of his reserves drained from the tank, he thought. They're busy, the police, they'll want to know what she knows; but do they want to know for the right reasons or the wrong ones? He steeled himself again and phoned Louise; he was leaving Candice to last, hoping she, at least, would raise his spirits. Louise answered almost immediately and she also didn't say hello.

'They were here again. The police. Nasty this time. Can you come over?'

'Bonsoir, Louise. How are you? Well? And how are you, Jacques? Ok. Passing well, you know. I can't come over now, Louise. Not tonight. I've had a very, very long day. I'll call on you tomorrow. Sometime in the morning. Ok. Sleep well.'

'I don't sleep, I don't eat. I don't walk. I don't talk. Tomorrow,' and she rang off. And that's another litre of my reserves drained off, thought Jacques. I wish I had a dipstick to see how much is left.

He waited ten minutes before calling Candice. He drank deeply to wash out some of the anguish. He didn't want to spread his anxiety onto her, she was too sensitive and caring and she had enough on her plate with the play. So when he did eventually call he was upbeat, and said how much he was looking forward to the play and that he might like to bring someone. Candice laughed and asked if it was a lioness.

'She's a tiger, I would say, yes, a tiger. But just a friend and she might not make it. I haven't asked her.' He had really just thought of it that second.

'She'll come. All the cats like to play,' replied Candice.

Chapter 39

Celestine visited the hospital where the victims of the robbery were still being treated. The man was still concussed, with blurred vision and wasn't able to say much. The woman was bandaged on both arms where she had been slashed, and she had a dark bruise beside her left eye. Celestine recognised her; she had seen her in the streets in Chartron and in a café where the ladies drank chocolate and nibbled delicate patisseries. The woman also recognised Celestine and seemed reassured that someone from her neighbourhood was investigating the incident. But at the end, Celestine didn't come away with very much.

Two young men, masked, speaking coarse French, carelessly violent and smelly. 'They smelled disgusting,' the woman stated, as though this in itself were an additional offence. They took jewellery, telephones, a little cash and credit cards. They kicked things over and threw things on the floor. Then they left and she could not imagine such a thing in a nice area like Chartron. And what are the police doing about these people?

'What are you doing about it?' At that point, Celestine thanked her for the information and promised to call on her at her home to give her an update, if they ever had one.

It was after eight o'clock when she parked her car next to her husband's in the car park outside the apartment. She didn't know if she was surprised, pleased or upset. She knew she didn't want another row with him. She just wanted to eat and sleep. The apartment was more like a hotel room to her now, rather than a home. When she opened the door she could smell cooking, and Vaillancourt appeared from the kitchen wearing a strange canvas apron.

'Dinner in fifteen minutes. You ready for it?' he said and almost smiled at her. She looked at him warily and thought he looked slightly ridiculous, standing there like a parody of domestic man.

'I suppose. Has the apocalypse come?' She saw the slight flare of anger in his eyes, but he quickly suppressed it.

'I cook sometimes. I cook. I thought it might be good to have a meal together, and you might need it, you always work so late.' Celestine shrugged.

'I have to shower first. I'll look out of the window to see what colour the moon is tonight.' She undressed and threw her clothes in a basket and laid her gun in its holster on the top of the dresser. When she came out of the shower she noticed that it wasn't there. Wearing silk pyjamas and a robe she walked into the kitchen and asked him why he had moved it.

'I was just tidying up,' he said. 'I don't like to see a gun in a bedroom. It's over by the hallstand. Let me get you a drink. I've opened a bottle of wine.' He pointed to the bottle on the dining table.

'No. I think I need something stronger. A martini. I'm not sure I can face this domestic harmony without it.'

'A martini?'

'Yes. I'll make it. Do you want one? Since we are doing civilised things.'

'No thanks, I'm drinking beer,' he replied and smiled at her. 'You look lovely in that gown, with your hair slicked back.'

Celestine ignored him. She poured herself a large drink and sat down at the table with her back to her husband in the kitchen. Now she had stopped she realised just how tired she was, how drained, she had no energy left to fight or even speak. She just wanted to eat and slide into oblivion. The table had been laid with cutlery but no plates.

'I'll dish this out here, it's easier,' Vaillancourt said. 'It's a bit sloppy, could make a mess on the table.'

Celestine waved her hand at him, she was too tired to take any interest at all. She heard him spooning food from a pan onto two plates and she heard the soft grinding of a pepper mill. Then the sounds of other utensils being moved and spoons touching the sides of bowls. Eventually, he walked to the table and placed a steaming plate of pasta before her. He placed his own plate opposite and sat down. It was when he looked up at her that she saw the desolation in his eyes, she was arrested by it, by the change in his face and even his posture; it was staggering and alarming.

'Jesus, Etienne. You look absolutely dreadful. The worst I've ever seen you. You look torn up inside. Are you ill? You look it. In fact, you look haunted. Are you ill?' And for a fleeting moment she wondered if all this secrecy, the moods, the distance was because he had some dread illness which he was coping with himself. But that wouldn't really explain so many things.

He smiled grimly. 'Just eat your food, Celestine. I don't want to talk. I want to feed you and look at you. But I'm not in a place to talk tonight. Just eat. I hope you'll like it.' He took a small forkful and placed it in his mouth, yet even this effort seemed like a struggle for him. But Celestine was hungry, and she pushed her fork into the dish and started to eat quickly. It was rich and too salty, but she sipped her martini and worked her way through it. Etienne, she noticed, was only picking at his, but he looked like a man who had no appetite left for anything, anymore.

'It was good. A bit salty, but good. Thank you. I'll clear up tomorrow. I'm going to bed now. I am exhausted,' said Celestine.

'You should do that,' he paused and gave her a strange, desolate look. 'I'm going away again tomorrow.'

She nodded. 'I don't think it matters anymore,' she said and stood up.

'No. I don't believe it does. Not anymore. Goodbye, Celestine.'

'Goodnight.' She felt a sudden surge of pity and sadness, and she walked around and kissed him on the top of his head. 'Goodnight. Thanks for the food,' she said.

She lay down on the bed in the spare room, and although the meal was lying heavily on her, she closed her eyes and drifted away within minutes.

Chapter 40

The apartment was on the second floor of a gloomy, neglected building behind the Rue Auguste Brutails. The door onto the street was wedged open and the foyer was dirty and malodorous. Jacques met no one on the stairs, and when he reached the second floor he tapped lightly on the door of number seven, listening carefully for any sounds from within. He waited five minutes before taking some thin tools from his pocket and applying them to the lock on the door. There was little resistance, and glancing around again he stepped inside and quietly closed the door behind him

When you've done hard physical work throughout the night, and you're sixty-three years old, without the recovery powers of youth, the first few hours when you finally lay your head down to sleep is when you go deepest, and any resurfacing ought ideally to be gradual. But if you are woken by a large, hairy, angry-looking man slapping you on the side of your face, you are not at your most resilient or resourceful, and you feel pretty shocked and defenceless. So it was with Lionel Meslier as he struggled to find his wits, wondering if what was happening was real, although the stinging on his right cheek suggested that it was, all too real.

He managed to say, 'what the fuck?' but that only resulted in him gaining a slap on the other cheek. He tried to rise, but the stranger was sitting on the bed covers and pushed a large hand onto his chest and forced him down. He found himself looking with horror at the man's face, a face he slowly began to recognise. He started to say, 'What the…' but changed it quickly to 'I haven't done anything. Get off.' Jacques pulled the pillow from under Meslier's head and held it in his right hand.

'Old men die in their sleep, Lionel. Happens all the time. All the time.' With that, he placed the pillow over Meslier's face and pressed down hard. The old man struggled in vain, it was more of a wriggle as Jacques brought his full weight to bear on him. Just as the struggling became more frantic he whipped the pillow away and with his face close to Meslier's said. 'You are going to talk. You are going to answer all my questions, without lying, without holding anything back. I have lost a friend and you are involved. He's dead, and I think you ought to join him, you miserable piece of cat shit.' There was complete terror in Meslier's red and sore-looking eyes. He looked around desperately as though there might be some respite, something in the dingy little room at the back of his daughter's apartment that might save him. 'You want to live or you want to die?' the man was saying.

'Live,' his voice squeaked out.

'What? Louder. Do you want to live or die?' repeated Jacques.

'Live, live, what, why.'

'Live. You want to live. Well, Armand Verville wanted to live, but he died. He's dead. He was murdered. Killed in a factory by the estuary beyond Valeyrac. Where you work Meslier. He was thrown into the water like a sack of rubbish. My friend Armand Verville. And you work there.' The old man looked even more terrified when he realised that Jacques knew where he worked.

'I don't know anything. I didn't see anything,' he whined, his eyes soft and watery now like dying jellyfish. Jacques placed the pillow over Meslier's face again and pressed down even harder. The old man flapped like a fish on dry land.

'Then you're no fucking use to me. So I might as well kill you.' Jacques growled. After half a minute he lifted the pillow, the old man was gasping for breath and his face was red and his eyes half glazed.

'All right, all right. He worked there. We worked there.'

'You still work there?' Jacques demanded. Meslier nodded. 'Tell me about the night Armand was killed.'

'We were just working. He went outside for a smoke. I kept working. He didn't come back. They said he'd left. Wasn't feeling well. But…'

'But what?' said Jacques and raised the pillow again.

'But it's away in the sticks. You can't just leave. How would you do that?'

'So what did you do?'

'Do. I didn't do. You don't. You keep your mouth shut. Jesus, they're brutal. You don't do and you don't talk.'

'I'll kill you if you don't talk,' Jacques said quietly. 'Did Armand go out of the big sliding doors at the back?' Meslier looked at him in terror and astonishment, as though he was some all-powerful, all-knowing demon.

'How the fuck do you know? Yes. Yes. To have a smoke.'

'Did you see who went out after him? Who was outside?' Meslier's eyes shifted to the left and Jacques leaned over and slapped him hard on the side of his head so that he jerked back and he made an effort to get up. Jacques placed his hand onto his throat and pressed until Meslier was choking. And then released it. 'This is the point when you save your miserable life or you die - a horrible, smothering death. Who went out of the doors after Armand?'

Meslier even then seemed to be trying to find a balance between his fears, but he came down on the side of the more immediate threat. At last, he said. 'Xabietta. A big guy. A big brute, runs the job.'

'Xabietta. A Basque?' Meslier nodded. 'Dark oiled hair, drawn back?' he nodded again. 'Anybody else? Anybody else go out?' Jacques demanded fiercely. It was almost worse having visited the scene, he could picture it all so clearly.

'Maybe one of the ducks.'

'The ducks. The Vietnamese?' Meslier nodded. Jacques sat back a little and Meslier made an effort to rise. Jacques pushed him down again. 'And you never saw Armand after that?' Meslier shook his head.

'And you didn't, you didn't try to find out… You just kept working there. You were fucking friends, weren't you? You worked together on that forgery job. I saw you in court.'

'Friends, no. We worked together is all.'

'Ok. And this job, what are you doing?' Meslier looked around desperately, shaking his head, his eyes wandering around in their sockets. 'Lionel. Lionel Meslier. You are in so much shit,' said Jacques. 'You will tell me what you were doing. Or I'll kill you.' He said it in such a reasonable voice, that at that point Meslier emptied his bladder in the bed. 'And when you've told me, you will continue working there, and you won't say a word to anyone about this. Or they'll kill you for sure. What were you doing?' And then he told him and Jacques knew it was true, and knew it was such a waste of a gifted man's talents and such a waste of a life. 'And the drugs?' he demanded and slapped Meslier again for good measure. The old man shook his head miserably.

'I don't know about drugs. We just did the metal.' Jacques picked up the pillow again. 'But I guess we knew there was something. The parts were all taken apart, during the day. We only worked at night.'

'Did Armand know?' Meslier nodded.

'He didn't say, but he'd seen something. He was bored, you know. He was fed up with the work. It wasn't good enough for him. He used to wander around the place, look at things when Xabietta was outside on the phone or in the lav. I think he saw something that day. He was worried and I saw him talking to Xabietta, pointing and things.'

'Are you lying?' asked Jacques fiercely. But he could just imagine his friend, curious, walking around in his ungainly, sloppy way, looking at things, picking things up.

'No, I swear,' entreated Meslier. 'That's how it was. He was worried. He kept saying; "This is a shit job, this is a shit job". And it is, but it pays well. I'm sorry. I'm really sorry about Armand. He was the best at the work. The best I've ever seen. I liked him,' he looked hopefully up at Jacques.

'I know he was the best,' said Jacques, who was suddenly sick of it all. He threw the pillow away and stood up. Meslier just stared at him, not daring to hope. 'Not a word, Lionel, not a word to anyone. Go to work today and just keep your head down. Then, at the weekend, walk away. Get well away. Go visit your Aunt Lulu in Saint Tropez.'

'I don't have…'

'Just keep your mouth shut and keep out of my way, and you might live to see a few more dawns.' Jacques stormed out of the apartment and Meslier sat up rigidly in bed. One part of him still hoped that he was waking from some particularly realistic nightmare, but the warm dampness on his legs and his stinging face suggested otherwise.

Chapter 41

Celestine was conscious of a vague sense of the daylight as her eyes struggled to open wider than a narrow slit. Her lids were heavy and she slipped in and out of consciousness. She ran her tongue around the inside of her mouth, grimacing as it stuck on the dry tissue of her gums. She groaned and turned her head on the pillow and became gradually aware of the smell. Forcing herself to emerge from sleep, she shook her head slowly and blinked several times, her scalp creasing up in pain. The smell was rank and bilious. She managed to raise her head and then she saw, on the cover beside her, a patch of drying vomit. She started, sitting up quickly and edging away from it; she had no recollection of being sick, and wondered for a moment if, in fact, someone else had puked on her bed - a message or a warning. But then she recognised last night's food in the mess and knew that the bedroom door was locked from the inside. She scrambled out of bed, not taking her eyes from the patch of vomit, as though it might be a moving character in the scene. She walked into the hall and called out for Etienne, but there was no answer. Of course, she always knew when the apartment was empty. Disorientated, feeling dirty and a little fearful, she went into the master bedroom and saw that her husband had slept there for at least part of the night. She cast off her clothes and walked into the bathroom, her head was pounding and there was a sour, acrid taste in her mouth and throat. She drank cold water from the basin before stepping into the shower. There were crusts of vomit in her hair and she rinsed it three times.

Sitting on the bed, allowing the beating in her temples to subside, she tried to work out what had happened. That she had been extremely tired the previous night, she didn't doubt, and she had eaten and drunk just before going to bed. Could she have been sick and not woken, or had she dropped straight back into sleep again after she'd thrown up? When she looked back over the last few days she could believe that her system was completely out of sync. She had gone without food; had bounced along for hours on the back of a motorbike; had placed herself in an extreme situation, where she had held herself tense for hours. Then, of course, the stress of coming to terms with her disintegrating marriage, and possibly her career. It was perhaps not really surprising that her body was objecting and reacting badly. She realised that she was crying out for a period of calm and repose, to look after herself, to give herself time to wash through her emotions and to find a route forward. There was always a route forward - she believed that. But as it stands right now, she thought, I am a long way from being at that point of repose.

She walked into the kitchen to pour herself a large glass of water and noticed that all the dishes and cooking utensils had been cleaned away and put through the dishwasher. She pondered that for a moment, it was out of character, but Etienne was in such an unhinged state it seemed, that perhaps everything was out of character. She swallowed two paracetamol and returned to sit on the main bed, with only a towel wrapped around her. She took a large notepad and began to make lists and diagrams on the pages. She knew that she needed to pull the threads together and then to sketch out a strategy for going forward. Up to now, she had been bouncing between incidents, like a marble in a bagatelle game, a mere responder to events. She wrote down and placed the salient points in boxes, and let her mind clear to allow the patterns to emerge and the links to appear. Small details that she had seen but not registered now came to the fore, and she noted them down, amazed sometimes at the intensity of the detail and the impression it left on her. She also noted the imponderables, those areas where she had little or no control; like the actions of her chiefs in the police force - would she get any help from them, or were they, in fact, an obstruction, more likely to derail her. Allowing for all of that, she sketched out a route map. She knew she had to discount all the personal and emotional issues she was facing and be fully focused on one thing – unearthing the evidence that would convict the murderers of Armand Verville and Ho Thi Quan.

Celestine's first call was at the laboratory, where she knew the director, Dr Miriam Rabelais, and asked her to arrange a quick turnaround on testing the pill she had taken from the factory. The other woman smiled at her and tilted her head to look more closely at Celestine. She clasped one of her hands and peered at Celestine's face.

'You have an unhealthy pallor, Chérie. Your skin is ….What have you been taking?' she asked quietly. Celestine shook her head lightly.

'Nothing. Two paracetamols for a blinding headache this morning. I was sick through the night. It's been a stressful time. I'm very busy.' The doctor looked unconvinced. She opened a cupboard and took out a small glass vessel.

'Since you are here, we can omit the stage where you visit your physician. Go in there and pee in that flask. I will run it through some tests, and if I am not happy I will call you and send details to your doctor. There is something my dear. I do not like the colour of the skin around your eyes, and indeed the colour of your eyes themselves.' She handed the flask to Celestine.

'I don't have time, really I don't…' The doctor put her hand on Celestine's arm.

'No pee, no quick turn-around. That's the deal,' she said and raised her eyebrows. Celestine sighed and took the flask, returning some minutes later with a sample. 'Good. Now go and work, but not too hard. I will call you when I have a result. Two results.'

Chapter 42

Vaillancourt stood outside the apartment door and breathed deeply, letting the strain slip away and the tension within him subside. This at least was a place of refuge, and he wanted to enter it in the correct frame of mind. He imagined she would still be sleeping at this time, so he opened the door quietly with his key. There was silence, and he stood inside the door and sniffed the air in which he believed he could detect her scent.

He tiptoed to the bedroom door, slipping off his jacket and draping it over a chair. The curtains were all drawn and the room was ill-lit, he couldn't make out any details, but it came to him that there was something missing. He eased open the bedroom door, excited, anticipating now to see the slender, languorous body of his young woman, stretching under the thin covers, smiling as she notices him, sitting up, the sheets slipping down from her perfect breasts. But there was no movement in the bed. He switched on the light and saw instantly that there were no covers, just a bare mattress.

He felt a sharp jolt inside his stomach and he looked around desperately. He tore open the door of the closet and the drawers of the dresser where she kept her lingerie. They were empty. He pushed his nose into one of the drawers, sure he could smell the silk and the lace, and her, but there was nothing there. He walked back into the living room and violently drew the curtains back. The room was bare; there was nothing on the table or the surfaces, there was no sign of her existence at all. He looked wildly around, blinking, hoping to clear his sight, to see the scene changed back again. But there were only four walls and the emptiness of a place vacated and a way of life ended.

As the realisation and the dark ramifications sank in, he dropped down onto the sofa, and with his head in his hands, he sobbed and sobbed.

Chapter 43

Jacques crossed the Place Longchamps and entered the gates of the Jardim Public. He took the path that curved around by the lake and sat down on a bench beneath the canopy of a chestnut tree. He stared up into the branches where the pink blossom stood vertically like broad candles. The scene was pretty and tranquil, but inside he felt wretched and ashamed of himself. He couldn't get the cringing face of Lionel Meslier out of his mind, and he wondered, not for the first time, what he had become. How could you act in that way? How could you threaten an old, a pathetic, old man and strike him and violate him, really? He tried to tell himself that it was justified to get the information he needed to find Armand's killer. Maybe he would have talked, just with a little encouragement. Perhaps you could have given the old man the chance to help; he was, after all, an old colleague of Armand's. You were so violent, so threatening, you have lost some of your soul, he thought to himself, and you have replaced it with something much darker and much uglier. And then he imagined his friend Armand, and he knew that he would never have slipped away from his humanity so easily. He sighed and looked at the rippling surface of the water and the leaves of the trees and shrubs, so fresh, so many different colours and shades as spring thrust itself into them. Where is the spring in you? he asked himself; you who have always cherished this time of the year above all others. You need to finish with this campaign soon, very soon, and then get yourself away, out of the city for a while. Time for the streets to be swept clean. He stood up and smiled at a young man who was holding the hands of two little girls, one of whom was chattering without a break, and he noticed that the father appeared to be listening as though it were the most fascinating tale ever told.

He left the park and walked around the edge of Quinconces, glancing at the statues below the Monument to the Girondins, and cursing himself for his stupidity and insensitivity; imagine suggesting to Celestine Courbet that she spend time looking there, as though that would help her in her marriage state. Full of self-loathing, Jacques pounded the streets, striding impatiently through the crowds in the long shopping magnet of Sainte-Catherine, until he came to the Gross Cloche. As always he looked up at the clock before walking beneath its arches and on to the Rue Buhan. Louise's door was locked, and he had to rap gently and call out before he heard the bolts being drawn back and saw her pale, uneasy face peering out at him from behind the chain. As he stepped through the doorway she grasped his wrist with her bony hand. He looked down at her face; it was drawn, almost skeletal, and her eyes were unfocused and scared. He put his arm around her shoulders and guided her to the sofa. He could feel the tension in her hunched-up shoulders, and he sat next to her, quietly, until she regained some calm.

'It's ok. It's ok. Tell me what happened and I will fix it. You know, with my tools and a little glue, I can fix anything.' She attempted a feeble smile and looked up at him gratefully. Then she re-arranged herself, and with her head bowed and her hands in her lap, she began to talk.

'They came back, yesterday, in the afternoon. Two this time, not the same one. Police, hammering on the door,' she paused, and a tremor ran through her body so that Jacques feared she might disintegrate in front of him and just leave a pile of dust on the furniture. 'Hammering and hammering. I didn't like it. I started going to the door but then I stopped, and I hid behind the kitchen door. They can't see in, but I thought they might hear me breathing, hear me teeth chattering and me bones rattling.' She tried to smile. 'Then they started shouting horrible things. "We know you're in there. You have to open the door. We'll break it down", and they shook it and rattled it, and I thought, yes, they will break it down. And then I thought of Jock and Vincent Antonietti, like we talked about the day. And I thought, if they were here, those policemen would have run ten kilometres, they would have kept their mouths shut, would have shown some respect. So, Jacques,' she took a hold of his wrist once more. 'I imagined they were there, between me and the door, so when they started shouting again there was someone else there. Like a ... a shield. But the words they used were horrible.' She shook her head.

'What did they say?' asked Jacques, a deep unease growing inside him.

'They said I was an old fool, and that I didn't see anything out of my window, and that they would personally pull my eyes out of the sockets if I lied like that again. And that they will come back and cut out my tongue as well, so I couldn't tell lies. And they said more horrible things, but by now I was rigid, I had slid down onto the floor. "We know you've been talking, telling lies. We'll cure you of that". Then "Goodnight, Mami", like we were family and it was some dreadful family squabble. But they were so harsh and ugly,' and she burst into tears.

Jacques did his best to comfort her, he made a pot of coffee and tried to get her to talk of other things. He told her he would fix it and that he knew who was involved, and who had passed the information on. He did know and he was furious, and the world had shifted a little. He left Louise when she was calmer, and he promised to return the next day, and she was not to open the door to anyone else. But in his own mind he realised that neither he, nor anyone he now knew, would be in a position to protect her completely until the bigger issues had been resolved. He walked out into the streets with his head in a thousand places. He found himself heading towards the river, and at a busy, noisy café by the Porte de Bourgogne, he sat down and took out his phone.

Chapter 44

Celestine looked for her husband's car in the yard behind the Hotel de Police, but it wasn't there. She stopped at the desk and asked the surly-looking agent to fetch the senior officer. She could see him leaning against one of the pillars, talking loudly to the female officer she had spoken to previously. She knew him; he was a capitaine and was known for his slowness and fastidious adherence to regulations. He seemed reluctant to leave his conversation but Celestine continued to stare in his direction, and he finally shuffled across to face her, his mouth pinched in annoyance. Celestine decided to plough straight in. 'Capitaine Lambert, who released the man Ho Thi Quan from the holding cells on Sunday and took him out of this building without recording it?' His head tilted back and she saw the surprise and wariness in his eyes.

'No one. No one did that. Why are you asking?'

Celestine replied quickly. 'No one, no one did that. And yet a man was in the cells and then he wasn't in the cells. Do you think he fucking vaporised? Don't you keep records of prisoners who just disappear, Capitaine Lambert?'

He stammered then and stood back from the desk as Celestine appeared ready to reach over and assault him. 'There is no record of this person. I have given any information we have to Commandant Martel already.' He turned away.

'CCTV. Lambert. You must have pictures. He was here, he was interviewed, then he left, then he was murdered.' She spoke so loudly that the others working at their desks looked up. She saw a couple of them shaking their heads. She pointed at the lieutenant who had been on duty when Linh had been there. 'You. Did you find out any more, did you?' The woman started to stand up. But Lambert walked over to her and waved for her to sit down.

'My staff and I have placed any relevant information in the hands of your superior officer. We have nothing to add to that,' declared Lambert. Celestine ignored him and continued looking at the lieutenant, she could see in the woman's eyes that she was apologising and had something to say, but Lambert stood in front of her, blocking Celestine's view. Furious, she entered the lift and rode to the third floor. Only Sorbot was in the office, working quietly on his computer. He smiled up at her cautiously, and then seeing her face he asked,

'Boss, are you ok? You look sick or something.'

'Yes, I'm sick, Jean. I had a bad night, but I could say the malaise runs deeper than that.'

'Martel's been looking for you, asking about you, yesterday and this morning. Wanting to know what you're doing. He's mad as hell.'

'So am I, Jean. But what have you been working on?'

'The guy in the alley. Drawn a blank. Nobody knows who he is. There's a lot of unregistered you know.'

'I know, Jean. His name is Ho Thi Quan. Came off a ship at Le Grave.'

'How do you know that, Capitaine? Martel said you were… well, making things up. Said you were having a breakdown or something. Said a lot of things. I didn't like it but he…Have you got any proof?'

'I have got proof, but I'm not going to introduce it yet. I don't trust Martel, and others could be in danger.' Sorbot bit on his lips and glanced uneasily at her

'He said you'd say something like that. Said it was a paranoia you had. Said it was sad, but you were unwell, mentally unstable.' Sorbot's jowly face looked so miserable, like a sad old hound. 'Perhaps you should take some time, boss,' he said. Celestine kicked out at the leg of the desk and started to speak again, but then stopped and walked away into her office. She didn't want to face Martel yet, she needed him a little off his guard. All of his actions suggested that he was thick in the mud of this. Mucky. She walked back out again.

'Have they placed that drug dealer under investigation for the murder?' she demanded. Sorbot shook his head.

'I don't think so, not yet. The examining magistrate was interviewing him this morning, but he was held up at his house.'

'Who's the Juge?'

'Trouffeau.'

'Trouffeau.' Sorbot nodded.

Celestine turned away and walked back to her office. Trouffeau wasn't the magistrate she would have chosen to take her evidence to. He was waspish and supercilious, especially in his dealing with female officers, but he was known to be thorough and very strong in his commitments. Maybe later she would contact him. Surely when he spoke to the drug dealer he would recognise that there was a lot of doubt there.

First, she completed her file on the robbery at Chartron; detailing the interviews with the victims, and then adding a few possible avenues to explore, fences to approach, informants to question. She printed it out and placed it on the edge of her desk, ready to hand to Martel if he came looking for her. Then she started to collate the file and the evidence on the two murders that she would hand to the magistrate. It still seemed very thin, and the process she was intending to follow was unorthodox. Normally the examining magistrate would be appointed by a prosecutor, and he would liaise with the senior officer on the case, which was Martel. It would be highly unusual for a junior officer to produce evidence independently from her boss, which, moreover, contradicted his evidence. Martel would undoubtedly start casting doubts on her reliability, probably already had. She still needed something more solid, more irrefutable. She was puzzling over this when her phone rang - it was Jacques Lecoubarry. She pushed her door closed and walked over to the window.

'Yes, Jacques.' For a minute all she could hear was his breathing, quite loud. 'Jacques.'

'You told. Who did you tell? That was in confidence. You said you wouldn't tell anyone. She's scared out of her wits. She's an old woman. What the fuck. Can't anybody be straight anymore? You bloody told somebody.' Celestine was taken aback by the vehemence in his voice.

'What are you talking about? You're rambling. Who's scared?' she demanded.

'Louise. I told you. She saw a police car at Le Sau. They came around, two of them. Two of Bordeaux's finest. Threatened to cut her tongue out, oh, and her eyes.'

'Jesus, I'm sorry, Jacques, but I didn't tell anyone.' But then it slowly came to her, and as it did so she recognised that a final piece had dropped into place, now there were no more doubts.

'I'm sorry, Jacques, I didn't mean to. I was goading him, seeing if I could discover which side of the fence he was on. I know now. I know where he stands now.'

'Who? Who did you tell?'

'Commissaire Vaillancourt, my husband. I told him to goad him.' There was a long silence. Celestine could picture the face of the man, thinking, running through the options, she could imagine that he was running his fingers through the hair on the side of his head, tugging it slightly, as though it might help to pull out the answers.

'So, he must have sent the two animals,' Jacques said. It wasn't a question.

'Instructed someone to do it. I have my suspicions,' Celestine added.

'You have your suspicions. I have enough of my own, and right now I've just added a new one. You. I thought you were an "untouchable".' His voice sounded distant and raw.

'Look, I am Jacques. I messed up. It was out before I knew. It was the heat of the moment.'

'Was it a trap for him? Cos, you're playing with the life of a very frail old lady here.'

'No, it wasn't a trap, not deliberately. It was just one piece of evidence I was throwing at him. I suppose I was testing him. I'm sorry Jacques, don't think for a minute that I would intentionally risk your friend. I'll apologise to her myself. Did she get their names?'

'She didn't let them in the door. Didn't see them, only heard,' replied Jacques. Celestine started coughing and Jacques waited until the fit had passed.

'You ok?'

'No, but don't ask. I'm busy compiling the file.' Jacques pondered for a moment.

'I have some detail for that file,' he said. 'I paid a visit this morning.' He stopped suddenly. 'Christ, are you lot able to record phone conversations?'

'Sometimes. It's not a simple process.'

'Ok. Face to face. I like to take lunch at the Black Cat on Rue Henry IV. It's small, dark and unpopular, except with the marginals.'

'You want me to come there?'

'Yes.'

'With the marginals. A police officer.'

'Are you wearing a uniform?' asked Jacques.

'No, I don't.'

'So, it will be all right. It's discreet. In half an hour. Try and look a bit sleazy.'

'I don't think so. And I am sorry, Jacques, really. There are some bastards in this place.'

'Oh yes there are. I'd like to bang on their doors one dark night and…'

Chapter 45

Vaillancourt left the city in the early afternoon, after returning to his own apartment to collect a few things. As he closed the door of his marital home, he heard the toll of the bells of the Church of Saint-Louis. As always the chimes sounded portentous, but today he felt nothing. He was numb, functioning but without feeling or awareness of anything around him. There was a leaden weight in the pit of his stomach and it was gradually seeping fear and self-pity into his body. He pulled out of the car park in his dark blue BMW, working his way through the streets on his way to the motorway, unaware of his surroundings, except for the minimum required to keep him on the right road, and certainly not aware of the small black Audi that had followed him from his street in Chartron, and that was sitting only a few cars behind him as he reached the edge of the city.

He took the autoroute south and east, collecting a ticket from the toll booth, and placing it carefully in the well between the seats, where a small plastic packet, almost full of a dirty white powder, was lying. He glanced down at it as he pulled away from the tollbooth, and the weight in his stomach stuck out two sharp blades and sent a stab through his bowels and genitals.

He drove steadily, he was in no great hurry. For the first time in a long while there was no expectation on when he had to reach his destination. He would have time enough to complete what he had settled on. This route he had driven many times before, always with a feeling of hope that maybe on this occasion the visit would be an agreeable experience, one to salve the old sores, to reset a relationship that had moulded so much of his life, so much of what he was. He had no such feeling of hope this day, no expectations, only a realisation that there would be an ending - and that was right. The road was quiet once he'd left the area around Bordeaux and he settled into a steady pace, only occasionally pulling out to overtake a truck or caravan. It was easy driving, and his shadow in the black Audi was content to sit back and follow relentlessly behind.

Chapter 46

Jacques wasn't wrong about the Black Cat. There were a few tables outside, for those who liked to blend their food with the sauce of tobacco smoke. Celestine ducked inside, into the gloom, where the tables were jumbled together, and men, only men, were eating and drinking with an avidity that suggested that they never took this process for granted. Despite their focus, they all looked up as Celestine threaded her way between the tables, and some jaws stopped chewing and glasses hovered for a second on their way to the mouths. Jacques enjoyed the discomfit of the moment, for the patrons but also for Celestine. He was still angry, but seeing her brushing past the gawpers and the leerers with her head held high and a hard glare in her eyes, brought out his admiration and he smiled broadly at her and stood up to pull out her chair. To his surprise, she kissed him on both cheeks like an old friend, as though this was the most normal of lunch engagements.

'So this is where they lunch when they leave prison,' she said quietly, 'I often wondered where they went.' Jacques laughed.

'An interesting clientele I admit, but incorruptible in their way. Where do the Bordeaux police have their lunch, Celestine? If there was an honesty contest…'

'Sometimes I think there are not three honest men in Bordeaux,' she said and picked up a rather soiled menu card.

'Mm. Who is the other one, unless you were not being gender specific? I would like to think you were an honest man. Are you?' he asked. She looked at him, but there was still a hardness in her eyes.

'It was a mistake. I have apologised. Now stop being holier than thou and tell me what I can eat in this place that doesn't include horse.'

Jacques looked at her carefully. 'In reality, you don't look robust enough for some of the dishes in here,' he said, 'you look…'

'Yes, I know. I look like shit. You are the third person to tell me that today. I've been sick. Over it now.' They sat back, the first round of verbal intercourse completed. Jacques smiled gently at her.

'The asparagus omelette might be the thing. Bit bland, but 'tis the season of the asparagus. In Basque Country, we cook it with hake and a dry white wine. You should try it sometime.' They ordered, and Celestine took out her notebook but Jacques waved her to return it to her bag. 'Very suspicious of the written word are these compatriots,' he said. 'I will tell you what I found out this morning.' He gave her a sanitised version of his visit to Meslier. She looked at him sceptically a few times but said nothing until he'd finished.

'So they are altering these machine parts to look as though they were from a different company?' she queried.

'Yes. They're bringing in cheaper components, I mean large components, you saw them, from Vietnam. They are, I guess, made of inferior metal, or maybe not up to the technical standards required.'

'Required for what?' asked Celestine.'

'For the nuclear power industry. They are adding numbers and details, to identify the parts as being manufactured by the major European makers. Forging identities for components, which are sold as genuine, and at a large premium.'

'And that's what Armand Verville was working on?' Jacques nodded. 'Sold to French nuclear power stations?' she asked.

'I guess, and others throughout Europe. You said Zubizaretta had a European client base. He's been supplying customers everywhere. Bloody nuclear reactors, and why not if there's money to be made…'

'So that's the link with Nguyen. The Vietnamese link. That's why he needs Zubizaretta. And the equipment is stuffed with illegal drugs as well,' added Celestine. 'You've got to hand it to them, it's a sweet arrangement.'

Celestine sat quietly, picking at her omelette when it came, forking out the green asparagus tips and chewing on them as she contemplated the enormity of the information Jacques had uncovered.

'Meslier, will he testify? In fact, I'll make him testify,' said Celestine fiercely.

'Behind armoured glass. He's not the heroic type. These are bad bastards playing these games,' replied Jacques.

'They are, they are. But this puts a whole new complexion on it. This is not just a drug smuggling case. This is a national, international issue.' She pushed her plate away. 'Now I think I realise exactly how much is at play here. No wonder I'm being blocked and kept away from this.' She told Jacques what Sorbot had told her. Jacques was incensed and he put his hand on top of hers and squeezed it. She didn't move it away. 'We are going to have to be really careful. I need to think this thing out. Think it out very carefully.'

'How is the dossier coming along? You can add this. Surely that will make someone pick up the ball and run with it.'

'Maybe, maybe. I wish I had pictures. I should have taken pictures yesterday, but I left my phone in that bloody leather jacket.'

'What about the pill? You've had it tested?'

'I haven't had the results yet. She'll get back to me today, I'm sure.' She thought for a moment of the doctor at the laboratory. 'She made me do a test, you know, on me, a sample. Said she didn't like the look of me.'

'Hm. Clearly a doctor with no taste,' said Jacques gallantly.

'No. I was ill last night, sick. I didn't even remember it. Not till I woke up. It was horrible.' She shivered and placed her hands on her stomach.

'Well that's a shame, as I was planning to kiss you on the mouth today,' said Jacques, his eyes rolling theatrically.

She smiled. 'Oh, were you? Well, don't. I am quite repulsive.'

'Yeah, you are. But I'm going to ask you anyway.'

'Ask what?'

'A friend of mine is directing a play. It opens tonight at the Corner Theatre. She's a good friend and I will go, despite all this. It's quite avant-garde, but it'll be good, she's very good. It'll take us out of ourselves. I think you need that, for a few hours at least. I need that. Anyway, I'm going and I have two tickets and one of them has your name on it, so you have to come. Ok.' He stopped, he realised that he was starting to gabble like a schoolboy. She was looking at him, following his words, but the hardness had gone from her eyes.

'A play. A theatre. I haven't been to a theatre in, I don't know, years. Etienne finds them pretentious and amateurish.'

'It won't be pretentious. Honest, enthusiastic, bursting with drama. It's just the being there. A chance to slip through the cracks into the dreams of others and see them exposed for you. I love the theatre.' He stopped again. She was still looking at him closely.

'Yes, I will. An escape into the dreams of others. What's the play called, what's it about?'

Jacques hesitated. 'It's about betrayal. It's simply called Betrayal.'

'Betrayal. Jesus. I could write the book about that, but there's always something new to learn about your specialist subject.'

Jacques grimaced. 'I'm sorry, but they don't do Moliere. More's the pity, but it's a different kind of theatre.'

'You like Moliere?'

Jacques nodded. 'It is not only what we do, but also what we do not do, for which we are accountable,' he quoted. 'That's quite close to home.'

'I'd heard something like that, but I didn't know it was Moliere. Yet another surprising facet of Jacques Lecoubarry,' said Celestine. 'What time?'

'Starts at eight, but we need to take a drink before. Come to the emporium for seven. Bring the dossier, you can leave it there.'

'Seven, ok.' But the lightness of their conversation slipped away, and the dark clouds gathered again. Celestine coughed. 'Be careful' they both said at the same time.

'This is very dangerous, Jacques.'

'For you surely. Don't worry about me.'

'For both of us. We need to be very sure-footed in the next forty-eight hours or so.'

Chapter 47

Vaillancourt changed autoroutes near Montauban and headed north before turning off at Caussade. He drove past row after row of fresh green grape vines winding up from their stubby winter stems. He pulled in by an ancient barn advertising vintages from the major chateaux. It was dark and cool inside and smelt of old stone and must. He wandered along the racks, pulling out bottles to look more closely at their labels. He chose a Domain de la Ramayne as a gift.

'Never look a gift vintage in the mouth', he sneered a little to himself. He bought, a Domaine de Moulin Florentin for himself. He would drink it alone, he thought, and it would be a rejection of all those fine Bordeaux wines he had drunk and which had been a part of the seduction. A rejection of Bordeaux, the whore who had ruined him. A wave of self-pity washed over him, and he had to stand and grip the bottles until he regained some control. He bought a large slice of Cantal Entre Deux cheese, a pate fritons de porc and some slices of dried ham. He took out his bank card to pay but then quickly changed his mind, instead drawing all the cash he had and placing it on the counter. He was too agitated to count it and the girl assistant pulled the notes together herself and handed him back a small amount of change. She would remember this later when interviewed, that and the haunted, distracted look on the customer's face.

He drove on, along the straight road into the Causses, where the woods came close to the road and there were few vistas. But then the road crossed a deep river valley and he pulled into a small parking place and stepped out of the car, just as a black Audi came alongside. If he had looked up he might have seen the driver and it might have started a new chain of thought in his mind. But he was looking away, and now he was standing on the edge of a cliff face, looking down at the river below. He could smell the energy and the freshness of the air as it rose up from the surging waters below. He closed his eyes and breathed deeply, swaying a little as he let the sweet air and the warmth of the sun envelope him. But then he opened his eyes with a start, and his stomach wrenched and he coughed up bile and froth and spat it out onto the stones. He could sense the vastness of the Causses, the high ground, stretching for hundreds of kilometres all around him. It made him feel small and shrivelled, like it had when he was a boy. It had always made him feel temporary and insignificant, and that is what he hated, that was one of the reasons why he had left.

He got back into the car and drove more quickly; the black Audi following discreetly like a shadow servant. He saw the first signs for Figeac and he could have turned away, it was his last chance, he knew. But there was just an inevitability about it now, and he had no volition left to change the course that had been set. It was six o'clock when he parked by the river, on a quiet street of the town, and as he stepped out to stretch his legs the church bells started chiming, and it was almost as though he had completed a passage from bell tolls to bell tolls, and he felt as if everything he did now had a resonance to it, everything was foreseen and would be marked by an announcement from the bells, somewhere He stood in front of the Church of Saint-Sauveur, where he had served as an altar boy, caught up then in the mysteries and mysticism of a religion that meant nothing to him now and could offer him no consolation. He turned away and walked back to his car.

The drive to his father's house took only five minutes. As he turned into the tight entrance he had to grip the steering wheel hard and grit his teeth until his heart rate fell and his breathing eased. He picked up the food he had bought, but then he took two slices of ham and half of the cheese and left them behind on the passenger seat. He chose the white wine and placed it in the bag with the other goods. He had to knock hard on the front door, as his father's hearing was poor, but eventually the door creaked open and a thinner, scrawny, much older version of Vaillancourt stood there. The expression on his face was of annoyance and distaste.

'Hello, Papa,' said Vaillancourt. 'I have brought you a present.'

Chapter 48

It was a little after seven when Celestine climbed the stairs to Jacques' rooms above the workshop. It was the first time Jacques had seen her in a dress and he thought she seemed more relaxed. He walked ahead of her, but at the top of the stairs, he turned and kissed her on both cheeks and looked at her in admiration.

'Methamphetamine. That's what's in the tablets. Probably manufactured in Myanmar,' she said, and frowned until he stopped staring at her and invited her into the room.

'Right, so definitely illegal then.'

'Yes, illegal, and in quantity. There must be millions of euros worth,' Celestine continued. 'I have to stop them getting onto the streets.'

Jacques nodded. 'You look stunning in that dress,' he said.

'Thanks. So this is where you live.' She looked around and then looked twice. 'It's like you isn't it? You think you've seen it, then you look again and there's something more, and it's nice, like that table, and there's another surprise.' She turned to him. 'Like peeling off different layers.'

'That's me. The onion man,' he laughed.

'Hmm. It's interesting. I don't suppose this room is like any other room, anywhere. And you have some beautiful furniture.'

'I've kept some of the best pieces over the years, when I could, and inherited pieces from my aunt and uncle too.'

'Yes. So you lived here, and you lived with them?' she asked, she was genuinely curious.

'I came here when I was eight, with my mother after my father died. We lived on the top floor. Then she died, then my uncle died, then my aunt died.'

'Poor Jacques.'

He shook his head. 'Poor humans. Everybody goes through it. You're just lucky if you get a good spell now and again and end it naturally.' They sat down. 'I'd show you more of the house, but it's a rich meal and I don't want you to get indigestion. Talking of which, did you get the test results?'

'No. It takes them a day or so. I'll find out tomorrow,' she paused. 'I want to go back there. I want some photographs.' She took a file from her bag and placed it on the sofa beside her. I'll leave this here. I might ask you to bring it when I make an appointment with the juge d'instruction.'

'Of course. When do you think that'll be?' Jacques asked. 'When I have a little more. I want photographs of the machine parts. I've put Lionel Meslier's name in the dossier. Ok?'

'Sure, has to be done. But you mustn't let the information get into the wrong hands. Do you know all of the wrong hands now?' She tossed her head and her lips tightened.

'No. Martel, I'm sure now. Etienne. I think I've traced the two flics who visited your friend. I cross-referenced the logs.'

'Nguyen. He's probably got dozens on his payroll. That's how they operate isn't it?' said Jacques.

'Maybe. I hope not. I hope it's just a few, powerful ones.' She looked sad and suddenly vulnerable. 'I've been ostracised, Jacques, by the people I've worked with for years. There was no one in my department this afternoon. It's as though I've got the plague and no one wants to be infected by me.'

'Is there no one in there?'

'Maybe, but they're young or afraid. Worried about their careers. That's something.'

'What is?'

'I realise I'm not worrying about my career anymore. I just don't care. It's all turned sour and I just want some justice, then I want to walk away for a time. I'm tired of being under this pressure. My marriage is at an end, I'm forty next year and I've hit the wall big time,' she paused. 'So if you'd rather cancel tonight's engagement I would understand. You can see the kind of company I'm going to be. And you're…'

'On your side. Come on, we need a drink, and I'll tell you some funny stories about Armand Verville, then you'll appreciate the fact that you are actually on the side of the angels.' He stood up, and taking her hand he pulled her gently to her feet.

'Can I, don't get this wrong, but could I see your bedroom? I just imagine it's going to be like another dimension again.'

'Ah ha. Prepare to enter the realms of mystery and mythology, where sleep is only one of the places where fantasies exist,' said Jacques theatrically. They walked along a short corridor and Jacques opened the door into a large room with a single, shuttered window and high ceilings, dominated by a huge bed with dark spiralled posts at each corner and an intricately carved headboard of spirals and what looked like the wings of an eagle.

'Portuguese travelling bed. Seventeenth Century-ish. Made for the tenth Duke of Braganza, who was a tyrant of massive girth and many unhealthy pastimes. Not at all a man like me.' Celestine couldn't help smiling. 'And the wall coverings are all tapestries, Spanish, French, Italian, Dutch. Some faded, some where the colours are as new.'

Celestine stepped into the room and looked around. 'They're beautiful, really beautiful, Jacques. Are they very valuable?'

'A little, but not seriously valuable. But the scenes they depict are of all human life. Well, up to the twentieth Century, there are no cars or aeroplanes.' He pointed. 'Humans: drinking water at a well, hunting, working in the fields, dancing, fighting, sailing on the oceans, making love.'

'Yes, I see, all of life. Is there any betrayal there?' she mused.

'Oh yes. Look at this chap here, he's stealing from his master, or this guy sneaking into the maid's bedchamber as his wife sleeps next door.'

'And this?'

'Men dressed as women, women dressed as men, hunters. There's nothing new.'

'No, I suppose not. Do you have a favourite?' she asked.

'No. I try not to get too attached. They're things, beautiful things, but I'm a human. It's the animals that count, not the objects.'

'You surprise me. Have I said that before? You surprise me, Jacques. I can't get a hold on you.'

Jacques grinned.

'Does that matter? Come on, you think too much. It's feeling not thinking as will do the job.' He laughed and took hold of her hand. 'If you keep me from alcohol much longer I shall not be responsible for my actions. Come on, out into the sunlight and let's drink and lose ourselves for a while. The dark stuff will still be there when we emerge.'

Jacques locked the door and they walked along the pavement, arm in arm. Across the street, in an unmarked car, a man took a number of photographs of them on his mobile phone, and as they turned the corner he stepped out and walked after them.

Chapter 49

Vaillancourt left his father's house after two hours. They hadn't talked much and they had eaten little. For much of the time they had sat looking at each other, wondering if there had ever been a link. His father was clearly irritated by the interruption and expressed little interest in his son's world.

'I have reached the highest point in my career. There is nothing I can achieve beyond this.' Vaillancourt had said at one point. His father had seemed to ponder this for a few moments.

'You always left a lot on the field,' he said and sipped on the dry white wine. As he stood up to leave, Vaillancourt held out a hand to his father, who held it lightly for a second, then turned to pick up the remote control for the television.

Vaillancourt snarled. 'I know a man who slit the throats of three other men, just for his father. You know, I wouldn't kill a rat if it was eating your bones, Papa.'

He walked out and drove through the town to the river. He crossed a bridge and parked by a low wall where he could see the waters running deep and swift. He took a knife from the glove compartment, and using the corkscrew end, he opened the bottle of rich red wine and took a deep swallow. Then he placed the cheese and ham on his lap and cut them into pieces. He prepared his meal. The sun was slowly setting and it cast a golden light on the spire of the Église Saint-Sauveur. He gazed at it, it had been a place of promise once. He was alone, there was no one in sight. He placed the food on the passenger seat, propped up the bottle of wine and stepped out into the evening. He walked over to the stone balustrade and leaned on top, wanting to feel the warmth and smell the fragrant air, the wisteria and jasmine, and the heady scent of may blossom. He closed his eyes and raised his head to take in a deep breath. His throat was cut through in an instant. Agony and astonishment forced his eyes open wide. He clasped his hands to his throat and felt the warm gushing of his blood before his lungs began to hunt desperately for air. And then he was falling, and the last sense was of the cold water folding around him, and the blue, then the black, then nothing as his corpse floated slowly beneath the arches of the ancient walls.

Vinh wiped the blade of his knife on the weeds growing from the foot of the parapet. He glanced around, but there was no movement, it was a place for fine killings, he thought. He walked swiftly over to Vaillancourt's car and reached in through the passenger door. He took the key pad and threw it into the river. He wasn't sure why, but it seemed like a kind of precaution. Then he noticed the food, the cheese and the meat on the seat, and he took them and the bottle of wine. He hadn't eaten since early morning and he was ravenous; action did that. He walked silently along the dark narrow lane to where his car was parked. He took a drink from the wine bottle and thrust a piece of ham into his mouth. He drove out of town carefully and then after about five kilometres he pulled into a stopping place under the trees. He needed to pee, and he thought he would drink the wine and eat the food in peace before setting off on the long road back to Bordeaux. He finished all the food and most of the wine, then he stepped out to stand behind a tree to urinate. Suddenly he was struck by a fireball in his stomach, and he lurched forward and vomited copiously, his mouth and his throat were on fire. He collapsed and crawled forward for a few feet before his brain was starved of oxygen and all consciousness left him. His body was found there the next day by a delivery driver. The door to his car was still open and there was a dao gam knife lying in the well between the seats.

Chapter 50

Jacques and Celestine stayed at the theatre for some time after the play had ended. They joined a gathering of the actors and others involved in the production. Candice came up to them and hugged them both so warmly that Celestine was taken aback. She looked at the face of the woman who was clearly appraising her with a genuine, but kindly interest, and she saw how Candice's eyes flashed when she looked at Jacques. Her husband was introduced, and he also embraced Jacques heartily and kissed her robustly on both cheeks.

Later, she said to Jacques, 'So, you didn't say you'd built the scenery. I thought it all looked quite amazing. The whole thing was ... fascinating, but a bit disturbing, and definitely thought-provoking. I was quite enthralled. But you didn't say before that you'd built the scenery. '

Jacques smiled and nodded. 'Yes. I did. It's a different kind of challenge. I like that. It's a challenge of interpretation, as well as woodworking.' he said. 'I'm sorry it wasn't comedy, it was very earnest. Candice and Philippe, they like to encourage people to confront themselves a little deeper, it can be uncomfortable. You should read some of Philippe's poetry, or better, listen to him reading it - it's extraordinary. But your nerves need to be robust when you do. I don't think this is the time.'

They were sitting outside on the terrace of a small bar by the Église Sainte-Croix. The bells chimed and Celestine suddenly shivered. It was a little chilly but good to be in the air, Jacques thought.

'Are you in love with her?' asked Celestine, holding him with her interrogatory stare. He took a deep breath and looked away. 'She's in love with you,' Celestine continued.

'No, she's in love with Phillippe. But she has a lot of love, a lot of passion.'

'Were you lovers?' Celestine persisted. Jacques hesitated, how much to reveal. He didn't want to be cornered or labelled, not by her.

'We have been. She's the most generous woman I have ever met.' He raised his hand as if to halt that line of conversation. 'Now shut up, and let me tell you another story about Armand Verville, so that you might know the man. He wasn't without fault, he definitely wasn't PC, but....' He poured himself another glass of wine and offered one to Celestine. She held up her hand.

'No thanks. I'm still feeling a bit ... tender. But you, you carry on, and tell me another story, Jacques. It all feels a little unreal tonight anyway.' Celestine sat back, wrapped her throw around her shoulders and looked up at the ornate façade of the building opposite.

'We were working in Nantes, on an organ and a church renovation, St. Benedicts.'

'An organ?'

'Yes, don't interrupt. Write down your questions and I'll answer them at the end. The organ was a mess, but it wasn't just the organ, it was the pews, the pulpit, the wrought ironwork on the confessionals. There was a mountain of work to do, and Armand had won the contract by promising a team of the finest craftsmen from all over France. Which was true in some ways, as I come from the Basque Country and Armand was from La Rochelle.'

'There were just two of you?'

'Yes, but still the finest craftsmen.'

'I don't doubt it. I'm sorry, I won't interrupt.'

'So, in Nantes. Not a really old church, eighteenth century, built to save the souls of the poor workers who'd migrated into the city to work in the factories and the mills. It had a few nice features, very gothic, but it had been neglected over thirty or forty years. No great architectural or historical value, but somebody had found some money from somewhere, so Armand and me, we were restoring it slowly and carefully.

Now, after a few weeks of working there, in that quiet place, with no noise except what we made ourselves, I suppose we became a bit calm, contemplative maybe; everywhere we looked there were religious paintings and artefacts, and we became a little detached from the everyday world. Armand was always one for thinking about unusual things; he'd pipe up with something most days; "Jacques, what do you think is humanity's greatest mistake?" something like that. Anyway, one day the big wooden door creaks open and a tramp comes in, homeless guy. Not that old, but with a lost, damaged look on his face. He came up to where we were working and Armand starts talking to him. He's a bit simple, slow you know, with his speech and stammered a little, vague but friendly. It was almost lunchtime, so Armand leans back against one of the pews and offers the guy some of his food. Good food too, we always ate well, you can't work without that.'

'No. That's where I've been going wrong,' said Celestine. 'Clearly, you haven't.' She was smiling now and enjoying listening to Jacques' deep, slow, southern voice.

'Ssh. So this character asks us what we're doing. Armand shows him the grill he's been repairing for the confessional, but he says, jokingly, "I'm making a cage to put the demons in", and the guy just sort of nods, but his eyes widen, and Armand embellishes it a bit. Because he always did. And the guy just says, "I hate priests".'

'I hate priests?' asked Celestine. Jacques nodded.

'Anyway, the next day he comes back, and Armand shares his food with him and asks him a little about his life; he doesn't say much, but he tells us his name - Monsieur Poulet. Not Jacques or Armand, but Monsieur Poulet. Then he asks Armand what he's doing today. So Armand says, today I'm mending the frame for these pipes, so they can blow the demons up to the sky where the angels can catch them, and the guy just nods, but his eyes get wider and he starts to say something, but the words won't come.'

'You remember all these details, Jacques. You'd make a good witness.'

Jacques grinned. 'Don't they say the devil's in the detail, but I think it's the other side, personally. Anyway, don't interrupt. The next day, Monsieur Poulet comes back again, shares some food, asks Armand what he is doing today. Armand picks up a metal rod with a small cross on top, part of a screen or something. "Today," says Armand. "I am forging a branding iron so that the demons can be branded with a cross before they're sent up the pipes, and then they can be easily recognised by the angels. And he embellishes a lot more. He's not taking the piss, he's just enjoying himself making things up, not thinking that the guy is taking him too seriously. It's all getting a bit surreal, and Armand keeps looking across at me and I can see the laughter in his eyes, and he's just about keeping it together. And the guy says, "I hate priests".

Fourth day's a Friday, and we're going home for the weekend, we're a bit demob happy, you know. We're just about to stop for lunch, I'm working on the screen behind where the organist sits, Armand has a bench in front of the altar and he's engraving. He's a beautiful engraver, and he's working on this big brass plaque to replace the one by the door, which is almost illegible. He's done about seven letters of the name. Monsieur Poulet comes in and Armand sits down on the steps leading up to the altar, gets out his food and hands some to this homeless guy. By this time he's been getting extra food in the morning to make sure he has enough to share. They talk for a while, then he says, "What are you doing today, Armand?" Well, Armand is now loose in the realms of anything goes, and he starts spinning this story about how the name of the man who will capture the demons will miraculously appear out of this magic plaque he's been burnishing. Now to me, it sounds wild but funny, and I'm starting to feel my belly rolling, and Armand, every time he says something I can hear it in his voice, he's getting slightly hysterical. And he looks at me and he says, "And the name of the man shall be revealed on the day of Judgement, when the angels and all the demons shall come forth"; and we're starting to laugh out loud now, and it's not against this guy, he's kind of laughing along with us, quietly, it's just Armand being funny. So the guy says, "Can I see it?" and Armand says, "Sure, but there's nothing to see, the name shall be revealed on the Day of Judgement", and the guy says, "Ok, ok, let me see". So they walk up to the bench and the guy looks down, his eyes nearly drop out of his head and his hands go up in the air, and he starts shaking in his shabby old clothes. "Benedict", he shouts out, "it says B-Benedict", and Armand pretends not to look at it, but the guy is bursting out now. "Not until Armageddon," says Armand, but this guy grabs him by the wrist and he's mouthing, "Benedict, I'm fucking Benedict". "You're Benedict", says Armand, "Jesus, that's a surprise", and now the guy is looking all around, maybe he's looking for Jesus. Well then Armand loses it for good, he starts laughing so much he's doubled up and he collapses onto the floor, taking great gulps of air, he's got the giggles you know, he's trying to speak but he can't, he's just creased up, and I'm rolling about behind the screen. I don't know how long we're lying there, and Monsieur Poulet is kind of hopping around the chancel, and the wave of giggles is slowly starting to abate, and Armand rolls over and looks up and there's a guy leering over him; he's a priest, some kind, and he's dressed all in scarlet, scarlet cassock, and he's just a little guy but he's absolutely livid and he's starting to shout at Armand and his eyes are starting out of his face and red, and he has two comb-overs, you know, on either side of his bald head, and when he bends over to scream at Armand they fall forward and they look for all the world like to two little black horns coming out of his head. Armand looks up at him and he calls out. "Hey, Benedict, your first demon's arrived", and he collapses into giggles again. Honestly, Celestine, I'm limp with laughing, I can't stand up, I'm aching with it. Then this tramp, Benedict, starts running around and he's shouting "Where's me fucking branding iron?" and he picks up the rod with the cross and starts towards the priest, who's off like a shot, legging it down the aisle towards the big doors and Benedict is lumbering after him. Armand keeps saying, in a voice just like the tramp's, "I'm B-Benedict, where's me fucking branding iron", and collapsing again. It takes another ten minutes before we're able to sit up, we were drained with laughing. Couldn't do any more work. We went home.'

Jacques looked across at Celestine, whose eyes were shining and her face was a little flushed, but there was a slight look of disapproval in the set of her mouth. He drained his glass of wine in one and shook his head, there were tears in his eyes.

'Armand. That was Armand. He never meant anybody any harm, but he did like to laugh, and he would always push it and push it until he'd squeezed every last drop out of a funny situation.'

'Did you keep the job?' asked Celestine.

'There was hell on, but they liked the work we were doing. We were there nearly six months, but we never saw the demon priest again.'

'And Benedict?'

'He didn't come back in, but we saw him in the street sometimes, and Armand always gave him something. It sounds funny, but when we did see him, he seemed more settled in himself, you know, like he'd been through something and it had straightened him out just a little.' Jacques shook his head again.

'That's kind of a weird story, Jacques. It doesn't feel quite right, you know. A bit insensitive. As you said, not exactly PC your Armand Verville,' said Celestine.

'No, he wasn't,' said Jacques sharply. 'He said and did things he shouldn't. But he ought not to be dead!' He poured himself another glass and drank deeply, his eyes still moist and angry.

Celestine reached over and laid her hand on Jacques' arm.

'Look, I've laughed more tonight than in years,' she said, 'so thank you for that. But I'm a bit blitzed now, and I must go home. I'll take a taxi. It's going to be a hard day tomorrow. But thanks again for tonight, Jacques. It's been … memorable.'

Jacques saw Celestine into a taxi and walked slowly back through the quiet streets of Bordeaux, thinking about her and about Armand Verville. He wanted to form a plan for the next day but his head was thick with the wine, and he was tired and emotionally battered. He let himself into his quarters above the workshop and collapsed on the bed. He was so weary he took off his shoes, wrapped a cover over himself and was asleep in seconds.

Chapter 51

Linh waited until the girl's breathing had settled before slipping out of the bed and tip-toeing from the room. There were no lights, so she felt her way down the stairs into the darkened restaurant. A pale light filtered through the window at the front, which bathed the tables in an unearthly green and left deep shadows between. She started at each dark shape and shivered at what she was about to do. She stumbled against one of the chairs which scraped noisily across the floor, and Linh hugged herself and stood in silence, feeling her heartbeat and listening to hear any sound from above. She crossed the restaurant and opened the door to the toilets; she imagined it would be harder for anyone to hear her speaking there. She switched on the phone and the light below her face made her look gaunt and spectral in the bathroom mirror. She was resolved, and taking a deep breath she dialled the number.

Celestine was still awake, her mind was picking over the day and the strange evening. She was sitting on the bed, with her notepad, trying to focus, when the telephone rang.

'Linh, it's late, are you ok?' she asked quickly.

'Ok. Monsieur Nguyen, Monsieur Zubizaretta here tonight. I listen.'

'Go on.'

'Tomorrow, they go to the factory by the river. Tomorrow at seventeen hours.'

Celestine was suddenly very much awake and focused.

'Seventeen, five o'clock, at the factory. You are sure they said the factory?'

'Sure. Monsieur Nguyen, he is very angry. Madame, they say your name. They say your name and Commissaire Vaillancourt.'

'Commissaire Vaillancourt, was he at the meeting?' asked Celestine.

'No. Very angry. Something happens. They are going to the factory. Problems.' She paused. 'Did they kill Ho Thi Quan?' Celestine heard the tremor and the anger in her voice.

'I think so. I'm pretty sure they did,' replied Celestine. There was silence for a few moments. 'Linh, you must be very careful now. No one must know you are speaking to me.'

'I know, I go now. Thank you.' The line went dead. Celestine sat looking at the phone. So they had mentioned her name, she must be getting to them. She shivered involuntarily. No Vaillancourt. Where was he, she wondered? But then she didn't, and she recognised how periphery he had now become to everything she was doing, and to her. She lay for some time, trying to pull all the ends together. A plan was forming, but there were still too many uncertainties. Her sleep, when it came, was troubled; the heads of the main characters in the drama kept appearing in her dreams, like untethered balloons. She woke several times, and each time the same questions waited for her, waited for an answer she wasn't ready to give.

Chapter 52

It was just before two o'clock in the morning when Agent Soulier cut two small circles out of the glass in the arched windows on either side of the door. He took the glass out carefully and placed it on the ground. He screwed the plastic spout onto the petrol can and pushed the end through the first circle. He poured slowly and carefully, listening to the petrol dripping quietly onto the floor inside. He did the same through the second hole until the can was empty. Then he took two petrol-soaked rags and pushed them into the holes, leaving a few centimetres outside. He took the can back to his car on the other side of the street and placed it in the boot. Then he walked back and stood listening. The street was deserted, quiet as the grave, he thought. For several minutes he just stood there, on the brink of another step that would take him further and further away from the place he had started out. Then he took a cigarette lighter and lit the end of the rag, it flared quickly and he moved sharply to the other window and fired that rag too. He didn't want to wait around, but he was interested to see the progress of the fire. He sat in his car, a little way down the street. He could see the flickering of flames through the murky windows. He thought he could hear crackling, and now and then a thud, as of a small explosion, and the whole window was lit up. He pulled off the dark jacket he'd been wearing over his uniform and drove off down the street.

The flames licked and caressed the dry, two-hundred-year old wood, and spat at the sawdust, and surrounded the glue pots and swallowed them with a flare. Each new conquest added to the power of the flames and they turned plastic into thick black smoke and wood into choking grey. Behind the second window, the metal tools resisted even as their paint was scoured from them, but the store of wood pieces, and thin strips of veneer caught alight with enthusiasm. The ancient workbench began to char and then burn like logs in a stove. In a very short time, the rooms below were thick with smoke, and the heat was building as each new stick was captured and devoured. Rosewood, wonderfully carved and shaped, mahogany, walnut rich in patina, leather tops, hundred-year-old marquetry, which despite its provenance was powerless to resist the flames. The ceilings and the doorframes were starting to smoke, then the windows blew out, and that's when Jacques woke up.

Unable to make sense of the density of the darkness, at first he thought he was still dreaming, but then he coughed and all his senses reared up. The thick smoke was filling his nostrils and scouring his eyes. He could feel the heat and hear the crackling of the burning timbers below. He turned quickly out of bed and rolled onto the floor, gasping at the clearer air a few centimetres from the ground. He reached up and felt for his phone and the file that Celestine had left, and which he had intended to read before sleeping. His bedroom was to one side of the central door, above the tools and wood store. He could hear the triumph in the sound of the fire as it claimed another victim down below. The smoke was his first enemy, so he crawled, face centimetres from the carpet towards the door. He had reached within a metre of it, but he could feel the heat beneath him and in front and he dared not open it. He crawled back, coughing and choking all the time, towards a small bathroom which led off the main bedroom. It was at the very back of the building and had a small window high up in the wall. He heard another roar and a small explosion as the fire scored another goal, and it was getting closer, he knew he had little time left.

He closed the bathroom door, threw some towels into the sink and turned on the tap. He tried to pack the wet towels around the door, but the smoke was starting to seep under and around the door frame. All this time, one side of his brain was repeating, this is the end, this is the end. He stood on the pan of the bidet and reached for the window clasp. How big have you become JL? he asked himself. Can you get through that window? There was another whoosh and suddenly the heat was growing and smoke was beginning to squeeze thickly through the door frame. He tucked the file into his shirt and the phone into his trouser pocket, and levered himself onto the window ledge. He pushed hard to get the window to open as far as it could go. Then he wriggled forwards so that his head and shoulders were protruding into the night sky and he gulped in deep breaths of glorious air. Below him was the corrugated roof of an outbuilding belonging to the house opposite, which fronted the main street. He had no option but to fall onto it, three metres below. But he was still manoeuvring his body through the window, caught fast as his shirt and trousers snagged on the window catch. He was half-in and half-out, and as helpless as a trapped rat. He stretched back his hand, his side was being pierced by the metal stopper on the frame, but he struggled and squeezed, and little by little he managed to free himself. And as the bathroom door began to buckle, he pulled himself up the last few centimetres and dropped, arms out to protect his head, and landed heavily on the roof below. The fall took the wind out of him, and his elbow and left shoulder, which took the brunt of the landing, were badly jarred, and he felt the pain searing up his arm and down his back. He lay uncomfortably for a few minutes, catching his breath and allowing the terror to subside. Then he took out his phone and called 112, but left no name. He had only thought about survival up to this point, but sitting on that roof, it came to him suddenly, that his world had ended. There was nothing that could survive those flames. He had no shoes on his feet, but he was fully clothed, luckily he had fallen asleep dressed or he could have been sitting out there naked. Gradually, as his breathing became more regular, and the air in his lungs was fully changed for clear, night air, his head also cleared and he had a moment of lucid coherence; his world was at an end so he must end the world of those who had taken it. Nothing more.

He edged along the roof until he came to a wall, and holding onto it he slid slowly down the corrugated sheets to the edge. Below was a yard, he could make out shapes, it smelled of decay, of dampness and a lack of sunlight. Holding onto the metal gutter, he swung his legs over the edge and managed to wrap his feet around the downpipe. Bare feet are useful sometimes, he thought, in his strange disassociated state. As he touched the cold and slimy ground there was another roar and flames came bursting out of a window on the top floor of the house. His house, his home.

The yard was enclosed on all sides by walls and the building. He tried the only door opening onto the yard, but it was locked. The windows were not shuttered, so he felt around on the earth, stubbing his toes repeatedly until he found a brick that had fallen loose from a low wall. Covering his eyes, he swung his arm back and hurled the brick at one of the windows nearest the door. It shattered, like the tolling of a thousand small bells. He picked up another piece of masonry and broke off the shards of glass that were sticking up from the window frame. He sat gingerly on the windowsill and swung his legs inside the building and cautiously lowered his bare feet to the floor. He shone the light from his phone and tried to pick his way through the splinters and fragments of glass. He yelped as his big toe and the ball of his left foot were sliced by a piece that was jammed against the leg of a desk. He passed through the room to the door and bent down to pull the glass from his foot, blood dripping onto the wooden floor. The door opened onto a passageway which led to the front entrance of the building. He was puzzled, he appeared to be in the offices of a firm of wine brokers, but there was no alarm sounding. He unbolted the main door, pulled it open, stepped out and crouched down to look out across the esplanade to the dark flowing waters of the Garonne. He was still breathless, the residue of the smoke still lingering in his airways, but he forced himself to remain calm and to focus on the facts and the options. They had tried to kill him tonight, and only by good fortune had they failed. He wasn't going to give them a second opportunity. Then he had a terrible anxiety for Celestine. If they had come after him, would they have targeted her also? They undeniably knew where she lived and they must have followed her to his house. He should have gone home with her last night. He had wanted to go home with her. He could hear the sirens of the fire engines hurtling towards the next street. They may save something, he thought, for a brief second, but then he quickly switched out that light. That existence, in there, has died. There would be no more carpenters in the Rue Carpentyre.

He had the file and his phone. He must stay out of the way for a while. Just then a police car, blue lights flashing, raced past on the road, then a second one and he crouched down tightly in the shadows. He needed to get off the streets. A singed, barefoot man would be noticed, even at this time of the night. Ironically, he thought, if I was in a difficult place in the past, I would have called Armand, who, even in the middle of the night, would have come hustling, carrying a pair of shoes and a hat for disguise. And he would have taken it seriously, as a personal affront that someone should harm or damage his friend, and he would have made a very funny story out of it at some time in the future when the wounds had healed. That was it, there is a theme running through this fandango, thought Jacques. He knew now what he needed to do. He pushed open the big door again and went back inside. On the left, there was an open office with several desks and computers, and he rifled around in the drawers of two of the desks and pulled out some items he could use, paper clips, pieces of plastic, small metal rods. He stepped out again and pulled the door closed behind him. There would be some very confused workers in that office in the morning.

Every step sent a shooting pain through his foot, and his arm and shoulder were aching where he had landed on them. He kept to the shadows by the edge of the buildings, standing still when the occasional car drove past. He turned by the Porte de la Monnaie and when he came to the Rue Carpentyre he looked up and saw the fire appliances, heard their loud engines, and saw the first shoots of water arcing up at the windows of his house. He moved as swiftly as he could past the road end and kept hobbling until he reached the dingy street where Armand and Maxine lived. He glanced around once but then stepped through the brown door and into the stale-smelling foyer. A dog barked in one of the apartments on the ground floor, and he heard the cry of a baby. He limped up to the third floor and reached the door of Armand's flat. He hoped, he was sure, that Maxine had not returned, although in some ways her hard-nosed affection would have been a fillip just then. He picked the lock easily with the items he had taken from the office and stepped inside, closing the door silently behind him. He switched on the light and looked around. He saw all the familiar pieces on the walls and hanging from the ceiling. The Armand frivolities, made from pieces of leftover metal, converted to animals and puzzles and surreal artefacts. The room smelled of

Armand and Maxine, and it was almost as though they might emerge, suddenly, and chastise him for staying away so long.

He was brought out of his reverie by the stinging in his foot, so he bathed it in the sink, took some tweezers and pulled out a small shard of glass. He saw himself in the bathroom mirror, his eyes were red, and there were streaks where tears had run down his smoke-blackened face. His beard and his hair were matted and sooty and his clothes stained and torn. Armand wouldn't mind. He stripped off and stepped into the shower. The water was cold and didn't run hot, but he stood and let it pelt him and run over his head. He ran soap and shampoo through his beard and hair and watched as a black sludge slid slowly into the drain. He dried and wrapped a robe around him. He realised that his lips were cracked and his throat parched. He found a glass and drank water again and again, and when his thirst was slaked he looked around for the other drink that he knew Armand would have. He found a bottle of old Armagnac and poured a deep slug into the same glass. He was starting to shake so he sat down to drink the brandy and get himself in order. His foot was stinging, so he reached down and poured a little brandy on it. He had no idea why he had done that, but it certainly makes me respect the depth of the wound, he said to himself. He poured another glass of Armagnac and sipped it this time. He couldn't think, he realised, he could only see; only see the pictures in his mind's eye, pictures of burning rooms, of corrugated roofs, of a strangely peaceful office, a disinterested space. He knew it hadn't sunk in yet, he was in shock, and in denial, in a dark limbo. He went into the bedroom, which was so tidy and proper looking. He clambered into the bed, switched out the light, and left himself to the mercy of the ghost of Armand Verville.

Chapter 53

A dull haze filtered the early morning light as Jacques made his uncomfortable way back through the streets towards the Rue Carpentyre. He was wearing an old raincoat and a cap of Armand's over his soot-blackened clothes, and he was hobbling in the largest pair of shoes he could find. He tugged the hat lower over his eyes as he entered the street and limped slowly towards what was left of his home. There was still a fire engine parked near the house, with a small group of fire-fighters leaning against it, not talking, just looking exhausted and defeated. The house had no roof, no windows, just walls stained with the black shadows of flames. Even at a distance, Jacques could smell the charred wood, the tarry, sooty stench of the fire's victims. He stared, and he could feel the tightness of the skin on his brow and the tension in his jaw, as he allowed the pain and the hate and the anger to rise. Thirty years of his existence had been cancelled in one night, into what was now a smouldering ruin. There was only one thing on his mind, he didn't care about himself anymore, he wanted revenge. He didn't go too close, he didn't want to be seen, just to check that his motorcycle was still in its parking place along the street from the house.

He turned and made his way through the waking streets, ignoring the curious looks of the other pedestrians. He ducked into alleys, and doubled back on himself, pressed into doorways, scanning and searching to see if he was being followed. Finally, reassured, he walked into the Rue Margaux and rang the bell of Candice's apartment. It was still only seven o'clock and it took some time for a groggy and dishevelled Philippe to open the door. His look of surprise immediately gave way to concern, and he bundled Jacques inside and sat him down in the kitchen. Philippe was talking to him about coffee, but Jacques' normally expressive face seemed frozen and his eyes were focused on something far in the distance or deep inside. He couldn't speak, he hadn't spoken since he had said goodnight to Celestine the evening before. Candice came into the room, alarmed, she took one look at him and wrapped his head in her arms. Philippe was standing helplessly. Candice glanced at him, her eyes questioning, but he shook his head. Candice held Jacques like that for several minutes until she could feel a slight thawing, a relaxation of the tension in his neck and forehead.

'What happened, Jacques?' she asked at last. 'What happened to you?' Only then did she notice the dark stains and smell the soot and smoke on his clothes. Jacques' eyes looked up and stared at her as she stroked the top of his head and cheek. The words finally came, struggling to emerge like the glue from an old forgotten tube.

'They burned it down. The house, all of it. They've taken away my life. My life in the Rue Carpentyre, they've erased it. You are looking at an ember, all that's left,' he said. After a time they managed to elicit a little more information from him and they sat drinking coffee around the kitchen table.

'It's the people who killed Armand, the gangsters, the dirty cops.'

'They tried to kill you?' asked Candice incredulously.

Jacques nodded. 'They kill anybody, anybody at all.' Stunned as she was, Candice went into action. She sent Philippe out to buy clothes and shoes for Jacques, and to get money to lend him. Then she made Jacques eat a breakfast, and she put antiseptic cream on the cut on his foot. She sat opposite him then and placed her hands on his on the table.

You're alive. Strong smelling, but alive,' she said, and squeezed his hands firmly. 'You have to stay that way, lion. You need to disappear, let this die down, let the authorities deal with this. You're alive,' she repeated. 'You have to stay that way.' Jacques said nothing; the words were kindly meant but they didn't impact on him at all. He knew what he had to do, and it would be tidy if he could end it and himself at the same time, so much tidier and simpler than trying to pick up the pieces again.

Philippe returned with the clothes, which were the camouflage trousers and dull-coloured tops he'd requested, and trainers at the outside range of the sizes available. He gave Jacques two hundred euros.

'If you need more, just ask. I imagine the banks take a long time to provide replacement cards,' he said.

'I have nothing, no ID, no passport, no driving licence or bank cards. I'm the invisible man.'

Candice snorted and slapped him lightly on the arm. 'Hardly invisible,' she said.

Chapter 54

Celestine dressed carefully, in clothes loose enough for movement and action, and chose comfortable, robust shoes. This was not going to be a normal day. She made two phone calls, but she didn't phone Jacques, she wasn't sure how to approach that one yet. At the last minute, something made her slip her old mobile phone into her bag, along with a pocket knife she used to carry when she was hiking and climbing in the wilderness, in the years before her marriage. The apartment already felt as though Etienne had gone, it had no sense of a home, just a fancy cage to perch in overnight. The morning was hazy and the air felt uncomfortable, as though the lightning was skulking somewhere close behind the horizon, waiting to fire up its shocks. As she drove she had an uncanny feeling of fatalism. All that had happened, everything that had been done was now in one place, and the lights were about to go up. There were no more rehearsals and she was the first actor on the stage, alone, ready to perform. I should go to the theatre more often, she thought, but then her phone rang. It was Dr. Rabelais from the clinic. The voice was very calm and quiet and Celestine had to strain to hear clearly, but she did hear one word and her stomach lurched.

'Poison, you're sure?'

'Cyanide. Small dose. A fortunately small dose. No lasting damage I would think.' Celestine was silent. The doctor continued. 'Capitaine Courbet, these substances, they don't appear by accident. They're not in nature in this form. A human being prepared this poison and a human being introduced it into your food or drink. Presuming that you didn't do it to yourself.' Again there was silence. Celestine had gone cold, she had so many questions, but then there was only one possible answer.

'Nothing permanent?'

'No. How do you feel today? Are your eyes clearer?' asked the doctor.

'Mm, yes, ok. So it must have been a small dose. How much more would a full dose be?'

'Difficult to say. But twice as much would have made you very ill indeed. I would think, but I may be wrong… that this was more of a testing dosage given to you.'

'A testing dose.'

'Yes. Rather than an attempt to do you grave harm. But of course, they may not have known. Are you all right, Celestine? You need to take this very seriously indeed.'

'Yes, I will take it seriously,' replied Celestine. 'I take everything seriously.'

'You should have yourself checked out when you can. See that there are no morbid symptoms remaining.'

Celestine was still thinking of this conversation when she pulled into the car park of the Hotel de Police. Again, there was no sign of her husband's car. The female lieutenant she had wanted to speak to was not behind the desk, so she walked up the three flights to her office. She noticed immediately how quiet it was. There was no one on that floor, none of her team, yet it was nearly nine o'clock. The door to Martel's office was closed and the blinds were down, but she could hear him talking loudly to someone as she walked past on the way to her office. She turned the handle, the door was locked. She almost jumped backwards, it was such a shock.

She tried the handle again but there was no movement. A voice then scraped its way down the corridor. She looked around. Commandant Martel had emerged along with two uniformed agents, Baylet and Soulier. So now she knew. It was those two who had visited the old lady. Important to know the enemy. Baylet was smirking, his thin face creased in a faux smile, a feeble triumph in his eyes. The other one, Soulier, just looked blank and thuggish, she thought.

'Capitaine Courbet, you will come into my office now,' demanded Martel. Celestine felt the strings of the net closing in on her, and she wasn't going to just flap there like a trapped fish.

'Why's my fucking office door locked?' she demanded and glared defiantly at Martel. He came closer, walking slowly, the two officers keeping pace behind him. He came right up to her, his face within twenty centimetres of hers, she could smell the tobacco and the too-young aftershave. His eyes were hostile but looked as though they hadn't rested for some time. His mouth was twisted and he was trying to intimidate her with the pressure of his hard, bull-like body. But Celestine was a long way beyond that; she stood her ground and stared straight back at him, putting as much contempt as possible on her face.

'Capitaine Courbet, you have been relieved of your duties. You are now under suspension.' Agent Baylet uttered a strange grunt and his smirk grew wider. 'You will come into my office now and hand over all the items of an official nature that you carry.'

'On what grounds, Martel?' she snarled at him.

'On the grounds that you're a nosy bitch,' said Baylet stupidly, in a high-pitched, grating voice. Martel turned angrily to him and put up his hand.

'You will come to my office and we will do this officially,' said Martel, his voice rising.

'Where is everyone else? Where's my team?' she demanded.

'Working, doing their job, obeying orders. Just like you're not doing. Now come with me.' He was shouting now.

'No way,' said Celestine. 'What do you want? Warrant card?'

'Gun, car keys, telephone, any official material.'

Celestine drew the gun from her holster, and the two agents shuffled nervously. Celestine sneered scornfully at them and laid the gun on the floor. Then she took her car keys and threw them along the corridor. Her old telephone she dropped over her shoulder and it landed on the screen which cracked and she stepped back and stamped on it. She flicked her warrant card in the air. The three men were looking uneasy now, even Martel didn't seem to know how to handle this.

'You're a fucking disgrace, Martel. This is not over, believe me. And you two, your careers are finished now.' She started to walk past them to go to the stairs, but Martel stuck out an arm and grabbed her elbow in one of his massive hands.

'I'm not finished with you. You will accompany officers Baylet and Soulier to the interview room D on the ground floor and wait there. You will be interviewed under caution. You are a suspect in the disappearance of Commandant Vaillancourt.' Celestine looked at him, stupefied.

'What do you mean, disappearance?'

'Well, where is he?' demanded Martel.

'The fuck do I know,' she replied, 'or care for that matter. Ask your Vietnamese friends or his whore.' Celestine saw Martel flinch and that was another question answered. She shook off his arm and pushed past the two agents.

'Keep her in that room. Use force if necessary,' he told them, but Celestine could hear that there was a little more uncertainty in his voice.

When she came to the car keys she kicked them as hard as she could so that they scudded along the floor and smashed into the glass panel at the end of the corridor. She knew it was petty, but she wanted to disturb them as much as possible. They went through the doors to the top of the stairs. The two officers came alongside her and the smirking one tried to take hold of her arm. She shook him off angrily and turned to face him. Now the anger really came out, the plug on the volcano blew. She looked at his smirking face and she smiled at him, then jerked her leg upwards almost springing off one foot, and kneed him viciously in the testicles. His eyes opened in horror and surprise and he collapsed with a groan. The other agent just stood there astounded and Celestine whipped her flat hand hard across his throat, knocking him backwards and then kicked him violently on the side of the knee. He buckled and tumbled down a few steps before hitting his head on a metal stair post. Celestine didn't wait; she sprang down the stairs three at a time, her heart racing and the blood pumping through her veins. She felt almost euphoric with the adrenaline, invincible and careless. She reached the bottom of the staircase and burst into the main reception area. She noted the surprised looks on the officers behind the desk, but she walked calmly out of the rear doors and into the car park. She wove her way between the cars, and just as she reached the exit she looked back. Martel was coming through the doors, but he wasn't looking at her, he was gesturing across the car park to a man standing by the door of a black SUV. She saw immediately that he was Asian and that he was starting to run towards her.

Chapter 55

Celestine dashed across the narrow street and along the wall of the Chartreuse Cemetery. The old wall was three metres high and she was in plain sight and felt terribly exposed. She turned the corner and hurtled along the street until she reached the cemetery gate. She glanced back to see a small, dark figure, no more than fifty metres behind her, arms and legs pumping like a manic clockwork doll, and she could sense his intent even from there. She turned into the cemetery through the high, ornate gates by the chapel. The alleys between the graves ran straight from this end to the gate half a kilometre away, and were wide, tarred and smooth like a running track, and she urged herself now to run as fast as she had ever done before. Her lungs were starting to gasp and her leg muscles burn as she reached halfway along the alley, and again she glanced back. The dark figure was coming on relentlessly, like a mechanical figure of nightmares, and he was gaining on her, not much, but enough to know that she wouldn't outrun him. He would keep going until he or she dropped.

She made a quick decision then. She suddenly veered off the main track onto one of the minor lanes that ran at right angles, then, after a few metres, turned off that lane, ran through the grass and ducked down behind one of the high mausoleums. She crouched by a low stone parapet and waited. She could hear the flat slapping of his feet and the change in tone as he ran around the corner and came to a stop part-way down the side lane. She could hear him breathing harshly, a weird, wheezing sound, squeezing out of his mouth along with words, strange words that she couldn't understand. He was talking to himself, it sounded like he was giving himself orders. She dared not raise her head, she could only listen, her ears pinned, tense and alert as a deer. The sound appeared to be moving slowly away, but he must know that she was stationary now, and hiding. He would hear her if she moved. Her breath was coming easier and her head was remarkably clear, her senses sharp as blades. She could still hear the whispering breaths, but also the trilling of a bird; and smell, she could smell cut grass from around some of the graves, and dank stone. Then all sounds stopped; she could hear no tortured breathing, no light footfall, no bird even, it was as though the whole world was in abeyance. She had one clear moment of illumination, of a realisation of just how exposed she was, of how strong were the forces ranged against her. For the second time in her life, she was facing the ultimate, a genuine life-or-death struggle, and she knew she must not freeze. The fear of that dark figure appearing suddenly from behind one of the tombs, like an evil spirit risen from the dead, encouraged her to start inching towards the end of the wall. She peered cautiously around it. At first, she couldn't see him, then a slight movement caught her eye and she saw him stepping stealthily, head down, towards another mausoleum forty metres away. He had his arms away from his sides as he moved silently, his head swaying gently from side to side like a bird listening, and in his right hand she saw a long dark thing, and as he turned slightly she recognised the glint of a blade.

She had walked through the cemetery often, sometimes with Etienne, as he had tried to explain his fascination with it and its attraction for him. For only a split second did she think of Etienne and wonder where he was, but in that second it came back to her, something he had told her. She began to crawl; there were steps, low walls, podiums and wrought-iron fences, and the low, shaped cypress trees. Using these as cover, she shuffled along the ground on her belly, stopping every few metres to listen for her pursuer. She was more afraid of being taken by surprise than facing up to him. She reached the next long alley that ran the length of the cemetery and there she stopped behind another mausoleum and stood up. She listened carefully; there was a sound, low, but clearly the voice of a man speaking quietly into a telephone. She thought the sound placed him some fifty metres away, close to where she had seen him before. She had to assume he was calling for some assistance. Two, or even three pursuers, would be impossible to evade. She knew she had one option and she had to take it quickly.

She was now no more than forty metres from the high outside wall, with a wide row of graves, statues and mausoleums, then another minor alley and a final row of graves to cross. The voice was still speaking in a strange, staccato way, and she decided to risk that he was distracted and wouldn't hear her steps. She braced herself and then raced across the alley and into the stone orchard, as Etienne had called it, weaving in and out of the graves. She had almost reached the next alley when she heard the cry behind her and knew that she'd been seen. Now it all depended on whether she could remember where it was, whose grave it was, if she missed it she was out in the open again. She ran now, not concerned with concealment. She bruised her leg on the side of a stone cross and nearly stumbled over a low wall, but then she was in the last alley and she looked desperately to left and right. Then she spotted the great stone pepper pot, which was the Cenotaph of Goya, and she knew she was close. She looked back, the small dark figure was coming, and she could hear his low, shrill screech. She ran twenty metres to the right then turned quickly behind a stone mausoleum, an edifice shaped like a small temple, with a cupola that looked like a melted bowl and with a Crusader's cross in front. Behind the cupola, the structure had been extended in the same dull grey stone. The whole looked like the fever dream of some architect obsessed with the East. One part of her mind remembered this description of Etienne's. Fortunately, the extension stretched back and almost touched the outside wall. Celestine took two strides and hurled herself at the structure, grabbing a handhold on the curved stone and dragging herself onto the top. She was now nearly at the same height as the wall, and she leapt from the mausoleum onto it and would have fallen hard onto the ground below, but as Etienne had pointed out, there was a lamppost felicitously positioned there, and she was able to grab it and ease her way down to land on the pavement below.

She didn't wait, she wasn't sure if her pursuer had seen her hurdle the wall, but she was outside, and she felt as though, at least for now, she had slipped the net. She ran along the wall for a few metres to a bus stop, where an old lady, weighed down with bags, was looking at her as though she was some kind of ghost escaped from the graves of Chartreuse. She crossed the street and turned onto another road. She was looking desperately for people, for a place where she could dissolve into a crowd, or lose herself in a maze of streets. But here there were only narrow, straight roads. It was a poor area, with low, single-storey, mean-looking houses. There were no gardens, no alleyways, and the house doors opened straight onto the pavement. She ran defiantly now, on the verge of collapse, her legs heavy and her lungs bursting, but she ran another two hundred metres until she came to a junction where four streets divided off and she turned down one and tucked in behind the corner of the first building. She peered back down the way she had come, she could see no one who seemed to be running. In fact, the street was completely deserted. It's a ghost town, she muttered to herself, a ghost town on the other side of the cemetery. She leaned back against the wall for a moment to let the air rush in and out of her tortured lungs. Think hard, she told herself. Where are you? Where can you get to? Where will they look for you? Everywhere. She knew now, everywhere. She was a fugitive; not only from a gang of sanguinary killers, but now also from her own police force. Yet, she needed one day, this day, she had to stay alive and at liberty for another twenty-four hours. She peered again down the road, this time she spotted a small dark figure standing there, looking in her direction and then looking to the left and the right. Now she could hear police sirens wailing not too far away. She needed to get off the street.

She started running again, along a road that seemed even poorer, with the same low, forlorn-looking houses, some with boarded-up windows, a few with dowdy lace curtains. There were no shops, although there must have been once, but the wide glass windows were dark behind the thick layer of dust. And then she saw it, a narrow alley running between two taller buildings. It could be a dead end and leave her trapped, or waste more time, but she had to get off the streets. She glanced around and then turned into the alley, which was gloomy and smelled of cat piss and old rubbish. She pushed past an upturned bin and came to the end of the buildings where it opened out into a wide overgrown garden, or rather to a place where plants, trees and low shrubs existed, untamed and unworked. The path that wound through the plants was half-hidden by the greenery, but still, somehow, it felt like a garden, and Celestine stopped and looked around. The garden was enclosed by walls, the buildings were empty and no one overlooked it, and she felt suddenly calmer, it was a haven, and she could become invisible for a while. The blossom on the acacia trees was pure white, with a delicate scent, and she could hear the bees buzzing there, excited, drunk on the nectar. There were four tall acacia trees near the back garden wall, and in front of them was a thicket of young acacia suckers, a few metres high and with thorns as sharp as razors. Celestine picked up a fallen branch and gently pushed aside the saplings, careful to avoid their thorns, and stepped through them to a shaded, hidden grotto beyond. There was an old wooden bench, which looked as though it had grown from the landscape. It was covered in moss but she sat down on it and let her head drop and her heart rate settle.

The place was a haven and a trap. If anyone found her she would have nowhere to run. But would they find her, it seemed unlikely, and if they came at her they'd have to break through the acacia saplings and she would swing at them with the branch she had laid by the side of the bench. No, this place could give her some time at least. She took out her phone, she knew she had to use it immediately because her voice would be a giveaway if anyone was in earshot. She called Jacques' number.

Chapter 56

Despite their reluctance to let him leave in his agitated state, Candice and Phillipe recognised that in order to break down the fibres of his anger, Jacques needed action. He left their apartment and headed through the back streets to a small workshop at the rear of the Hospital St-André. The large wooden doors were closed, but a small trap door opened when he pushed it, and he stepped into the gloom inside. The stench of oil and dirt hit him, it seemed to coat every molecule of air. The place was lit only at one side by a long fluorescent tube hanging loosely from the ceiling, and a stark white halogen lamp focused on a workbench against the far wall. There were two, new-looking motorbikes on stands, and other bike parts littered the floor. There was no one standing at the workbench, but as Jacques moved towards it a figure came out of the shadows, a large wrench in his hands. Jacques smiled.

'You working on big trucks now, Xavi?' he said. The man's hands dropped to his side.

'Jacques. Can't be too sure. Getting worse. Kids, bad kids, worse than ever.' He held out an oily fist to Jacques who bumped it with his own. He was a small man, at least twenty centimetres shorter than Jacques, with a round, pockmarked face and stubby black hair. He was wearing overalls that may have started out as blue but were now black with years of encrusted oil, and were shiny at the elbows and knees.

'How's it going, Jacques? Heard about Armand. Fucking shame. They got the bastard who did it?'

'Getting closer,' replied Jacques. Xavi shook his head.

'Police. Couldn't catch Covid.' Jacques just nodded.

'I need a key for a BMW 1000'

'Yours?'

'Yes.'

'Lost it?'

'Kind of.' Xavi tipped his head back slightly and narrowed his eyes.

'You know you can hot…'

'Yeah, I know. But I need to be quick and not obvious. Have you got one or not?' he demanded.

'Yeah, ok, ok. I have, I have a tin of them. You'll have to take a few, bring the rest back.' He disappeared into a small backroom and emerged several minutes later with a string of keys attached to a grubby, oil-stained label. He handed them to Jacques.

'And a helmet, I need a 62,' Jacques said.

'You lost your helmet too. Bit careless, Jacqui-boy. Sure you've still got the bike,' said Xavi, grinning and showing the dark gaps in his teeth. '62, you might need to go to NASA for that,' he wheezed and chuckled to himself.

'Still got the bike. Almost all I have got.' There was something in the downbeat tone of voice that made Xavi stop and look at him more closely.

'You don't sound too good, Jacques. Not like you. Generally have a laugh. You all right?' Jacques bit his lip.

'They burned my fucking house down. So I'm not real cute right now. Have you got a helmet?' Xavi looked at him, wondering for a second if he was joking.

'Jesus, your house, the workshop?' Jacques nodded. 'I heard the engines in the middle of the night. I was doing a little night fishing, you know. Keep my hand in,' he sniggered. 'Nice little haul, nothing too big. Fucking burned your house down. Who? Who would do that?'

Jacques leaned over him a little. 'Xavi, I need a helmet, and I need to get out of here. And I haven't been here, and you haven't seen me for weeks. I'll come back in a few days with the keys and the helmet, but in the meantime, keep your mouth shut. Please.' Xavi disappeared again into the backroom and emerged with a black motorcycle helmet.

'Try that on,' he said. Jacques placed it over his head.

'It's good. How much?'

'Nothing. You don't owe nothing. Jesus, it's a messed-up life, no?' said Xavi, shaking his head and wiping a greasy hand over his mouth. Jacques placed his hand on Xavi's arm.

'It's going to get a whole lot more messed-up for someone,' he said. 'Not a word.'

Jacques stepped through the wooden door and the air outside seemed like a different species to that inside. How the hell did I get to be on such terms with these characters? he asked himself. After this, if there is an after this, you really do need to raise the standard of your social acquaintances. But then he thought of Candice and Phillipe, and he thought you couldn't get a lot higher than them. He kept out of the main thoroughfares as he made his way to the Rue Carpentyre. Within two hundred metres of it, he could smell the soot and the charred timbers, and for the first time a real sense of loss kicked in. The beautiful workmanship of the furniture, lost: the fine tools, acquired and honed over decades, ravaged, annihilated in one indiscriminate immolation: and there was emerging within him a sense of guilt that he had brought an end to a century or more of family history. That was when the pain really racked him, and the fury that he had even got himself caught up in this, and how much of this was he honestly doing to gain justice for an old friend and how much because he was chasing a piece of tail. He was muttering to himself and shaking his head as he limped along the backstreets. And then his phone rang. He stepped into a doorway and pulled it from his pocket. When he saw it was Celestine, he hesitated, he didn't want to answer it. She was deeply involved in his anger, but he opened the call. She was whispering and he spoke sharply.

'Speak up. I can't hear you,' he said.

'I can't, Jacques, I'm hiding. They're trying to kill me. Can you come and get me, please?' He could hear the fear in the voice that was ordinarily so clear and confident.

'Where are you?' he asked.

'Back of Chartreuse cemetery, off Rue de Lacanau, Rue Lugeol.'

'Where?'

'Rue Lugeol, where it crosses Lacanau. Quick Jacques. Be careful. There are police and Nguyen's men. I'm hiding. Don't call me. Send me a text when you get there. I'll hide till then.'

'I'll be on the bike,' said Jacques, put the phone in his pocket, and hurried on to the Rue Carpentyre. The fire engine had gone, but there was a police car parked almost opposite the house and a small truck where two men were erecting metal barriers on the pavement around the building. He put on the motorcycle helmet. It was too late to turn back, so he walked past the police car without looking at the agents inside. He crossed the road to where his motorbike was parked next to an old scooter. He had been feeling the keys to see if any of them felt familiar, and he had narrowed it down to three. When he reached his motorbike, he swung his leg over the seat immediately and pretended to be adjusting something on the side as he tested the three keys. The second one fitted and he switched on the ignition and tried to start the engine. He saw that the door of the police car had opened

324

and one of the agents was getting out and looking in his direction. He tried again and the engine almost turned over. In desperation he tried again as the police agent started walking towards him, his hand in the air. The engine fired and Jacques swung out, flicking up the stand with his heel and roaring off down the road. In the mirror he could see the agent standing there, his hand still in the air watching him, and then he saw him tilt his head to one side to speak into his radio.

Using the main routes, it took him less than ten minutes to reach the corner of the Chartreuse Cemetery, and there he headed into the back streets. It had been a while since he had walked through this area, but it was still familiar to him from his years of wandering and mapping the streets of the city in his mind. He spotted the first police car at a junction off the Rue Brizard, and he rode past and cursed as he would have to take the long way round and come back down on the Rue Pierre. But it was a one-way system and he found himself at the road end, facing the wall of Chartreuse again. Another police car was posted there so he took a sharp right, following the one-way system. He was now within a minute or so of the Rue Lugeol. He saw a small shop on the left, selling and repairing computers. He pulled up in front of it and took out his phone. He texted the word "here" to Celestine. He looked back down the road. The police car hadn't moved. The streets were quiet. He looked in the other direction; an old man on a bicycle, a young woman pushing a buggy and staring at her phone, two men dressed in dark clothing, walking towards a black SUV parked further along the street. They stopped by the vehicle, one of them was on the phone, and they were both looking down the road towards Chartreuse. Jacques pulled his motorbike onto the pavement beside the shop window, the engine still running and leant it on its stand. He climbed off, and as he glanced back he saw that the police car had entered the road and was heading towards him. He pushed open the door of the shop, which buzzed excitedly and kept buzzing until he had closed the door again. He looked between the notices on the glass door. Behind him, he could hear a man shuffling.

'Monsieur?' he said. Jacques glanced around but then turned back to the window.

'I wish to thank you for your wonderful service,' he said. The police car was almost level and Jacques leaned away from the window to face a confused-looking man behind the counter. 'Yes, excellent work. I will recommend you.' He turned back and looked up the road; the police car had stopped beside the SUV and the two men were talking to the agents inside. 'The bastards,' he said out loud. The man behind him remained silent, confused and not a little afraid. Jacques watched the police car pull away and the two men climb into their SUV and set off after them. 'Merci. I will return,' he called as he went through the door.

He climbed quickly onto his motorbike and headed down the street. The Rue Lugeol was the first street on the right and he turned into it, watching, scanning all ways. He had no idea where to find Celestine, so he rode slowly along the narrow street with the cars parked on one side, any one of which could contain trouble. He remembered these streets; the low stone houses, the shuttered windows, the paint peeling from everything. He came to a crossroads of five branches, there was no sign of her. He wondered if she'd been caught, but the police car and SUV had not come down this street. He rode carefully over the crossroads, glancing in all directions, each road looked the same, underfunded and forgotten. And then he saw a movement, a brief glimpse of a head peering out from behind a wall, and as he pulled alongside, Celestine was there, rushing out and throwing herself onto the bike behind him, her arms grabbing him tightly, pinching his skin.

'Go fast and far as you can,' she yelled at him. He throttled up and the bike jerked away. Celestine was gripping his shirt and forcing her head into his shoulder blades. He rode quickly, switching from road to road in an irregular route, scanning all the road ends and looking constantly in the mirrors. He had no clear destination in mind, only to get out of the area, maybe out of Bordeaux, but then he realised that he had been heading all the time towards the Barriere du Medoc and the roads that lead to the estuary of the Gironde.

Chapter 57

They sat at the rear of the Auberge, a dark, unsmiling couple, withdrawn and intense. The few other patrons had looked at their faces when they'd come in but had quickly looked away again. There was something in their eyes that was hard and implacable. The waitress sensed it, and she simply took their order without any of the usual casual talk. Jacques and Celestine had said hardly a word from the moment Celestine had clambered onto the motorbike until now. Sitting facing each other in this quiet eatery, in a small, out-of-the-way village, they seemed paralysed by the enormity of what had happened to them; not wanting to speak for fear that they would be unable to bear the words themselves, to let out the fear and the pain, almost as though that was all that was keeping them whole. They kept looking at each other's faces and eyes, almost like strangers, as if they hadn't seen each other for months and had both been through a time of trauma that the other could know nothing about. Finally, Jacques managed to say, in a thin, whispered voice.

'Celestine, last night they burned down my home.' Celestine just stared at him, unbelieving, then looking at the pain in his eyes, believing. She gasped, her mouth open, her hand raised to her face. He told her then, coldly, matter-of-factly, what had happened since they'd parted with affection the previous night. When he had finished, he said simply; 'That is over, there is nothing more to say. Now tell me…' And Celestine told him of the poison, and the confrontation in the commissariat and the pursuit. And Jacques said nothing, just gritted his teeth a little more and tightened his fist. When she'd finished, he didn't comment but looked out through the window at the trees beyond.

They ate the food listlessly and without pleasure. Then, when the waitress had taken away the plates, Celestine breathed deeply, raised her head and sought Jacques' eyes.

'Now it must be finished. This day. I think we can. I have made some arrangements. I would like your help. Do you want to help?'

'What arrangements?' asked Jacques.

'I will explain…outside,' she said, 'but are you up to it?' Jacques turned his face away towards a wall where a picture of hunters carrying a slaughtered deer was hung.

'There's no point in offering a helping hand to someone who wants to drown,' he said quietly. Celestine looked at him, perturbed and uncertain.

'What's that?'

'Basque proverb,' he said. She stood up, and he followed her outside to where the motorbike was parked beneath an oak tree. Celestine outlined what she had planned. 'And you think they'll come?' he asked once.

She shrugged. 'Yeah. When, I don't know.'

Another time he asked, 'Who is this guy? Do you want him involved? See what's happened to the rest of us.'

'No. But I don't have a choice,' she replied. They stood in silence as Jacques digested what she had proposed. He picked up a fallen twig and snapped it into smaller and smaller pieces, before throwing the last piece on the ground.

'So this might not end it?' he said.

'No. It might not. But if I can get the proof, I can turn the tables on them, I can bring them down, I can be vindicated, as a police officer,' she said fiercely, her eyes wielding daggers of light.

Jacques shook his head. 'Proof of the crimes, the drugs, machine parts. But proof of the murders, I am not convinced. But we will do all that we can,' said Jacques finally. 'We'll do as you say, but afterwards, you know it won't be easy to remain out of sight, and there may well be random predators out there, not caught up in the net, with revenge on their minds.' Having said it he gave a huge shrug and his face lightened a little. 'We'll do it.'

'I know. We may not get out of it. I've thought that. But, it's all slipping away in any case, so what the fuck. That makes us dangerous,' said Celestine, and then to Jacques' surprise, she came close to him and kissed him hard and full on the lips, almost biting into his mouth, and he could feel the wildness and the passion and desperation in her. 'There,' she said, stepping back, 'I hope I'm not so repulsive today.'

At four-thirty, they parked the motorcycle under the chestnut trees near the little village square. There was no one around. We could have a nice peaceful afternoon, sitting in that café over there, watching the world not go by, Jacques thought. Celestine pointed the way and they walked down the narrow street to the harbour. Alain Jarre was waiting for them, sitting on a capstan, as Celestine had once imagined. He stood up and smiled at them shyly as they came onto the bank. Jacques saw the softness and slight wariness in his eyes when he looked at Celestine, then the uncertainty, but frankness when he shook Jacques' hand. He seemed calm, but excited, and after the first greeting he stood there, a little uncomfortably.

'Monsieur Jarre, Alain, I was asking Celestine what kind of boat you have. But I see. It has good lines. Oak keel?'

'Yes, the keel is oak.'

'Oak and teak, proper woods for a proper boat,' said Jacques, and nodded sternly, unable to smile. Celestine shook her head.

'Jacques is a carpenter. He will talk wood to you all day, but not this afternoon. Now we have more serious work to do.'

The boat was hauled close to the wooden jetty, and although the tide had peaked some hours before, there was still plenty of depth in the channel. Alain climbed in first, then held out his arm to help Celestine. Jacques climbed down the ladder easily and with surprising grace. The way he stood, and the manner in which he looked quickly at all the relevant parts of the boat told the others that he was at ease, and that this was not a new environment for him. Alain handed them life jackets. The sun was piercingly hot, pressing hard on their heads, and the thick extra layer made them prickly with the heat. Alain pointed to a small pile of waterproof jackets.

'There'll be a tempest with this, lightning, rain, wind. It might not last long, but it will be lively.'

'Lively,' mused Celestine.

'Yes. Getting more frequent now. Sudden storms, winds that tear up the trees, a month's rain in an hour.' He shook his head. 'It's the wind, it whips up the waves.'

'When do you expect it,' asked Jacques, looking towards the western horizon.

'Could be an hour, could be two. We'll hear it grumbling for a while before it starts up,' and he smiled and chuckled at his own words.

'Well then let's go,' said Celestine, and sat down firmly on the bench at the rear of the boat. Alain fired up the engine and Jacques slipped the ropes. Celestine noticed again that he seemed very comfortable and certain in his actions.

'You know boats, Jacques?' she asked. He stored the ropes and then sat down next to her.

'Yeah. Spent some time on them. In the forces.'

'The forces. I didn't know,' she said, surprised.

'Long time ago,' he replied and turned away to look out at the waters. They sat there for a while, then Jacques rose and went to stand next to Alain.

'What time will the tide turn, Alain?' he asked.

'Oh, not for a long time yet. Nine, ten tonight.'

'It must get a bit interesting when that happens.'

'Can do,' Alain agreed, nodding. 'It can get a bit interesting in a lot of situations on this estuary: high tides, full rivers, winds and currents. Moving and changing all the time.' He seemed to be talking to himself, but Jacques was impressed by his calmness and the quiet, firm way he steered the boat. The water was flat, it looked as though it had been ironed by the hard atmospheric pressure. Jacques felt sticky and uncomfortable.

'Back on land we'd be bitten to death by crazed insects now,' he said.

'Ah. You don't get much problem out here, but when you come into shore, thundery weather like this, those insects must feel it, drives them a bit insane, must feel the pressure on their thin, membranous bodies.' Jacques grinned.

'I think you're a bit of a poet, Alain. The Poet of the Estuary.' Alain looked to see if Jacques was mocking him, but there was only good humour and sadness in his eyes. Then he turned to look back at Celestine and shook his head.

'Poet of the Estuary,' he said.

They seemed to skim over the water, it was so much calmer than Celestine's last voyage. She sat looking at the river bank, but not seeing much, just running over details in her head. The land curved gradually to the left and the far bank seemed much farther away as the estuary started to widen. She recognised the village of Valeyrac from the tall spire of its church and the narrow inlet that pierced the lush flat fields. On the margins there were mud banks that had emerged from the retreating tide, and a line of birds stood, ankle-deep, pecking repeatedly at the stranded creatures on the sand. Jacques sat down beside her again.

'You don't have your gun now, do you?' he whispered. She shook her head. 'So no heroics, just in, photo what you can and get out. Should be enough.' Celestine nodded. They were speaking very quietly, below the noise of the boat's engine.

'I want you to open that door for me again, then go back to the boat. If I have to run, I can cover the ground more quickly,' she said.

'I am no slouch.'

'No, you're not, but you're no leopard either,' said Celestine, frowning at him. 'Photo, back to Bordeaux, complete the file and somehow get it to Juge Trouffeau. I think I can do that. Then turn invisible.' She raised her eyebrows and smiled wanly at him.

'Turn invisible,' replied Jacques, 'I've started that process already.'

After another ten minutes, Alain turned to them. 'Soon,' he called out. 'You know where it is?'

They went to stand on either side of him, scanning the river's edge on the port side of the boat. There was a slight promontory, and then behind that Celestine recognised the jetty and the long metal building with its fringe of trees.

'There, Alain, there,' she said and pointed.

They were still several hundred metres away, but as they came closer they saw that there was another boat tied up to the concrete pier. Alain pointed to it and looked at Celestine questioningly. She cursed under her breath.

'Go in close, Alain. We'll keep out of sight. You're a fisherman. See if there's anyone on the boat.'

'That's not a fishing boat,' he said sharply, but he changed course gradually towards the shore. 'Lots of mud around here. That's a pleasure boat, fast-looking.' He seemed to be talking to himself, but for the first time, there was a slight nervousness in his voice. Jacques and Celestine crouched down behind the small cabin, Celestine peering out carefully. Alain brought the boat in closer and closer, making small swift changes to avoid any shallowness of the water. Celestine could see the boat quite clearly now; it was longer and sleeker than the *Belle Étoile*. It was white, with a black stripe along the side of the hull, and the cabin at the bow was almost all Perspex and shaped like the bonnet of a very fast car. She could see no one on the boat, which was moored halfway along the near side of the jetty.

'What do you want me to do? Can't see anyone,' asked Alain, clearly uneasy approaching an unknown quay. Celestine thought quickly, or recklessly.

'Go alongside the jetty on the other side, or at the end. Call out quietly. If there's anyone on the boat they'll come out. Just say you thought they were in trouble.' Celestine looked back at Jacques, who was half-hidden in the doorway of the cabin. She could see the darkness in his face, she knew what he was thinking. Alain manoeuvred the boat expertly alongside the end of the jetty, Celestine dropping the buffers over the side on his orders, as before. He throttled down the engine and called out softly,

'Anyone aboard?' There was silence and no movement from the other boat. Celestine made a quick decision. She grabbed the rope from the stern, leapt out of the boat and fastened the rope around a ring set in the concrete. The bow of the boat swung out and Alain threw her the other rope.

'Don't tie it. Pass it through the ring and back to me. In case we have to leave quickly.' Celestine looped it through the ring and threw it back to him. He hauled the boat tight to the jetty so that Jacques could climb out. Celestine looked at Alain and whispered fiercely.

'If there is any trouble, cast off, leave. This is not for you to be involved.' Alain pushed his tongue into his cheek and blinked, and anyone could see that he was as solid as the keel of his boat.

'Tempests coming quickly.' He lifted his head towards the horizon where the dark clouds were gathering. 'Best hurry,' he said.

Chapter 58

The voices were raised and they echoed around the metal building, their volume enhanced but the clarity dulled and confused by the feedback. Celestine strained hard to catch the words. Zubizaretta's low, grumbling, guttural voice made a flat sound, difficult to differentiate between the words. Nguyen's voice was higher, harsher, like a crow or a jay, she thought, rasping, clearer but still distorted by the echoing walls. There were no other sounds in the building, and when they stopped talking for a moment, the voices seemed to linger, muttering in the upper reaches of the roof and the corners. She could only see the four men, they were standing in the centre of the floor, a floor still littered with pieces of metal, just as she'd seen it two days before. Zubizaretta was standing stolidly, arms by his sides, blunt head tucked into his shoulders; it was a defensive but aggressive pose. Next to him stood a taller, younger man, with slicked-back hair and a dark beard. Celestine was sure this was the Basque, Jacques had talked of, Xabietta. Opposite them stood Monsieur Nguyen. She couldn't see his face, but it had to be him, in a dark suit, his hair thinning. He stood as still as an ice statue. Next to him was a man of a similar height and build and wearing a kind of nautical cap, which made Celestine think it was most likely the skipper of the boat they had seen moored outside. She hadn't considered that Nguyen might come along the river, but now it made perfect sense, it was more discreet and if the building was being watched it would be from the front, the road side.

She lay on the floor of the gantry, holding her phone by one of the stanchions, taking photographs of the four men. The light wasn't very good and she prayed that the flash wouldn't suddenly come on. She was waiting for Nguyen to turn around, but the four men were stationary, squaring up to each other, and she sensed there was a kind of tension holding them in their place. There was silence for several minutes, then Zubizaretta spat angrily on the floor and raised his head like a bull about to charge. He looked into the face of Nguyen. They were two metres apart, and Zubizaretta's eyes bulged and his thick round head seemed ready to burst out of his collar. He lusted so much to shout at this miserable, emotionless creature, this dark, imperturbable man. But he had no ammunition. This was his operation, his part of the project, and it was lying in pieces all over the floor. So he let the heat seep out of him, something he had learned to do, something his father never could, and he forced himself to reply calmly to the question.

'Five more days. In five days this will be transported to our warehouse in Lyon,' he paused. Nguyen's face had not shown any sign that he was satisfied with the answer, so Zubizaretta struggled on, his anger rising again. 'Five days.' He looked sideways at the brutal-looking man standing next to him. 'Xabietta?' The tall man shrugged.

'Mm. Five, with another two workers.'

'Five. Five is all you've got.' Zubizaretta swore at him as an outlet for his anger. Nguyen turned to his own man.

'You will clear the last of the pills tonight?' he asked, harshly and quietly.

'Yes,' the other man nodded, his eyes fixed on the ground. There was no one else in the building, just these four. The few workers had been told to stand outside in the car park at the front. Nguyen looked slowly around each corner of the building. Then he turned back to look at Zubizaretta.

'When Dang removes the remainder of the drugs tonight, that will be the end of my association with this building. Everything that is left is your responsibility, your risk,' he paused. 'Yes, your risk. Always things must be done to a time. Every hour after that time adds to the danger and the risk. Your risk, not mine.' Zubizaretta ground his heel on the concrete floor.

'Vaillancourt? The woman?' he asked. Nguyen's eyes became hooded while he considered the questions.

'Commissaire Vaillancourt has not been heard of for some time,' he said coldly, and even Zubizaretta felt a slight shiver in his spine. 'The woman, Capitaine Courbet, remains a fish waiting to be trapped in a net. She is now completely alone. A matter of time.'

'You said that two days ago,' said Zubizaretta, wanting to regain some territory. Hardness seemed to slide down Nguyen's face but he didn't respond.

Twenty metres away on the gantry, the fish had taken her last photograph. She moved back from the edge and sat up, closing her mobile phone. She stayed there for a moment, thinking of what she had seen, and steeling herself for the perilous retreat she must make. She began to realise that something in the sounds were different. It was muffled in that tin space, but there was definitely a change in the nature of the sounds outside the building. She heard a door open hurriedly and slam closed again immediately afterwards. There were quick footsteps on the concrete. She lay down again to peer through the rails. She saw a man dressed in blue overalls she could see he was agitated as he picked his way through the metal parts on the floor. He spoke so loudly and shrilly when he reached the men, that Celestine could hear every word.

'Inspectors here, fucking nuclear inspectors and gendarmes here. They want to come in.'

She saw Zubizaretta's shoulders drop, but Nguyen pointed at the man and snapped out a command.

'Lock that door. Keep them outside for ten minutes. Go.' He turned to Zubizaretta. 'You come with me.'

Celestine knew exactly what was going to happen next. She sprang up and rushed to the exit door, flung it open and bounded down the metal staircase. She was running half-way across the wasteland when she heard the large doors sliding open behind her and heard the cry. She didn't hesitate, but flew along the path towards the boats. Even in her haste, she was aware of the dramatic change in the weather since she'd been indoors. The wind was now violently twisting the branches of the trees, and the surface of the estuary seemed to be erupting in waves and spume. She could see Jacques' head protruding above the bank, but then there was another shout and she saw him turn and scurry back along the jetty. She slid down the bank, and by the time she got to the boat, Jacques had untied the stern rope and was holding it against the quay, ready for her to jump in. She glanced back once, she could hear the sound of running feet. Jacques grabbed her hand as she leapt into the rear of the boat and then jumped in after her. Alain already had the engine running. He was wearing a full set of waterproofs, and he threw out the bow rope and they accelerated away from the jetty. Celestine looked all around her in surprise, she couldn't believe the strength of the wind that had risen while she'd been inside the building, and the waves that were now nearly a metre high. Jacques passed her a life jacket and she struggled into it, her heart pounding, her fingers shaking as she tried to fasten the straps. Jacques leaned over and clipped them into place. Their eyes met for a moment, Jacques' seemed full of questions, but she looked past him towards the shore. Two men were clambering down the bank and running along the jetty, Nguyen was being helped, his arm held by his captain. Zubizaretta was the furthest behind, his bulk heaving as he came through the gates where Xabietta was waiting to help him down the low bank. Celestine saw him throw off the arm that was extended and hobble to the boat. Alain Jarre had said nothing, but his head was moving in different directions, he seemed to be gathering information from all quarters. Celestine called out to him.

'Alain. They may follow. Can they catch us?' She heard him mutter something under his breath but she couldn't make it out. She stood up unsteadily and moved over to stand beside him. 'Can they catch us?' she asked again. He nodded. He seemed distracted, she thought it was fear, but then she realised that he was calculating. He looked up at the sky which was darkening by the second.

'Put the waterproofs on,' he said, his voice shrill in the wind.

'Can they catch us?' she asked a third time.

'Much faster boat in open water,' he replied, finally. 'They're going to try and catch you?' he asked, a strange note of anger and affection in his voice.

'I think they will. I think they'll try to catch us. They want me,' she shouted. Alain nodded and returned to his calculations.

'Sit down. And, Jacques, keep low, it's going to get choppy. Keep low, away from the sides. Waterproofs,' he said out of the side of his mouth.

She could see the intense concentration on his face and in the way he was gripping the wheel. There was a sudden explosion as the thunder cracked above them. Celestine started, and stumbled as she made her way back. She couldn't believe how rough the water had suddenly become; waves were lapping over the sides and the boat was bouncing, it seemed, from crest to crest. She grabbed two waterproof jackets and sat down next to Jacques. He was looking at her with a hard expression, although he seemed remarkably calm. She glanced back, the other boat was pulling away from the jetty, its sharp nose pointing like a blade directly at their stern. She turned back to Jacques, and he could see the fear and the wildness and the triumph in her eyes; she was grinning, almost laughing, though not with humour.

'You nearly got caught. Again,' he said. 'Who the hell is in that boat? Did they see you in there?' Celestine shook her head wildly, her hair swaying around her face before being pulled away again by the wind. She brought her face close to his.

'Nguyen, Zubizaretta, your big Basque mate. Yes, him. They're running because they've been busted. Fucking busted. I didn't think they'd come so soon.' She wagged her head, it seemed everything amazed her.

'Who? The police?' Jacques asked, surprised.

'No. ASN, with some gendarmes,' she was shouting now in the teeth of the wind.

'ASN?'

'Autorité de Sûreté Nucléaire. I told you, I called them this morning. The nuclear safety people. I called them this morning. Told them the major players would be here at five o'clock. I never thought they'd come, not so quickly.' She was shaking her head still, and she grabbed Jacques' arm. 'Bastards red-handed. Got the bastards.'

'Except they haven't. They're in the boat behind us,' said Jacques, trying to gather up all the pieces, and with a growing sense that there were large areas of information that had been withheld from him.

'I've got pictures, even a video of them talking in the shed,' she said breathlessly. Jacques took hold of both of her hands and glanced back behind them

'Well, you'd better send them to someone you can trust, now, because that boat is gaining on us quickly.' Then. 'You knew. You knew they would be there today.'

'At five o'clock. Yes,' she replied.

'How the …you didn't say. You didn't say any of that. Photos you said. Proof,' he tightened his grip on her wrists.

'I needed proof, photos of them in the place, amongst all that machinery. And there's still drugs there,' she said, and cast her head back and laughed wildly. 'You wouldn't have come,' she shouted. 'Maybe you wouldn't have come. I had to do it. I had to.'

Jacques released his grip and looked at her askance, wondering at her callousness. 'And him. Alain. Did you have to involve him in this?' She shrugged and took out her phone.

'I'm going to send them to a few people, just in case,' she said.

Chapter 59

The sky was now so dark that it was getting harder to see the boat behind them, but then a vicious flash of lightning spewed white liquid over everything and Jacques could see the distance between them was now less than a hundred metres. He edged his way to the front to stand next to Alain, and when he stood up the wind almost blew him over, and he braced his legs as the boat lurched from side to side as it butted into waves that were now higher than the side of the boat itself. He leant towards Alain and shouted in his ear.

'They're getting closer. Can we lose them somehow?' he asked. Alain didn't respond for nearly a minute. He was gripping the wheel tightly, but his face was absorbed and calm, his eyes flicking from side to side, up to the sky and down to the surface of the water.

Finally, he said; 'Wind's sixty knots. Going to be a maelstrom. Don't want to get caught broadside to this.' He said it in such an unemotional, matter-of-fact way, that Jacques somehow got the impression that Alain knew exactly what he was doing. 'Going to get very tight. Keep low down, low in the boat. Keep her down. Hold on to the thwart. Going to get rough,' he said again, without looking at Jacques or stopping his scanning of the elements all around him.

Jacques eased his way back and told Celestine what had been said. Then the rain started, dense sheets of it which turned suddenly to hailstones, battering and bouncing off the surfaces of the boat and off their unprotected heads. Jacques encouraged Celestine to lie down on the bottom of the boat between the seat and the bow, and he crouched down beside her, protectively. He looked back every few minutes to check on the progress of the boat behind them. He realised that Alain had gradually changed their course and that they were now running upriver, parallel to the bank. The movement of the boat was different, no longer bracing the waves, but running against the ebbing tide, bouncing between the crests and the troughs. Another flash of lightning showed him that the shore was no more than a hundred metres away. He looked back; the other boat could only just be seen through the rain and the darkness, but when the lightning flashed it reappeared as a dark shield in a weird negative, it was following exactly their course, and it was gaining all the time. Jacques put his arm over Celestine's shoulders, she was crouched like an animal, hands over her head. He could feel the tension in her, no longer wild and triumphant, holding herself, awaiting the inevitable. He could never remember being on water like this, it felt as though there was a battle going on beneath, where unstoppable flows battered against immovable forces. As though all the currents were mixing and throwing themselves against each other, deep down and at every depth until the result on the surface was a frenzy of leaping, twisting waves, breaking out suddenly like molten spurts from a cold volcano. The boat was being tossed and punched, lurching from right to left, assailed as a trespasser in this personal battle of the estuary. The storm had whipped up a wind that was screaming across the surface of the water, keening like mourning women in the gloom, and drilling the rain into Jacques' head when he raised it. It was too loud to think and it felt like there was madness in the air. Yet through it all, Alain stood resolutely at the wheel, legs braced widely, forearms pushed through the spokes to grip and hold the course. The chasing boat was only twenty metres behind when he suddenly turned round and shouted.

'Hold at the next flash. Hold on at the next flash.' Celestine didn't hear him. She was retching now. Jacques could feel her body heaving below him. He took one quick glance back, the dark boat was fifteen metres behind. The lightning flashed and for a second he saw the tall figure of the Basque, Xabietta, face drawn back by the wind, he seemed to be staring at him, teeth bared, his face a ghastly white in the lightning glare. Then he felt the boat turn sharply and he was thrown over Celestine as the port side rose up alarmingly and the starboard dropped low into the waters which rushed over the side and poured over their heads. Celestine tried to rise, spluttering, looking around desperately. They seemed to stay in that slanting position for an age, time stood still, the boat seemed to hover between righting itself and oblivion. The wind screamed the same wild note, as though stuck. For Jacques it could have been a second or an hour, his mind was in mental limbo, conscious only that he was holding onto Celestine and straining with all his body not to be toppled into the water. And then slowly the boat righted itself as it turned away again from the driven waves. Jacques thought he heard a scream, a human scream, flung helplessly into the screeching wind. The lightning flashed and he looked back, fearfully expecting to see the other boat almost on top of them, but somehow it seemed to have stopped, to be suspended, as though it was in a different time to them. It was stopped, but on its beam end, like theirs had been, the port side high in the air and the starboard wallowing deep in the water. Suspended, but only for a second, as he saw the next wave smash into the hull of the boat and it was as if all the forces were heaving and tearing at it. It lurched once, almost jumping it seemed, then turned over on itself and was bounced along by the flood, with its keel in the air.

All was dark, and Jacques caught hold of Celestine, wanting to tell her what he had seen, but she started retching again so he gripped her tightly, his mouth pressed into her hair. The lightning flashed again and he looked back quickly. There was now a distance of fifty metres between the boats. He could see the stark white hump of the hull, a sharp blemish in the negative, and he saw the waves crashing over it like a victor toying with the vanquished. He turned to look at Alain, who seemed unmoved by it all, and was steering a course parallel to the shore again. Jacques gripped Celestine more tightly, raising her body slightly from the waters swilling around the bottom of the boat. He wanted to shout out, to whoop, but he was too drained and traumatised. Even when it's your enemies, he thought, there is something terrible and unholy about watching them perish like that.

They motored on for another ten minutes while the sky started to lighten and the rain to ease off. The waves were still high and deranged; there was a pattern to them, but it was broken time and again by renegade waves and currents. Jacques sat up and looked about. Celestine was rigid, but as he encouraged her, she uncurled herself and raised her head. The water streamed from the ends of her hair and her face was white and pained. Jacques thought he had never seen anyone look so wretched but so fine. She sat up, holding her stomach and looking out of the back of the boat. There was incomprehension on her face, as though she had woken from a dream in a different place than where she'd gone to sleep.

'Where...?' she managed to say, her throat retching again, but only a trickle of bile came out.

'They're gone,' said Jacques, and then described to her what he had seen. He watched the dawning in her eyes, the realisation.

'Could they... I mean, swim, get to shore?'

Jacques shook his head. 'They're drowned. The waves were too high, the currents, nobody could.'

'You're sure?' she asked earnestly, searching his face for certainty.

'I'm sure. They're dead.'

Celestine sat there, head down, holding her stomach, and Jacques left her to gather herself and went to stand next to Alain.

'There's water in the box there, in the cabin,' he said, not looking away from the wheel. 'And brandy. That would be a good idea.' Jacques stood looking at the side of Alain's head, and eventually he turned, his eyes wavering somewhere around Jacques' nose.

'So what was that? You knew,' Jacques said. 'You were leading them to that.' Alain flicked his eyes up once then turned back to stare at the waters ahead.

'Sandbanks,' he said finally. 'Knew they had a deeper draft than this one. Tide was starting to uncover them. I know where they are, but you can't see them, just the line of the water, the way it behaves. Difficult mind in this mess.'

'You turned just as you got to the sandbank,' said Jacques, incredulously. 'That was ….risky, bloody risky.

'It was, it was. But we got a shallower draft than that other craft, and she's more robust, more stable, broadside the wind like that, solid keel. The other one's slicker, lighter in the water, but they get skittish when they're not running straight.' He nodded to himself, but then Jacques saw his face crumple and he almost doubled upon himself, only his grip on the wheel was holding him up. Jacques put an arm out to support him. He looked up at Jacques, full in the eyes this time. 'I hope those men were bad, real bad. I have never done a thing like that in my life. It's like I killed them. You don't do that on the water.' There were tears in his eyes and Jacques could see that all the tension and the concentration had drained him and the reality was bearing in on him. He put his hand on the man's shoulder.

'They were very bad, Alain. They would have killed us and not thought two figs about it. They killed my friend. Those bastards killed my friend, my innocent friend. Now they've killed themselves, they killed themselves on the tempest. Don't weep for them, my friend. You are a hero. You saved her.' He nodded towards Celestine.

'Is the lady all right?' asked Alain, straightening up and wiping his face. 'There's water and brandy,'

'I know. I'll get it,' said Jacques.

'And there's a baler. Need to get some water out of the boat. Making her sluggish.'

Jacques reached into the doorway of the cabin and opened a large icebox that was there. He took a bottle of water and handed it to Alain, who drank thirstily. Then he took another bottle to where Celestine was now sitting upright on the bench. She drank it keenly and rinsed it around her mouth.

'If it's all the same, I'm not going to kiss you on that mouth for an hour or two,' he said.

Then he took the baler and began scooping water out and hurling it over the side. He struggled to keep his feet, but the physical activity was good for him, it gave him a different focus. He scooped and threw, scooped and threw, almost in a frenzy, until there was only a thin stream of water swilling around on the bottom of the boat. He noticed Celestine staring vaguely at his hands.

'How…what do we do now?' she called out to him. 'I can barely breathe… and please stop this boat from wallowing around like that. I've nothing left to puke.' Jacques sat next to her and put his arm around her shoulder. Her dark eyes were wide, as though aghast at the world and at what could happen in it.

'Drink some more water. I'm going to get you some brandy,' he said and started to rise. She pulled at his arm to hold him to her.

'Just stay, just stop there. It feels better. Hold on to me, I'm a void, I could float away. I've nothing inside me anymore.' Jacques held her more tightly to his side, and they stayed like that for ten minutes while the boat rode the lessening waves and the air lightened. Jacques could see Alain trying to reach the brandy bottle in the ice box, so he extricated himself from Celestine, who moaned lightly but had no strength and seemed almost to be sleeping. He handed the brandy to Alain.

'Sorry, I got caught up there. She's not in a great state,' he said.

'No,' replied Alain, glancing around and taking another swig of the brandy. 'Water's settling again. The tempests passed over to there now, over Bordeaux. See.' Jacques looked in the distance where he could see the dark, black/green clouds and the shafts of rain that were clearly visible. 'That's over Bordeaux. They're going to know a storm there.'

'They certainly are,' replied Jacques, and took the brandy bottle back for himself. He pondered for a while, holding hard onto the rail on the top of the cabin. It was a lot to ask of this man who had already done so much, but he couldn't see any other way of getting there. Finally, he turned to Alain again.

'Do you carry a lot of fuel on board? What sort of distance can you cover?' he asked. Alain considered the question carefully, his head nodding slightly.

'About forty litres now, give or take. That'll get you to … La Rochelle, bit to spare.'

'La Rochelle, well. I was thinking more inland,' Jacques hesitated. 'I'll tell you what I was thinking, Alain. And you can tell me if it's a possibility or a non-starter. You decide. You've done way and beyond what anyone could reasonably ask.' Alain's eyes narrowed now but he was listening carefully. 'I have a place, upriver,' Jacques continued, 'past Bordeaux. I want to take Celestine there. She's not out of danger yet. A few things have to happen first. I want to keep her safe. Do you understand?' Alain turned his gaze back to the course ahead and adjusted the wheel slightly as the near shore began to curve away.

'You've got a place upriver. Upriver of Bordeaux?' he asked slowly.

'Yes. She'll be safe there. Until we can sort some things out.'

'Near the river?'

'Yes. Just near, where the Canal de Garonne joins the river. Past Langon,' explained Jacques.

'Langon! That is a long way up. Long way past the city,' muttered Alain, more to himself than to Jacques.

'Yes, I know. And it'll be dark.'

'Dark doesn't matter. We've got lights.'

'Well. It's a long way and I don't like to ask. Not for me. But she's all in. Someday, I'll tell you everything, everything that's happened, and how that woman has fought against them all.' Jacques said, his voice cracking a little. Alain took some time to ponder this.

'She, Celestine, is a police capitaine. But I don't think this was all police business was it?' he asked, turning to Jacques.

'It was, Alain. Police business. Those guys were smuggling drugs in machine parts, inferior parts they were then forging, to sell to the nuclear industry. That was all police business. Trouble was, some of the police were in on it, which is why she had to act on her own.'

'With you,' he jerked his head up slightly.

'Yes, with me.'

'But you're not police. I don't think so,' said Alain.

'No, I'm just a carpenter, mate. A carpenter who lost a good friend and wanted to get justice for him.' Jacques took another pull from the brandy bottle and handed it back to Alain. 'Tell you what though,' he continued, 'you are one hell of a sailor. Not many would have even tried to pull off that manoeuvre.' Alain looked pleased and coughed slightly as the brandy caught in his throat.

'There's emergency blankets in there, small cupboard. You want to wrap one around her, and you. You're soaked to the skin.'

Jacques noticed that his teeth were chattering, even though the air was mild and muggy. He reached into the cabin and came out with the foil blankets, neatly folded. He took one to Celestine where she was sitting hunched up, like a drowned rabbit. She was shaking and when she looked up he could see that her eyes were glassy. He opened the blanket and wrapped it around her, over her head and enclosing her whole body. She didn't move except to help him a little, but then hung her head again and returned to her trance-like state.

'Langon?' He heard Alain say.

'Yes, past Langon. There's a jetty there. I know it. To tie up. Proper concrete jetty.'

'That's good then. Take a few hours. Yes, a few hours,' he paused. 'There's coffee in a flask and sandwiches in the other box. Help yourself,' he said, in a voice so calm now that it was as though they were on a pleasure cruise along the river.

'You are a legend, Alain,' Jacques called back. 'A bloody legend.'

Chapter 60

They came through Bordeaux just as the final rays of the sun were gilding the roofs and the higher parts of the buildings on the waterfront. The storm had passed on, and Jacques could imagine the streets gleaming with the torrential rain that had fallen. Alain kept the boat on a course nearer the opposite bank to the city. They came cautiously through one of the arches of the Pont de Pierre and Jacques felt the old surge of affection for the city in which he had spent thirty years of his life. He could see the top of the Porte de la Monnaie; in his mind, he passed through the gates, turned right onto the Rue Carpentyre and stopped before the burned-out shell of his house, of his past. Celestine was stirring, she raised her head from the foil blanket and looked around. He went to her.

'We're in the city. Where are we going?' she asked in a voice that was weak and wavering.

'We're going somewhere safe. Somewhere no one knows about. It'll be ok. We're going there,' replied Jacques. She looked at him, wanting to question, but there was no energy there, and she lowered her head again. Jacques went to talk to Alain, who seemed immovable.

'Do you want me to take the wheel for a while? Give you a chance to stretch, have a coffee.'

The waters were running full and strong, but the waves had dropped and it was now more of a swell. The last of the light was draining out of the sky, and the land on either side glowed like a final tribute to the day. It's ethereal, this time of the day, thought Jacques. It's when the myths and the phantoms drift into the world. When the lion emerges from the woods. But not that anymore. No more Lion des Bois. They left the outskirts of Bordeaux eventually, and continued along the quiet river as the darkness seeped into the sky and the sound of the engine and the light wind on the water were the only things they could hear. Alain took back the wheel and switched on the lights, which were low but separated the boat from the life outside, and they travelled in isolation, a capsule through the darkness. Jacques went to sit with Celestine again, and she responded when he took hold of her hand and squeezed it between his own.

'Where are you taking me, Monsieur Lecoubarry?' she said quietly, and there was a flicker of life back in her eyes.

'I'm taking you into the unknown, literally. Where travellers have no names. Where no one is alert. Where no one knows you.'

'Riddles, really,' she replied and managed a pale smile.

'Yes, riddles. Safer that way,' he said, and peered out at the night and the black shapes on the river bank.

'I'll explain when we get there. Alain is taking us all the way.'

'He's a brick, just a brick,' said Celestine. 'He's got brandy too. What a brick.'

'He's got coffee if you want some.'

She shook her head. 'Brandy and ... milk. Yes, brandy and milk,' she repeated.

'Milk. I'll ask the steward to bring you some. I'm sure they keep a cow on board,' said Jacques.

'You're funny, Jacques. You're funny,' she said.

They were alone on a dark ribbon, and then the lights of the town of Langon flowed out onto the surface of the river and they were suddenly back in the other people's world.

Jacques and Celestine instinctively shrank into themselves, both feeling vulnerable and exposed. But then they were in the quiet darkness of the countryside again. A little later Jacques called out to Alain.

'I believe that's the metal bridge at Castets. The jetty, it's immediately after that. You can take a course between the right pier and the land. There's plenty of depth.' He stood up next to Alain and pointed out the line. They could see a few pale street lamps. They passed under the bridge and Alain brought the boat gently alongside the quay. Jacques managed to climb wearily onto the concrete and fasten the bow line around the tall metal pillar. Alain threw him the stern line and he fastened that too. He sat there for a moment, looking up at the lights of the medieval chateau which hung over and dominated the small settlement. Then he climbed back into the boat. He put his arm under Celestine's elbow and helped her to rise. She was unsteady, but she shrugged off the blanket and made tentative steps towards the side of the boat.

'Help me to get her on shore, Alain,' he called. 'You push from here and I'll haul her from the top.' She wasn't heavy and between them, they managed to lift Celestine onto the jetty, where she sat, legs under her, like a stunned mermaid. Jacques climbed back into the boat again and stood facing Alain.

'Do you want to come? You could stay the night. It's a long way back.'

Alain shook his head.

'No. It'll be nice and peaceful. That'll be just right for me,' he said.

'Look. We'll be a few days, a few days off-grid until things are sorted. Then I'll come looking for you. Pick up my motorbike. You'll keep an eye on it, will you? It's in the village square.'

'It'll be all right. She'll be all right?' Alain lifted his head towards Celestine.

'In due course. I'll take care of her.'

'You will. I would too,' he said, and there was a gentleness and a sadness in his eyes. Jacques put his arms around him and hugged him massively.

'You, I will never forget. Never,' he almost roared. Alain handed him the half-empty brandy bottle.

'I'll come and find you,' Jacques said again. Then he hauled himself out of the boat and untied the ropes. The bow of the boat eased away from the jetty and headed a little upstream before slowly turning around. Alain waved once, before staring ahead as he headed back down the river to his haven in the little village by the Gironde.

Jacques sat down on the jetty next to Celestine, pleased to be on land, but cold and very weary.

'We have to climb these stone steps, they're quite narrow. Then we have to walk about a kilometre,' he said.

'I can walk,' muttered Celestine. 'I can walk. I would like this ground to stop moving. I could revisit that brandy bottle, I think.'

'Come on. Walking will sort you out.' He stood up and helped her to her feet. He put his arm around her waist.

'You're big, Jacques, you know. You are a big man. Solid, really solid.'

'Thank you. And you're a bit shaky. Beautiful but shaky,' he said, helping her take the first steps.

'Beautiful but shaky,' she mused. She took a swig from the brandy bottle, coughed and quickly took another one.

They climbed the stone steps and then hobbled along the quay, gradually getting the strength back into their legs, which seemed still to be on board the *Belle Étoile*. They joined the road which ran along by the canal and walked in silence, Celestine leaning gently on Jacques' side. She kept taking small sips of the brandy, which burned in her emptied stomach, but in her confused mind, she saw it as a cauterising, she was lining the walls and scorching out the last dregs and vestiges of the poison that her husband had given her.

It was late, and the town was quiet and deserted and their faltering footsteps seemed to ring along the street. The night air was cool but sweet with the scents of the flowers in the gardens and the ornamental trees that edged the road and the canal side. After a short while, they left the town, still on the road by the canal. Then Jacques stopped abruptly and Celestine started and her momentum swung her into his chest. She looked up at him.

'I'm not so shaky now, Jacques Lecoubarry,' she said. 'We are walking into the darkness. Where are you taking me?' She jutted out her chin, her eyes slightly unfocused.

He turned her so that she was facing the canal. 'Walk,' he said. They stepped off the road onto a short path that led to the towpath by the canal. A little way along the towpath they stopped beside a dark shape, which Celestine could only just make out.

'Another bloody ship,' she said comically, and holding his hand, swung her arm out wide.

'True. Another bloody ship,' said Jacques. 'But this is my ship, or barge as we say in nautical circles. This is the *Incognito*, and this is where we will take refuge and restore ourselves.' He led her to a spot near the boat and told her to stand while he found the gangplank and the lights. She stood with her arms out, watching him, curious. He climbed onto the boat and fiddled around with various things and suddenly the lights came on, and he came to the side, beaming, and laid a small ridged board between the boat and the canal side. He held out his hand to her and she tripped over the board until he grabbed her and drew her onto the barge.

'It's a bit cold, but I'll put the heating on. It won't take long,' he said. He helped her down the short stairs into the galley of the boat and through into the salon, where he sat her down carefully on the bench. It smelled damp and musty, unlived-in and cheerless. She hadn't spoken since she'd entered the barge. 'I'll make some coffee,' he said. She just nodded. He went into the galley but returned quickly. 'You need to get dry. Get out of those wet clothes. Go in there.' She looked at him dumbly. He took hold of her arm and led her into the next section where there was a narrow wooden bed. He took two large towels from a cupboard and laid them on the bed.

'You need to take off your wet clothes, all of them and dry yourself. Wrap yourself in these towels.'

She just nodded. 'You could take off my clothes,' she said and sat down on the bed.

'I could, but I won't. You do it and don't be long. I'll make the coffee.' He left her there, his own clothes sticking to him and weariness starting to overpower him. He adjusted the heating and locked the cabin door. He made two cups of coffee and tapped on the door to the bedroom. There was no answer, so he eased the door open with his elbow and carried in the two cups. Celestine was lying on the bed, wrapped in the two large towels, her eyes closed. He took a duvet from a box under the bed and cast it over her. Then he stripped off his own wet clothes and towelled himself dry in the small shower room next door. Celestine was sleeping soundly, so he slipped into the bed on the other side and pulled the covers over him. He heard her call out once in the night, she'd moved closer, her body soft and warm beside him. He dreamed of nothing until daybreak.

Chapter 61

Bodies washed up. Etienne Vaillancourt, half a kilometre down the River Lot, snagged in the trailing branches of a tree, head twisted upwards, eyes like dark river stones glaring through a few centimetres of water at the young angler, chilled to the marrow. Nguyen and Zubizaretta, excreted face down on the same river bank, only metres apart - spotted from a fishing boat, curious about the frenzy amongst the gulls scrapping over the carcasses. Captain Ngoc, his body floating into the little port at Goulée, looking for a berth after being toyed with by the ebb and flow of the tides. Several days later, an excited cocker spaniel sniffed at the bloated corpse of a large male, beached among the bladderwrack on the margins near Saint-Palais-sur-Mer. Nearly made it to the ocean, remained unidentified.

Jacques and Celestine spent a day in seclusion, barely venturing out of the cabin of the barge, eating from tins and dried goods. Celestine slept a lot, but when she did wake she wanted Jacques to hold her. They didn't talk much, they didn't want new information, they had too much to process from the previous days. At one point though, Celestine, wrapped in a towel, wandered into the galley as Jacques was boiling rice in a pan on the stove. She looked around, opening drawers and peering at charts and maps on the wall.

'So, this barge,' she said finally. 'Nobody knows about it. It's yours, but you don't come here very often. Clearly.' She looked around again. Jacques turned to face her.

'It's an escape capsule. I come here to decompress. Nobody knows about it because I don't want anyone to know about it. That way, I can't be found if I don't want to be,' he tried to explain. She came close to him and wound her fingers in the hair at the side of his head.

'How long have you had this escape module? And how long have you had these feelings that you needed to escape?' she asked, slightly mocking him, but he just smiled.

'Look, I got it about four years ago. I took it instead of payment. I was doing some work in a chateau near St. Émilion. English guy, total twat, but the work was interesting. But then he couldn't pay me. Which I didn't take well. So, from his prone position, with my boot on his neck, he offered me this, the Lady Madeleine, as it was called. It needed work but it was…'

'Love at first sight?'

'A kind of comradeship built up, I would say. Based on mutual need.'

'And what did you need?' asked Celestine, still teasing, but watching his face as he wrestled to explain his motivation, this need for anonymity, to have a life apart.

A little later he said, 'You know this canal crosses all of Southern France and ends at the Mediterranean Sea, near Narbonne.' She nodded.

'I knew that,' she said, 'Before I looked at those maps on the wall by the stove.'

'Yes. Well, I might do it. No. I'm going to do it. I'm going to take the *Incognito* right across France to the Med,' he paused. 'It was a pipedream - too long, a business to run, money to earn… but now I've kind of dropped off the edge. So…' He looked at her, a little shyly. She had picked up a coffee cup and was cradling it in both hands, then she sipped from it, like soup from a bowl.

'You should come too,' he said suddenly. 'Take some time out. This has been a hell of a thing. Maybe still is.'

'On a boat? Live on a boat?' she asked, as though it was the strangest suggestion she had ever heard.

'Obviously, I'd make some alterations,' he said quickly. 'Build a wardrobe for your Dior dresses and such. Hey, leave it, just a thought. We can't make decisions yet, there's too much out there still. Today we are in *Incognito*.'

Monsieur Trouffeau, the examining magistrate, was surprised to receive a visit from an eminent local poet in the late morning, minutes before he planned to leave to take his lunch. More surprised still when the poet presented him with a dossier relating to a case in which he was engaged.

'May I ask you, monsieur, where you obtained this information and the photographs?'

Phillipe looked at him, keen to appear confident despite the nervousness he felt inside. As always, he chose his words carefully.

'I can say that this is water from the source,' he said finally.

Early the following day, Jacques recovered the motorbike, and they entered Bordeaux in mid-morning, almost surprised that everything appeared to be normal. People were walking in the streets, although Celestine had the impression that they were all extras, acting a role, ready to turn and pursue them on a director's cue. Jacques left her at the foot of the steps outside the Hotel de Police and watched as she walked through the glass doors.

Nobody came on the first day. The restaurant was closed. Then the police came and hammered on the door. They were looking for someone who was not there. Only Linh and her friend remained, bunkered down, feeling that a storm had passed over them, uncertain of when it was safe to go outside

Then Linh received a phone call from the lady with the fierce eyes and the kind mouth. She packed a small suitcase with her belongings. She walked through the back of the restaurant to where the rubbish bins were kept, and there she deposited her silver slippers. She raised her head and walked out into the street.

When Jacques and Celestine met two hours later, at a café by the Gross Cloche, the Great Bell, they were both bearing a new wound which showed in their faces and the cast of their shoulders.

'Etienne is dead,' Celestine said, as she sat down. 'They found him in the river near Figeac. That's where he came from. He'd been… his throat…' She closed her eyes, and her breathing was sharp and rapid. Jacques placed his hand on hers, but he had very little sympathy to spare. He took a sip of his coffee.

'Louise died yesterday. Just there below the clock. She hadn't left her flat in fifteen years, but, the neighbour said, she just walked out yesterday afternoon and collapsed as she got to the clock. Heart gave out.' He was shaking his head as though to clear it of the images and the guilt. They both lifted their faces to look at each other closely.

'I'm so sorry,' said Celestine. 'Sorry she had so much trauma in her life. I'm sure you were a lifeline for her.' They sat in silence for a few minutes, beyond common discourse. Then Celestine stood up. 'Come on, let's go over there, to the Great Bell. I have an announcement to make. What better place.' They walked along the narrow street, up to the great medieval bell tower. They stood looking up and Celestine stretched her neck to stand tall. Then she said in a strong, clear voice: 'I hereby announce to the good and the bad people of this city, that I have today resigned from the Police National of Bordeaux.' She gulped slightly after she'd said the words, but continued standing straight and looking up at the bell, thirty metres above. Jacques looked at her in amazement.

'Seriously,' he asked once. She slowly nodded her head. No one passing by seemed to pay any attention. Jacques went to stand below the arch and looked down at the ground.

'Was it here, where she died?' Celestine enquired gently.

'Yes. Below the arch.'

On the wall beside them was the plaque with the words in French, taken from the Latin inscription on the bell. Only the last line had been omitted on the plaque.

'You know, Armand turned down the job to engrave this,' said Jacques.

'He did?'

'Yes. Because they didn't want the last line to be included. Said it was too morbid for the tourists or some such. Armand refused, said something like, "It was an insult to the authenticity and the original sentiment of the ancient people of this city".' Jacques smiled grimly. 'You see. He had integrity did Armand Verville.' He looked at Celestine closely, to see how she was coping with all the traumas of the last few days. 'It's all change now, isn't it,' he said. 'Are you ok?'

She nodded, then linked her arm in his and started reading out aloud the words from the Great Bell:

'I call to arms; I announce the days; I give the hours; I chase the storms; I sound the festivals; I scream at the fire.'

She paused and squeezed Jacques' arm. Together they inserted the last line.

'I weep for the dead.'

AUTHORS NOTE

This story is the prequel to the first Celestine Courbet novel, **The Devil's Point**, and throws Celestine and Jacques reluctantly together for the first time, as they seek justice following the violent murder of Jacques' friend. The title of the book refers to the inscription in Latin inside the belly of the *Gross Cloche* or Great Bell in Bordeaux. This inscription lists the occasions on which the bell should be rung. I have seen a number of translations into French and English but settled on the one shown in the book which includes the last line, *I weep for the dead.* I chose this because I wanted to give the victims of the crimes a voice throughout the book and to show them as real people and not just as numbers on a detective's score sheet. I also wanted to reflect on how their deaths affected the main protagonists. The current *cloche* was cast in 1775, and was baptised Armande-Louise.

Bordeaux is a wonderful city, with history, culture, superb architecture, great wine and a fascinating cemetery. The Cemetery of Chartreuse does appear with great regularity in the book. We were recently talking to some Australian visitors and suggesting sites to visit in Bordeaux when I realised that we kept mentioning Chartreuse and had to explain that we were not, in fact, related to the *Addams Family*. The Gironde Estuary and the Medoc Peninsula are the backdrop for much of the other action in the book, and these are wonderful, picturesque settings, but they also have a mysterious and sinister side. The strong tidal currents of the estuary can be perilous for the unwary, as some have found out.

Above all else, this book is a work of fiction; and the themes of police corruption and Vietnamese criminal gangs are not based on real people or real events but on the fevered imagination of the author. I do hope you enjoyed reading this crime novel. The trials and investigations continue for Celestine and Jacques as they sail slowly down the Canal du Midi on the good barge *Incognito.*

If you would like to follow their progress, please send your contact details and we will let you know when the next book is available.

Tom

    Email: tom@tombecketauthor.com
    Facebook: tombecketauthor@gmail.com
    Website: www.tombecketauthor.com

Tom Becket

Tom Becket is the author of the Celestine Courbet crime thriller mystery series. Living in the South of France with his wife and an energetic spaniel, Tom draws his stories out of the rich history and colourful landscapes of this beautiful region. He writes about authentic characters in conflict who inspire affection and concern in the reader. His research for the novels takes him outdoors, walking the long-distance footpaths and cycling along the towpaths of the French Canals.

Tom taught English and ran his own company for many years before committing to writing fiction full-time. He invites you to join him in discovering the mysterious and fascinating France described in his novels.

Printed in Great Britain
by Amazon